"Where are you, Emily? You seem a million miles away." Zach's thumb rubbed across her fingers, and a shiver went through her.

"I'm not, really. I was just thinking about how I got here, about the difference you've made in my life."

"Have I?" he asked with a hint of vulnerability. If her heart hadn't already opened to let him in, that tiny insecurity would have done the trick.

"You know you have. You've helped me see what I really want in life. And that's a priceless gift."

"You've changed things for me, too," he confessed, bringing her closer. His hands moved up her arms to grasp her shoulders and he leaned toward her. Emily closed her eyes, knowing he was going to kiss her, her insides quaking with excited anticipation. Tenderly Zach touched his lips to each of her eyelids. Then his lips trailed down to the corner of her mouth and bestowed small, soft kisses.

She needed more. She wanted him closer, closer than she'd ever wanted anyone before. As if he heard her wishes spoken aloud, his arms tightened around her, bringing her body into contact with his from head to toe. . . .

DESERT FLAME

ANNE HARMON

DIAMOND BOOKS, NEW YORK

This book is a Diamond original edition, and has never been previously published.

DESERT FLAME

A Diamond Book/published by arrangement with the authors

PRINTING HISTORY
Diamond edition / December 1992

ISBN: 1-55773-824-6

Diamond Books are published by The Berkley Publishing Group, 200 Madison Avenue, New York, New York 10016. The name "DIAMOND" and its logo are trademarks belonging to Charter Communications, Inc.

PRINTED IN THE UNITED STATES OF AMERICA

10 9 8 7 6 5 4 3 2 1

To my parents,
Juliette and Gabriel Herrmann,
who encouraged me to go after my dreams—
whatever they might be.

To Don and Colleen Shinn,
Eleanore Cannon,
Millie Carson,
for all you've given me.

To Karen Hoagland,
proofreader extraordinaire,
with thanks.

And

To Ted, Joe, Jen,
Alisa, and Mimi
with love.

AUTHOR'S NOTE

Ostriches were really raised in the United States in the late nineteenth century to fill a demand for feathers by the fashion industry. According to Charles C. Colley in his article "Ostrich Plumes for Milady's Bustles and Bonnets" (Ninth Annual Arizona Historical Convention, April 19–20, 1968), "Between 1882 and 1886, small ostrich farms were established in Florida, North Carolina, Texas, and California. . . . In 1887 the first ostriches were imported to the Salt River Valley of Arizona, soon to become the ostrich raising capital of the United States."

Several articles on ostrich farming in the United States appeared in popular magazines of the late nineteenth and the early twentieth centuries, including *Scientific American* and *National Geographic*. The industry died at the start of World War I when the worldwide demand for ostrich feathers declined sharply as fashion trends changed drastically. Nonetheless, ostrich farming represents an interesting sidelight on American history.

The book referred to in Chapter Three, *Ostriches and Ostrich Farming* by Julius de Mosenthal and James Edmund Harting, really exists and was one of the reference books we used. It was published in a second edition in 1879.

We wish to thank the staff of the Arizona Historical Society, Central Arizona Division, in Phoenix for their assistance in providing research material for this book and Bruce Dring, vice president of Safari at Six Flags Great Adventure, Jackson, New Jersey, for sharing with us his expertise on raising ostriches and for letting us hold an ostrich chick.

CHAPTER

1

Billy Crabtree looked at his cards in disgust and threw them onto the table.

"I'm out," he said and leaned back in his chair. The other players were strangers, men passing through town just as he was. They were hard men, drifters if he was any judge. The game had started out friendly enough, but had turned grim as the pile of money on the table grew.

"It's your bet. You plannin' to fold or sit there all day admirin' your cards?" the dealer asked the man to Billy's left.

The man said his name was Zach, but who knew for sure? Strangers would as soon lie to you as tell the truth, especially about something personal like that. On the other hand, of all the men in the saloon today, this Zach was the only one Billy would trust by his side in a fight. The rest weren't worth a plug nickel all together.

"Take it easy, Ray, ol' buddy," Zach drawled, addressing the dealer. "I'm just planning my strategy."

He wasn't drunk as far as Billy could tell, but the whiskey they'd all been drinking had given a lazy edge to his deep voice. After contemplating his cards for another few seconds, Zach pushed his remaining dollars to the center of the table. "I'll see you, brother, and raise you another fifty."

Ray Hudson narrowed his weasel eyes and glanced at the saloon's ceiling. The movement was so quick, a man could have easily missed it. But Billy had been around a long time and knew what to look for. Tucked into the fancy scrollwork above Zach's head was a tiny peephole. You had to know exactly where it was to spot it, and Ray Hudson knew just where to look.

So, it seemed, did Zach.

"Why you cheating, no-account son of a bitch!" he growled and reached for his gun. Before anyone could so much as take a breath, he had it cocked in his hand.

Ray Hudson and his brother Carl froze in place, their hands barely reaching their sides, let alone the handles of their guns. Zach had simply been too fast. The other men at the table pushed back their chairs, out of the line of fire.

At Zach's command, the Hudsons put their hands in the air, out of reach of their guns. A deathly silence filled the room as everyone waited to see what would happen next. The penalty for cheating was known to them all. If Zach decided to pull the trigger, not one man in the saloon would object. The town was too small and too isolated to boast a sheriff, so the decision was Zach's.

Billy wiped his forehead with a bandanna. Maybe he was getting too old for this, he thought. Cold-blooded murder was definitely not to his taste, even if the culprits deserved it. But Zach was another story; maybe he felt differently. After all, a man didn't get that fast without a lot of practice. And no one practiced that much unless he intended to kill. Billy squelched that line of thought. Zach didn't impress him as a killer, and after more than fifty years of life, Billy prided himself on being a pretty good judge of character.

"You boys local?" Zach was asking the dealer, his voice low and hard.

"N-no," Carl answered for his brother when Ray kept silent.

"Who's up there? Call him."

Ray merely glared defiantly at Zach.

"Gus, you better come down," Carl cried out, his voice shaky.

Gus looked no more than sixteen as he came down the stairs, a skinny boy with a hangdog look.

Zach motioned him toward his friends.

"Where're your mounts?" Zach asked.

"At the livery stable," Carl said with a nervous look at his brother.

"You," Zach called to the lanky youth. "Go get the horses and bring them here." He tossed a coin to the boy, who caught it in midair and dashed out the door.

Billy realized that killing wasn't in Zach's plan. Apparently Ray had come to the same conclusion.

"What're you plannin' to do?" Ray asked, his tone belligerent, his hate and fury unmistakable.

"I haven't decided yet." At Zach's words, Carl Hudson made a whimpering sound, but Ray silenced him with a look.

Ray lowered his hands slightly, the right one moving subtly toward the side where his gun waited.

"I wouldn't try that if I were you," Zach said in the same lazy drawl he'd used earlier, except this time, there was nothing lazy or the least bit slow about the way he moved or the way he held his gun. Without turning his head, he pointed to Billy. "You with them?" he asked.

"No, sir," Billy answered. "Can't say that I am."

"Good. Then get yourself out of that chair and relieve these two *gentlemen* of their weapons." His voice dripped with sarcasm. "From behind," he advised. "I don't want you getting between my bullet and the man it's meant for."

Billy jumped out of his seat and approached the two brothers carefully. At Zach's nod he reached around them one at a time and carefully eased their guns out of their holsters. Neither brother tried to stop him.

"I got 'em," he said. "Now what?"

"Check their boots and their backs. I don't want any unpleasant surprises."

"You got no right!" Ray sputtered when Billy started patting him down.

Zach waved his Colt under Ray's nose. "I've got all the right I need right here in my hand. Don't tempt me to use it."

"Found a knife and this beaut here in his right boot." Billy tipped his head to indicate he was talking about Ray. In his hand, Billy held a small pearl-handled pistol, a woman's gun, but deadly nonetheless even if it only held two bullets. "The other one's clean."

"Good. Now I want you two boys to stand up very slowly and back to the door. I plan to follow you to the edge of town, so don't make any detours. Just get on your horses and ride out."

Ray stared at him, not moving. "What about my winnings?"

Zach didn't even look at the pile of money on the table.

"What winnings?" he growled. "Seems to me you should be happy enough just to leave with your lives. Of course, if you'd prefer not to . . ."

His voice trailed off, and Carl grabbed his brother's arm and pulled him toward the entrance.

"Come on," he urged. "Let's go."

"We can't go without our guns," Ray protested. "We'd be easy pickings for any desperado. It'd be exactly like killing us to send us out unarmed."

"You'll get your guns back once you're out of town. Now get going."

The Hudsons backed out the swinging door, and Zach followed, his eyes alert for trouble, either from the brothers or from inside the saloon. That hole in the ceiling hadn't gotten there by itself. More than likely this bunch had a deal with the saloon owner for a cut of the profits.

Billy watched until the three men were outside. Then he scooped the money from the table into his hat and followed them out. No one objected. The whispers started as the door swung shut behind him, but no one else dared come outside, not with a professional gunslinger loose.

Zach stood on the plank sidewalk, his gun still in his hand, as Ray and Carl mounted their horses.

"Now what?" Ray snarled.

"Now you ride. I'll send Gus out later with your guns. I don't expect to see you 'round these parts again. I've a good memory for faces, so stay clear."

The two galloped off down the makeshift main street of the town. Gus glanced after them, a worried frown creasing his brow.

"I'll be back in a minute. You stay here," Zach said to Gus and started to walk away.

"Wait!" Billy cried out. "What about the money?"

Zach stopped and scratched his head. He looked consideringly into Billy's hat. "How much did you lose?" he asked.

Billy told him.

"I lost at least a couple of hundred myself," Zach said and counted out his money. "Why don't you take out what you lost and tell the others to do the same."

"What should I do with the extra?"

"I don't rightly know. Seems to me there's no call to return anything to those cheatin' bastards 'cepting their guns, since I said I would. I guess we could split it. What do you think?"

"Sounds fine to me," Billy concurred, and grinned at Zach. His instincts had been right. This man was no killer. But why did he wear his guns tied down low on his legs? And how in tarnation had he ever gotten so fast on the draw? There was a mystery here, and Billy loved mysteries.

By the time he'd handed out the money to the other players, Zach had returned on his horse.

"I'll ride you to the edge of town," Zach was telling Gus when Billy came outside. "Then you can go join your friends."

"I'd watch my back if I was you," Billy called out. "You made some mighty fierce enemies just now. I wouldn't trust them to come after you fair and square."

"Don't worry, old-timer. I always watch my back. Better men than them've come after me before."

Zach motioned Gus to move out and turned his horse to follow. Billy stood on the sidewalk watching them. Suddenly he remembered he hadn't given Zach his share of the extra money. He called out, but the two riders didn't seem to hear him, for neither of them looked back.

Though he hadn't planned on it, Billy decided to spend the night in the local boardinghouse. That way Zach would know where to find him if he wanted the money.

By morning there was still no sign of the younger man. Billy frowned and figured he'd head out of town in the same direction.

The sun was bright and high in the sky, but a cool mountain breeze wound its way through the towering fir trees. Snow covered the peaks of the Rockies, and if you looked in the shady corners, you could find some snow at this elevation. At night the temperatures fell to near freezing up here, but during the day the air warmed up comfortably.

The only sounds Billy heard were the buzzing of insects, the rustling of tree branches, and the creaking of his saddle as his horse plodded uphill. A bird call sounded, and Billy put his hand to his forehead to shade his eyes as he squinted into the distance. Vultures. Circling in the sky.

Billy dug his heels into his mount's sides, and the horse quickened its pace. The packhorse trailing him resisted the pull of the reins at first, but Billy yanked sharply on the lead, and the reluctant animal obeyed, breaking into a trot.

The trail narrowed and passed between two rocky outcroppings, and that was where he saw them. Two men lay sprawled on the ground; a dark color stained the dirt around them. Blood. His horse could smell it and shied away from the spot.

Billy jumped down from the saddle and ground-tethered his animals upwind of the bodies. Drawing his pistol, he approached cautiously. One of the men moaned. After scanning the area to make sure no one else was near, Billy hurried forward.

He recognized them at once. The boy, Gus, with a bullet to the heart, lay dead. Zach lay near him, groaning softly.

Billy ran back to his horse and grabbed his canteen and blanket. He carried both to Zach's side and lifted the younger man's head so he could sip some water. Zach's skin felt warm to his touch—too warm. But warm was better than dead-cold like Gus.

"What happened?" Billy asked when Zach's eyelids flickered.

The injured man's eyes didn't seem to focus. Billy covered him with the blanket and gave him another sip of water.

" 'Nough," Zach complained, his voice hoarse and scratchy.

"Can you tell me what happened?" Billy probed again.

"Ambush," Zach explained, breathing hard with the effort of talking. "I gave Gus the guns . . . and sent him off. . . . Heard a scream." He paused and closed his eyes. Billy put the canteen to his lips again, but Zach pushed it away feebly.

"You have to drink, mister. Can't have you dying on me. Bad for my reputation."

"How's . . . Gus?"

"Dead. Shot twice. Once in the arm and once in the chest."

"Damn . . . bastards. He was . . . one of their . . . own."

"How'd they get you?"

"Stupid . . . fell for the . . . oldest trick. . . . Stopped to check . . . on Gus, and . . . they shot from . . . above. . . . Pretty . . . stupid, huh?"

Billy looked up to the tops of the cliffs on either side of the narrow gulch. Zach had been stupid, all right. The place was an obvious ambush site. But what man with any shred of decency would have anticipated that anyone, even the Hudson brothers, would bait a trap by shooting one of their confederates, and a young boy, at that.

Zach's head fell back as he passed out again. Billy checked him over and found two gunshot wounds, one a simple graze on his thigh, the other in his shoulder with entry from the back. Judging from the size of the bloodstain on the ground near Zach, he couldn't handle much traveling. Billy knew he had no choice. He had to find someplace close where they could make camp.

He dragged Zach into the shade and off the trail, then dressed his wounds before leaving Zach and his packhorse and setting out to search alone. After backtracking a ways he found another, less used trail. It led around the side of the rocky outcropping, then down the side of the mountain, ending at a small stream. At least they'd have water. Billy followed the stream a short distance until he found a small cave hollowed out of the stone by wind and rain. As long as the weather held up, it would serve them well. He hurried his horse back up the mountain.

Zach hadn't moved while he was gone. A couple of the vultures had come down for a closer look and perched on a boulder by the side of the trail. As Billy rode up, they took off again, squawking their protest at having their find disturbed.

The packhorse whinnied, and an answering snort came from nearby. Billy scanned the woods and made out the other horse, still saddled and trailing its reins where Zach must have left it.

He brought the animal over to Zach, then bent to shake the other man. Zach's eyes opened but quickly closed. Billy shook him again.

"I've found a place we can make camp. It's a short ride. Think you can make it?"

"My horse?"

"I've got him here."

"Okay."

Before helping him up, Billy rummaged through his pack and pulled out a couple of bandannas. He rewrapped Zach's leg more tightly and bound his shoulder where the bullets had struck.

Zach flinched once and bit his lip, but made no protest. With a lot of straining, pulling, and heaving, Billy got Zach up in the saddle.

Once there, Zach simply collapsed, barely maintaining his seat. Billy debated his plan. Maybe he ought to have tied Zach across his packhorse rather than trust him to stay in the saddle. But by now there was sweat on his own brow and his cheeks were plenty red to boot. He had absolutely no desire to try to get Zach off this horse and onto the other. They'd just have to take their chances.

The pain was unrelenting, prodded to new peaks with each step his horse took. Zach didn't know which was worse, the pain from his shoulder or the pain in his leg, and after a while, it made no difference. The pain was everywhere. He wished it would stop, but nothing he did made it go away.

He wanted to give up, but a strange voice kept needling him, ordering him to hang on, to keep going, just a little farther, just a little farther. The phrase kept repeating itself in his mind, sometimes in that strange voice, sometimes in his own. It kept him going, like a prayer or litany. One more step. Just a little farther.

After a while the motion stopped, but the pain didn't. Zach felt it burning inside him, consuming him with its fire. His mind churned and whirled, images forming and fading, twisting and turning in a confusing swirl of memory and reality. Sometimes he knew he was dreaming. He would see his parents and sister again, smiling and happy, sitting around the table, sharing their hopes and plans for the future.

His parents had had small dreams. All they'd wanted was a modest home of their own, a place to raise children and live out their days in peace.

Then gold had been discovered nearby. Top dollar was offered for their land, but Jeremiah Hollis had refused to sell out. Gold didn't interest him. He valued the land itself, the place that had welcomed him and let him fulfill his dreams. The other settlers sold out one at a time, some willingly, some after "persuasion." But Jeremiah had held firm.

The images Zach saw changed, becoming more real. His mother's worried face, the threats, his father's determination. The sky was dark when they heard the first riders. Zach and his sister had already climbed to the loft to go to bed. Jeremiah and his wife were completing the last of their nightly chores.

"Quick, Zach. Get down here and grab a rifle," his father called up the ladder. "Sarah, you and Becky get ready to reload for us."

"You expecting trouble?" Zach's mother asked, her voice quavering. Sarah wanted to sell, Zach knew. He'd heard her pleading at night with his father, telling him they could start over somewhere else, that it wasn't worth it to fight the inevitable.

Jeremiah had refused to budge, saying that outlaws and thugs couldn't be allowed to get their way. He wouldn't be driven off his own land. There was plenty of gold elsewhere; they didn't need his quarter.

But the Darnells were greedy. They wanted every last bit of land in the area, and Jeremiah was the last to hold out.

"I don't know if there'll be trouble, Sarah. I just want to be prepared," Jeremiah said to his wife. "Hurry, now, and keep your head down near the windows."

The family scurried about, getting all the guns and the two rifles ready, making sure the extra ammunition was on the kitchen table, which Jeremiah and Zach had pushed up near the front windows.

The riders came up to the house but didn't stop. Instead, they circled around it. In their hands they carried lit torches. The flames looked golden in the darkness of the night and illuminated their faces for the few seconds before the men threw them at the roof of the house.

Sarah looked at Jeremiah in horror. "They're burning us out. God help us."

She clutched at her daughter as helpless tears ran down her face.

"The guns are loaded, Pa," Zach said. "What do we do now?"

At eleven, Zach was on the border between man and boy. He still did his lessons with his mother, but oftentimes he helped his dad out on the range. He was a fair shot, though he didn't get much practice—ammunition was too expensive to waste. His father had taught him never to lift a gun unless he meant to use it, and then he'd better use it right. Injured animals were a menace to all. A shot had to be quick and clean. Deadly.

But Zach had never shot at a man before, never even thought about it. Now there wasn't any time to think. If he didn't shoot them, he sensed, they would have no compunction about shooting him.

"Grab that pistol and wait to see what they do. Maybe they're just out for a good time and will leave soon. Sarah, take Becky to the back room. You'll be safer there. The fire on the roof hasn't taken. The wood's too wet after our last rain. Hurry now," he urged.

As Jeremiah finished speaking, the first shot came through the window, narrowly missing him.

"Quick, quick!" he cried. "Get out of here. Zach and I will hold them off."

Jeremiah flattened himself against the outer wall of the house by the window the shot had come through, and bided his time. Zach followed suit across the room by the other window, once a luxury, now a curse.

"I see someone, Pa," he whispered.

"Hold your fire till I tell you," his father whispered back.

The man outside had no torch. Thinking the darkness hid him, he was creeping toward the house on his belly, heading for the window Jeremiah guarded. When he got close, he raised himself to a crouch, preparing to sprint to the house. Jeremiah's bullet hit him right between the eyes.

"Hell, Bart was shot," a voice cried from behind the stand of trees fifty yards from the house.

"He all right?" another voice cried out.

"Can't tell," the first voice called back. "He's not moving."

"You know what to do. Do it now," a third voice called out, a voice Zach recognized. It belonged to James Darnell, the man who'd been buying up all the properties nearby, the man who wanted the Hollis place.

"Hang on, boy," Jeremiah warned. "Shoot to kill. We won't get a second chance."

Those were the last words either spoke as the woods came alive with torches and gunshots. Suddenly there was the smell of kerosene. It was burning, the house was burning. So hot, so hot. Mama, where are you? Where's Becky? It's so hot, too hot!

Against the backs of his eyelids, Zach saw their faces again, the man with the first torch, the men with the buckets of kerosene, the man who had shot his father, and the men who had caused it all, James and Earl Darnell. He would never forget. Never.

The fire burned hotter, consuming him from within. The images ebbed and flowed like the tides, leaving him high and dry, then floating him away, carrying him along in their currents. He no longer knew if he was alive or dead or someplace in between.

At last the fire cooled, the images faded, his mind slowed down, and he became aware of himself again. He opened his eyes and saw nothing but gray everywhere he looked.

"You back among the living yet?"

The voice came from far away, piercing the gray haze surrounding him and bringing with it pain. Zach shut his eyes and tried to escape back into the oblivion. The voice wouldn't let him.

"Not so fast, young man. I'm a-talking to you. Come on, now, open up them peepers and give us a look-see."

The persistent voice sounded familiar. Zach could remember its soothing presence amid the burning confusion he'd been living. The voice had brought him cool water, the comfort of another presence, the encouragement to survive. Zach turned his head to the side and cracked open one eye.

"That's more like it. Sure you can't do no better?"

Staring back at him, not more than six inches away, was a bright blue eye, a bit rheumy with age but clear and knowing for all that—and cheerful, too, if a single eye could be so described.

"Who're you?" Zach croaked through chapped lips. His mouth felt like sandpaper, gritty and dry.

"Why don't you see if you can't guess?"

The blue eye pulled back about a foot, and Zach could now make out its mate, a slightly crooked nose, and a shock of whitish-gray hair.

"Recognize me yet?"

"Billy? That you? What're you doing here?"

"Well, now, where else did ya think I'd be?"

"I thought you was heading for Denver. What happened?"

"Well, you never showed up to take your share of the money, so I decided to come after you. Lucky for you I did or you'd be dead and gone for sure."

"I thought I was for a while there," Zach said.

"I thought you might be, myself. But you're a strong 'un, boy. You pulled through. Now, you take some of this, and no more fighting me off."

Billy propped up his head and held a metal cup to his mouth. Zach took a sip. The water ran down his throat, clean and refreshing. Suddenly he wanted more—he was thirsty and he was alive, and that was all that mattered.

"Hey, boy, you better slow down. Don't want you getting

sick on me now. I'll give you more in a bit," Billy promised as he pulled the cup away. "You'll feel better in a minute, and I'll give you something to eat."

Zach was too weak to fight him. When Billy lowered his head back to the ground, exhaustion overtook him and he fell asleep.

When he woke again, it was dark. He opened his eyes to the sight of flames; a scream formed in his throat. Not again, not again.

"Ah, you're back, are you?"

This time he recognized Billy's voice. He looked more closely at the flames and saw that Billy had lit a campfire. That was all. The scream died, taking with it the old primal fear and the stench of death. He was alive, and soon he would be well. He would resume his quest. He would find the last remaining men Darnell had used on his raid of the Hollis homestead—most especially the elusive Earl Darnell. Earl was a master at escape, at hiding his tracks and moving on, almost as if he anticipated Zach's arrival in time to make his getaways.

Zach had been tracking him on and off for nearly twenty years. Of all the men involved in the murder of his family, Earl had been the worst, showing no mercy as he inflicted the greatest pain.

Zach had thought he was getting close to Darnell, but his latest hunch had turned up dry. The only information he had left to work with was the possibility that the man he sought might be in Arizona. That would have to be his next destination.

"Hungry?" Billy asked. "I ain't got much, but I boiled up a rabbit I caught earlier today. Made you some soup. Want to try some?"

Zach didn't, but he knew he had no choice. If he wanted to

get well fast, he had to eat; he had to fight the overwhelming weakness that held him in thrall.

"Why're you doing this?" he asked the older man a day or two later. He was feeling better now, well enough to realize the extraordinary effort Billy had made on his behalf. He didn't like it, didn't want to be indebted. But Billy had given him no choice.

Billy sat nearby, just inside the mouth of the cave, whittling a twig with his knife. "Well, now, let's see, kid. Maybe I just took a liking to you. Or maybe I need a favor." The older man's eyes lit up brightly.

"What kind of favor?" Zach asked warily. No one had simply taken a liking to him since his family died. Some had been too afraid of the Darnells and their long reach; others had had no patience for an angry youth with no family or fortune to speak of.

"Well, now, it's more of a proposition than a favor."

The other man gave him a sly look that Zach couldn't quite interpret, as if he were privy to some secret he wasn't prepared to share. In recent years, as Zach's reputation as a shooter had spread, people had tried to hire him as a gunslinger. Gunslingers were supposed to do their dirty work and disappear, leaving the good citizens of the town to continue their moral existence unsullied by contact with the seamier side of life—even though they were willing to pay to get the deed done. Zach wanted none of it.

"To do what?" Zach asked, still unwilling to commit himself.

"It's kinda a long story, but the short of it is, I got me an investment. A ranch. Think you could run it for me for a while, kind of get it on its feet?"

"A ranch?" Zach couldn't have been more surprised. Not because Billy didn't look like he could own a ranch. Hell, the man had probably won it in a poker game or conned some poor sucker out of it. Even more likely, Billy himself had gotten suckered, accepting the ranch sight unseen as payment for a gambling debt. Despite his conniving ways, Billy seemed to have a soft heart.

"Yup, a beaut of a ranch. 'Cept for one thing. I ain't never lived on no ranch. Wouldn't know which end of a steer to milk to save my life."

Zach laughed at that. "Your life wouldn't be worth much if you tried to milk *any* end of a steer."

"Well, there you are, then. You interested in the job?"

"Why me?"

"Why not you? You seem smart enough, from what I've seen, 'cepting for the day you got yourself shot, of course. And you look like an honest man, more or less. What you got against it? Seems to me like you need a place to get yourself together for a while."

"That's for sure." Zach rotated his shoulder a little and winced from the pain. His whole arm felt stiff. It would be a while before he could whip his gun from its holster faster than an eye could see.

"Ranch's out Arizona way. I know it's a ways from here, but . . ."

Arizona. Zach couldn't believe it. Maybe his luck had suddenly changed. This was just what he needed, a place to recuperate, to get his shooting speed back up. A place where he could pursue his search for Earl Darnell with no one the wiser.

"Arizona, huh?" he said musingly. "Sounds kind of interesting."

"Does that mean you'll take the job?"

"I can't stay for long. I got some things I got to do. But I could come for a while."

"Sounds good to me."

Billy's entire face smiled, and Zach could almost see his

thoughts whipping through his brain. Zach only wished he had the faintest inkling of what those thoughts might be. Maybe he was making a mistake. He hardly knew Billy, after all, nor did Billy know him.

"Well," Zach said with a sigh that turned into a groan as he tried to shift into a more comfortable position, "I don't reckon you know what you're getting into, taking me on."

"Why? You planning on cheating me or something?"

"No," Zach was forced to admit. "But you can't know that."

"You insulting my capabilities?" Billy charged, his satisfied smile of a minute ago replaced by a menacing scowl. "You think I'm too addlepated to judge a man's character?"

"Hold on, there, Billy. I never said no such thing. You're damn right, I'd never cheat you. I'm just surprised is all."

"Well, in that case you don't got no choice. If you don't agree to what I'm saying, I'll know you don't trust my judgment."

The look of hurt and outrage on Billy's face convinced Zach of the older man's sincerity.

"All right. When do we head out?"

"As soon as you're feeling a might more fit. I can only go with you a ways. Then, like you, I got some things I got to do. But I'll tell you how to get there so you won't have no trouble finding it."

The gleam was back in Billy's eyes, but Zach was so tired from his exertions that he didn't pay any attention to it.

"Well, now that that's decided, I better get some sleep. Sooner I'm put back together, the sooner we can get moving."

"Right. You just settle yourself and rest. I think I'll set out here a while longer and finish this up."

He picked up his whittling and took out his knife. Zach knew Billy'd be out there for a while now and went to his blanket. The feeling of being lost and without purpose that always followed a serious injury was absent tonight. He knew what he would be doing tomorrow and the day after that for many days to come. It warmed something inside him, something he'd barely let himself be aware of since he'd set himself the challenge of avenging his family's death.

There was something magical in having plans, in building something positive instead of always chasing after evil. It would be nice to have some roots for a change, even if they were only temporary ones, to come home to a place where he was in charge, where the people looked at him as if he belonged rather than as a stranger passing through. For once someone had seen beyond his gun and found value in him as a man. Billy was right. He owed the man a debt of gratitude, not so much for saving his life as for giving him a sense that his life had been worth saving.

His eyes were closed, and visions of the lush green ranch danced in his head. In seconds he was asleep, a look of satisfaction on his face.

Billy chortled with glee. He'd done what he set out to do—found somebody to run Emily's ranch. Emily's money was going to triple in no time with this investment. And it had all worked out so perfectly. Zach wanted to go to Arizona—that much and more Billy had gleaned from Zach's fevered ramblings over the first couple of days after the shooting.

Billy had instinctively known that Zach would feel honor bound to help him, but this was even better. While getting a favor done, Billy would also be helping Zach with his quest.

Billy frowned. The more he thought of it, the less he liked the idea of what Zach was doing. Spending his whole life avenging the death of his family would be a terrible waste.

Zach had already done enough. If he didn't let go of the past, he would never be ready to face the future. There must be something he could do to help Zach find another path.

It didn't take Billy long to figure out a plan. It was a gamble, but then, that was Billy's weakness, and somehow, no matter the odds, Lady Fortune had always smiled fondly on him.

The stagecoach bottomed out as one wheel skidded into a rut. Emily Crabtree bounced against the inner side of the compartment and suppressed a sneeze. The dust, which had blown into a cloud around her, settled again in a light-colored layer over her dark traveling coat and every other flat surface.

"Not used to travelin' much?" asked the plump middle-aged woman in the seat across from her.

"Not like this," Emily admitted, glad of the distraction. Ever since Opal had fallen asleep she'd had only her own thoughts to keep her company. Not very happy ones, unfortunately. "I feel like I'm turning into one giant bruise."

The stagecoach lurched in the opposite direction, and Emily reached for one of the leather straps attached to the sides of the coach with her right hand while she steadied Opal with her left. The two men sitting next to the older woman on the other seat slept slumped in their seats, seemingly oblivious to the rigors of the trip.

"The drivers don't like to waste no time on this stretch," the woman explained, hanging on to her own leather strap. "Been too many holdups lately."

Emily's throat constricted at this unwelcome announcement. The trip was harrowing enough without the threat of robbery or worse. She never knew when these westerners were pulling her leg because she was a novice from the East or when they were telling the truth, but the woman looked serious enough. What had she gotten herself into, Emily thought, leaving home so impulsively? And bringing Opal along on such a harebrained trip. What must she have been thinking of?

"You travel this route a lot?" she asked, hoping for more information.

"Often enough," the woman allowed. "My name's Beatrice Keller. You can call me Bea; everybody does. Where're you headed?"

"Phoenix. And I'm Emily. Emily Crabtree," Emily responded, having adjusted to the friendlier western style. Back home in Connecticut she would have waited for a proper introduction rather than being so forward, but out here no one stood on such formality. She nodded to the sleeping woman beside her and said, "And this is my aunt Opal." No need to go into any of the confusing details of how Opal was really related to her.

"Right pleased to meet you. I'm headin' to Phoenix myself, then on to Bethel Springs. It's a small town in the middle of nowhere, not that Phoenix is any great shakes."

"Why, I believe I'm heading through Bethel Springs myself. We'll be visiting my uncle's ranch."

"Got a lot of ranches out our way. The Salt River Valley is a good place for growing things, what with all the irrigation canals and such. Where exactly are you headed?"

"The Double F Ranch. Have you heard of it?"

"Heard of it?" Bea Keller started to laugh; she laughed until tears rolled down her cheeks. In between gasping for breath, she kept saying, "I'm sorry . . . I'm sorry," but the peals of laughter just kept coming. She laughed so hard her bonnet fell forward over her eyes, but she was shaking too hard to straighten it.

Emily wasn't sure what to make of Bea's reaction. She suspected Uncle Billy must have done it again. He was fa-

mous for getting into strange scrapes—which was why
she'd dropped everything to come out here, after all. Bea's
laughter was definitely not a good sign.

Finally, with a small hiccup, Bea stopped laughing. "I am
truly sorry. I just don't know what got into me." She pushed
her bonnet back into place and swiped at her eyes with a
large grayed handkerchief she recovered from a hidden
pocket in her skirt, then smiled at Emily. "Now, what would
make a nice young girl like you come all the way out here to
Arizona? Don't you have any family back east?"

Emily had plenty of family, but all of it was on her husband's side, including Opal. Since his death nearly a year
and a half ago she'd spent more time trying to avoid their
company than craving it. Opal was the only one to show her
any consideration, but then, Opal—like Emily herself—was
a Crabtree by marriage only, not by blood. Emily wasn't sure
what to say to Bea. She didn't like lying, but she didn't feel
ready to share such personal confidences, either.

"I just thought this might be a good time to see how Uncle
Billy is doing," she said, hedging. "He wrote to me about his
new place, and it sounds interesting."

"Interestin', eh? That's about as good a word as any," Bea
conceded, and once again chuckled. "Now, promise me this.
If you get out there and change your mind about stayin',
don't be shy or nothin'. You just head right back into Bethel
Springs and look me up. I own the dress shop there—the
only dress shop, so everybody knows me."

"Is there something wrong with the ranch? Will it be safe?
I don't want to put Opal in any danger." By now Emily had
nearly forgotten the unpleasantness of the ride, her curiosity
and concern over her new home wiping out all other consid-
erations.

"I wouldn't say there was anything *wrong*, but you'll see
soon enough. Your aunt might want to stay in town until you

get settled, though, being elderly and all. You don't look much like a country girl. Lived in a city back east, did you?"

"Yes, I did."

"With your family?"

Emily glanced at the two sleeping figures on the other side of the coach and then at Opal, wishing one of them would wake up and share the burden of conversation with her. Suddenly she didn't feel like talking anymore. Beatrice Keller was entirely too curious.

"Not exactly, no," Emily mumbled.

"Now, don't you mind my pryin'. I just don't got nothin' better to do," Bea said with amazing perspicacity. "Small town folk do like their gossip. I just can't help but wonder what could possibly cause you to leave home. I certainly wouldn't have if I'd been given the choice."

Emily blushed. "I guess I didn't feel I had much of a choice, either."

"Well, you're here now, so there's no use lookin' back. Just make the best of things as they come to you, I always say."

The stagecoach picked that moment to slow down, and the ride smoothed out.

"We're past the Willard place, I'd guess," Bea put in, releasing her grip on the leather strap. "Reckon I'll just rest my eyes a bit before we get into Phoenix."

She shifted around until she was wedged into the corner between the seat and the side of the stage, then closed her eyes. After a minute or so she opened one eye. "You best catch some rest yourself, dearie, like your aunt. You'll need it. It's been a long day, and we still have a ways to go. No use worryin' about your decision now. What's done is done."

"Yes, ma'am," Emily said and wondered if Bea Keller was able to see her thoughts. When Bea continued to watch her, Emily reluctantly closed her eyes, though she knew she couldn't stop worrying.

Closing her eyes opened the door on her memories. Once again she stood in the library office, getting the first of a series of blows that had led her to this spot on this day.

It had all started two months ago. She'd gone to her job at the library as usual, only to find that soon she would not have one. Her small subscription library was being merged with the Hartford Library Association, and they would no longer need her services.

Then that night she'd received the telegram from Uncle Billy: "Bought a ranch. Everything under control. Your money will double before next year. Much love. Uncle Billy."

The money she'd planned to use to tide her over until she found a new job was being frittered away by her dead husband's crazy uncle.

As if things weren't bad enough, her father-in-law had up and sold the house in which she and Opal were living. She had no job, no money, and no home. And Opal to care for. Not that she minded caring for Opal. Despite the difference in their ages, she and Opal had become close friends—two widows with no one else to lean on, single women in a world that demanded couples.

Opal had cheered her on, sharing with Emily her wisdom and just plain common sense, filling the voids in Emily's life. When Billy's telegram arrived, Opal had encouraged Emily to trust her own judgment where Billy was concerned. Worried about leaving Opal behind to an uncertain fate, Emily had broached the subject of Opal accompanying her out West. Opal looked on it as a great adventure and readily agreed. Emily wasn't sure whether to be excited or dismayed, but it was too late for worrying about that now. She had no choice but to see what Billy was up to. Two days after her last day at her job, Emily had packed up Opal and all their belongings and left for Arizona.

The stagecoach hit another hole, jarring Emily out of her restless slumber. She sat up, made sure Opal was still comfortable, and then gazed out the window. The terrain here was so different from that of Connecticut. She was used to lush green hills and fertile valleys, not the stark desert wilderness that surrounded her on all sides. She hoped she and Opal could survive all the changes in their lives, starting with this alien landscape and whatever surprises the ranch held.

Bea Keller yawned and sat up straighter. "We'll be in Phoenix before you know it," she said, glancing at the passing scenery. "And right after that, we'll be in Bethel Springs."

Emily stretched in her seat, easing the kinks out of the back of her neck. "It can't be too soon for me."

Bea smiled. "I know what you mean. The food on these trips is barely edible. And the dust . . ." She waved her hand in front of her face, as if to clear the air. "First thing I'm goin' to do when I get home is wash everythin'."

Emily sighed. She wished she knew more about where she was headed, enough to know if there would be a bath waiting for her at the other end.

The stopover in Phoenix was short, and Emily soon found herself in the small town of Bethel Springs. The main street was barely more than a couple city blocks long, but crammed into its short length were several small shops, a saloon, a public bath, a general store, and a bank. The name on a sign—Bea's Dress Shop—caught her eye.

"Now, don't you worry about Opal none. She can stay here with me until you're settled," Bea said as they all stood on the side of the dusty street in front of the livery.

"Why, thank you, Bea. It's so kind of you to offer," Opal

chirped. "What would you prefer, Emily? I wouldn't want to be in your way, but if you'd rather not go alone . . ." Her voice trailed off in a question.

Emily wasn't sure herself. She didn't want to face whatever was out there on her own, but if there were real problems, she didn't want to deal with them and look after Opal as well.

"I think it might be better if you stay in town, at least until I see exactly what we're up against."

"Don't worry about her," Bea said. "We'll get along just fine. The ranch ain't too far from town, Emily. Last I heard, it was livable, or I wouldn't be lettin' you head out there by yourself. You just go into the livery here and tell Jackson I sent you. He'll know how to help. Now, I'll just let you say your good-byes in private, and when you're ready, Opal, I'll be at the back of the store."

Opal and Emily watched as the large woman made her way up the street toward her shop.

"Are you sure you want me to stay in town, Emily? You might need me."

"I'll be fine, Opal. I think Bea would have said something if she thought I couldn't handle it. I'll come and get you as soon as I'm settled and know what we'll need. I only wish Uncle Billy were here to meet me."

"Maybe he didn't get your telegram," Opal said.

"Why Laurence left Billy in charge of everything is beyond me."

Opal shook her head commiseratingly. "That Laurence. He never had the good sense God gave a turnip, if you don't mind my saying so. But he sure hid it well. I don't think many people had an inkling what he was really like."

"I guess not," Emily said.

Even Opal didn't know the half of it. Laurence hadn't just lost their money, though that would have been reason enough for Emily to feel lost and vulnerable. He'd also had terrible mood swings, one day feeling lighthearted and reckless, the next, without warning, falling into the deepest despair.

When he was in an elevated mood, he spent money lavishly, flirting with the ladies and making outlandish plans. He would forget he had a wife and a home to come back to, staying away for days at a time only to return smelling of cheap perfume and cheaper wine. When he was down, he would cry in Emily's lap, begging her not to leave him, promising to reform, and threatening to kill himself if she abandoned him.

His death had been the end of a nightmare, a blessed escape from a marital prison. She still felt guilty over her relief at being free, but now was not the time to let any of her lingering anger and frustration show. What good would it do? Her husband was dead and had achieved in death what he'd never had in life: the respect of his family. No one, except her, seemed to remember how he'd squandered their money and violated their marriage vows.

"Now, dear, you mustn't let one bad experience sour you like this," Opal was saying. "For all you know, William is nothing like his kin say. After all, you always said you liked him."

For Opal, liking was always the most important thing. She'd never met Billy, but Emily had, a couple of times, when he'd traveled back east.

"Yes, I guess I did. He was extremely personable"—the better to swindle the unsuspecting, her mother-in-law had insisted—"and interested in everything we were doing"—so he could assess your value and know exactly how much you could be cheated out of, her sister-in-law warned—"and just . . . I don't know, cheerful and happy"—so you'd let down your guard, her brother-in-law declared with haughty contempt.

"Sounds like an all right gent to me. Besides, as far as I can see, the less the Crabtrees like him, the better he probably is."

Opal was familiar with the family stories about William Crabtree, since she'd married his younger brother, John. Though Emily was sure all the stories had been embellished, she worried that there might be a grain of truth somewhere in those tales. What little she had left in the way of money was now tied up in this ranch, and she was going to make sure the investment prospered.

"I'm sure Uncle Billy has done the best he could. I just wish Laurence hadn't decided that only a man could possibly have the business acumen necessary for managing money and left Uncle Billy in charge of my finances."

"Better William than one of his other miserly relatives, you know. It could have been worse. I know John loved him dearly, and while younger brothers often idolize their older brothers, I think John knew what he liked and what he didn't. After all, he married me, even though the family all thought I was too old for him. Twelve years his senior and still I outlived him." Opal wiped a tear from her eye. "John was a good judge of character, and he liked William. I don't care if the rest of the family thinks of him as some sort of confidence man, making and losing fortunes at the drop of a hat. What do *you* think?"

It was nice to have someone ask what she thought instead of lecturing her on what she should be thinking.

"I can't say. Uncle Billy never confided in me, but from all I've heard, he never contradicted any of the others, either. He'd just sit there and smile."

"Sounds like a man who knows when to keep his own counsel."

"That's what I like most about you, Opal," Emily said with a laugh. "You always see the best in everybody."

"So do you, child, or you would never have stuck it out with Laurence."

Emily sighed. This was old ground, and now that Laurence was dead, there was no point in belaboring the obvious. "Laurence isn't the issue, I'm afraid. Uncle Billy and the ranch are. I should know where we stand with the ranch within a few days," Emily said, changing the subject. "I'll come and get you then."

With those words, Emily hugged Opal good-bye and watched the older woman enter Bea's store. Now all Emily had to do was find transportation out to the ranch. She entered the livery stable.

The buckboard pulled through the gates and into the courtyard of a large adobe building with a red-tiled roof. The walls were a dirty gray, but at least they all were standing. This was more than she had expected. Of course she hadn't seen the inside yet.

"There she is, ma'am," drawled the aging cowboy who had driven her out from Bethel Springs. Uncle Billy had made arrangements with the livery stable to care for anyone traveling out to the ranch. Emily thought that strange, but was so relieved she didn't question it.

"Is my Uncle Billy here, do you know?" she asked.

The cowboy wiped his hands on his pants, squinted at the yard, and finally said, "Don't rightly know, ma'am. All's he said was to bring you out here."

This was the longest speech Emily had heard from her taciturn companion. He'd carried her trunks and Opal's from the stage depot, and loaded their belongings on the buckboard after mumbling something about Billy having sent him.

"When did you last speak to him?"

"Never did. He just left instructions with the boss. He did say a neighbor boy would be coming over to help with the . . . stock." He stumbled over the final word.

She didn't like the sound of that, but before she could ask what he meant, a young boy came bounding around the far corner of the house. His face filled with laughter as he kept glancing over his shoulder.

Emily followed his glance. What she saw following him left her so thunderstruck she couldn't speak or move. Emily wasn't normally the type of woman to faint, but if she had been, now would have been the perfect time.

CHAPTER
2

Zach leaned back in his saddle. The creaking leather reminded him of how long it had been since he'd sat on anything but a horse. He stretched his shoulders and felt a twinge in his right arm. The wound was healing nicely, but he wouldn't bet his life on the speed of his draw just yet. He turned his head, shading his eyes with the brim of his hat, and looked around. From where he sat, he had a good view of Billy's spread. It wasn't exactly what he'd expected. He'd gotten directions in Longtree, the last town he'd passed through, and was pretty certain this was Billy's property. He just wasn't sure he'd call it a ranch.

There didn't appear to be any outbuildings, just a large adobe structure built around three sides of an open courtyard. On the fourth side, between two side wings, was the gate to the courtyard which now stood open. He'd never seen a ranch laid out like this before.

Twisting in his saddle, he looked around. There didn't appear to be any grazing land nearby, either. The cattle must be over near the mountains on the other side of the house, 'cause he was darn sure nothing could live on the scrub he saw growing around him.

Gently kicking his horse, he ambled down the slight incline toward the large building. It needed a coat of whitewash, but otherwise it wasn't in bad shape. Billy'd mentioned that the town of Bethel Springs wasn't too far away and he could get what he needed there. Billy'd even set up an account at the local general store for him. Yup, the first thing on his list would be whitewash.

Just as he reached the gate to the large courtyard, a terrible screeching startled his mount. He tried to settle the horse, but the screeching grew more strident and insistent, and it was all he could do to keep his mount from racing away. Then from around the far outside corner of the building came the strangest sight he'd ever seen. First came a woman with her skirt hiked up around her knees and then the oddest-looking bird, a bird as tall as she was. As he watched, they raced by, neck and neck, out into the open range.

He sat for a moment dumbfounded, unsure what to do. He'd only seen a bird like that once before, and that had been in a picture book in Chicago. An ostrich from the heart of Africa. But he'd never expected to see one in the wilds of Arizona.

When he heard the woman yell, he knew he had to do something. He turned his horse, kicked the beast's sides, and raced after the duo. Within a few moments he'd caught up with them. Then he did the only thing he could. He leaned over in the saddle and scooped the woman up off the ground. At the same time he slowed the horse to a stop, turning it away from the ostrich's path.

He felt the pull on his right arm even though he'd picked her up with his left. The gunshot was certainly a pain in the . . . Before he could finish his thought, he felt a sharper pain in his forearm. It took only a second to discover its source: The woman had bitten him.

"Let me go. . . . Let me go. If you lay a finger on me, I'll have my uncle come after you," she gasped as he automatically tightened his arm around her. He could feel the warmth of her body through the cotton of her blue dress, the softness of her curves, so different from his own. He was startled by the depth of his awareness. He had been prepared for her to blush and then smile, give her thanks, and offer him a cool drink. He wasn't prepared for the bite or his reaction to her femininity. And he certainly wasn't prepared for what was happening now. She had started kicking and screeching louder than the bird.

"You idiot. What in the name of all that's holy do you think you're doing?" she yelled, thrashing out with her arms and legs.

"Saving you," he said succinctly, loosening his hold to let her breathe more easily.

He pulled the reins to the right and turned the horse back in the direction from which he had come. He wanted to put her down just as much as she wanted to be down, but he couldn't leave her in the middle of the range. His mother had taught him always to respect a lady, even if this lady wasn't exactly acting like one. Imagine showing her legs to all and sundry.

"Let me down this minute or I'll have the sheriff lock you up for good."

"Why don't I just take you back to the house?" he said in a soothing tone. He wasn't the least bit intimidated by her threat. Besides, being chased by a bird of that size probably had her frightened half to death. She had to be in some sort of shock from her near escape; he could think of no other reason for her behavior. After all, ladies just didn't act this way, at least none he knew. Not that he had that much experience with ladies, but he did remember the way his mother had acted, and she was certainly a lady.

"You fool. I don't want to go back to the house. I have to

get that bird. And she'll be halfway to Bethel Springs if you don't put me down," she said and pounded on the forearm she'd already bitten.

"*You* have to get the bird?" he asked as he pulled the horse to a stop inside the courtyard gates. "I thought *he* was chasing *you*!" He swung his leg over the saddle and slid down onto the sandy soil, still holding her close to his side.

The woman quickly pushed herself out of his hold and finally did the first ladylike thing he'd seen her do. She checked the buttons down the front of her shirtwaist and gave a sharp tug at its bottom, settling it into place. Then she quickly repinned the strawberry blonde hair that had fallen out of her bun.

"Who do you think you are?" she demanded, having finally regained her breath. Her brown eyes snapped with anger. She didn't appear to be the least bit embarrassed about what had happened.

"Are you all right?" he asked, ignoring her question.

"This is my property, and I don't like strangers thinking they can do whatever they like on it."

It appeared they were going to play a game of never answering each other's questions. Well, he could play that game as long as she wanted. He was good at it, as a matter of fact; he'd spent a lifetime keeping his own counsel.

"This is your property?"

"That's right," she said with an emphatic nod of her head.

At least she'd started answering his questions. Maybe this wasn't a game, but she was a woman, and he'd found out long ago that they were always playing one game or another. He just hadn't found hers out yet.

"I was under the impression that Billy Crabtree owned this spread."

"How do you know about Billy?"

"So this *is* his land."

"Only in the eyes of the law," she replied with a tinge of . . . defeat in her voice, if he didn't know better. And then her voice changed. "He used my money to buy this ranch—and these birds, and I plan to see that he doesn't lose it all in the blink of an eye."

"Birds?" he questioned. What in hell had Billy gotten him into, the crazy old coot? Zach certainly owed him, but ostriches? He wasn't altogether certain he could handle a herd of cattle by himself, much less alien birds.

The woman ignored his question. She had turned her head to gaze out at the horizon as soon as she'd finished speaking. Watching her, Zach forgot all about the birds. He was mesmerized by the soft outline of her silhouette. "Soft" was the only word to describe it. The delicate pinkness of her rounded cheeks, the small up-tipped nose, the fall of her thick lashes, and the long white line of her throat belied the fierceness of her voice when she'd berated him. Her hair shimmered in the desert sun. He wanted to reach out and touch the fire, even though he knew he'd be burned. She was certainly a study in opposites.

"Oh, good. Here comes Baby now," she said with relief in her voice. "I'm surprised you didn't scare the life out of her."

Zach watched as she and the bird walked toward each other. When they met, she gently placed her arm around its neck.

"Baby?" he asked as the five-foot-tall ostrich inched its way forward.

"The neighbor boy named her," she murmured softly as she petted the creature. "And, like a baby, she likes pretty, shiny things. She likes to steal them, too. Don't you, girl? That's why I was chasing her. She stole my silver thimble," she said fondly, then suddenly looked anxious. "I don't see the thimble. I hope she hasn't swallowed it." She ran her hand up and down the bird's long, almost hairless neck and cooed to it just as if it were a baby.

"If he did, it'll just get chewed up in the gizzard—if these here ostriches have gizzards, that is. He seems mighty tame for a wild thing," Zach added, not coming any closer. Better safe than sorry.

"She," the woman corrected, though how she could tell was a mystery. "Seems Oswald, the neighbor boy, plays with her every time he comes to care for the stock. I guess I've taken Oswald's place in Baby's eyes. Just as well, since he won't be coming anymore now that I'm here."

"He won't be coming anymore because *I'm* here," Zach repeated with changed emphasis. As soon as the words left his mouth, he knew he'd made the decision to stay. He'd conquered tougher things, though whether he'd be able to conquer her was another question altogether.

"I told you *I* own this land," she said, planting her hands on her hips. She looked ready to take on the world.

"And Billy hired *me* to look after it. How many men do you think would take on this ranch after seeing this oddity?"

"Since I only got here yesterday, I have no idea how many men will be calling at my doorstep," she replied in a prim, schoolmarmish voice. "Exactly when did Billy hire you? How long ago was it that you talked with him?"

"I'd be obliged if we could do this jawin' in a more comfortable place. I've had a long ride. And it's hot out here."

"But—"

Zach merely shook his head. He was dusty and tired, and the relentless beating of the sun had added a sharp edge of impatience to his temper. He took off his hat and wiped the sweat from his brow with his forearm.

She watched him as he put the hat back on, then gestured for him to follow her to the ranch house. For a distance, neither said a word.

"By the way, my name's Zach Hollis," he said, removing his dusty brown hat once again. She was a lady, no matter how she acted. Best to start treating her like one and stop any wayward thoughts.

Emily wanted to ignore him, but her well-brought-up, better-mannered self told her she couldn't. After all, she'd already acted like a . . . she didn't know what, with her skirt hiked up around her knees and her hair falling all over her face. She couldn't imagine what this man was thinking. Of course she really didn't care what he thought, but a small niggling voice, the voice of her mother, reminded her to act in a dignified manner. She was glad she wasn't wearing gloves, for she had no desire to shake his hand. "I'm Emily Crabtree."

"Billy's daughter?" he asked, his astonishment evident as he tied his horse to the hitch in front of the main house entrance.

"No, I'm his niece by marriage," she haltingly admitted. She didn't want to give this man any more information than was necessary. He certainly didn't look like a ranch foreman to her, not that she had a lot of experience with hired hands. There was something about him she didn't trust. Whether it was the gun strapped low on his leg or the look in his eyes, she couldn't say. Something just didn't sit right where he was concerned. And it wasn't just the way she'd felt when he'd had her pulled tight against the side of his hard body, either.

"Maybe I should be talking with your husband then, ma'am."

"My husband passed away," she said, turning away from the house. "You'll have to do whatever talking you're going to do with me." She started up the steps of the porch that ran along the front of the living quarters, and then remembered the ostrich and started shooing her off. "You have to stay

outside." She hoped he'd think the command was for him
and not the bird. He didn't.

"My sympathies on your loss, ma'am. Was it recent?"

"I lost Laurence eighteen months ago." My, he was nosy,
but she was beginning to learn these westerners weren't as
reticent as her eastern neighbors had been. Besides, her loss
of Laurence was really much more than eighteen months
ago. She'd lost whatever she'd thought he was long before
that. Their last few years of marriage hadn't really been a
marriage at all.

"I wouldn't mind something cool to drink, if you could
spare it," Zach said, hitting his hat against his leg to rid it of
dust, obviously uneasy with the silence.

"Come inside and I'll get you some water," she said, indicating the front door. "And then you can answer some of my
questions."

She didn't want him inside, but she did want to know what
was happening with Billy. Once she found out what he knew,
she could send him on his way.

That Billy sure was a sly one. He had to have known she
wouldn't just let him get away with sending a telegram. And
if he'd thought she would be coming out here, he might have
sent someone like this Zach Hollis to make sure she didn't
get into any trouble. She didn't like being maneuvered this
way. She'd thought when Laurence died she'd be able to run
her own life. After all, she was a grown woman of twenty-
five. Now it looked as if Billy was putting Zach Hollis in
charge.

She opened the front door and walked into the main living
area. The neighbor boy had told her a wealthy English gentleman owned the ranch before Billy. She was still amazed at
the contrast between the indoors and out. If she didn't know
better, she'd think she was still in Hartford. The Englishman
had obviously been a literate man. She'd found a number of

books, including a couple on ostrich farming, already on the shelves and had added her own eclectic choices to the collection. With her fringed scarf draped over the small round table by the settee and a few knickknacks arranged about, the room almost felt like home. When Opal got here and added her things, it would be quite nice.

"If you'll have a seat, I'll bring you some water." She turned to face him as she spoke. Outside, he'd seemed large enough, but in the confines of the sitting room he loomed even larger and more overwhelming. His brown shirt and pants only accentuated his size. She could still remember the feel of his strong, muscular arm holding her against his leg and the side of the horse. He produced a feeling in her she didn't want to remember or admit to. The sooner he was out of her house and her life, the better. She could handle her own business.

She hurried into the kitchen and ladled some water into a glass. It really was convenient that the Englishman had left most of his furnishings. Emily had never considered that aspect when she'd made her mad rush to the West. Nothing out here was what she'd expected—not the desert, not the ranch, not the ostriches, and certainly not Zach Hollis.

She returned to the sitting room and handed him the glass of water, then sat down on the settee directly across from his chair.

"Thank you, ma'am. It's been a long, dry trip," he said after draining the glass, implying that a real drink would have been better. Well, that was just too bad. Emily didn't approve of spirits. They'd done their dastardly deed on Laurence, and as long as she had her say, there would be no alcohol in the house.

"Exactly where are you coming from, Mr. Hollis?" she asked bluntly. She didn't want to waste time with polite conversation, even if Zach Hollis was capable of it, and she doubted that he was.

"Out Denver way," he replied in a lazy drawl.

"And when was the last time you saw Billy?"

"When was the last time *you* saw him?" he countered.

She knew it had been too much to ask that he follow her lead, answering all her questions without demur. She would have to answer some of his in exchange for the information she wanted.

"Billy and I correspond mainly through my solicitor, except at the holidays. I haven't seen him in person for over three years. He couldn't make it back for Laurence's funeral."

"I understand."

What did he understand? She didn't like the knowing look in his hard eyes nor the way those hazel eyes stared right at her. Actually they were more green than hazel, she thought, then caught herself up short. She was too acutely aware of him without knowing why. He made her uncomfortable, she decided, unwilling to acknowledge any deeper feelings.

"As I was saying, I take it you've seen Billy recently," she said.

"About a week ago, more or less."

"And that was in Denver?"

"Thereabouts."

"Did he send a message?"

"Can't say."

"And why can't you, Mr. Hollis?" she asked sharply.

"He never mentioned you'd be waitin' here for me," he replied in a lazy drawl.

"I am not waiting here for *you*. And for that matter, he never mentioned you to me, either." This man was totally aggravating. He gave only as much information as he felt like giving and not one word more.

"As the saying goes, we seem to be in the same boat."

"No, I don't believe we are, Mr. Hollis. I'm in the boat. You're swimming alongside. Unless, that is, you have a letter or a contract from Billy stating your position." She'd had enough of his evasions. Either he produced proof or he was gone.

"You out here all alone?"

"Don't think I'm some poor helpless woman. I assure you, Mr. Hollis, I'm not, and if this is some kind of subtle threat—"

"Miz Crabtree, 'helpless' is not a word I'd use for you."

For a brief moment Emily knew a stab of disappointment. She had been brought up to think of herself as a young lady of respectable social standing, and as such she ought to be thought of as helpless in some sense and worth helping. All the etiquette books said so, and Emily didn't want to be different from other young ladies. Yet she knew she was. Laurence had seen to that. Well, if Zach Hollis thought of her as self-sufficient, then she'd show him exactly how self-sufficient she could be.

With the dignity of a queen, Emily stood up in front of the settee. She lifted her chin and looked down at her visitor. "I suggest you find lodgings for the night, Mr. Hollis. It becomes quite chilly here, I've discovered."

That statement brought him out of his chair, just as she knew it would. What she hadn't planned on was his menacing height. He topped her five feet five by a good seven inches, and every one of those inches was now poised on the brink of explosion. She could read it on his face.

"What do you mean by lodgings, Miz Crabtree?" he asked in a quietly menacing voice.

Emily couldn't quite believe he dared ask the question. "Well, you can't think you'll be able to stay here in the house."

"And why not? Billy said I could."

"Because *I'm* staying here. It . . . it wouldn't be proper."

He didn't answer, but she could tell by the look on his face that he had no qualms about staying in the living quarters of the building with her, even if she did. The West was certainly different.

"And where do you suggest I bunk?"

"Bethel Springs has a very—"

"If you think I'm going to ride all the way into Bethel Springs tonight, just to cater to your sense of eastern propriety, you're wrong. You're in the West now. Remember that."

"Then what do you suggest?"

"What's in the rest of this building? You don't seem to be using much of this place to live in."

"The bedrooms are in the northwest wing, along that side of the courtyard." She pointed out the window to the adjacent wing of the adobe structure. "This part of the building houses the kitchen and dining room in the back and the parlor runs along here in front."

"And what's in the other wing over there?"

She turned around to face the wing that ran along the third side of the courtyard. It was much larger than the bedroom wing.

"The barn extends from the front to the back and the back section has a bunch of storerooms. Most are full of junk. I haven't had a chance to go through them yet. There's also another living area. It looks as if it was used as a bunkhouse at some point."

"Sounds good enough to me. I'll bunk down there tonight, near the barn. We'll continue this discussion in the morning." With those words, he turned and walked out the door.

Emily stood staring after him in amazement. The volume of his voice had never changed, yet she'd known he was very upset. She'd assessed him from the very first as a cowboy—a not very cultivated denizen of the West, despite the romantic tales she'd read in the newspapers. And that spoke for itself. But she was finding out that wasn't all he was. There was something dangerous and untamed about him, something that threatened her at the most basic level. Not that she thought he would attack her physically, he'd had plenty of opportunity if that had been on his mind. No, his threat was much more subtle and elusive. And that made him all the more dangerous.

An hour later, when the sun had started its lazy trip down to kiss the tops of the mountains to the west, Emily decided she had acted much too hastily. Suppose Uncle Billy had invited Zach to the ranch as the foreman. It wasn't impossible. And if he had, she'd done the unpardonable. She'd thrown a guest out of the house. One of the rules of etiquette that had been drilled into her since she was old enough to understand kept running around in her mind: "A conscientious hostess puts her guests' wants and needs before her own."

With her chin up and a practiced and polite apology on her tongue she was about to walk over to the storage area where he was bunking when she saw him in the courtyard. He was bending over the water pump, his pants pulled tight over his backside and clinging to his powerful thighs. From what she could see, he was shirtless.

Emily caught her breath. She knew she shouldn't be staring, it simply wasn't the respectable thing to do, but the man before her was mesmerizing. Where Laurence had been soft and white-skinned, Zach was hard and bronzed from the sun. His muscles rippled as he sluiced water from the trough over his head and shoulders.

There was something intimate about watching a man at his evening ablutions, even if he wasn't aware he was being watched. Emily's heart raced in her chest, and she decided she'd better turn away before he caught her staring through

the window. But just then he straightened up, and the water
ran in rivulets down his back, glistening in the slanting sunlight and shooting golden points of light to her eyes.

His shoulders were broad and powerful, she noticed, and
his hair gleamed shiny and dark, almost black now that it
was wet. He tossed an errant lock off his forehead with a
sharp sweep of his head and turned slightly. That was when
she saw it.

High on his right side, up at his shoulder, the angry wound
gaped. Emily pressed her hand to her chest and looked
again. The wound was recent and only partly healed. The
skin around it still looked red and tender. Emily couldn't tear
her eyes away. She'd never seen anything like it, yet knew
instinctively what it was—a gunshot wound.

Zach swept his wet hair back with his left hand, then
picked up his hat and put it on, again with his left hand.
Emily recognized now what had only vaguely registered in
her mind before: He favored his right arm even though he
was obviously right-handed. She hadn't understood it
earlier, but now, faced with the evidence of his injury, it all
became clear.

What kind of man was he? she wondered, suddenly afraid.
She'd been dismayed when she'd first seen how he carried
his gun, but the reality of it hadn't really sunk in until now.
People who wore tied-down guns didn't only shoot; they
also got shot. What if he'd lied about Billy sending him?
What if . . .

The thought wasn't completed because at that moment
Zach turned toward the house. Emily shrank away from the
window, half hiding behind the heavy, faded curtains so she
could still watch him.

Spying was really what she was doing, she admitted to
herself, and now her curiosity was fueled by fear. As he

walked toward the window, Emily could see his muscled chest with its covering of brown curls, but what caught her full attention was the companion injury on the front of his shoulder. Larger and more roughly shaped than the wound on his back, it told a story of its own.

He'd been shot from behind!

Before she could think things through, her legs were carrying her out the door and onto the porch.

"What happened to your shoulder?" she called out.

For a moment Zach looked startled. He grabbed for his shirt with his right arm, then winced.

"You've been hurt," Emily said, stepping down from the porch.

Zach watched her warily as she approached. She was slim and of medium height. In the late afternoon sunlight, her reddish-yellow hair glowed, framing her face like an angel's halo. Everything about her was fair and delicate, except her eyes. They were brown like the earth, richly fringed with dark lashes that ended in golden tips, and full of knowledge beyond her years.

"It's nothing," he said defensively and managed to swing his shirt over his shoulder. The last thing he needed was for her to learn about his stupidity. Besides, the wound was almost healed. He could damn well take care of it himself.

"It didn't look like nothing to me. I think I should take a look at it."

She gestured to the low step of the porch and indicated that he should sit. He ignored her. She gave him a look that might have cowed an easterner, but Zach was made of sterner stuff. He stood his ground.

"There's no need. I told you, it's nothing much."

"If it's nothing much, then you can't mind my taking a peek, now can you?" she said with a logic he couldn't refute.

"Besides," she went on, "if you're injured, you probably shouldn't be traveling."

That did it. Zach wasn't a man to pass up an opportunity when it virtually hit him in the face. He'd been looking for an excuse not to have to fight her about staying on at the ranch, and she'd just handed him exactly what he needed.

"You might be right at that," he said, grimacing more painfully than his injury really warranted at this point in his recovery. "Traveling can be mighty painful at times." And that was surely no lie. The slight evening breeze picked up a lock of her hair and spun it out like gold, gently curling it before setting it softly across her cheek. Zach watched, fascinated. She flicked it back with one hand, tucking it into the knot she wore at the back of her neck, the gesture quintessentially feminine. The breeze gave a little twist when it reached the end of the courtyard and blew back against her, pressing the soft cotton fabric of her dress against her skin, revealing the soft swell of her breasts to Zach's discerning eye.

Zach could feel his body tighten. He didn't need or want this. He didn't want to think of her as a desirable woman, and he was suddenly very aware of his need. What's more, he sensed her vulnerability, and he didn't like that, either. He had no time for such nonsense. He had a job to do. Period.

"What're you doing out here in the desert on your own?" he demanded.

"As I said before, I'm protecting my investment."

He took a step forward and looked down at her from his greater height. "And who's protecting you?"

"I thought you said you were," she threw back at him. "Isn't that why Billy hired you?"

She was quick, he had to hand her that, and she had sand, standing up to him the way she did.

"He hired me to take care of the ranch, not to wet-nurse some greenhorn lady while she plays at being a ranch hand."

"Nobody asked you to wet-nurse me. If anything, you're the one who needs nursing. Now, are you going to sit and let me look at your injury or are you well enough to leave the same way you came?"

Zach was as stubborn as the next man, and not one to be outwitted by a lady, no matter how charming she looked with her cheeks all flushed and the breeze wreaking havoc on his good sense. But he'd learned to be subtle over the years, to win his victories by subterfuge as much as brute strength, to make his opponent think he was yielding when he was merely biding his time in search of an even stronger position.

With a conciliatory shrug, Zach sat on the step.

"You need help getting that shirt off?" Emily asked.

Her gaze skittered along the ground by his feet. She might be a widow, but she wasn't so brazen that she liked undressing a stranger. Zach toyed with the idea of pushing her a little just to equalize things, then decided against it. He sensed that her bravado was just a facade. And while he might not be reckoned a gentleman by all who met him, his mama had taught him to tread gently with all who were weaker than he was.

"I can manage," he said softly. He slid the shirt off, and this time his grimace had nothing fake about it. The shoulder still plagued him when it got too much use, and the past couple of days he'd been feeling better, so he'd exercised the damn thing too much.

The sun was still bright enough in the sky that it felt warm against his bare skin despite the flirtatious breeze that spun about the courtyard raising little eddies of dust and straw. He closed his eyes as Emily drew close and breathed in the scent

of her. Violets. In the desert. How incongruous and yet . . .
how right.

She touched him with her fingertips, and they burned hotter than the sun. Her skin was soft, unused to hard labor. Her
breath was sweet as she leaned over him.

"How'd you get shot?" she asked, her voice wavering as
she felt around his bruised shoulder, delicately assessing his
wound.

He was all too aware of her, of her scent and her warmth,
of her nearness and femininity. It had been too long since
he'd last had a woman, he suddenly realized. Way too long.

He shifted uncomfortably, then opened his eyes, needing a
distraction. It was a mistake. Her breasts were just inches
from his face as she leaned over to examine his shoulder
more closely. They were full and sweetly rounded. Beneath
the scent of violets, she smelled clean and inviting. Zach
could feel himself hardening. What was it about this lady
that caused him to act like a boy with his first real woman?

"I was shot the usual way. By a gun," he replied bluntly.
As he'd hoped, his words made her jerk away. He took a
deep breath and bunched his shirt into his lap before she saw
anything untoward.

"That much I figured out," she said tartly with her fists
planted on her hips. "Is it also usual to get shot in the back?"

"That was stupidity." He stood up still holding the shirt in
front of him. "Now, if you're quite finished, I've got work to
do."

"You need to get that bandaged first. You'll get an infec-
tion if dirt gets in it."

He knew she was right, but he didn't trust himself near her
for much longer. "I can take care of it myself. I've managed
just fine so far. If you'll excuse me, I still have some things
to straighten up in my room."

Zach stalked back to his makeshift bunk, more confused

now than before. That woman was a total enigma. Stubborn and strong, yet gentle and pliant, concerned about his wound even though he knew she didn't want him anywhere near *her* ranch. He couldn't figure her out, and that was dangerous. He liked to have everyone's measure, be it man or woman. That way he knew where he stood.

He massaged his right leg as he looked around the room. This was hardly what he'd imagined when Billy had asked him to come here. He'd been looking for roots, if only temporarily, for a feeling of belonging, of investing something of himself in the ranch. Instead, he was being shunned as an outsider yet again, consigned to this tiny room in the back by the barn. Emily couldn't have made it clearer that she was tolerating his presence only by dint of his connection to Billy Crabtree, and she treated even that with suspicion.

Maybe it was something about him. He'd been a loner for so long, he wasn't sure he knew how to deal with people anymore, at least not in close proximity, and certainly not with ladies like Emily. He had his friends, few enough but true and loyal, and maybe he should be satisfied. But deep inside he hungered for something more, something this ranch had represented for a few brief moments by the campfire, something out of a dream.

He sighed. He knew enough of dreams. Look at his parents. They'd had a dream, too, and what had it gotten them? No, he'd best keep his mind on his job, on taking care of things for Billy until it was time to get on with his real purpose for being here—finding Earl Darnell and then the remaining members of the Darnell gang.

Clenching his jaw, Zach surveyed his new domain. It was a far cry from what he'd expected, but not impossible. He'd managed to move some old furniture out of the way and concocted a bed out of an old divan. This would work until tomorrow when he had a regular bedroom. In the house. Emily

Crabtree might not realize it, being an easterner, but this was still an untamed land. They didn't have policemen on every corner out here like they did back east. He'd feel a lot better when he was closer to her and able to do more in the protection line. Being this far out and not having a good shooting hand wouldn't bode well if there was any trouble.

He was just about to go do a final check on his horse for the night when he heard a soft knocking at the wooden door. He knew it could only be one person and was tempted to ignore her. Her uppity eastern ways grated on him; his response had nothing to do with the smell of violets or the softness of velvety brown eyes. He was tired and he was sore and he wasn't ready for any more of Emily Crabtree.

But he couldn't just ignore her. For one thing, he was sure she wouldn't allow it. When the knock sounded again, he opened the door.

She stood at the open doorway, her hands clasped in front of her, holding some bleached white material.

"Mr. Hollis, I thought you could use this bandage for your shoulder," she said, stepping inside and holding out the material in his direction. "And I wanted to apologize for my earlier behavior. I wasn't expecting any company, and my manners were less than they should have been. It won't happen again."

"I see," he said, though he wasn't sure where this was leading. He made no move to take the white bandage material from her hand.

"Uh, if you'll take this, I'll be going."

He took the fabric and tossed it carelessly onto the divan. "Well, if that's all?"

When she didn't answer, he assumed she had nothing else to say and ushered her out the door, closing it behind her.

Zach could almost feel her shock and surprise through the door. It was no less than he was feeling. He'd never been so rude to a lady in his life. She'd offered to help with his shoulder, even if she'd been a little condescending about how he was shot, and she'd even apologized for her earlier attitude—something Zach himself should have done. Granted, she'd rubbed him the wrong way ever since they met, but that was no reason to act the way he had. But something about her got under his skin, and he felt he had to keep her at a distance any way he could.

Still, there was no call to be nasty to her. He'd have to find some other way. After all, he'd made Billy a promise, and he planned on staying right where he was. It appeared she felt the same way; neither was about to budge. They'd have to come to some sort of agreement if they were going to make this work. After he settled and fed his horse, he'd go and make his peace.

By the time he found fodder for his horse, it was dark. He'd come across an old lamp still filled with kerosene in the storeroom when he was making up his bed and had lit it before going out. Now he was glad he had. The moon was a faint sliver in the sky, and the stars provided scant illumination.

As he walked back toward his bunk, delicious aromas assailed his nostrils. His stomach growled, and he realized he hadn't eaten since morning. Whatever she was cooking sure smelled good. The lights inside the house were a beacon in the darkness. Maybe this was as good a time as any to make amends. He changed direction and headed around the barn to the back door by the kitchen.

When he reached the open door, he could see her seated at the table, spooning potatoes onto her plate. He could also see a roast on the table. Zach's mouth watered, setting off a clamor that triggered his stomach to growl once more. He must have made a sound, for she looked up in his direction, but she didn't say a word. She merely turned back to her plate and began eating.

When she didn't invite him in, Zach knew she wouldn't let him off the hook so easily—not that he could blame her. She'd steeled herself for her own apology, and he'd all but thrown it back in her face. Now she was going to be just as stubborn as he'd been. At least they had something in common. Not that being stubborn was an admirable trait, but it might be a start.

"Evenin', Miz Crabtree."

She didn't answer, but she did put down her fork.

"I was thinking we might call a truce, Miz Crabtree. What do you say?"

She didn't answer right away. Then, just as his patience was about to snap, she said, "Exactly what kind of truce, Mr. Hollis?"

"A truce that will allow us to work together until we can get this misunderstanding straightened out."

He watched her as she considered his suggestion and then stood up.

"Would you care for some supper?" she asked as she moved to the sideboard and began preparing another place setting.

"That's mighty kind of you. It's been quite a spell since I've had a home-cooked meal."

"Well, it's plain fare you'll be getting here, I'm afraid. I only brought a small supply of food out from town. I wasn't sure what I'd find when I got here."

"Whatever you're having smells mighty good," he said and moved to the chair she indicated.

"I'm . . . We're lucky the former tenants left so much behind. I couldn't have done much without all their cooking utensils."

Zach hadn't missed her stumble. More than anything else, it showed she was willing to meet him halfway. He couldn't do less.

"Do you know anything about the people who owned this ranch before Billy?" Zach asked conversationally as he speared a piece of beef and put it on his plate.

"Oswald said the former owners were English nobility of some sort. They couldn't make a go of it out here, I guess. This land is rather rugged."

She offered him some peas.

"Takes a special breed to make it out here," he agreed.

"And apparently they didn't have what it takes, but I'm grateful for the things they left. Quite frankly, I didn't think to bring kitchen utensils with me from the East."

"Where in the East are you from?"

As she told him about her life back in Connecticut, he thought how different it was from his own. Her family, her friends, her work. A normal sort of life. The kind of life he might have had if the Darnells hadn't deprived him of it.

"And do you have family, Mr. Hollis?"

"No, ma'am. I've only myself to worry about. Makes traveling a whole lot less complicated," he answered lightly, but he knew he would give just about anything to have his family back. For years he'd plotted his revenge, trailing the men who'd murdered his family. He wouldn't rest until he'd found every last one of them, he reminded himself. Until that day, he had no room for finer feelings, for putting down roots or enjoying the scent of violets. . . .

"And do you have a lot of experience as a ranch foreman?" she asked, interrupting his thoughts.

"Enough," he replied. He didn't really have any experience as a foreman, but he had no doubt about his ability to do a good job, even if the stock consisted of ostriches instead of cattle. He'd run cattle from one state to another and back. He knew he would have no trouble handling a spread this size. "I think I'll ride out in the morning and see what shape everything is in. Then I can decide what needs to be done."

"I'm afraid you're stretching our truce beyond its boundaries, Mr. Hollis. Just because I invited you to have supper with me doesn't mean I'm turning over the running of this ranch to you. Unless and until Uncle Billy tells me otherwise, I plan to oversee everything that goes on here, and that includes being a part of every decision that is made."

She rose without giving him a chance to respond and started collecting the dinnerware from the table.

Zach was in too good a mood after being fed and having rested a bit to challenge her. There'd be time enough in the morning. There was no way he'd let his own judgment be overridden by a greenhorn, as she'd find out soon enough. But for the moment he wanted nothing more than to prolong his feeling of well-being.

"Here, let me help with the cleaning up. It's the least I can do after you've fed me," Zach said as he came up behind her.

"There's no need, Mr. Hollis," she said in a surprised voice, as if she didn't expect him to offer. She deliberately stepped back, moving out of his way. It was almost as if she didn't want him to touch her. "I'm perfectly capable of handling these dishes . . . and anything else that comes up on this ranch."

"We'll see about that," he said in a voice too soft for her to hear, then louder, he added, "In that case, thank you kindly for the meal. I'm sure we'll be seeing more of each other, Miss Emily."

He was out the door before she could retaliate. Thinking about it, he realized he'd had too good a time over dinner. If he didn't keep up his guard, there'd be hell to pay, on all sides. But if Zach was an expert at one thing, it was at keeping his guard up, and tomorrow wasn't too soon to start. He'd show her who was boss and convince her a ranch in the desert was no place for a lady. Then he'd get back to his real reason for coming here.

CHAPTER
3

The morning was cool and dry, a far cry from the blistering heat of the previous day. The air was crystalline, reflecting the light in every direction.

Emily poured the water she'd prepared the night before from the light blue pitcher into the matching bowl on the dry sink and quickly washed. Then she dressed in her oldest shirtwaist and a light cotton skirt, forgoing her usual layers of petticoats in favor of only a light chemise. It might be cool now, but that was no guarantee that the rest of the day would be as comfortable, if yesterday was anything to go by. Besides, who would see her out here anyway?

She had her answer when she looked out the front window and saw Zach striding to the barn. She knew he'd be at her door before long. She wasn't sure she was ready to face him so early in the morning. He'd unsettled her last night with his attitude and his body.

She could still remember the resilient feel of his skin beneath her fingertips, and the memory sent shivers running down her spine. He was so . . . male, in an exciting and untamed way. None of the men she'd known back east had exuded the same air of power, though she'd known her share of powerful men. But they had been different. Theirs had been the power of money and law. They'd sat in their offices and banks and dispatched others to do the dirty work, buying and trading souls as easily as they exchanged cash—all from a distance.

But Zach's power was more immediate, more physical, more personal. It reached out to her, cracking the defenses she'd set up after her marriage as if they weren't there. She couldn't imagine him letting anyone else do a job he'd decided was his. She couldn't see him breaking his word once he'd given it.

She closed her eyes and once again saw the smooth muscles beneath his sun-bronzed skin, touched his warmth and vitality with her fingertips, felt his pain and betrayal in the wound that marred his masculine beauty. Her senses had been captured by him, making her aware of him in every corner of her being.

Compassion had flooded her when she saw his injury. To be shot from behind! What kind of amoral place had she come to? But he seemed to take it in his stride, calmly walking away with that air of self-assurance. How she envied his self-confidence, his sense of himself and his place in the world! She'd had to fight so hard to stake out her own little corner, and now she would have to fight again, but this time against a more worthy adversary.

Emily tamped down her compassion. Zach claimed he could manage by himself. She would take him at his word; it was too dangerous to do otherwise. And besides, he seemed oblivious of the effect he had on her. She couldn't afford to let herself be weakened by emotion, to once again let a man take over her life. She'd learned from bitter experience that men were too greedy. They weren't satisfied with controlling just her life; they wanted her very soul. And she'd had to fight too hard to get hers back to risk it on a man who made her heart flutter in her chest and turned her knees to jelly. Her judgment had been faulty once; she wouldn't trust it so quickly again.

As soon as he was well, she'd give Zach his marching orders. That would be time enough. After all, she wasn't heartless, and despite his protestations, the man must still be in pain from that nasty-looking gunshot wound. Besides, she rationalized, maybe Billy really had wanted him to care for the ranch. She'd take it one day at a time, but she wouldn't let Zach—or any other man—walk all over her. That was a promise she'd made to herself long ago, one she vowed never to forget.

While she ate her breakfast, a quick affair of a few biscuits left over from dinner and some hot tea, she decided she would take a closer look at some of the books on ostriches she'd found around the house. One in particular had caught her attention. It had a purple cover with a running ostrich embossed on it in gold, its feathers boldly displayed.

"Ostriches and Ostrich Farming," Emily read on the inside page. How perfect, she thought. The book—written by a Frenchman, Julius de Mosenthal, and an Englishman, James Edmund Harting—had been published only a few years earlier in the hope of enticing Europeans to raise ostriches for the fashion industry. The feathers were highly prized as ornamentation and increasingly hard to obtain from the wild because indiscriminate slaughter had nearly led to the birds' extermination.

Emily figured the advice on ostrich farming intended for Europeans couldn't be too different from what an American would need to know, so she propped the book up on her lap and paged through it while she ate.

"In regard to food," the book said, "the ostrich may be said to be omnivorous. Seeds, berries, fruit, grass . . ." The list seemed endless and included sand, stones, and even bits of metal. "So indifferent, indeed," the book continued, "does the bird seem to what is palatable or nourishing that it is said to feed upon whatever it can swallow."

Well, she'd had personal experience with that, Emily thought with a wry smile, thinking fondly of her recently eaten silver thimble. Apparently Baby's proclivity for anything shiny was not unique.

A sudden commotion out front in the courtyard brought Emily to her feet. What on earth could Baby be up to now? Emily rushed to the window and looked out. Baby was nowhere to be seen. Instead, a wagon laden with trunks and bags was standing in the yard. Two women were climbing down from its high bench.

"Watch yourself, now, Eula," the blond one called out. She was dressed outlandishly in a low-cut, overly tight red dress that clung to every generously endowed curve. She wore a matching hat set at a rakish angle. A shining white feather swooped backwards on one side, then curved high over the hat's crown before cascading down over its brim.

"I'm fine, Jewel," her mousy companion replied in a softer voice. Her dress was as loose as the other's was tight, as colorless as Jewel's was bright. Even her hair looked faded, a dull, musty brown gathered into an untidy bun at the top of her head. "Are you sure this is the right place?"

"Near enough. If not, they'll let us know. Come on. Let's see if anybody's here."

Emily opened the door a crack. "Who are you?" she called out. "What do you want?"

"This here the Double F Ranch?" the woman named Jewel yelled back. "This Billy Crabtree's place?"

"Yes," Emily replied and opened the door far enough to step out. "Have you seen Uncle Billy? Do you know where he is? Is he coming back soon?"

"Hold your horses there, girl. One question at a time. You must be Emily, eh?"

"How'd you know?"

"Billy said he thought you might show up. Sent ya this, in case. Hang on a minute and I'll find it."

Jewel rooted around in an immense travel bag, then pulled out a wrinkled piece of paper and held it out triumphantly.

"Here ya go," she said with a big smile. Her lips were painted redder than her dress, and as she sashayed over to Emily, her hips waved from side to side provocatively.

"You can read, can't ya?" she asked, a worried frown creasing her powdered brow.

"Oh, yes," Emily admitted, a bit startled at the question.

"Good. I was worried there for a minute. Couldn't help you much otherwise, seeing as I can hardly read myself."

She handed the piece of paper to Emily. "Old Billy said to give you this if'n we saw you. Said it would explain everything."

She smiled again and flicked one end of the long feather boa she wore round her neck over her shoulder. "Sure is getting hot, ain't it?" she commented.

Embarrassed, Emily said, "Oh, I'm terribly sorry. Won't you come in?"

She'd been the recipient of western hospitality often enough on her trip out to realize she had broken the first tenet of neighborliness. She stood back from the door so the two women could pass.

"Maybe you better read that letter first," the mousy woman said, her voice tremulous.

"Now, Eula, don't you worry none," Jewel said and patted the other woman's arm. "Billy said he'd take care of us. And he's a man of his word, Billy is. Ain't that right, Emily?"

"Why . . . yes. Yes, of course he is." She gave the woman a bemused smile and gestured once more for them to come in. "It's cooler inside," she added, "and I can offer you some tea. You must be thirsty after your trip here."

In truth, both women looked rather dusty. On closer inspection, she saw that even Jewel's bright red dress had seen better days.

"Why, that's very kind of you," Jewel said. "Come along now, Eula. We're keeping poor Emily out in the sun, too."

"Oh, my," Eula murmured. "Oh, my, yes. We mustn't keep you out. You're so fair."

She bustled into the house behind Jewel, leaving a thoroughly befuddled Emily to follow them in.

Jewel quickly took over the kitchen. "Now, you just take a seat and read your letter, dear, and leave us to take care of ourselves. We don't want to be no bother. Besides, you must be dying to know what Billy has to say."

"Do sit," Eula seconded. "We surely don't want to be no bother."

She stood near the wall, wringing her hands. Emily felt sorry for her. She seemed so nervous, as if she expected someone to jump up and yell at her at any moment. It was her nervousness that made Emily acquiesce, that and the hopeful way both ladies—if that was the proper word—looked at the letter.

"The tea's right on the stove and there are some cups in the cupboard over there." Emily indicated which cupboard with her hand, then sat at the table, unfolded the crumpled missive, and began to read.

She looked up a few minutes later to find Eula and Jewel standing still as statues, watching her, a combination of hope and fear lighting their faces. It came to her in that instant: They had nowhere else to go. Like her, they were women alone, women with no men. Even here in the West that meant an uncertain future if the man in your life had not left you well-provided-for.

"Billy writes you're to stay here," she said, getting right to the point. She caught the anxious glance that passed between the two women. "Will that be a problem? Would you rather go somewhere else?"

"N-no," Eula mumbled. "It's just—"

"We wouldn't want to impose," Jewel put in firmly. "Seems to me you got a right to an opinion, too, being as how you're living here now. Billy was none too sure what we'd find when he sent us."

"If he wasn't sure, why'd he send this letter?"

"In case you was here. Said he wasn't sure what your plans would be once you heard about his investment."

Emily shook her head. It did no good to get exasperated with her wily uncle, especially when he wasn't even here.

"Well, my opinion is that you can stay if you want to. There isn't much here yet, and I still have to get my aunt Opal out from Bethel Springs. But if you can put up with us, we could sure use the company."

"Good." Jewel smiled again and took off her hat. "If you don't mind, we'll have that tea now. It's been a dry and dusty morning, if you don't mind my saying so."

Eula didn't smile, but she did look less nervous.

"That sounds fine to me. When you're ready, I'll show you to your rooms. . . . Oh, and one other thing. There's also a man—"

"Well, glory be. Will you look at that?" Jewel interrupted, her blue eyes growing round in appreciation as she looked past Emily to the door. "My, my, my."

Emily jerked her head around to see what had caught Jewel's attention.

Zach stood there, his hat in his hand. His hair was neatly combed and still a little damp. His eyes scanned the room quickly, then came to rest on the two visitors.

"I saw the wagon outside. Thought I'd check on who was visiting."

"Well, come on in," Jewel invited, her false eyelashes batting an invitation of their own. "I'd be more than pleased to have you . . . check me out."

Emily didn't know whether to gasp or groan at Jewel's audacity. Or to laugh. There was an almost childlike quality to Jewel's behavior.

"Uncle Billy sent a letter," Emily said, grateful to be able to change the subject. "He's invited Miss Gardner and Mrs. Smith here to stay for a while."

Zach narrowed his eyes. "He say anything else?"

Emily looked away. "Yes," she admitted reluctantly. "He also mentioned that you'd agreed to help him look after the ranch. For me," she added defiantly.

Let him make of that what he would. After all, Uncle Billy had not said Zach would be in charge, merely that he was there to help. That meant she could not in good conscience send him away, but she didn't have to follow his orders, either.

"So you're staying here, too?" Jewel cooed. "How nice. It's always good to have a man about the place, if you know what I mean. Especially someone as strong and . . . capable as you seem to be."

Her voice was husky and filled with a playful invitation, a sexual invitation. Emily was surprised. She couldn't imagine encouraging a man in that way. Having been married, she was not sexually inexperienced, but what little she knew had not endeared the subject to her. The romantic novels and magazine stories she'd read exalted love, making the union of two people in love sound like the ultimate experience. The reality had fallen far short of her expectations.

But Jewel was making no secret of her admiration as she made her way to Zach's side, her skirt swishing with the exaggerated swaying of her hips. She placed her hand in the crook of Zach's arm.

"My name is Jewel. Jewel Gardner, that is, but let's not stand on formality."

"Pleased to meet you, Miss, uh, Jewel, ma'am." Zach seemed to be looking anywhere but at Jewel, though every once in a while his gaze would skitter over in her direction, pause briefly at the revealing neckline of her gown, then dart away again.

"And this is my friend Eula Smith," Jewel said, pointing to the other woman. "We're traveling together, you might say."

Eula managed a quick birdlike nod, her hands once again clasped nervously together.

"Ma'am," Zach said, also nodding.

"Now, have you had your breakfast yet?" Jewel asked, not bothering to see what Emily might or might not want.

"Uh, no, ma'am." Zach shot an uncomfortable look at Emily. After their parting the night before, she guessed he wasn't sure of his welcome.

"Well, then, come on in. Eula and I like nothing more than feeding a big, strapping man like yourself."

"First I'd like to hear what Billy has to say. Miss Emily?" he prodded, forestalling any more talk of breakfast.

Emily felt a quick rush of relief. There weren't any more biscuits to offer. She'd just been planning to make another batch when Eula and Jewel arrived. She held up the letter and quickly scanned the rest of it.

"Seems he bought the place from an Englishman, second son of a duke or some such. He was supposed to increase the family coffers but gambled away more than he earned. The family finally ordered him home. That's how Uncle Billy was able to make such a good deal." She couldn't quite keep the skeptical edge off her voice, but the others seemed not to notice it, so she went on. "There's no mention of any hands or anything. From what Oswald said, the ostriches were the Englishman's latest gamble. There aren't many others in this area, and the only other ones are in California. No one knows too much about how to care for them."

"Ostriches?" Jewel asked. "What're they?"

"Birds, ma'am," Zach said with a straight face. "*Large* birds."

The look he sent Emily invited her complicity. His light hazel eyes crinkled at the corners with the shared joke. She felt something warm come to life inside her.

Unable to resist, she smiled at him. At that moment she knew their thoughts were perfectly attuned. They were both remembering the episode with Baby, the way Zach had ridden up to "rescue" her when she'd been chasing the beast. Then she remembered how he'd swept her up against his hard, firm body, the way her heart had raced from anger and something more, something she could no longer afford. She quickly lost her smile and chewed on her lower lip.

Zach watched the play of emotions across Emily's face. What was she upset about now? She was probably still simmering over letting him stay, and now that they had received Billy's instructions, she really had no choice in the matter.

The ranch was his responsibility, like it or not, and that included making sure everyone was safe and cared for. That was why he'd dropped everything to come check out the visitors. And what visitors they were!

He wondered if Emily had any idea what Jewel did for a living, and then decided she surely did not. Ladies were not known for keeping company with soiled doves—not if they wanted to keep their reputations, that was for sure. What on earth could Billy have been thinking of?

But before he could pursue that line of thought, Jewel was talking again.

"Whatever do you want birds for?" she asked Emily.

"Why, Jewel, you should know better than anyone, dear," Eula put in softly. "You love wearing feathers. Why, it'd be my guess that those feathers right there are from ostriches." She pointed at Jewel's boa. "But I never heard of them growing out here. I thought they were from some foreign place."

"They are—Africa," Emily confirmed. "Now someone's had the idea of trying to raise them here."

Jewel looked up from studying her feather boa. "I'd sure like to see them birds. I've never seen a bird that was pink or green or even purple for that matter. Must be a pretty sight."

"Pink and green and . . . oh, no." Emily gave a laugh and her brown eyes sparkled. For a moment Zach wished they would gleam like that when she looked at him. "They don't grow in those colors. Your boas are dyed. The book says—"

"Book?" Her words brought him out of his musings. The last thing he needed was for her to get some highfalutin ideas about ranching from a book. She was trouble enough as it was. "You don't need a book. Just look out the window. You'll see them dang birds. They're black or gray. Not a pink or green one among them, unless you're not sober, that is."

"Well, I still can't wait to see them," Jewel said. "Especially if *you* have the time to take me around." She batted her eyelashes at Zach.

"But, Jewel," Eula protested, "he hasn't had his breakfast yet. Shouldn't we feed him first?"

She sent her first tentative smile in Zach's direction. Emily sat up straight. It was bad enough that Zach had cut her off in mid-sentence, acting as if he knew it all. She didn't need to have *both* of her guests fawning all over him, too!

"I'm afraid I don't have anything prepared. I'll have to stop at the mercantile when I go into Bethel Springs today. I'll need much more than I expected."

"Surely there's the fixings for biscuits," Eula said. "I can whip some up right quick."

"And eggs," Jewel put in enthusiastically. "Birds lay eggs, don't they? I mean, even big birds? Maybe we could scramble some."

"That's all right, ladies," Zach put in quickly. "I don't think we better bother those critters until we've had some time to figure them out. Besides, I don't know if their eggs are even edible."

"They are. I just read about it in my *book*," Emily said. "They taste kind of like a chicken egg, except they're a lot bigger."

"Well, that doesn't mean we have to try one now. I still have some trail grub with me, so I'll be fine. While you ladies are eating, I can unload your wagon for you, and then Miss Emily and I can head into town."

"I'm quite capable of going into town on my own," Emily protested.

"This is unsettled country out here. You can't go wandering about without protection. And anyway, I need to buy some supplies myself. Billy gave me a letter of credit for the mercantile."

"He what?" She couldn't believe it. She'd come west to gain control of her life, and now it was all slowly slipping away. Not only did Billy have control over her money, it now seemed as if he'd handed that control over to a complete stranger. Worst of all, there wasn't anything she could do about it. She had spent most of her meager savings getting Opal and herself to Phoenix. She'd been counting on convincing Uncle Billy to give her some of her inheritance. Now she had to deal with this . . . this . . . There weren't words to describe the arrogant cowboy adequately.

Zach gave her an exasperated look. "Where shall I put their trunks?" he asked, ignoring her question.

Emily glanced at the two women. Eula was looking nervous again, and even Jewel seemed a bit uncertain. This was no time to pursue her standing with this man. There'd be time enough when they were on their way to Bethel Springs.

"Follow me, ladies. You can have your pick of the rooms. None of them is in perfect condition, but they should be easy enough to fix up once we all settle in."

"Which room is yours, sir?" Jewel asked with a sly smile on her face.

"I'm not staying here in the house, ma'am." He sent a look in Emily's direction.

"Not staying in the house? Then where?" Jewel demanded.

"Mr. Hollis has his own quarters," Emily put in hastily.

"He does?" Jewel asked. "I didn't see any other buildings. Did you, Eula?"

"I didn't, either, but I could have been mistaken," Eula said diffidently.

"There aren't any other buildings," Zach informed them. "This ranch must have been built by Spanish settlers. Everything's in one building set around the courtyard where you pulled in. The main living area's at this end. The animal quarters and storage rooms are back over there." He extricated his arm from Jewel's grip and gestured toward the other wing of the large adobe structure.

"And where do you stay?" Jewel asked.

"My room's on the back wing, along with the quarters of the other hands."

"Other hands?" Jewel's eyes lit up with interest. "How many are there?"

"There aren't any right now, but I'll be taking care of that shortly."

Before Emily could react, Jewel said, "So there's no one else around?" She frowned worriedly. "I must say, Mr.

Hollis, I surely don't like the idea of you being so far away. What if something happens? There are Indians and outlaws roaming these lands, or so I've heard. Billy said you'd be protecting us."

"I'll do my best, ma'am," Zach said. "Try not to worry too much."

"But how can you help us when you're so far away? You might not even know something's happening. I think Mr. Hollis should be in the house with us, Emily. You, being from the East and all, might not know how dangerous it can be out here, but I'd feel *much* easier if we had a man in the house. I'm sure Billy would agree, if he was here."

Emily was about to object when Eula said, "I'm afraid she's right, dear. Unless you have any objections, Mr. Hollis?"

Needless to say, Zach had none. "Why don't you ladies choose first," he said with a smug grin that set Emily's teeth on edge. "I can make do with whatever room is left."

It looked as if Zach would be in the house now whether she wanted it or not. Emily couldn't even look at him after that, couldn't bear to see the victory written on his face. It seemed no matter what she did, he came out ahead. But she wouldn't let that continue, not at all. He would get his come-uppance. She would personally see to it.

Pulling herself together, she smiled reassuringly at Eula, then led the way down the hall toward the bedrooms.

As if he sensed her new resolve, Zach went out the door without another word and started to unhitch the mule.

The sun shone down with unremitting intensity, sending heat waves shimmering from the ground in every direction. Ordinarily Zach would have waited until later in the day to make the trip to Bethel Springs, but with Emily along, he wanted to make sure they could make it there and back in daylight.

Zach pulled a bandanna out of his pocket and swiped at the sweat beading his forehead. He glanced at Emily seated beside him on the wagon bench. She was wearing a neatly trimmed straw hat with a spray of silk blossoms attached to the front. The brim was longer in the front than in the back but barely wide enough to shade her face. An easterner's hat—impractical and nearly useless.

Zach couldn't deny that it made her look even more attractive, though, setting off her fine profile and balancing that stubborn chin. She'd changed into a fancy dress, too, one that outlined her figure. The collar was crisply starched and stood up straight; the bodice had a military cut, with two rows of buttons from neck to waist, while the skirt was fuller in back than in front. Its rich brown color matched her eyes and made her hair look more golden, especially where the damp tendrils clung to her face. The finely tooled buttons on her bodice traced the soft line of her breasts and curved in deeply at her waist.

Zach's imagination sprang free of his control as he wondered what she would look like without all the concealing layers of cloth. His fingers itched to open each button one at a time, to lay her naked before him as he loosened her hair from its elaborate twist and spread it on a pillow to frame her face. How would she look when passion claimed her?

He shifted in his seat and stuffed the bandanna back into his pocket. His clothes felt too tight, and his shirt clung damply to his back. The heat was to blame for part but not all of it. The rest was the fault of the woman sitting silently by his side, as regal as a queen with her cream-colored parasol held tightly in her hand.

The tightness of her grip revealed how nervous she was. Zach couldn't blame her. This barren country was a far cry from the world she had left behind. What had made her do it? he wondered. Looking after her investment was a feeble excuse for leaving behind everything familiar. Surely there were others who could watch over the ranch for her—the men in her family, for one thing.

"Don't forget to take a drink now and then," he reminded her. "You can get sick out here before you know it in this dry heat."

He reached back for the canteen with one hand and held it out to her. "Watch out that you don't get burned by the cup. It's hot from the sun," he added.

"I am not a child, Mr. Hollis. I can think for myself."

"Fine," he said with exaggerated patience. She had a knack for getting on his nerves. Why'd she have to be so stubborn? "Don't say I didn't warn you."

He took the cap off the canteen and took a deep swallow himself. "Sure you won't have any?"

She looked from his mouth to the canteen, a soft frown marring her brow. Rolling his eyes skyward, Zach looped the reins around his arm and reached for his bandanna once more, then wiped off the top, before pouring some water into the cup for her. "Here. Drink this. It'll make you feel better."

She chewed her lip uncertainly. "How far are we from Bethel Springs?"

"I don't know. Not far, I'd guess, from what Billy told me."

"All right, then." She took the cup and drank the water down thirstily. "Thank you."

"You want some more?"

"No, I'd better not."

He was about to ask her why, but she looked too uncomfortable. Then it came to him. If she drank too much on the way, she'd want to make a stop, and there wasn't any place very private as far as the eye could see. He sighed. Things were a lot more complicated with a lady than he'd ever realized, probably because he'd had so little to do with one before. He'd spent his days wandering, first in hiding to save his life, then as the hunter, out for revenge.

That was one of the reasons he was coming into Bethel Springs today. He wanted to check out the town, get a feel for what the law was like here, whether he could trust the sheriff. He also wanted to send a message out to Frank and let him know where he was. Frank was Zach's closest friend, a man who'd seen him at his darkest and not turned away. Frank would be surprised to hear he was in Arizona. Last he'd heard, Zach was heading up Denver way.

The town came into view at last, looking sleepy and abandoned in the afternoon heat.

"It's siesta time," Zach said as they drove down the main street. "Out here they follow the Mexican customs. Everyone closes down in the heat of the day. The stores will open as soon as the temperature starts to cool."

"What can we do in the meantime?" Emily asked.

"I'll drop you off at the dress shop and check around town. We can meet later on so you can do your shopping."

Emily wasn't sure she liked that, but what other choice was there? She wanted to see Opal and make sure she was all right, and Zach no doubt wanted to do whatever it was men did in a town this size. They'd already passed a saloon and dance hall so she had a fairly good idea of what he could get up to if he was so inclined. She wrinkled her nose in distaste. Or was it disappointment? She didn't want to examine her feelings too closely for fear of what she might find.

"You got a problem with that?" Zach asked in that overly patient way of his, almost as if he knew how aggravating it was.

"No, that's fine. Bea's Dress Shop is just up the street a ways. I'm sure she'll let me in even if she is closed."

She pointed out the way, and Zach pulled up in front of the store. He climbed off the wagon, then turned to help her down. He looked ruggedly handsome standing there, his blue shirt contrasting with his sun-darkened skin, his hazel eyes framed by dark lashes, his hat pulled down over his forehead. He reached up and extended his hand to hers. A frisson of excitement ran down her arm. His hand was long-fingered and capable. He held her gently but firmly as he helped her from the buckboard, lingering for a second longer than was strictly necessary once she reached the ground. It was as if he, too, had felt that brief flash of desire, that ache for something deeper.

Then he stepped away and said, "I'll be back in a while," without meeting her eyes.

She wanted to ask him to wait, to tell her what he was thinking, where he was heading. To act as if she mattered, even if only a little, as if she had a right to know where he was going and what he was doing. But that would put an obligation on her, too, and she wasn't ready for that. If he let her into his life, she would have to let him into hers, and experience had taught her what devastation a man could wreak without half trying. So all she said was "I'll see you then," and turned her back on him.

The door to Bea's store opened just minutes after she knocked, and she heard the wagon move off as she entered the cool darkness of the building.

Both Opal and Bea rushed over to see her.

"So, what was it like? Did you find everything that you need?" Bea asked.

"Enough to manage," Emily replied. "That Englishman left behind a lot of his things and they all came in useful."

"What Englishman?" Opal asked.

"The one who owned the ranch before," Emily explained and proceeded to tell them about the ranch house and the ostriches. Bea started to laugh as Emily described Baby's antics.

"See? Now you understand what I was goin' on about in the stagecoach. Them birds are a sight, aren't they?" She chuckled again.

"Sounds like a lot of work for just one person," Opal said.

Emily could feel her cheeks heating up. She'd omitted mentioning Zach in her story. She wasn't too sure how to bring him up tactfully.

"Well, I wasn't totally on my own," she said diffidently. "Oswald was there. He's been taking care of the place for Uncle Billy."

"Oswald Barnes?" Bea put in. "Why, he's just a boy. Not that he doesn't work hard, but he's hardly any protection at all."

"He's been most helpful. And . . . well, Uncle Billy hired a ranch manager. He's only just arrived himself."

If Bea had been a dog, her ears would have pricked forward.

"A ranch manager, eh? What's he like?"

Emily didn't know what to say. She could hardly confess that she'd seen the man half naked and found him more handsome than she should have, or that he was far too bossy for her taste.

"I've hardly even met him," she said instead, then quickly changed the subject. "Oh, and Uncle Billy sent two of his, uh, friends to stay, too."

This subject seemed even worse, especially considering Jewel's obvious background. Emily wished Bea weren't quite so curious, but true to form, Bea leaped into the fray.

"Friends? What kind of friends?"

"I don't know all the details. Just that they're traveling together and need a place to stay for a while. They're going to help with the ranch house. Eula says she can do the cooking, and Jewel is willing to help with—"

"Oh, lady friends. Well, that's all right, then."

Emily didn't have the heart—or maybe it was the courage—to correct her. "Lady" was hardly the word to describe either of her guests.

"I can hardly wait to see the place for myself," Opal declared.

"Now, Opal, you mustn't push yourself. You're more than welcome to stay on here with me and—"

"That's very kind of you, Bea, and I've had a lovely time," Opal interrupted, "but I really think it's for the best if I get a look at what poor Emily is up against, don't you?"

Opal sent Emily a silent message, promising retribution if she dared contradict.

"Opal will be just fine," Emily put in reassuringly. "The ranch is really in pretty good shape, and once I stop at the mercantile and purchase a few necessities, we should be quite comfortable."

Opal smiled, pleased, and said, "I'll just go upstairs and pack my things. I should be ready whenever you are."

With that she bustled out of the room, leaving Emily to handle Bea on her own. At once Emily understood Opal's need to leave in a hurry. Though she was very kind, Bea was also insatiably curious and given to asking questions that would have been considered exceedingly rude back home. But she did it with such kindly interest, it was hard to deny her.

By the time Zach came back to get her, Emily was exhausted from the strain of protecting her privacy without hurting her hostess's feelings.

"So what do you think?" Emily asked Opal as they sat at last in the older woman's new bedroom at the ranch.

"The room's very nice and, as you said, quite comfortable considering we are truly at the back of beyond."

"That's not what I meant," Emily said, fixing Opal with a meaningful stare.

"No, I didn't suppose it was." Opal took a wrapper from her trunk, shook out the dust that had permeated every one of their belongings, and folded it again carefully before placing it in the tall mahogany armoire that stood on one side of the room. She looked up at Emily, a twinkle in her eyes. "We did say it would be an adventure, didn't we?"

"Yes, but who would have thought Uncle Billy would invite all these . . . people to stay?"

Opal must have heard something in her tone, for she stopped emptying her trunk and came to sit beside Emily on the bed.

"Is it the people who bother you, my dear, or just one of them?" The twinkle had been replaced by a look of understanding that Emily didn't want to deal with.

"What do you mean?" she asked, evading the truth. "I'm not singling out anyone in particular. It's just hard having to accommodate strangers when I've barely adjusted to the place myself."

"Zach Hollis seems like a fine man to me," Opal replied, refusing to let her avoid facing the real issue.

"I didn't say a word against him."

"You didn't have to." Opal sat in silence for a few moments, watching her. "Do you want to talk about it?" she asked at last, "or would you rather I minded my own business?"

Emily stood and began to pace. "There's nothing to talk about. You know as well as I do what it means to have a man in charge of your life. Look what happened to you. John's father was ready to throw us out on the street for a few dollars. Where do you think you would have gone? The house was

yours. Your husband left it to *you*. But that didn't stop him,
and no one would have lifted a finger to help you."

"Not all men are like John's father . . . or like Laurence,
for that matter. You can't judge them all by one bad experience."

"You don't know the half of it, Opal. Laurence didn't just
spend money. He broke every promise he ever made to me."

Opal sighed. "I know more than you think."

Emily stiffened and stopped pacing. Slowly she turned to
face Opal. "What else do you know?" she asked, her voice a
hoarse whisper, her hands clenched at her sides.

Opal looked away, her expression filled with regret. "I
know there were other women. I saw him once." She looked
back at Emily. "Oh, he didn't see me, but I don't know as he
would have cared. When he was on one of his spirited jags,
he didn't think anything could stop him or get in his way. I
don't think he meant to hurt you, Emily. I think he had a
sickness, something that took over his life and his mind. If
he'd been well, he could never have treated you so badly.
You have to believe that."

Emily looked away. She knew Opal meant well, but
sometimes she wondered about her own role in the collapse
of her marriage. Had Laurence treated her badly because of
some lack in her? Had she failed to satisfy him in some es-
sential way? When he'd died in the arms of one of his
women, she'd felt anger and guilt and, worst of all, relief.
There had been no one to talk to, no one who would have understood or cared to hear about such terrible things. Or so
she'd thought. Maybe she could have talked to Opal, though
what good would that have done? It wouldn't have changed
Laurence or saved her from his abuse.

"Laurence is not the issue here," she said, closing the door
on the topic. It hurt too much to talk about, and besides,

Laurence was gone now, out of her life forever. "He's gone now and there's no going back."

"Is he gone? Or will his shadow mark the rest of your life? I'd hate to see you lock your heart away because of him. It's too high a price to pay for his mistakes."

"I made a mistake, too. I gave him control over my life. I'll think twice before I do that again for any man."

"And so you should," Opal agreed. "But don't close yourself off too soon. Don't judge each man by Laurence. Believe me, nothing is sadder than growing old alone, unless it's never having known the happiness love brings. At least I have my memories, good memories. I want you to have some, too."

Emily came to Opal's side and gave her a hug. "Thank you for caring, and don't worry about me. I'll have lots of happy memories. This is a new life for us, a new chance. I can't wait to start. You'll see. Even without a man, things will be better."

Opal hugged her back. "Yes, things will be better," she murmured, then added in her heart, But I want even more for you. I want the best.

And for Opal the best meant only one thing: a man. She closed her eyes, and the image of Zach Hollis came to her—tall and masculine, with dark hair and light eyes and a need for love that matched Emily's own, if he'd only admit it. Maybe she could help. There were ways. . . .

Opal smiled to herself. This new life would indeed be an adventure.

"Well?" the impatient voice demanded from the dark corner.

"I did just like you told me. I hung around town, but didn't let anyone get too close," Jabber Sidel said, squinting his eyes, trying to see the man sitting in the corner of the darkened room. He'd only seen him once, and that brief glance had been far too short to recognize him again.

"And?" the voice demanded from the shelter of darkness.

"Two women came out from back east on Thursday last. The older one stayed in town while the younger woman headed out to the ranch."

"Did you check out the ranch like I asked?"

"Followed her out there. And then went out again today. She's not alone."

That statement brought the legs of the chair crashing to the floor. "What!"

"There's a man out there with her."

Jabber heard a muted swearword, then heard the man in the corner slap his leg with his hat.

"Recognize him from town?"

"Nope, can't say I do, and I've gotten to know most folks by sight," Jabber replied, eager to soothe the older man's displeasure.

Silence filled the room. Jabber wanted to be gone. There was something dangerous about the hidden man. He'd noticed it from the first.

"It doesn't matter who's at the ranch," the voice declared with ominous intensity. "I want everyone off that property. Do whatever you have to to see that it happens. Got it?"

"Right, boss," Jabber murmured and slipped out the door as a chill ran down his spine.

CHAPTER
4

The streets of Bethel Springs were deserted as Zach rode into town. He'd been at the Double F Ranch for more than a week now and was glad of some time on his own. Handling four women alone, if you wanted to count an older lady like Opal Crabtree in that category, might be some men's idea of how to live the good life, but Zach was finding it a strain. When he wasn't being mothered to death by Eula and Opal, he had to contend with Jewel's not-so-subtle sexual signals and Emily's snooty indifference.

Not that Emily was totally indifferent. Oh, no. Just let him try to do anything on that blasted ranch without checking it out with her first and she threw a regular hissy fit. It'd been all he could do to get into town on his own today, she was that suspicious of him. He'd had to promise up and down that he wouldn't do anything she didn't know about, at least as far as the ranch was concerned. He'd made that limitation perfectly clear, and if her expression'd been anything to go by, she had a much more exciting afternoon planned for him than he had for himself.

"Afternoon, Jackson," he said, touching the brim of his Stetson with one hand as he rode into the livery yard. "I'd like to leave my horse for a few hours, if you've got the space."

Zach peered into the gloom of the large livery barn, trying to see if he recognized any of the other animals. He couldn't see much from outside.

"No problem. I still got a space or two," the livery owner said and grabbed the reins near the horse's mouth, steadying the beast as Zach dismounted. The big roan danced sideways a few steps, then settled down as Jackson began crooning to him.

"I'll be back before dark," Zach told the man, following him into the barn. Once he was away from the bright glare of the sun, he could make out the familiar outline of the buckskin gelding in the back corner. Frank had arrived.

"No hurry. We'll be here," Jackson said dismissingly, already preoccupied with seeing to the animal rather than its owner.

Zach took his leave and headed for the saloon. That was where he'd most likely find Frank—his friend had an eye for the ladies and would waste no time scouting out the neighborhood.

Zach pushed open the swinging door and entered the barroom. Over to one side, a piano player was plunking out a familiar tune and chatting softly with the bartender, who was idly polishing the already burnished mahogany and brass fittings of the bar. The room was fairly empty at this time of day, except for a table in the back corner. Even from across the room, Zach could make out the sound of giggles and provocative taunts.

Zach sauntered over, taking his time to look over the bevy of saloon girls gathered around Frank. They were like so many he'd run into before, no longer fresh-faced and eager, though trying to hide that fact as best they could. This land was hard on men, and even harder on women, especially women alone.

His thoughts turned suddenly to Emily, to her soft, fair skin and golden red hair. She, too, was a woman alone, but she seemed to thrive on it. He could see the glow in her eyes every time she made a decision, especially if she had to cross him. Sometimes he yielded; other times he fought back. He was a man, after all, and used to being in charge. He could indulge her up to a point, but he couldn't let her do anything that would seriously harm the ranch or anyone on it. He had a responsibility, to Billy and to himself, to make sure everything turned out all right, and whether Emily wanted to acknowledge it or not, she was part of his responsibility.

He liked that thought, somehow. It put his recent inner turmoil into its proper place. Emily was his responsibility. That was why he felt so protective, why his heart kicked up its pace when she drew near, why he was so aware of her scent. That was all there was to it.

A high-pitched squeal from one of the saloon girls jarred him out of his musings. This was neither the time nor the place to be thinking about Emily. He'd come here for another purpose, a purpose he dared not forget, even for a moment: revenge.

"Hey, Frank," he called out, suddenly impatient with himself. "I see you wasted no time finding yourself a place to settle in."

Frank Ross looked up past the feathered hairpiece of the floozy on his lap and squinted at him.

"Hello, Zach, you old dog. There's plenty of room here if you want to join me. I'm more than willing to share. And so are they—ain't that right, girls?"

Another round of giggles greeted this remark, and Frank grinned, pleased with himself. A couple of the women gave

Zach a professional look-over; then one got up from her chair and sashayed to his side.

"You a friend of Frank's?" she asked in a sultry voice.

She must have been pretty at one time, but now there was a hard edge to her. Invitation was written in every line of her body, from the silk-stockinged toes peeking out of her high-heeled slippers to her sulky pout, but her eyes were blank. Zach felt a stab of pity for her. What had brought her to this?

"Yeah, I reckon so," he admitted. "But I'm afraid Frank and I have business to discuss, important business, so . . ."

He let his words trail off apologetically. He had no interest in her. His thoughts were filled with other things.

She reached down to the front of his Levi's and ran her fingers up and down the button fly. The gesture left him cold. With uncompromising firmness, he pried her hand away.

"Maybe another time," he said softly, knowing there would not be another time. She wasn't the right person. He didn't know why or where the thought came from. He only knew it was true. Everything had been changing since he arrived in the Arizona Territory, and this most of all, though he couldn't say why. "Take this for your trouble," he added, slipping her some change.

She gave him a startled look, but didn't turn down the money. Then she looked consideringly at him. "I guess you already got a lady of your own," she said before leaving his side.

He didn't. A man in his situation couldn't afford to have a lady of his own, no matter how much he might want one, but if thinking so made it easier for her to accept his turndown, he'd let her.

"Come on, Frank," he said, his voice brisk. "We got some catching up to do." He gave the other man a meaningful glare, and Frank took the hint.

"Got to go now, girls," he said with a friendly leer. "But don't none of you go far, ya hear? I'll be back in a jiff."

Frank extricated himself from the clinging arms of his new friends and threw some money on the table to pay for his drinks.

"Where you want to go?" he asked.

Zach looked around the room. "Somewhere more private."

Zach still wasn't sure about the town. The sheriff had been friendly enough, but Zach wasn't going to take any chances. The less anyone around here knew of his business, the better.

"Let's go outside. We can find us a place to talk," Zach suggested.

"I'm right behind you, partner."

The midafternoon heat hit them in the face, almost searing their lungs.

"How'd you come to pick this godforsaken town, anyway?" Frank demanded as he pulled a bandanna from his pocket to wipe his face. By the time he had it ready to swipe across his forehead, his skin was already dry.

"It's a long story," Zach answered. He started walking down the plank sidewalk as he told Frank about being shot and meeting up with Billy.

"You're kidding me!" Frank exclaimed. "You really planning on settling down and ranching? I never thought I'd see the day." Frank smiled widely.

"It's not like that, Frank. I owed Billy and I needed to be down here. It just seemed like a good plan at the time."

Frank frowned. "And now?"

They'd reached the end of the sidewalk and stood looking out into the street. Zach took off his hat and ran his fingers through his hair. "That depends on what you've found out. The ranch is only a few miles out of town. It's only got four females living there aside from me, and—"

"*Four* females! All to yourself? No wonder you weren't interested in Lila." Frank chuckled deep in his chest. "I tell you, boy, if'n you don't have a way about you! Not one, but *four*. My God, don't that beat all!"

"It's not like that, Frank," Zach protested, knowing his friend was most likely pulling his leg. But what would Emily think? How would she feel if she knew Frank was talking about her like that, even in jest? She was a lady, a widow at that. She deserved more respect. And Opal. Why, she was a dignified older lady, not someone to be used as Frank implied.

Frank must have caught something in his tone, for he stopped chuckling and narrowed his eyes. "Whatever you say, Zach. You know I was only trying to get your goat. I didn't mean nothing by it."

"I know."

Zach leaned against the wall of the nearest building, his hat tipped half over his eyes as he scanned the area around them. No one was within earshot. "So what'd you find out," he asked softly, his voice carrying only to the other man.

"Not too much," Frank replied, his voice equally soft. He bent down and grabbed at a clump of dried grass growing by the foundation of the building and poking up past the raised sidewalk. A blade broke off and he stuck one end of it in the corner of his mouth.

Zach knew Frank was using the time to gather his thoughts. Frank was one of the government's sharpest minds, a U.S. marshal who was rarely fooled for long by anything or anyone. Part of his skill was that no one realized just how sharp a mind he hid behind his easygoing-cowboy demeanor. Now, watching him settle into business, Zach saw that steel-trap mind begin to work.

"There's not much to go on," Frank drawled at last. "Just a few scraps of information gathered from here and there.

You know how it is. Earl Darnell is a slippery cuss. Rumor has it he's changed his name again. He sold out all his holdings in Colorado, but no one knows where the money went. The thinking is he had this hidey-hole all set up, name change and all, in case he needed it."

"What tipped him off? How'd he know we were getting close? We've been so careful." Zach could feel the frustration curl inside him. Earl Darnell had escaped again. All that work for nothing.

Frank shrugged. "Darnell's a rich man. Who knows how many men he could have bought off. It's not as if the government pays us all that much."

"You think someone let him in on our plans?"

Frank blew the grass out of the corner of his mouth. "Could be. I got no proof, mind you, but I can't rightly come up with any other explanation for how he knew to leave. We were closing in on him. You know that. I've never lied to you, one way or the other."

"I know that, Frank. If you hadn't helped me catch James, I'd probably be in jail now myself. I owe you a lot."

And he did. Frank was the one who had persuaded him to let the law handle James Darnell, Earl's older brother, instead of a bullet from Zach's gun. James had been put in prison and later hanged for all the murders he'd committed. The man had cheated more than just Zach's family out of their land and their lives. But for years no one had been able to catch him.

Most of the witnesses, like Zach's family, were dead. Those who had survived knew better than to talk lest they, too, end up in the churchyard. The law had been powerless to intervene, or so it had seemed to Zach when he decided to take matters into his own hands.

Fortunately he'd run into Frank first, and the big man had stopped him. With the impatience of youth, Zach had resisted until Frank had told him he was a U.S. marshal assigned to fighting land fraud and related crimes. Together they'd baited a trap and lured James into it.

Made brave by the fall of the powerful man, his surviving victims came forward, eager to be in at the kill, to exact a small measure of revenge. But for Zach it hadn't been enough. James had not acted on his own, nor had he been the worst. There were others with debts to pay, and no one more so than James's brother Earl. Of all the Darnells, Earl had been the meanest, the most depraved, and Zach wanted him the most.

Zach had worked with Frank on and off during the intervening years, bringing various members of Darnell's gang to justice, but Earl had always managed to escape. Just as he had this time.

"So what do we do now?" Zach asked. "Does anyone know anything about Earl?"

"We traced him a ways south from Colorado. Some habits never change, you know. He's still vicious with women, and the whores were willing to talk after we promised them enough money to leave the state. We lost track of him north of here, but we think he was heading this way."

Zach winced at Frank's words. No one knew better than he how vicious Earl Darnell could be, but that was something he kept to himself.

"Anybody in the area been forced to sell out recently?" he asked.

"Nope. That's why we feel he had his hiding place lined up long ago. Could've even bought it legitimate-like, just in case. Would make it harder to trace, you know."

A steely glint appeared in Frank's eyes, and Zach knew Frank's patience had finally worn out. It would be just like the time they went after James: a no-holds-barred chase.

"How do you want to handle it?" Zach asked in deference

to the older man's position. Zach had ideas of his own, but he owed it to Frank to listen first.

"I got a few handpicked men. We'll be doing this on our own. If Washington don't like it, too bad. Nobody's going to give Darnell the jump on us again."

"You and your men could stay at the ranch, if you want. I was planning on hiring some hands. It'd be a good place to search from, and nobody'd think twice about a bunch of strangers suddenly appearing if they posed as cowboys."

"What about the ladies? Won't they mind?"

Zach shrugged with deceptive nonchalance. "As long as the men behave and do their chores, they won't mind in the least."

"I'll telegraph the boys now. Tell 'em to head straight out," Frank said, taking Zach at his word.

Zach only hoped things would go as smoothly as he'd promised. Eula and Jewel wouldn't mind, as far as he could tell. If anything, Jewel would really take to the idea. Emily was another question. Zach could hear her now, furious with him for having made a decision about the ranch without consulting her first. Well, there wasn't anything he could do about it now. Besides, this was one issue where he couldn't afford to give her a choice. Too much was at stake.

Emily had spent the day moping about the ranch, feeling at loose ends without Zach around to keep an eye on. Not that there wasn't plenty to do. The ostriches needed tending—the yearlings in their special pen and the three breeding pairs out in their wire-fence enclosures back behind the house, beyond the small rise that hid them from view. Emily brought them water and the extra feeding of soft grain, molasses, and hay she had read was needed to supplement their feed. The main part of their diet was the alfalfa that grew right in their enclosures.

To keep them from cropping all the feed so short they would starve, each pair was assigned two paddocks. Oswald had instructed her on moving the birds from one enclosure to the other as needed. Fortunately they seemed to be doing fine so far. Emily wasn't sure she relished the idea of tackling one of the eight- or nine-foot-tall cocks on her own. They seemed exceedingly rambunctious and territorial, typical behavior during the mating season, which seemed to extend over most of the summer with the hen constantly adding eggs to her clutch.

The younger birds had to be fed separately because they had quickly cropped the alfalfa in their pen nearly to the ground. All their food had to be brought in and their area raked clean. Zach usually saw to the lean-tos provided at various locations inside the pens to shade the birds from the merciless Arizona sun.

By late afternoon Emily had completed all of her outside chores and was glad to get in from the heat.

"What have I said about going outside without a hat?" Jewel admonished her when she walked into the kitchen. "You'll just destroy your lovely complexion. Ain't that right, Eula?"

As always, Eula was ensconced in the kitchen, cooking or baking as the mood struck her. At the moment she was kneading the dough for her light, fluffy wheat bread, which melted in your mouth when it came warm from the oven. Emily could feel herself beginning to drool at the thought.

"This desert sun is a lot hotter than you're used to," Eula said. "You don't want to get burned none, not with your fair skin."

"I was wearing my hat until that mean old cock out by the spring took a swipe at me. Stupid bird thought I was invading his territory."

"What bird?" Opal inquired, coming into the room.

"Emily, you didn't go into one of the pens with Zach gone, did you?"

"What's Zach got to do with it? I'm perfectly capable of handling those birds by myself," Emily declared, even though she had been reluctant to enter the pens on her own. She was simply tired of everyone thinking Zach was the only person on the ranch who could do anything right.

"But if something should go wrong, dear, none of us would know what to do to help you," Opal explained.

"Besides, Zach would be mighty put out if he found you'd been reckless and gotten hurt," Eula added, to Emily's annoyance. "We just don't want nothing bad to happen to you, dear."

Had it been anyone other than Eula, Emily wouldn't have hesitated to let her know she was overstepping her bounds. As it was, it was rare indeed that Eula felt comfortable enough to give her opinion about anything, so Emily bit her tongue and swallowed her sharp retort.

"Well, you needn't worry. I stayed outside the pens and dropped their feed through the fence. If that cock had been near the nest the way I expected, nothing would have happened. As it was, he only grabbed my straw hat and took off. By now he's probably eaten the thing for dessert."

"He could have pecked you badly. You should be glad he only took off with your hat," Jewel said with a shudder. "Quite frankly, I don't know how you stand going near those birds. They scare the willies out of me."

"You don't have to worry, Jewel. They're not really pecking birds. It's their legs that are dangerous. They can kick right through a plank if they're riled up enough, from what I've read in my books."

"Well, getting kicked don't sound much better than being pecked to death," Jewel said with a sniff. "Especially by birds whose knees work backwards. I ain't never seen anything like it."

"Speaking of Zach," Eula said, though Zach hadn't been the subject of the conversation for a while, "when do you expect him back? I want to make sure my bread is ready. I'm sure he'll be starving when he gets here."

"Oh, my gosh, you're right," exclaimed Jewel, looking out the window at the sun. "It is getting on, and I promised Zach I'd make him my special potato cakes. He said they're his favorites. Now where did we put the leftover ham from last night's supper?"

Jewel began to bustle around the kitchen, and Opal offered to go to the root cellar for the potatoes, leaving Emily as the only one not engaged in preparing for Zach's return. And why should she? He had more than enough attention from the other women. They weren't going out of their way to prepare anything for her, and she was the one who'd been working all day. God only knew what Zach had been up to in town—and Emily wasn't too sure she wanted to know, either.

For reasons she couldn't understand, she felt a sharp pain in the region of her stomach every time she thought of Zach going to town on his own and what he could do there. She tried to convince herself it was just her worry about what he might be up to concerning the ranch, but her more honest self admitted the funny hollow ache went deeper than that. Well, whatever he was doing, it was none of her business. Hadn't she reconfirmed just this past week that she would never make herself vulnerable to a man again?

Firming her jaw and squaring her shoulders, Emily marched off to her room to get cleaned up before dinner—not for any man, but for herself. It was a matter of pride for a lady always to look her best, no matter who was going to see her. And besides, the others were so busy at their self-assigned tasks, they had no time for her anyhow.

A short while later, having given herself a quick sponge bath to wash off the grime of her day in the sun, Emily was feeling a lot better. The ranch really was shaping up well, she thought, and she was generous enough to admit that Zach deserved a good deal of the credit. In fact, she had missed him today, missed their verbal sparring and the constant challenge of trying to cope with their unusual charges, missed his help and even—dared she admit it?—his good advice. He might not take the time to read the books, as she had, but he possessed more than a fair share of sheer common sense.

More than once this afternoon Emily had found herself turning to ask his opinion or make an observation, only to remember he wasn't around. When had their sparring become more than a contest of wills? When had it taken on the exhilaration of matching wits? Emily had no idea. All she knew was that today, for the first time in a long while, she'd felt lonely. And Zach was the reason why.

The sound of hoofbeats in the courtyard drew Emily to the window. She peeked out from behind the curtain, unsure what she'd find since it had sounded like more than one horse. Sure enough, there were two mounts standing in the courtyard, one of them familiar as Zach's strawberry roan. But to whom did the other belong?

She heard Zach call out to the house, letting anyone inside know who had arrived. At least he was being considerate of the others. They weren't expecting two men and might be worried. Sure enough, at the sound of his voice, Jewel opened the front door a crack. Emily heard its distinctive squeak.

"That you, Zach?" Jewel called out and stepped outside onto the porch.

Emily hurriedly made her way to the front door. Zach had made no mention of bringing a guest back from Bethel Springs. What was he up to now? It was bad enough having Zach staying here with a house full of women. She didn't need to cope with yet another stranger.

By the time Emily reached the front door, Jewel was sashaying off the porch, taking little running steps since her skirts were too tight to allow for more.

"Almost didn't recognize you," she was saying to Zach. "Did you get all your . . . business done in Bethel Springs?"

Her voice lingered over the word "business," suggesting he'd had much more to do than just work. It was just her way, and they'd all gotten used to ignoring the innuendo in every sentence that came from her mouth. But the stranger was not so inured.

"Excuse me, ma'am, but I'm afraid we haven't been introduced. I'm Frank Ross, and I must say, I am more than pleased to make your acquaintance." He jumped off his mount and strode to Jewel's side.

"Why, Mr. Ross, the . . . pleasure is mine." Jewel batted her eyelashes and smiled broadly at the tall man. "I'm Jewel Gardner."

"Mighty pleased to meet you, Miss Jewel," Frank said, tipping his hat.

"You, too, I'm sure," Jewel said, never taking her eyes off the newest arrival. "Will you be staying long?"

The man would have had to be dead not to appreciate Jewel's fading but still compelling beauty and her openhearted manner, Emily thought with a sinking feeling, watching the byplay between the stranger and Jewel. Zach would have competition when it came to the special treats Jewel had been plying him with in the last week.

Frank Ross smiled and then nodded his head toward Zach

who was coming up behind him. "Depends on him, but I sure hope so. I understand you need a foreman."

"Jewel, would you be kind enough to show Frank around while I have a few words with Miss Emily?" Zach suggested as he, too, dismounted.

"Of course," Jewel agreed and then turned back to Frank. "Mr. Ross, why don't I start by introducing you to Eula and Opal? They're in the kitchen."

Emily stepped back from the door to let Jewel and the man come into the front foyer. Zach was right behind them.

"Miss Emily," Zach said with uncharacteristic hesitancy, "let me explain about my friend here." He gestured toward Jewel and the stranger.

"What's there to explain?" Emily didn't want to be inhospitable, but she knew she wasn't going to like what was coming next.

"Why, Emily, you'll never guess what Zach did," Jewel said, excitement tingeing her voice. Without waiting for Emily to reply, she added, "He invited Frank Ross, here, to stay at the ranch as foreman. Isn't that grand?"

"It sure is, pretty lady," Frank put in. He continued to look at Jewel who, much to Emily's surprise, was starting to blush. Then he swung his gaze toward Emily. "Pleased to meet you, too, ma'am," he said, his smile fading at the edges as he caught her disapproving glare.

"I'll just show Mr. Ross around the house while Zach fills you in on the details," Jewel put in hurriedly. With an instinct for avoiding trouble, she ushered the stranger toward the bedroom wing.

Emily was livid. She was losing control of her life—had been, in fact, ever since Zach arrived. Everything she'd hoped for in coming to the West was slowly being taken from her. The only way she could combat the panic growing inside her was to convert it to anger, anger against the most obvious source of her problems: Zach.

"How could you? You told me you were not going to town on ranch business! You promised to consult me before you did anything affecting this ranch."

She paced back and forth in front of him, unable to control her blazing emotions.

"Listen, Emily," Zach started to protest. "I didn't plan for this to happen, but once I ran into Frank, hiring him seemed like the logical thing to do."

" '*Ran into* Frank'?" she repeated in angry disbelief. "You mean to tell me he just *happened* to be coming through Bethel Springs?"

Zach had the grace to redden as he explained the situation. "No, of course not. I telegraphed him when I first arrived, just to let him know where I was."

"You telegraphed him? Were you planning to take over the ranch all along? God, I don't believe this! Everything I wanted, everything I—" her voice, which had risen to a higher pitch, almost seemed to be coming from someone else, someone who was driven by demons she could no longer control—"planned is coming apart. What makes you think you can get away with this?"

"Stop it, Emily," she heard Zach say, but she was too consumed by her wild thoughts to slow down. Things were turning out just as they had with Laurence. What was she going to do?

She felt his hands on her shoulders, stopping her frantic pacing. The air between them shimmered with electricity. Zach's light hazel eyes darkened to green, and his nostrils flared with every breath as his face came closer and closer.

And then his lips were on hers, firm and warm, yet gently coaxing. Her heart stopped beating, then started again, its cadence quickening as her blood raced through her veins. His hands left her shoulders and slid down her back, drawing her more intimately into his embrace as his mouth tormented hers. With a sigh, she parted her lips and brought her hands up to his chest. A far corner of her brain told her she should be pushing him away, but she ignored it, overwhelmed by his dark, spicy taste and the sensual roughness of his tongue against her own. All she could think about was Zach.

Her fingers curled into his shirt and she felt the hard strength of his muscles beneath, then the rapid beat of his heart. She angled her head in response to his urgings, and he deepened his possession of her mouth, seeking her most secret recesses, then withdrawing until she followed, daringly exploring on her own. His teeth were smooth, their edges sharp. He gently nipped the tip of her tongue, then ran his own tongue over the same spot to soothe the hurt.

His hands tugged her body even closer to his until she could feel the hard evidence of his arousal pressed against her and felt her knees go weak. Making love with Laurence had never been like this—and so far, Zach was only kissing her. But it was a kiss like none she'd ever received, a kiss that was meant to arouse, a kiss that was meant to be shared, a kiss that reached down into the deepest part of her.

And suddenly it was over. Zach was still holding her close, his arms wrapped tightly around her as he leaned his cheek against the top of her head.

She didn't want it to be over, didn't want the feeling of belonging to ever end.

"This isn't the right time or place," Zach whispered, and she stiffened. He was right. What had she been thinking? What about all her promises to herself? Did they mean nothing at all?

Emily pulled away from him, and Zach reluctantly let her step back, but he didn't let her go completely. He kept his hands on her shoulders, savoring the contact. She felt small

and fragile in his arms and utterly feminine. Her eyes were
so dark they looked almost black, like pools at midnight. He
wanted to drown in them, to lose himself so fully in her he
would never find his way out. He could imagine how she'd
look in his bed, her lips red and swollen from his kisses, as
they were now, her hair spread like a river of gold on his pillow, her naked body curled into his. His already tight body
throbbed, and his hands squeezed her shoulders.

She looked at him with eyes filled with confusion, as if
she didn't fully comprehend what had just happened. Her reaction surprised him. She'd been married before, and surely
been kissed. Why did she look so unsure?

He was about to ask when a shriek pierced the air, followed by a bellow and then running footsteps.

"Stop her! Stop her!" Jewel's cries shattered the silence.

"Don't worry. I'll get her," Frank shouted as he ran past
them out the door and around the far side of the house.

"What happened?" Zach demanded as Jewel came running up behind him, her hair in disarray.

"That pesky bird. She stole my tortoiseshell hairpin. I just
set it down on the windowsill for a minute and she ran off
with it."

Jewel took off out the door, pulling up her skirt so she
could take longer steps.

"I better go help," Zach said apologetically. Though Zach
had told his friend all about the birds on the ride out, he
wasn't sure what Frank would do if he actually caught up
with Baby.

Zach could still see a hint of confusion in Emily's eyes,
but he wasn't ready to explore what was happening. In a
way, he was grateful to Baby for providing this distraction.
He had a lot to think about, and from the looks of her, so did
Emily. This . . . this feeling, whatever it was, had come upon
them suddenly and unexpectedly. Already Zach was remem-

bering that he couldn't afford to get involved, not with a lady like Emily who needed someone permanent in her life.

He had obligations to the past, a past he could not ignore, and until he had fulfilled those obligations, he was not a free man. Pulling himself together, he added, "We'll talk about Frank later," then shot out the door.

Dinner was a strained affair. Everyone could see Jewel was upset about Baby. The young ostrich had taken a perverse liking to the one person on the ranch who was truly uncomfortable about the birds. Maybe it was because Jewel always wore such bright colors and shiny ornaments or maybe because she wore more ostrich feathers than the birds themselves. Whatever the reason, wherever Jewel was, Baby would not be far behind.

And now Baby had committed the cardinal sin: she'd eaten one of Jewel's prized possessions, the hairpin given to her by the owner of the first saloon where she'd worked.

"It had sentimental value," Jewel said through tears.

"There, there," Frank crooned as he stroked her arm. It was not the sort of thing a proper gentleman would do in public, but clearly he was too involved in trying to console Jewel to worry about such niceties.

Nor did Jewel seem inclined to object, for she launched herself into his arms and cried on his shoulder.

Eula and Opal clucked sympathetically, though Emily caught a gleam of wicked amusement in Opal's eyes as she watched the pair across the table from her. Emily didn't dare see how Zach was reacting.

Ever since her wanton response to his kiss, she dreaded being alone with him. What would he think of her? What did she think of herself? She wasn't sure. Even before Laurence died, his behavior had killed something in her. She had entered her marriage full of hope and promise, intending to

create the type of home every young lady was taught to
make. A place where her husband could find shelter from the
demands of daily life, where her children would be brought
up to take their place in the world, where she would fulfill
her destiny as loving wife and mother.

But that was not to be. One by one her dreams and illusions had been stripped from her. Or so she'd thought. She
could not remember when she'd last felt the stirrings of
desire—until Zach touched her. Just thinking about that kiss
made an ache of longing come to life low in her abdomen.

"If everyone's done with dinner, I'll start to clean up," she
said abruptly, needing to escape by herself for a few minutes.
"The rest of you can go on into the parlor. I'll bring in the
coffee when it's ready."

"Are you sure you don't need any help?" Opal asked.

"No, no. I'll be fine," Emily replied and quickly picked up
her plate and utensils. Once she was in the kitchen, she
opened the back door and looked out at the desert. It was so
different from her home back east, so dry and barren-
looking, though it really wasn't barren at all. Even in the dri-
est parts, cactus grew to tremendous heights, and other small
plants dotted the arid landscape.

The shallow rise hid the lusher irrigated areas from her
view. The alfalfa fields where the ostriches were kept were
the same green as the hills near her home in Connecticut, but
in Connecticut, that green had come naturally, fed by the
rains that fell all year round. In Arizona the green had to be
carefully cultivated, nurtured by the rancher against the in-
sults of the burning sun and drying air. The Salt River Valley
was fertile, but it needed to be irrigated to yield up its richness. So far, on the Double F, only certain sections received
water while the rest stayed in their original state.

Emily had thought she had become like the land—sucked
dry of all outward signs of life. But she was discovering

she'd been mistaken, both about the land and herself. Given the proper nourishment, they both could yield up a great richness; they both could come to life.

She heard a noise behind her.

"Just put everything down on the table," she said without turning around. "I can handle the dishes tonight. I said I would."

When no one responded, Emily turned to see what was the matter and there, leaning back against the table, was Zach. She caught her breath. This was the first time they'd come face to face since their kiss earlier today. Just thinking about it, she could feel the heat in her cheeks.

"Oh, it's you," she said, flustered. "I thought you were someone else. I . . ."

Her voice trailed off, and her nervousness increased. Zach looked so male and imposing in the kitchen. His eyes glinted with reflected light from the oil lamp, and his dark hair was neatly combed.

"It's okay. I'm sorry about Frank—not that I hired him; he's a good man. I just didn't mean to make you feel bad or nothing." Zach ran his hand through his hair, ruffling it, then smoothed it back into place. "I'm not after your ranch, Emily. I'm just doing Billy a favor. He asked me to come here, and I couldn't rightly say no, after all he'd done for me. I've got a responsibility here, and I gotta do what's right. I hope you understand."

"I do," she answered, but a part of her felt bereft, as if a lovely treasure had been placed within her reach, then suddenly yanked away before she could grab hold of it. Obviously their kiss hadn't affected him in the same way it had affected her. Zach looked as wary and distant as he had at their very first meeting. He was fulfilling his responsibility to Billy. Nothing more, nothing less. "Well, you're right that we need the help. I guess Mr. Ross will do, since you know him. Where will he be staying?"

Zach felt a wave of relief wash over him. Once again her graciousness in the face of the inevitable impressed him, just as it had the first night she'd shared a meal with him. He didn't know what he would have done if she'd adamantly refused to let Frank stay. He would have been caught in the middle, between the man who'd become like a second father to him and the woman who was coming to mean more than he could allow.

"I've put him in the room I fixed up when I first came. In a few days we'll be hiring a few more men to help out, so I'll work on the big room down by the barn for them."

"Do we need so much help?" she asked.

"We will soon enough. Those birds are laying eggs left and right. Once they start hatching, we'll need new pens for the young. I want to extend the irrigation ditches so we don't have to haul water so far, and this place needs some tending. This here adobe won't last forever if you don't take care of it. I'll see to it that the men are busy, don't you worry none."

She seemed to accept his word, which made his conscience gnaw at him, for he hadn't been totally honest with her. The men would be busy, all right, but not just at the ranch. They would be helping him find Earl Darnell, and once he was found, they would help hunt him down. But that was his private business and definitely not a story to tell a lady.

"You seem to have everything well in control, Mr. Hollis. Am I to be allowed to have any say at all in what goes on?"

She'd drawn herself up to her full height—not even five and a half feet—but she was full of spirit nonetheless. One look at her flashing eyes and he knew he'd done it again.

"You know you have a say. Don't you agree that those things need doing?" he asked, unable to keep his exasperation from showing.

"Yes, I do. But I'm getting tired of reminding you to check with me on what needs doing and when to do it. I don't seem to be getting through to you at all."

"You want to be consulted, then fine. Come on out to the back storeroom and see what you can make of the junk Billy sent."

"What junk?" she asked him suspiciously. "Why didn't you mention it sooner?"

He couldn't make himself tell her the truth—that her kiss had knocked every thought from his head and left him thinking only of her, of how smooth her skin felt, how soft her body was snuggled next to his, how sweet she tasted, how eager she made him feel, as if life had possibilities he had yet to dream of and they were all within his reach.

So instead he said, "I meant to, but with all the excitement over Baby, I plumb forgot. Would you like me to show you the stuff now?"

Emily looked around at the mess in the kitchen. "I really should straighten up in here first," she said with obvious reluctance. "Could you wait a few minutes?"

"Wait for what?" Eula asked in her usual solicitous way as she walked into the kitchen carrying the last few plates. "Can I be of some help?"

"Miss Emily's been wanting to see the box her uncle sent. Frank and I brought it in from town today and put it in the storeroom," Zach told her.

"Well, why don't you take her out to see it? I can finish up in here."

"Would you?" Zach said before Emily could protest, and if the expression on her face was anything to go by, that was what she was planning. "That'd be wonderful. Come on, Miss Emily. We can head out this way."

He put his hand beneath her elbow and guided her out the door. He held his breath, waiting for her to dig in her heels and refuse. But for once her stubbornness was nowhere in evidence, and she let him lead her outside.

CHAPTER

5

Zach was still uncertain about Emily's reaction to his presumption, so he wasted no time hurrying her around to the other side of the building.

"So what do you think?" he asked as he showed her in through the storeroom door. He held the lantern high so she could see the medium-sized box sitting in the center of the floor.

"How can I tell if it's all wrapped up in the shipping crate? Can we get it open?"

"I can try."

Zach looked around for something to use as a crowbar and found an old shovel, which he used to pry open the shipping carton.

"Oh, look. It's an incubator," Emily cried as the inner package came into sight.

"What for? Can't those birds hatch their own eggs?"

"Of course they can, but you take fewer risks if you hatch them in this. The hen will just lay more eggs if some of them disappear, kind of like a chicken."

Zach looked skeptical. "Where do the eggs go?"

"There's a drawer here for them." Emily pointed to the

middle of the box. "And hot water goes down here to keep everything warm. The eggs have to be kept at over one hundred degrees so it's just like their mother."

"Their mother? It seems to me it's the cock who does most of the work. The hens barely sit on the eggs for three or four hours a day. The cock sits on the nest and guards it the rest of the day and all through the night."

"Well, I'm sure the cocks are just as warm as the hens. The point is, the eggs have to be kept clean and warm so they have the best chance of hatching. This is supposed to be a business, you know. I'm just glad to see Uncle Billy has enough sense to treat it as such. Did he send a message?"

"No. The stationmaster simply had an invoice showing that William Crabtree had paid the bill in full."

Emily shook her head. "That man. What can he be thinking of?"

Zach had no answer to that, so he kept his silence. Besides, he was much more interested in watching Emily than in worrying about the crafty old confidence man who was probably having the time of his life wandering from one card game to the next. The light from the lantern lit up Emily's hair like a golden aureole, and her eyes were bright as she examined the contents of the box.

She knelt in front of the package, and Zach caught sight of her ankle where it stuck out from under her skirts. Her foot was narrow and beautifully shaped, and her stocking clung to every curve of her trim ankle and calf. For dinner she'd put on one of her fancy eastern dresses, with a snug bodice and flounced skirt. The sateen top was delicately patterned and had two rows of lace edging down the front. The flounces on the skirt were edged with the same lace. The dress was totally unsuitable for a ranch in the West, and yet it suited her perfectly.

She was as delicately feminine as any article of clothing

she wore. He could feel his blood rushing to his center, filling him till he was ready to burst with wanting. She seemed oblivious to his condition, to the effect she was having on him. And that was probably for the best, he decided.

"We'd better be getting back to the main house," he said, his voice sounding harsher than he'd intended. "You can look at the rest of this stuff in the morning."

She looked up at him with her startlingly dark eyes. "I'm sorry. I didn't mean to detain you."

There was only the slightest hint of rebuke in her tone, the barest reminder that he was the one who had asked her out here, not the other way around. He bit down on his tongue.

"I didn't mean it that way. It's just that it's getting late. I thought you would want to get back to the others."

She stood gracefully and straightened her skirts, then walked past him to the door.

"I'm sure they're getting along fine without me," she said. "It's warm out tonight, don't you think?"

She stepped outside and wrapped her arms around herself while he closed up the storeroom.

"It seems nice enough," he allowed. In the distance from over the rise came the strange sounds of the ostriches. "I ain't never heard such weird cries before," he said, nodding in the direction of the birds.

"Me, either. They say lions sound like that, roaring at a distance. I've never heard a lion roar, though, so I couldn't say."

She started walking toward the main part of the house, but paused at the fork in the path where one branch led out back to the ostrich enclosures and the other to the house.

"If you're not in a hurry, we could go check on them birds, just to be sure they're all set for the night," Zach offered.

They both knew the birds were fine. It was just an excuse

to stay together a little longer, to savor the intimacy of the moonlit night without the presence of the others.

"I'm in no hurry," she said softly.

Zach had no explanation for the feeling of elation that shot through him, nor did he want to inquire into it too closely, not now. It was enough that she wanted to be with him as much as he wanted to be with her. He took her hand into his and started down the right path, taking her away from the house and up the slight incline of the rise.

At the top of the low hill, they looked out over the ostrich pens. In the moon's silvery light, the birds resembled dark clumps of foliage in the distance. Only their long scrawny necks remained upright, like ghostly sentinels. In a far pen, one of the cocks stood up from the nest to stretch. The white plumes at the ends of his wings stood out sharply against the black feathers covering his body. He flapped his wings several times and seemed to reach to the sky with his beak. Then his neck swelled and he issued a deep-throated challenge to anyone within hearing distance before settling himself back on the nest.

"He's a nasty one, that 'un," Zach commented as he drew Emily closer to his side.

"He is at that. He ate my hat today."

"He what? How did he get it?" Fear shot through Zach. Those birds were dangerous, the males more so than the females. Had she no sense at all? Independence was all well and good, as long as she didn't do anything foolhardy. What would he do if she got hurt?

"He just grabbed it over the fence when I was getting him his special feed. Before I realized what he was up to, he was gone. And my hat, too."

She chuckled and her breast brushed against his arm.

"As long as he didn't get anything more than your hat," Zach said softly.

The light breeze brought her scent wafting in his direction. Violets and Emily—the two scents were becoming one in his mind. He slid his arm around her waist, and she looked up at him. Her lips were full and glistened in the moonlight, as if she'd just licked them.

Another ostrich emitted his low-pitched primal sound, and Zach knew just how he felt: protective and male, ready to take on all comers to preserve what was his, ready to stake his claim. As if propelled by a force outside himself, he bent his head to do just that.

If anything, she tasted even sweeter than before. He opened his mouth more fully over hers, needing to devour her, to take her into himself until there was nothing else in the world, just the two of them. When he reached out with his tongue to gently lick her lips, she responded immediately, opening to him in invitation. He groaned deep in his chest and crushed her to him, feeling her every curve move pliantly against the harder planes and angles of his body. His tongue plunged into the welcoming warmth of her, simulating the other throbbing rhythm he craved.

His hands moved restlessly against her back, learning every valley, every indentation. Her hands moved, too, kneading his chest through his heavy shirt, then slipping underneath as a button gave way. A shiver ran down his spine as he felt her warmth against his bare skin. She stilled, and he feared that she would pull away.

"Don't stop," he pleaded against her cheek and pressed his hand over hers so she could not withdraw them.

He felt her relax and spread her fingers, tangling them in the hair on his chest. He let her go then, and of its own volition his hand mimicked the motion of hers, finding the sweet upper curve of her breast, then slipping lower. She filled his palm with her softness, and her hands slipped up past his shoulders to the back of his neck. He turned her slightly so he could press her against him and still have access to her soft breast. She moaned as his fingers found her nipple through the layers of fabric. He could just discern its hardness and knew she'd/swelled to meet him just as he was swelling below.

He'd never felt such intense desire. He wanted to ravish her and possess her, to conquer the world so she would admire him and follow him to the end of their days. He'd never longed for forever before, certainly not in a woman's arms, but suddenly the dream of a lifetime together echoed in his soul.

Emily couldn't get enough of him, even with her hand pressed to the back of his head and her fingers buried in his dark brown hair tugging him closer and ever closer. His rich male taste overwhelmed her, and the way he thrust his tongue into her mouth left her with no doubt that he was thinking of the same things she was. How wanton she felt—and how cherished. He wanted her, she could tell, but he handled her as if she were infinitely precious, not the way Laurence had. Zach took his time, waiting to see if she responded, sensitive to what she liked without her saying a word.

His tongue was like rough velvet as it swept across her lips, then plunged once again into her depths, drinking from her very soul. His arms were so strong as they held her, taking her weight when her knees turned to liquid. And when he gently brushed his fingers against her breast, she thought she would come apart.

The ostriches' bromming made a primitive background music to their passion, underscoring their desire with its universality. When the need for air became overwhelming, they stood, leaning against each other, her head nestled against the hollow of his shoulder, his head resting on hers. Emily took a deep, shuddering breath and felt Zach's chest rise and fall with hers. Even their hearts kept pace with each other, their pulses racing as if they'd run up a hill far steeper than the small rise where they stood silhouetted against the moon.

"We'd better get inside before they come looking for us," Zach whispered in her ear.

She nodded without speaking, unwilling to break the special spell that held them in thrall. This was a night like no other, a moment out of time, a moment that could occur in no other place on earth—only here with the silvery moon shining from a diamond-clear sky and the otherworldly sounds of the ostriches below.

Zach slowly released her from his embrace, then shifted her and placed his arm around her shoulders. He hugged her and they started down the hill toward the house. She leaned into him as they walked, her arm around his waist. She soaked in his heat and the male essence that surrounded him, hoarding the memory like a treasure so she could take it out when she was alone and savor once again the moments in his arms.

At the back door he brushed his lips against hers and said, "I'd better let you go in alone." And then he was gone, swallowed by the darkness.

She waited outside until her heartbeat had slowed and she felt the swelling in her lips had faded. They still tasted of him, but at least no one would be able to see the more obvious signs of their activities on her face. She went to her room, grateful that the others were preoccupied in the parlor and she could avoid their scrutiny. She didn't want to explain what she hardly understood herself.

In her room, she undressed quickly and fell onto the bed, her mind filled with fanciful tales. She didn't know when she slipped into sleep, the dreams were so much like her fantasies. In all of them Zach appeared, and when she awoke, she blushed and was glad no one could read her thoughts.

* * *

Emily was washing up the breakfast dishes when she heard the back door open.

"Did you have any trouble with them?" she called out, thinking it was Eula returning after hanging up the clothes they'd just washed, most of which seemed to be Zach's.

Ordinarily Emily would have argued that Zach should be doing his own laundry. After all, the women did theirs in addition to their other chores on the ranch. She'd never understood why it wasn't right for a man to wash his own clothes, as Eula argued. But today was different. Today she hadn't minded in the least touching his shirts and even his more personal garments. It'd been all she could do to keep from blushing when she recognized his scent rising from the steamy water—a mixture of laundry soap, honest sweat, and something that was Zach's alone and had imprinted itself in the deepest recesses of her mind last night.

"Depends on what you mean by trouble," a decidedly masculine voice responded.

Emily turned quickly and found herself looking into Zach's eyes. She couldn't tear her gaze away from him. His shoulders seemed broader than before, his rugged masculinity more pronounced, now that she was familiar with the strength of his muscles, the hardness of his chest. He looked dusty and hot, and it was a minute before she realized how grim his expression was.

Whatever romantic notions she'd entertained about their first face-to-face encounter after last night's kiss shattered into a thousand pieces when he spoke.

"What?" she asked, not quite connecting his answer to her question, since it had been directed at someone else.

"How many of those ostrich books have you read?" he asked, ignoring her confusion and response.

There was no acknowledgment of their deeper intimacy of

the night before, either in his words or in his look. Stung by his attitude, Emily withdrew into herself. If he was going to pretend nothing had happened, then so would she. It was probably better this way, she tried to console herself, keeping her own expression under strict control. It would only add to her humiliation if he ever guessed what fairy tales she'd been spinning in her head . . . and to think she was the one who'd promised never to place herself at the mercy of a man's moods again.

"I've read one and browsed through some of the others," she said, matching his detached tone. "Why?"

"I need to know something, that's all."

His manner put her immediately on edge. Something was going on, something more than just what was happening between them—if, indeed, anything was.

"What happened? Is there a problem?" She thought back over the morning. It had been unusually quiet. A sudden thought struck her. "Where's Baby?" she asked with a touch of panic. Could something have happened to the wily young bird? She hoped not, for the silly thing had stolen her heart.

"Baby's fine. I just wanted to know what your books had to say about how those birds handle their eggs."

She looked at him and saw the faint worry lines creasing his brow. She dried her hands, still wet from doing the dishes, and draped the towel over the back of a chair.

"I know that each female can lay eggs anytime between February and August, and it takes forty-odd days for them to hatch. They have to have—"

"Do they ever break their eggs?"

"Sometimes, I guess," she said as she leaned against the counter holding the dishpan, "but the book says for such clumsy creatures they're quite gentle with their eggs. Besides, I think the shells are extremely hard."

"If you have the time, it might be a good idea if you come out to the corral with me."

"Are you going to tell me what's going on?"

"I think you'd better see for yourself. Then you can make up your own mind."

For the first time he was treating her as an equal, actually asking for her help on ranch business. The thought should have made her ecstatic, but in the circumstances, it only increased her concern.

"Let me change and I'll meet you out back," she said as she took off her apron and laid it over the drying towel on the chair. "I'll be right out."

As Emily slipped off her skirt and shirtwaist, she thought about what Zach had said. Until today he'd made no secret of the fact that he thought her books a waste of time. Knowing his stubbornness, it must have taken a lot for him to ask her for help. Whatever had happened must have been bad.

She hurriedly straightened her work skirt, then reached for a bonnet to protect her head from the glare of the morning sun. She just wished she had some gloves, and not the prissy gloves she'd brought from Connecticut. She needed strong, heavy gloves—like the ones Zach wore—if she really planned on making this ranch profitable. She'd have to see about getting some the next time she went into town.

"I'm ready," she said as she rushed out the back door.

"This way," Zach said and started walking ahead of her. None of the solicitousness of the night before was evident in his manner. Did he regret their kiss, or was he just upset about whatever he was taking her to see? Emily didn't know and was insecure enough about men not to ask. Laurence had been moody, too, and more than once had let her know she was not capable of holding a man's interest for long. Could the same thing be happening with Zach?

Her heart ached with a deep pain. She'd married Laurence

with her illusions intact, but he had never made her feel half the passion Zach had evoked with a single kiss. How could that be? And what had Zach felt? She wished she could read men better—*Zach* better, to be exact—but wishing had never gained anyone a thing, just more disillusionment. Quelling her churning thoughts, she followed in Zach's footsteps, her eyes searching anxiously, seeking anything out of order.

By the time she and Zach had walked to the paddocks in back of the house, perspiration had dampened the front of her shirtwaist on the inside and she was feeling light-headed. She was sure she would never get used to this heat. Then she caught sight of the ostrich pair frantically dancing around in their secondary enclosure instead of guarding their nest, and all thought of her discomfort fled.

"What happened?" she demanded. "Why aren't they near their nest?"

The birds were extremely territorial and protective of their eggs. One or the other of them would always be hovering near the nest if not actually sitting on it.

Zach gestured with his hand. "See for yourself. I didn't want that cock nearby while you were taking a look."

She took the few steps that brought her to the edge of the slight hollow the birds had dug in the sandy soil to serve as their nest. A sharp gasp escaped her. All the eggs were broken. There was nothing but jagged shells and pale yellow yolk.

Emily leaned over and picked up a shard of shell. The creamy liquid ran off the side.

"Are the others like this, too?" she asked, bewildered by the sight before her.

Zach nodded, his lips pressed into a thin white line, his jaw angrily clenched.

Just yesterday there had been three nests, each with over

ten eggs. Now there were no nests and only broken shells. She'd planned on getting the incubator into operation today and putting at least half the eggs in it. Now she'd have to start from scratch.

Using her hand, she shaded her eyes against the brilliant glare and scanned the distant paddocks where the other pairs were housed. They were too far away to make out.

"How did this happen?"

"I thought you might have some idea. I mean, you've had a chance to read the books."

"One thing I know: The ostriches didn't do this. Not every single egg. This was done on purpose. Do you see how thick this is?" she asked, holding up an egg shard. "A man could walk on an ostrich egg without breaking it. You'd need a hammer to do this to it."

"I thought the same."

"Why would somebody do something so senseless?" she asked as she looked from the shard in her hand to the damaged nest. "Why?"

"Exactly what I'd like to know," Zach said, kicking one of the shells as he cut across the enclosure to check a neighboring nest.

Emily followed him to the fence and watched him squat down beside the dug-out hollow and look inside. Out of the corner of her eye, she caught sight of the male ostrich streaking toward Zach. Apparently this pair had not been moved out of their pen like the other.

"Zach! Watch out!" she cried out in warning. She knew the damage an ostrich could inflict on a man.

At the sound of her voice Zach rolled to one side and the ostrich's leathery foot flew out over his head, missing him by only a few inches.

Zach started to get up when Emily remembered something she'd read.

"Stay down and tucked into a ball," she yelled at him. "And for heaven's sake, don't stand up. They can't kick you as long as you stay low. I'll try to distract him."

She looked around for something to use to get the angry bird's attention.

"Never mind distracting him," Zach called as he slowly rolled toward the fence. "He seems to have found something else of interest."

Emily breathed a sigh of relief as the bird trotted off in another direction and Zach crawled out to safety. She hadn't found much she could have used to stop the ostrich's attack other than a few stones and sticks to throw. "Thank goodness you got out of his territory before he landed a blow. Their kick can kill a man."

Slowly Zach got to his feet and picked up his hat. He beat the dust from it, with his left hand, Emily noticed.

"His territory, huh?" Zach said and rolled his shoulder as he walked toward her, wincing slightly. "I noticed the birds were mighty protective of their nests, but I didn't realize they claimed a territory."

Emily wanted to say, Are you all right? Did you hurt yourself when you hit the ground?—but she didn't. Though the kiss they had shared should have created an intimacy between them, Zach's lack of reaction this morning had put a certain distance between them, a distance Emily couldn't breach. She took shelter from her feelings in talking about the ostriches. Here, at least, was safe common ground.

"Each male ostrich has a home territory for himself and his mate. When anything or anybody invades it, he protects it, just as we humans protect our homes. But once you leave his personal territory, the male loses interest in you and goes about his own business. At least that's what the book says."

"Did it tell you how to protect yourself, besides rolling

into a ball? I don't reckon on having to do that every time I want to check on the nests."

"We could try making an ostrich stick."

"What's that?" he asked as he put on his hat and then pulled it low over his forehead until his eyes were almost hidden.

"It's a pole several feet long with a fork on the end, usually made from a young tree. You hold it up against the ostrich's chest and push him away. They use them in Africa."

"Found out about all that stuff in the books, huh?"

"Yes, I did." She waited, unsure of what his reaction would be.

He merely nodded and started walking toward the gate. When he'd didn't say anything, Emily decided not to pursue the subject, but instead followed him to the next nest. Until this moment she hadn't fully realized how dangerous the ostriches could be. Baby had become a pet, and because of her love for the curious bird, she'd lowered her defenses. Never again.

As they walked by the last nest, the male ostrich charged at them, his wings flaring as he puffed himself up to look twice his size. Fortunately he was on the other side of the wire fence and showed no inclination to come through it. Since he couldn't fly, there was no danger that he'd come over the top, either. When they passed out of his territory, the male backed off and, like the first bird, went on to other things.

"Do you have any idea who might have done this?" Emily asked, breaking the silence.

"Can't say that I do."

"You've been to town more often than I. Did anyone question you about the ranch? Seem more than just curious?"

"Nothing more than casual conversation. This place has

been the talk of the town since the birds arrived last spring. Everyone has a few questions. Besides, the people who did this wouldn't come talking to you face-to-face anyway."

"I guess you're right. Maybe we should ask the others if they heard anything last night. I certainly didn't." Emily squinted as if trying to see something. "Did you?"

"No, and I don't think we should mention this to the other ladies, either, since there's nothing they can do. It would only upset them needlessly. Don't you agree?"

Emily was astounded. Zach was actually asking her opinion for a second time today. Of course she was the one who'd come to the rescue with the information she found in the books, so maybe he felt he owed her. If he'd had a choice, he probably wouldn't have confided in her at all, but he'd obviously felt that he needed her help. She found she liked the idea of him needing her, even if it was just with the ostriches.

"I don't see any reason to tell them, do you?" Zach reiterated when she didn't answer.

"I'm not so sure. Jewel and Eula both seem to know what the world has to offer." Emily stopped by the gate and looked over at Zach. His face had turned a ruddy hue, and he looked as if he might be choking.

He certainly was a strange mixture. Being embarrassed because she knew that Jewel was a woman of the world, but having no compunction about kissing and touching her as he had last night. Emily guessed that doing and talking were two different things out here in the West.

"I think Eula and Jewel should be told, and I know Opal can handle anything. We have to have them on guard so they don't put themselves in danger."

"You're a lady, so you probably know best about these things," he mumbled. "Well, I guess I'd better get this cleaned up."

It was obvious he no longer wanted to talk about such delicate subjects.

"All right. I think I'll keep some of the broken shells to scatter around the yard for the ostriches to eat so they'll have enough calcium to make strong new eggs."

"Why don't you go inside out of this heat? When Frank gets back, we'll handle the cleaning up. Ladies' work is inside the house, anyway."

Just when she thought they were finally understanding each other, Zach would come out with something like that! But she was too hot and disappointed to argue. She had to make a living on the ranch or find someone to buy it. And since a buyer would be even harder to find than Uncle Billy, wherever he was, she'd have to get to work.

"I refuse to argue over this again. This is my ranch and therefore my responsibility." Not wanting him to argue, she decided to change the subject. "What effect do you think this will have on the birds?"

"Don't rightly know. They do seem a bit high-strung. Sorta like they know what's going on. I think it'd be best if we cleaned up the shells right away," Zach said after looking around. "Why don't we stack them over in the corner?"

With his concession on the division of work, Emily felt she'd at last scored a small victory. Maybe Zach was beginning to accept her authority, after all.

"Shall I start collecting the pieces from that first nest?" she asked. "I can carry them in that old washtub."

Zach looked in the direction she pointed and nodded.

"I'll go out by the spring and see if I can find a sapling with a good fork in it before I venture back into those other paddocks," he said. "Don't go in there yourself until after I've moved those birds, you hear?"

"I hear," she said saucily, more pleased than annoyed by

his solicitude, especially now that she'd won her concession from him.

He took a step closer to her, his gaze locked on hers. Her breath caught in her throat. Surely he wasn't going to kiss her again!

Instead he slowly reached into his back pocket and pulled something out.

"If you insist on doing man's work, you'd better use these. Don't want you messing up your hands. I'll go get the ax."

She reached out automatically to take what he held, fighting her unreasonable disappointment. Then, before she could take another breath, he leaned over, kissed her on the lips, and was off to the barn.

Emily stood stunned, her mouth tingling. Damn the man. What was he up to now? She looked at her hands to see what he'd given her, and her heart skipped a beat—she held a pair of leather work gloves in a perfect size six.

Jabber sure didn't like the strange meeting places the man set up. He stepped hesitantly into the dark mine shaft, not even able to see his hand at the end of his arm where he groped along the wall so he wouldn't trip over anything.

"That's far enough. Take a seat and face this way," the familiar voice rasped from the back, breaking the ominous silence and startling him. "What have you got to report?"

The man wasted no time, not even a pleasant greeting, Jabber thought with a hint of anger. Well, his news would change that.

"I did pretty well, if I do say so myself," Jabber said with smug satisfaction. "I snuck onto that ranch and broke all them critters' eggs. They won't have no reason to stay on now, not with their profit all shot to hell."

"And nobody saw you?"

"Nary a soul. Though I tell you, them birds is pretty fierce until you get a bag over their head. That was a pretty smart idea."

Jabber might not like the man behind the voice very much, but he sure had to admire him. Jabber'd never met a more devious cuss.

The man merely grunted. "You better be right. I want to see them off that land soon or there'll be hell to pay."

Jabber didn't hear a sound after that warning, but in the next instant he knew he was alone in the mine shaft. He felt a strange premonition—like someone'd walked on his grave, as his mother used to say. But why should he feel threatened? He'd done exactly what he'd been told to do, hadn't he? It was those others who'd better worry, those people on the ranch. They might not know it, but his boss was getting impatient, and if they knew what was good for them, they'd take heed.

The dark of the damp shaft closed in on Jabber, and he skedaddled out of there and into the warm sunlight, glad he didn't have nothin' the boss would ever want.

CHAPTER

6

Emily was pulling off her new gloves when Eula, Jewel, and Opal came into the kitchen.

"You and Zach sure were out there an awful long time," Jewel said, easing herself into one of the kitchen chairs. Jewel had on another of her colorful dresses today. Her clothes might not have been of the best quality and were a bit on the worn side, but she certainly did have a rainbow array. Today's dress was turquoise with broad yellow satin insets from shoulder to ankle.

"You two must be gettin' along a good sight better," she teased, draping her matching yellow boa over her shoulder.

Emily felt a sudden influx of heat flood her face. She was sure no one could have seen her with Zach last night. Now that she thought about it, maybe they had stood out against that bright silver moon when they were on the top of the rise. She glanced at Jewel but saw no deeper knowledge in her eyes. Her telltale blush would only give her away.

She turned her head to one side to avoid any close scrutiny and said, "Jewel, I'm a widow of almost two years, and hardly the sort of woman someone would want to dally with in the corral."

"Why, I wouldn't say that at all," Jewel declared, sounding shocked. "I think all of us have a little dalliance in us. Don't you agree, Miss Opal?"

"I don't know about all of us," Opal replied. "But I can't imagine any red-blooded male looking at our Emily here and not getting ideas, even if she won't admit it."

At Opal's words, Emily's face again flooded with color. "My goodness, Opal," she whispered. "What are you saying?"

She didn't know whether to be more shocked that Opal thought such things about her or that she had the gall to say them out loud for anyone to hear.

"You two, stop teasing Emily. Just look at her blushing," Eula reprimanded the other ladies.

"Thank you, Eula. I'm glad to see someone here has maintained her sense of decorum," Emily replied in her best librarian voice.

"Now, Emily, you know we don't mean anything by teasing like this. We're all women here and have had our share of experiences, one way or another, so don't fret. We wouldn't say anything like that in front of the gentlemen," Opal said soothingly. "Isn't that right, Jewel?"

"Oh, yes, Miss Opal. We wouldn't say a thing in front of the menfolk. The less they know, the easier they are to manage, I always think. And you must admit that Zach is a good-looking young man, almost as good-looking as Mr. Ross."

Jewel looked dreamily at the ceiling, clearly remembering an interlude with Frank. Emily couldn't help but notice how different Jewel's behavior was toward Frank compared to Zach. With Frank, she seemed more straightforward, showing her true self instead of hiding behind her usual unremitting sensual banter. Emily wondered where all this was leading and hoped Jewel wouldn't be hurt.

"Yes, well," Opal said, "be that as it may, I must say, I

haven't seen you looking this pretty in many a month, Emily."

Emily felt her cheeks flare as they had earlier, but before she could frame a suitable reply, the kitchen door opened and Zach and Frank entered.

"Have you told them?" Zach asked, absently slapping his hat against his thigh, before placing it on the hat tree. Frank stood slightly behind him.

"They haven't given me a chance," Emily replied, not quite meeting his eye. The earlier conversation had left her feeling exposed.

"I'm mighty sorry about the loss, Miss Emily," Frank said, taking off his hat and setting it next to Zach's.

Emily nodded her thanks for his sympathy.

"What loss?" Jewel asked, looking from Emily to Zach.

"It seems someone was out prowling around the property last night," Zach said in response.

"Last night! Are you sure?" Eula asked with a tremor in her voice.

"I'm afraid so," Emily said and patted her hand. Poor Eula was afraid of her own shadow. Emily wished she could do something to help her, but for now all she could do was make sure she wasn't more frightened than could be helped.

"Did they do any damage?" Opal asked.

"Nothing too serious, yet. They broke most of the ostrich eggs and left the shells scattered around," Zach explained in blunt detail.

Emily glared at him. Didn't he realize he was scaring the ladies? But then, hadn't she been the one who'd said the ladies should be told? She should have realized by now that once Zach decided something should be done, he went straight to the heart of the matter.

"Oh, no. You were just gettin' ready to put 'em all in that there box, weren't you?" Jewel asked Emily.

"Yes, we just got the incubator together, but now we'll just wait for the next batch," she said calmly to reassure the others. "We'll have more eggs before long."

At least that was what she hoped, as long as this invasion of their territories didn't put the ostriches off laying.

"Zach and I will be taking extra care . . . especially at night. So there's no need for you ladies to worry none," Frank said. Though his words were intended for all of them, his eyes were trained on Jewel.

"I'm sure you'll take great care of us, Mr. Ross." Jewel's lashes were batting as fast as Baby's . . . and they were nearly as long. "As for myself, I wouldn't feel any safer if we had a U.S. marshal staying here."

Emily wasn't sure what Jewel had said, but she saw Zach stiffen and send Frank a meaningful glance. Whatever Zach saw in Frank's eyes must have satisfied him, because he nodded and visibly relaxed.

"Well, I'm mighty pleased you feel that way, Miss Jewel. Now, if you ladies will excuse—" Frank was interrupted by a sudden banging on the front door.

"Opal? Emily? You in there? It's me, Bea. Bea Keller."

"Oh, my goodness, we have company," Opal exclaimed, then rushed to answer the front door, checking to make sure all was in order as she went. "How nice to see you, Bea," she gushed as she pulled wide the door.

Jewel and Eula crowded in behind her, as eager to get news of the outside world as Opal, even though they hadn't yet met Bea.

"Bea. What a lovely surprise," Opal continued. "Do come in and meet our other guests. You'll stay to dinner, won't you?"

"Some sittin'-down time would be right welcome," Bea replied. "Besides, I brought some of my homemade hazelnut cake for dessert."

Emily arrived in the front room in time to see Bea lift a wicker basket from beside the front door and look around her with the undisguised curiosity that was her hallmark.

"Mr. Hollis," Bea said with a slight curtsy after she'd taken stock of all the new faces. "It's nice to see you again."

"And you, Mrs. Keller," Zach drawled. "To what do we owe the honor of your visit?"

Emily gasped, appalled and completely taken aback by Zach's lack of social grace. Good manners dictated that one never ask why a guest had come to call. One conversed circumspectly until the answer was revealed of its own accord; one never blatantly demanded to be told.

"Don't look so scandalized, Emily," Bea said with a smile and waved her hand in a dismissive gesture. "I'm used to plain speakin'. And your Mr. Hollis is right. I have a reason for comin' and not just to see you all, as pleasant as that will be. If someone can see to my horse, I'll be happy to tell you my news over our meal."

Opal and Eula had prepared the midday meal while Emily and Zach were cleaning up the broken eggs, so within twenty minutes they were sitting down to dinner.

"Now, Mrs. Keller, you were saying . . ."

"Zach, really. At least let Bea take a sip of tea," Emily protested.

"I can understand his impatience, after hearin' what happened here last night. You know, I hadn't thought of it, but maybe the two events are related."

"What two events?" Zach asked.

"Why, your eggs being broken and what's goin' on in town."

At that, the two men sat forward in their chairs.

"Maybe you better tell us your news right quick," Zach said, and Frank nodded.

Emily would have protested again, except both had such

serious expressions. She felt a quiver of fear unsettle her stomach. She'd been so worried about the birds and their eggs that she hadn't given serious thought to who had done the damage or why. But obviously Zach and Frank had.

"Zach's right, Bea. Please tell us everything you know, especially if it has anything to do with our birds," Emily urged.

Zach shot her a glance that contained both surprise and approval at her sudden change of heart before he looked expectantly back at Bea.

Bea milked the moment for all it was worth, basking in her role as the center of attention. "Well," she said consideringly, "I'm afraid my news isn't good. I don't know if you all have met Reverend Putney yet. He's our new minister. He hasn't been in town very long at all, not like our old one. Now, that was a fine man. . . ."

"Uh, Bea, dear," Opal cut in with a meaningful nod of her head toward the two men, "I think you'd better stick to the point. We do want to hear what happened before supper."

"Oh . . . oh, yes, of course." She smiled at the men, and when they didn't smile back, she hurried on with her tale. "Well, to put it short, Reverend Putney's been talkin' about all the goin's-on here at the ranch."

At Bea's words, Emily felt a shiver run down her spine. The only thing she could think of was that the pastor was talking about how she and Zach had been out here alone before Jewel and Eula came. She looked across the table at Zach and found he was watching her. Quickly she looked away. Maybe before last night she would have pooh-poohed such an accusation, but not now.

"How does he know what's going on out here?" Jewel demanded, outraged. "I haven't seen him doing any calling in this direction."

"Oh, he knows what's out here. He's been told all about

them birds by some of the church members. They were delivered right through the middle of town, you know. Caused quite a commotion at the time. It's only been the past couple of weeks that he's started preachin' about 'em, though. In his sermons and all," she added in explanation as the others looked at one another in confusion.

"What in the world could a preacher have to say about a bunch of ostriches?" Frank asked.

"Just what the Bible says. It's got him all fired up. He's rantin' and ravin' about the heathens out on this ranch keepin' birds the Lord holds up to such disdain."

"He says we're heathens?" Emily asked, hardly able to believe what she was hearing.

Before she came here, no one had ever said a disparaging word about her, nor had anyone had cause to. In fact, quite the contrary: She was often praised for her library and charity work. Now that she thought about it, she almost liked the sound of what Bea was saying. Imagine prim and proper Emily Crabtree with a tarnished reputation. What an interesting prospect!

Emily looked over at Zach, and their eyes met. He was smiling, too. Together they broke out in laughter, both of them trying to hide behind their napkins.

"Emily, this is nothing to laugh about," Bea reprimanded her. "I know we're a small town compared to where you've come from, but talk can ruin your reputation all the same."

"You're right, of course, Bea. It's just so surprising. I mean, I know the ostriches look funny and all, but they're really quite harmless as long as you stay out of their way," Emily replied in a more sober voice. She tried to keep the corners of her mouth from turning up.

"Well," answered Bea, somewhat mollified, "if you want my advice, I think it'd be best if you come into town for services next Sunday. That way everyone'll see you're not hea-

thens. And besides, you'll get a chance to meet some of the
townsfolk. Once they see you, they'll know the reverend is
mistaken."

"That's a wonderful idea," Emily agreed. "I've been
meaning to get to church, but with everything that's been
happening here, I haven't had time to do more than think
about it. Next Sunday I'll be sitting in the front pew."

"And so will I." Zach's tone challenged anyone to dis-
agree . . . most of all Emily. But she didn't say a word, keeping her eyes trained on her plate.

She wasn't sure what scared her more, spending the day
with Zach by her side or knowing he was coming because he
suspected someone in the town had caused the destruction of
the ostrich nests. Was Bea right to suspect that the preacher's
words had incited some zealot to commit such a misguided
act? If so, what could they do?

Maybe Reverend Putney would be open to reason. Surely
if they invited him out to see the birds he would realize how
harmless they were—at least with a fence between you and
them—and he would retract his earlier criticisms. Emily
could only hope so.

They ate the rest of the meal in relative silence, the others
apparently as immersed in their own thoughts as Emily was.
But when the dessert of hazelnut cake was served, they became more animated. The talk turned to the news from
Phoenix and whether the latest newspaper from the East
showed any new dress styles.

By midafternoon the ladies had talked themselves out, and
Bea was getting ready to head back to town. The men had
left soon after the meal to get on with their chores. No one
was expected, so the knock on the door came as a surprise.
Who else could possibly be coming to call, especially this
late in the day?

Jewel, being the closest to the door, went to open it and

came face-to-face with Baby. The young bird had been pecking at the metal frame surrounding the small window set in the door.

"Bless my soul," Jewel screeched as she came eye to eye with the feathered beast. Jewel's bellow scared the baby ostrich and sent it flying backwards over the front porch.

Before Emily could do more than give a startled gasp, Jewel was out the door and down the steps, cooing over the bewildered animal.

"Oh, you poor thing. Did ol' Jewel scare you? Well, of course I did, poor Baby. Here, let me see if you're all in one piece." Jewel began running her hands over the ostrich's body and wings, looking for any misshapen parts.

While Jewel was looking for broken bones, the other women came out to see for themselves what had happened. Even Frank came from around the corner where he'd been patching a worn spot on the adobe wall. The ranch residents exchanged puzzled looks as they watched Jewel tend to her arch nemesis.

Concluding that everything was in order with the young bird, Jewel walked Baby back to the barn and returned to the group. By the time she reached the bottom step, everyone on the porch was laughing.

"Well, what are you all carrying on about?" she demanded, placing her fists on her hips.

"I thought you were none too fond of that there animal," Frank offered, trying unsuccessfully to swallow his chuckles.

"I'm not," she conceded, "but somebody had to help the poor thing after she fell. Besides, she's only trying to be friendly. She can't help it if we both like the same things."

"I guess not," Frank said with another hearty laugh.

Fully suspicious now, Jewel looked back over her shoulder, only to find herself once again nose to nose with Baby.

The ostrich batted her impossibly long lashes and watched Jewel with a fascinated stare.

"Get back to the barn, you crazy bird," Jewel admonished. "I can't have you following me everywhere I go."

But Baby seemed to recognize there was no real anger in Jewel's tone, so she didn't move a step.

Exasperated, Jewel threw up her hands, the ends of her feather boa flying in the air. "Oh, I give up," she declared and strutted up the steps.

When she was barely halfway up, she looked over her shoulder. There was Baby, her strange, two-toed foot already on the bottom step.

Jewel glared at the group standing on the porch. "Aren't any of you going to do anything?"

"Now, Jewel, I think this all might just be your fault," Eula ventured in a tentative voice.

"What do you mean, my fault? All I did was see if the dang thing had any busted bones. I didn't save its life or anything."

"I don't think it's what you did, but what you wear." Eula leaned over and lifted the end of Jewel's boa. "See, I think she thinks you're her mother, what with all these feathers you have on."

"Her mother! Well, I never," Jewel said with an indignant squawk. She looked ready to stomp her foot.

When the others began to chuckle again, Jewel became even more indignant. She seemed just about ready to explode when Frank came to her rescue.

"Personally, I think it's charming." He gallantly offered his arm and helped her to the top step. Then with a flourish he kissed the back of her hand.

"Why, Mr. Ross, how kind you are." Jewel smiled, her mood suddenly improved.

"Please call me Frank."

"My pleasure, Frank."

The two of them seemed oblivious of the others as they stared into each other's eyes.

"Why don't I help you get that young bird penned up out back with the rest of the yearlings?" Frank offered, his voice turning husky.

"Why, how very kind of you," Jewel agreed. She almost looked demure, except for the tight dress and fluttery feather boa.

Frank offered her his arm, and Emily thought the air fairly sizzled between them. She was sure if she had a match, it would burst into flame just from being held near the pair.

They walked back down the stairs, arm in arm. Within minutes Baby had joined the procession, her long-lashed eyes glued admiringly on Jewel's retreating figure as she hurried to keep up.

Then, as if she had just remembered her manners, Jewel called back over her shoulder, "Bea, it was real nice meeting you. Have a safe trip back to town."

Opal, Eula, and Bea shared meaningful smiles as they all watched Jewel disappear with Frank. Emily wasn't sure what to think, so she simply sighed and shook her head. What other surprises would this strange place bring?

"I hope we're doing the right thing," Emily fussed as she sat beside Zach on the wagon seat. They'd been traveling quite a while and would soon reach the outskirts of Bethel Springs, in plenty of time for Sunday services. Opal was sitting on a makeshift seat in the back of the wagon.

"Whether we're doing the right thing or not, it's too late now to change our minds," Zach said and flipped the reins, urging the horses on.

He'd been the one to decide it would be best if only the three of them made the trip into town for Sunday services without the other two "ladies" or Frank. Only Emily had objected. Jewel and Frank were more than happy to stay at the ranch and get to know each other better. Eula promised to have dinner on the table by the time they got back.

Zach knew none of the men Frank recruited to help work the ranch had any desire to be in church on a Sunday morning. But that hadn't stopped Emily from insisting that they should be invited. The men had trickled in over the past week in response to Frank's telegrams and had taken over various chores. None of the women seemed aware of the men's other purpose for being at the ranch.

"I still think everyone should have come with us," Emily continued to insist.

"I know exactly what you think, Emily. You've told me over and over, and I've told you that the less the town knows about our business, the better. Besides, this whole charade should please you, what with me going as your ranch foreman and you as the owner."

"Zachariah Hollis, I've never wanted you to feel like a . . . a servant or anything," Emily said in honest astonishment. "All I want is to be myself and do what I think is right. Laurence used to—" Emily stopped abruptly.

He watched as she took a deep breath, and then continued in a less agitated voice, "All I want is control over what's mine. Nothing more. Besides which, this whole foreman thing was *your* idea."

She clasped her hands together in her lap and seemed to be making a concerted effort not to look at him. She'd revealed far more than she'd intended; he could tell by the look on her face. Her brow was crinkled, and her eyes held a sad faraway look—a look which, if he let it, could have gotten him more involved than he'd ever been in his entire life. He had to watch himself; he could easily drown in those sad eyes and never come up again. He had to remember that he didn't want any ties, and after their kiss last week . . . Well, he'd have to be careful how he proceeded.

Emily was a lady and therefore expected the men she knew to act like gentlemen. No one had ever considered him a gentleman. . . . Probably no one ever would. And he certainly hadn't acted like a gentleman when it came to that kiss. But then, the way she'd reacted had surprised him as well. She'd turned to liquid fire in his arms, and it had been all he could do to stop at just the kiss. If he'd had his way, he'd have taken her to the nearest bed and spent the next week there. Just thinking about the feel of her silken skin next to his stirred his body to life even now, sitting here in the hot sun on a hard, bouncing wooden seat.

He shifted his position, trying to ease the building pressure in his pants. This was mighty embarrassing, especially with Opal Crabtree sitting in the back of the wagon. Never in his life had a woman affected him as much as this bossy, irritating lady from the East, with her independent ways.

When he'd dreamed about a normal life, he'd never imagined sharing it with anyone like Emily. He'd always thought he would want someone demure and submissive, the way he remembered his mother was, acceding to his father's every wish. But with Emily, everything was different. She didn't know what the word "submissive" meant, though Zach had to admit their arguments were almost as exciting as their kisses.

And it wasn't just her beauty that attracted him; her need to be in control of her own life sparked an answering chord in him. He sensed her vulnerability, knew with an instinct born of his own pain that her independence had been bought at a price. How he wished he were free to pursue her!

But that was not to be. He was still fighting a crusade that had started when he was eleven. It wouldn't be fair to her to start anything he couldn't see through to the end. If it hadn't been for the trouble on the ranch, he wouldn't even be here now. He'd be using his day off to scout around for Earl Darnell—and he intended to get started on that as soon as he figured out what was behind the attack on the birds. He owed Billy that much.

And Emily, too, a small voice inside him proclaimed, but Zach silenced it quickly. He couldn't afford to hear it. Not now—and maybe never. He was bound by a promise he could never revoke, a promise made on his father's grave.

"We're almost to town," he said as he spotted the low-slung buildings in the distance. "Remember, now, be careful what you say."

"I really don't see why all this pretense is necessary," Emily said, having regained her composure. "Why can't we just go into town and tell everyone what's going on?"

"Because we aren't sure what's going on. And until we know, it's better to play our cards close. For all we know, it might have been the minister himself who came out to the ranch."

"How can you say such a thing about a man of the cloth?" Emily asked in a scandalized voice.

"I'm not accusing Mr. Putney of anything. I'm just saying better safe than sorry. We don't know who's doing what. Or why, for that matter. It'll be best if we say as little as possible. Agreed?"

"I suppose so," Emily conceded with ill grace.

Zach flicked the reins and set the horse to a trot. Services would be starting in a short while, and he didn't want to be late.

They rode down the main street, heading for the church located on the western edge of town. When they pulled up, people were just going in, so Zach tied up the horse and helped the ladies down.

"Mornin', Emily," Bea called from across the street as she scurried toward them. "Glad you could make it."

Emily and Opal hugged Bea when she reached them.

"Mr. Hollis," Bea acknowledged.

"Mrs. Keller," Zach said, tipping his hat. "Is the good reverend in sight?"

"That's Mr. Putney over there, standin' by the side of the church. The one dressed all in black."

"He certainly doesn't look like sweet Mr. Barclay back home," Opal commented. "Reverend Barclay has such an open, friendly face. This gentleman looks like he's just eaten something sour."

Zach agreed. The man looked none too pleased. He greeted people as they passed inside, but a smile never touched his face.

"Until he started goin' on about the ostriches, I thought he was doin' a good job," Bea said. "He's only been here a few months, but he seemed to be fittin' right in."

"I think we should be moving along inside. We don't want to be the last ones in, especially since we don't want to call attention to ourselves," Emily urged. Taking the two older ladies' arms, she started toward the church doors.

Before he followed them into the building, Zach looked around. Since they'd pulled up to the church, he'd felt that he was being watched. His brief inspection of the area showed nothing out of the ordinary, but he sensed that something wasn't right.

An hour and a half later, after the service, Zach was again standing in the same spot and still had the feeling he was being watched. Emily and the ladies spotted him as they trailed out, having stopped every few feet for Bea to introduce them to another of her friends in town.

"Who would have ever thought there were so many references to ostriches in the Bible," Emily commented.

Opal nodded her head in agreement. "Doesn't look like the good Lord has anything nice to say about them, that's for sure."

"At least not by Mr. Putney's interpretation," Zach added.

"Do you think he's making all this up?" Emily asked, her eyes growing round at the prospect.

For someone who thought she could take care of herself and a large ranch, she could be incredibly naive.

"Wouldn't want to say nothing bad about a man of the cloth," Zach said wryly, "but I have known one or two preachers who twisted things the way they wanted them."

"The fact is, when he saw you all, he sorta changed his whole line of thought and started in on the ostriches again," Bea observed.

"Noticed that same thing myself. I wonder if he's having help deciding on what to preach?" Zach considered.

"You mean someone's pushing him to talk out against us?" Again Emily sounded shocked.

"Maybe" was all Zach said. He didn't want to reveal more than he needed to. His gut was telling him something, and that something didn't bode well for the ranch. But until he had more to go on than just a hunch, he'd better curb his tongue.

Zach was trying to pin down his feeling of being watched when he saw a man heading straight in their direction.

"Miz Crabtree. Let me introduce myself: Dan Ebbert, at your service," said the bearded man as he came to stand between Zach and Emily. "I've heard a great deal about the revolutionary experiments at your ranch and wanted to make sure I met you."

"Mr. Ebbert, I'm pleased to meet you," Emily said, placing her hand in his. "But I wouldn't call what we're doing revolutionary. It's done in Africa all the time."

Zach watched Emily as Ebbert leaned over and pressed his lips to the back of her gloved hand. The man was of medium height and solidly built. Though he was older than Zach by a few years, he was still in his prime and not nearly as unattractive as Zach would have liked, even with his full beard. In fact, if Emily's expression was anything to go by, she found him handsome enough. It was all Zach could do to not grab the guy by his neck and warn him off, but he knew Emily would never forgive him if he made an ass of himself in the middle of the churchyard, so he kept his hands at his sides and bided his time.

"Let me introduce you to my friends," she was saying.

Zach heard Emily make the introductions, but he couldn't take his eyes off her hand. Just when he decided he didn't care how big an ass he made of himself, Ebbert freed her hand.

"Weren't you afraid to talk with us after what the preacher said in his sermon, Mr. Ebbert?" Opal asked. "I know if I'd just heard all that, I might have been."

"I make my own judgments. Nothing against the parson, you understand. I've found you have to see things with your own eyes."

"Very commendable," Opal said and gave Zach a significant look.

Zach shrugged his shoulders. What did she expect him to do? Best to just let this conversation run its course and then get back out to the ranch. They hadn't learned much so far, and Zach didn't want Emily anywhere in the vicinity when he started making his inquiries.

"Maybe I could visit you at the ranch sometime and see the birds for myself," Mr. Ebbert was saying. "If it wouldn't be too much of an imposition, of course." He sent Emily a toothy smile.

Zach clenched his jaw. In his role as foreman, he knew it wouldn't do for him to bark out orders—not that Emily would have taken them, anyway—so he kept silent. She hadn't asked for his help before, and she probably wouldn't be pleased to hear his opinion now.

"You're welcome to visit," she said with a smile. "We're far from experts, but things are coming along. The feathers are in high demand. As long as the fashions don't change, we should do quite well. I've written to a feather merchant in New York and hope to harvest some feathers in the near future."

"But surely life on a ranch must be quite a change from what you are used to. Don't you find you have a hankering for town life?"

"Oh, no. The ranch is most interesting, and I plan to see it become a success."

Her determination warmed Zach, especially when he saw Dan Ebbert frown.

"Don't you care for ranch life?" Zach challenged the man.

Ebbert barely glanced at him, dismissing him as though he really were just a hired hand. "Actually, I live on a ranch, myself," he said to Emily, acting as if she had asked the question. He shifted his position slightly to cut Zach out of the conversation. "So I know it can be a risky venture. You might do well to find a buyer, if you can, and put your resources into something more secure."

"You're very kind to show such concern," Emily replied, "but at the moment I'm enjoying the challenge. It may not sound like much to a man of your obvious talents, but for me it is quite the most exciting thing I've ever done."

"Well, in that case, I wish you well. But please, if you ever need help or advice, do call on me. I'd be most pleased to put my talents at your disposal."

He seemed ready to kiss her hand again, and Zach ground his teeth together.

Fortunately, Opal took that moment to intervene. "I think we'd best be getting back to the ranch. There's the midday meal to prepare and the birds to water," Opal said to no one in particular, "and this heat is starting to make me feel a bit unwell. You do understand, don't you, Mr. Ebbert?"

"Of course, of course. It was very nice meeting you all. I'm sure we'll be meeting again real soon."

He took his leave, bowing slightly before walking over to a group of men standing by the front door of the church.

"Quite a nice man, don't you think, Zach?" Opal opined.

Zach looked at Opal as if she'd lost her mind. He could have sworn she didn't like Dan Ebbert any more than he did.

"Can't say, Mrs. Crabtree. Never did like making snap judgments."

"Well, he certainly liked Emily well enough. Couldn't take his eyes off her. Did you notice?"

"Can't say I did."

"Oh, well, it makes no never mind. We'd best be saying our good-byes to Bea," Opal said as Bea waved from the far side of the churchyard.

Opal headed in Bea's direction, and Zach looked over at Emily. So far she hadn't given her opinion one way or the other where that fancy Mr. Ebbert was concerned. Nor did she now. She merely smiled and followed Opal.

Zach was silent on the way home, and Emily was unsure why. She knew it had to do with her conversation with Dan Ebbert, but she didn't know exactly what had bothered him. She still hadn't figured it out when they pulled into the courtyard of the ranch. Before she had a chance to think about getting down, Frank was by her side helping first her and then Opal off the buckboard. It almost seemed as if he had been waiting for them to get back.

Emily's suspicions were confirmed when he turned to talk to Zach as soon as he had Opal settled on the ground. Whatever had happened wasn't good, if she had to guess by the look on his face.

Emily was uncertain how she felt about Frank turning to Zach like that. On one hand, she wanted to be included in everything that had to do with her property, but on the other hand, she found herself trusting Zach more and more when it came to decisions concerning the ranch.

She wasn't sure whether it had to do with the relationship that was beginning to develop between them or whether she'd realized Zach always had the ranch's best interests at heart. Or was she yielding to more personal reasons, letting Zach make more decisions in the hope that he'd stay on?

"When Jewel and I were watering the birds, we noticed something," Frank began ominously.

"What?" Zach asked.

"Nothing good, I'm afraid. Seems one of the wire fences was cut."

"What about the ostriches?" Emily asked, concerned that the newly laid eggs might have been tampered with.

"They're fine. The fool cut the wire on one of the twin paddocks housing a single pair of birds. The birds couldn't get free. They just drifted over to the other section of their pen where the greens were growing higher."

Zach laughed, but his brow still carried a worried frown. "Well, that's good, at least," he said.

"Whoever's doing this is mighty sneaky," Frank added. "The men kept watch most of the night. The last shift only came in at dawn."

"I know they're doing all they can," Zach assured him.

"I'm not looking to blame them, but maybe we'd better set up a better schedule. This time nothing serious happened, but we might not be so lucky the next time."

Frank nodded his agreement.

"Was there anything out there to indicate who's been doing this?" Emily asked. "Or why?"

"Nary a thing," Frank said, shaking his head. "They're mighty smart or mighty lucky. The tracks show only one horse and rider. He must have kept watch, and when the men came in, he decided to do his dirty work."

"Too bad he didn't get caught in the paddock with the ostriches like I did," Zach said. "He'd think twice about messing with those birds again if he had. I can still see that cock bearing down on me. It's not something I'll forget for some time, that's for sure."

"I could use your help stringing some new wire on the west paddock, Zach, if you got the time," Frank said and then turned to Emily. "You'll be changing them birds over soon, won't you?"

"Yes, I'd planned on switching them all sometime this week. The alfalfa is pretty well trampled in their current pens and hard for them to eat. Once they're switched, it should all grow back. When they eat all the alfalfa in their new pens, we can switch them back again."

"Why don't I go out with Frank and get that fence back up this morning? Then this afternoon I can help you move the ostriches," Zach offered.

Emily was relieved. She'd dreaded having to move the breeding pairs by herself. She was uncomfortable handling the more aggressive males. "That sounds fine," she agreed quickly.

"Good. How about moving them right after lunch? That okay with you?"

Emily nodded as Zach took her hand and gave it a

squeeze. It was the first time he'd touched her since the conversation with Dan Ebbert at the church. She nearly forgot about the ostriches' plight in her relief that he seemed to have gotten over whatever was troubling him.

"Frank, you ready to head out?" he asked as he let go of her hand.

"Any time you are, partner," Frank replied, and then with a roguish twinkle in his eye, he said to Emily, "I'll be looking forward to seeing you at lunch, ma'am."

Emily watched them walk toward the barn. Her hand still tingled from the warmth of Zach's touch. She feared she was losing her heart to him and didn't know what to do. Though he'd told her little about himself, he'd made one thing clear: He didn't want any permanent ties.

Sometimes she wondered why Zach had come here, aside from his promise to Uncle Billy. There was something else, she was sure. She recalled all the occasions when she'd come upon him staring into the distance, a sad and grim expression on his face. What was he thinking of then? What had he been doing when Uncle Billy met him?

She knew now that he wasn't the irresponsible drifter she'd thought him to be on first acquaintance. If anything, he took his responsibilities too seriously. Was that what was bothering him? Did he have some other responsibility, something that would someday make him leave the Double F?

Emily shivered even under the blazing heat of the noonday sun. Though she had never thought she would feel this way, the one thing she was sure of was that she didn't want Zach to go. But how could she get him to stay if she didn't know what demons haunted him? And how could she get him to tell her?

She wasn't sure what to do, but she knew she wouldn't sit meekly by and let events carry her where they would, as she had with Laurence. This time she would take her destiny in her own hands and fight for what was hers, whether it was the ranch . . . or maybe something more, something that was still just a dream.

With a last lingering look at Zach's retreating figure, Emily turned to follow Opal into the house.

"Well?" the man asked from the back of yet another dark alley. This one was on the far edge of the town.

Jabber didn't like meeting outside, especially in a place this deserted, but he was being paid for doing as he was told.

"Come on, man. Speak up," the voice commanded, sounding colder than ever. Little bumps rose upon Jabber's skin even though the evening was on the warm side.

"Something's happening out there on that ranch, that's for sure," he said, speaking quickly. The sooner he was done with his report and out of here, the better he would like it. "Five men rode in this week. They look like they're settling in for a while, at least."

"Have you done what I instructed?" the voice demanded impatiently.

"Haven't been able to. They're keeping too good a watch. On guard round the clock."

"They can't be on guard every minute. Have you even tried?"

"I sure did," Jabber protested. "Why, I got so close, one of the men darn near stepped on me," he added without thinking.

"What? Did he see you?"

The voice sounded even colder, if that was possible, with a hard, steely edge.

"No, no. How could he? It was dark."

"Not totally. There was a moon," the voice countered from closer than before. "You're a fool, Jabber, an incompetent fool. If there's one thing I can't stand, it's incompetence. I've decided to take you off the job and do it myself."

Those were the last words Jabber heard. The knife cut deep, shredding his insides before he even guessed what was happening.

"Wh—" he gasped and fell to the ground.

CHAPTER
7

Emily heard a strange rumble as she closed one of the paddock gates. Carefully she placed the ostrich stick up against the outside of the fence and picked up the basket of eggs. In the past few days there had been no further incidents disturbing their peace, and Emily had begun to hope the worst was behind them. Even the ostriches had started laying again.

Now the strange noise was an intrusion, one she had to investigate. Whatever its cause, the sound was getting closer, so Emily hurried back toward the house. As she reached the top of the rise, she saw what was making the loud racket. A distance from the gates of the ranch came a procession of buggies and buckboards. Emily looked at the watch pinned to her dress above her breast. It was only ten o'clock, far too early for callers.

She hurried down the slight incline, stopping only long enough to put the eggs in the shade by the entrance to the storerooms before heading for the courtyard.

When she reached the front of the house, she found everyone else already assembled inside the courtyard, waiting for the caravan of vehicles to reach them. Obviously, they had heard the noise before she had and had opened the large gate to greet the newcomers.

Frank and Zach were standing out in front of the group while Jewel and Opal hovered close behind. Eula hung back by the porch, ready to rush inside if anything alarming should happen.

Emily walked forward and joined Zach and Frank.

"Do you have any idea who they might be?" Emily asked as she stopped beside Zach.

"From the looks of them, I'd say they're some of the people from church."

"Isn't that Bea?" Opal said and pointed out one of the wagons.

"Seems like it," Zach replied, but didn't look any less tense.

Zach's concern put a different interpretation on what was happening. When Emily'd first seen the line, she'd thought that the townsfolk had come out to see the ostriches and get a better understanding of what they were doing. Now the visitors looked less neighborly, more menacing.

"Well, if these people are looking for a fight," Jewel said, echoing Emily's thoughts as she wrapped her pink boa around her arm to get it out of the way, "I'm willing to oblige."

She looked it, too, with her body held taut and a fierce expression on her face.

"Now, don't go gettin' all riled up, Jewel, honey. Let's wait and see what they have to say," Frank cautioned Jewel with a hint of affectionate amusement in his voice.

"If you say so, Frank, but I think we should be prepared," Jewel conceded, though she still had the light of battle in her eyes.

"We are, Jewel. Don't you worry," Zach said.

When Zach was reassuring Jewel, Emily noticed the gun

tied low on his right hip. He hadn't been wearing it around the ranch. As a matter of fact, she'd seen it on him only one time in the last few weeks and that was the morning he'd discovered the broken eggs. She did know that when he went out on patrol with Frank or one of the hands, he strapped it on, but never inside the confines of the house or courtyard.

"I wonder what's brought them out here?" Opal asked, edging forward the slightest bit, but making sure she stayed well behind Zach and Frank.

"I don't think you'll have to wait too long to find out," Frank said with a touch of sarcasm.

No sooner had Frank finished speaking than the first buggy rolled into the courtyard. When the five vehicles had stopped, Bea made quite a show of pulling around the lot of them and maneuvering right up next to Zach and Emily.

"Thought I'd better come along when I heard what they were a-plannin'," Bea whispered only loud enough for Zach and Emily to hear as Frank helped her down from her conveyance.

"Mornin', folks," Zach said as Bea moved in beside Emily. "To what do we owe the pleasure?"

"We've come to talk," the man in the first buckboard said. From the way he took charge, it was clear he was the spokesman for the group of about fifteen men and women.

Zach stood with his legs braced apart, ready for whatever was to come, and looked back, his eyes narrowed. Emily realized she'd better intervene before the men let things get out of hand. This situation needed a deft feminine touch if trouble was to be averted.

"Let me introduce myself," she said quickly. "I'm Emily Crabtree and this is Zach Hollis."

"Ma'am. Sam Dawson," the leader introduced himself, tipping his hat, but that was as far as his sense of courtesy would take him. He neither smiled nor offered any other pleasantries.

"Just exactly what is it you folks want to talk about?" Zach said, cutting off any further attempts at politeness. Though his words were pleasant enough, Emily could tell by his tone that he wanted some straight answers, and soon.

"Those birds you've got out here is what we want to talk about," the man said, his tone less amicable than the first time.

Before Zach could answer, Emily broke in, "Then Bea passed on our invitation?" She looked around expectantly, but only Bea answered.

"That's right. Told 'em you'd be glad to show 'em everything you were doing here anytime they wanted to come out."

"How nice of you to call so promptly. We have a lot of things for you to see," Emily continued, hoping some of the women in the wagons would respond.

"No offense, ma'am, but we don't want to see the birds," Sam Dawson replied. "We're here to tell you to get rid of 'em."

"Get rid of the birds?" Emily gasped, not believing what the man had just said. She'd known the parson had been spreading all kinds of resentment against the ostriches, but she hadn't realized it had gone this far.

"That's right," a burly man in the second wagon called out. "We want those birds gone." He'd risen and was standing up on the seat of his wagon. "And if'n you can't handle it, we can."

"Set back down, Jed. We all agreed I'd do the talking," Sam called back over his shoulder.

"That's right, Jed. Hush up and let Sam do the talking," a woman called from one of the back wagons.

With ill grace the man sat back down, but he didn't look any too pleased with the reprimand.

"You heard the parson in church last Sunday. He said no good will come from having those birds in our midst," the leader said.

"I'm sure you'll be able to see for yourselves that the ostriches aren't going to cause you any problems," Emily tried to reassure them, looking from one wagon to another, hoping to see one friendly face. There were none.

"They're the devil's instrument, and they need to be gotten rid of. The parson said so," Jed called out again. He was leaning forward in his vehicle, clearly itching to do more than just talk.

"Won't you just come and see the birds for yourselves? It won't take but a minute to walk to their pens," Emily pleaded, ignoring the burly man's comment. She didn't want a confrontation with a bunch of men all wearing guns, especially with Jewel, Opal, and Eula so close by. Neither Zach nor Frank had said anything in quite some time. She didn't like their silence. She didn't really know what Zach might do. He was a gunslinger, after all. He had the guns and the scars to prove it.

"Well . . ." the leader hedged.

Just when Emily thought she might have convinced them to at least look at the ostriches, a voice called out from the crowd, "They'll peck you to death, you know."

"They will not, you crazy old fool," Jewel retorted, standing on her toes to see who had made the comment.

"Jewel's right. They won't hurt you. Besides, they're fenced in," Emily said, and then added, "just like cattle."

"Well, if they're fenced in . . ." Sam said, on the verge of conceding.

"Hell, no, we don't want to see them playthings of Satan," Jed yelled out, jumping off his wagon and coming forward.

He stopped not four feet from Zach, his hand on his gun. "We don't cotton to folks who disrespect the Good Book."

As he finished speaking, he pulled his gun from its holster. Emily's heart lurched, and fear pumped through her like lightning from a storm cloud. No one in the wagons moved, and a tense silence settled over the crowd.

Emily saw Frank reach for his own gun, but Zach sent him a look that, while it didn't make him move his hand from the gun, did keep him from drawing.

Zach didn't move an inch. Emily sensed his complete attention was trained on the man standing before him.

"I have the greatest respect for the Bible, as I'm sure you do, my friend," Zach said in a calm, friendly tone. "Let me ask you a question. Have you ever seen a plaything of Satan?"

The question surprised the man, and for a moment he didn't answer.

"Uh . . . no," he said, clearly confused. Obviously it wasn't a question he'd ever heard before.

"Do you think you'd recognize one if you saw it?" Zach questioned, still in the same friendly tone.

This time the man was less unsure, and he answered almost before Zach finished speaking.

"Damn right I would."

"Then why don't you come and take a look?"

"I don't know," Jed said doubtfully, but he eased down his gun arm so the weapon now pointed to the ground.

"If you do, you can be sure for yourself," Zach coaxed. Emily held her breath. Jed seemed to be yielding. Maybe this would all end peaceably after all.

"See them for myself?"

"You seem like the kind of man who likes to make his own decisions. Right?"

The man nodded, but still looked suspicious about where Zach was leading him.

"You wouldn't let some greenhorn tell you how to handle your horses, would you?"

The man shook his head.

"Then I'm sure you're not going to let someone else do your thinking for you, either."

"Hell, no."

"I thought not. Just put away your gun, then, and let's go look at those birds."

Jed looked down at his hand as if he was surprised to see the weapon still there. He quickly holstered it. Zach gave him a nod of approval, then turned and started for the back of the house.

Emily watched in amazement as all fifteen men and women descended from their vehicles and trailed him around the house, followed by Frank, Jewel, Opal, and Eula. She'd underestimated him earlier. He'd avoided a serious confrontation with as much skill as anyone could hope for— maybe more.

Emily was about to turn the corner of the house herself when the sound of hoofbeats stopped her. Her heart sank. The last thing they needed now was someone else arriving and stirring things up again.

She turned and saw a lone male rider pull up by the well. He held the reins of his horse in one hand and the lead of a packhorse in the other, and he looked vaguely familiar.

"Emmie, you're certainly a sight for sore eyes," the man called to her as he dismounted and came over to give her a hug.

"My goodness. Uncle Billy?" Emily said, her voice muffled against the shoulder of his jacket. Billy was the only person who'd ever called her Emmie.

"Right as rain, darlin'," he said, holding her away from

him. "And you're lookin' prettier than I last remember. Must be this weather—or the company. Maybe both?" he suggested, and raised one of his bushy eyebrows.

Emily felt the heat sting her cheeks. Would she never stop blushing? She hadn't blushed this much since she was a schoolgirl. To cover her embarrassment, she used the anger she had felt back in Connecticut when his telegram first arrived.

"Billy Crabtree, where have you been?"

"Workin' my way here. Where else?"

"Where else? *Where else?*" Emily repeated, astounded by the question. "Why, right here looking after this place, that's where."

"*You* were here, weren't you?" he asked as if he'd done nothing out of the ordinary.

"You had no way of knowing that," Emily protested. "Why, this place could have gone to ruin if I hadn't come in time."

"Do you mean Oswald didn't do a good job? If so, I'll—"

"No, of course not. Oswald did a wonderful job. He saw to everything, and he taught me a lot, too."

"Knew he would," Billy said in a satisfied tone. "Now tell me about these here wagons. Got company, have we?"

No matter what she said, he interpreted it to his own advantage. She'd question him more closely later, when she had time to think. Right now she needed to get around back.

"Some of the townsfolk have come to call. Seems they're not too pleased with the investment you've made."

"Why in the world not?" Billy blustered.

From the sound of his voice, he didn't like having his judgment questioned. Just wait until *she* got done with him, Emily thought. He had a lot of things to answer for as far as she was concerned.

"The ostrich isn't held in the highest esteem by the local

minister. As a matter of fact, ostriches have been the main topic in several of his sermons, and now the members of his flock are up in arms. Seems they want *your* ostriches off the face of the earth."

Not for the world would she have let Uncle Billy realize how much the birds had come to mean to her. No, she'd let Billy stew in his guilty feelings for the time being.

"Never heard of such foolishness. I'll have to see about this," he muttered. "Where'd they go?"

"Zach's taken them to see the birds. He managed to control the situation quite well, I might add."

"Knew that boy had something goin' for him. Liked him on the spot." Billy looked at her and raised one eyebrow.

Emily merely looked back, not saying a word, and motioned him to follow her.

As they walked toward the ostrich pens, the last words Billy said kept echoing in her mind: "Knew that boy had something goin' for him. Liked him on the spot."

Well, she hadn't. At least she didn't think she had.

She remembered the day he'd arrived and the feel of her body pressed up against Zach's when he swept her up on his horse. That wasn't liking, though; that was something else altogether. But she had come to like him since then, more than she wanted to admit even to herself.

The way he'd acted today was just another in the list of things she'd found to admire in him. He had calmly and patiently talked that man out of using his gun. She knew there would be times when he wouldn't be able to talk his way out of a situation, but she was glad to know that when he could, he did.

By the time Emily and Billy reached the ostrich pens, the townspeople were heading back to their wagons. They waved at Emily as they passed, and Jed personally reminded her to stop in and visit when she came to town.

Emily sent Zach a questioning look, but he merely shrugged with just the slightest touch of pride in his stance. Then his eyes shifted to the man standing by her side. A look of surprise crossed his face, and then his mouth widened into a big grin.

"Why you old scalawag, it's about time you showed your ugly face in these parts," Zach said as he pounded Uncle Billy on the back.

"Knew you'd handle everything till I did," Billy returned with a satisfied grin of his own.

"Let's go up to the house and get a cool drink, and you can tell us all about *where you've been*, Uncle Billy," Emily said, taking control of the conversation and letting him know he wouldn't be getting off so easily.

"I'd better hurry back and get things ready," Eula said in a soft voice before hurrying into the house.

"Right nice seeing you again, Miz Smith," Billy called out, his eyes never leaving Eula's retreating figure.

Zach left the main house and headed for the storeroom to check on the incubator. He'd had all the socializing he could take for one day, what with all those folks out from town and then Billy showing up out of the blue.

He hadn't expected Billy to appear quite so soon. And for some reason, he wasn't entirely happy about his arrival. Not that he wasn't glad to see Billy; he was. He just thought he'd have more time. More time for what, he wasn't sure. Then again, maybe he did know, but was afraid to admit to it.

Leaving the door open only long enough for his eyes to adjust to the murky darkness, he crossed over to the incubator. He'd have to see about getting some light in here. Emily couldn't work with the eggs if she couldn't see what she was doing.

There he was again, trying to please Emily. The sense of

protectiveness he'd felt when he faced down Jed this morning still burned in the pit of his stomach. His need to protect Emily had been foremost in his mind the entire time he'd been talking to the angry man. He didn't know what he would have done if things had gotten out of control.

Not that he couldn't have shot Jed first. He'd been practicing out on the range, out of earshot of the house, and though he still wasn't up to full speed since his injury, his aim was as good as ever now. Only another gunman would be able to tell he hadn't shaved all the extra time off his draw.

But what good would it have done to shoot Jed if all it did was start a free-for-all? That would have been much more dangerous. Someone would have been bound to get hurt, and his biggest fear was that that someone might be Emily.

This need to protect her raised conflicting thoughts and feelings inside him. It reminded him of his dead family, and all the horror from long ago surfaced until he felt only the pain. The wall he'd constructed to protect himself over the years threatened to rise again, to shield his heart from daring to want more than he could bear to lose. Then he remembered Emily, the way she'd looked at him when Jed had finally put away his gun. There was more than gratitude in her eyes. There was admiration and respect.

The dream he'd briefly entertained when Billy sent him down here was starting to come true. He was making a place for himself here and doing it all without his gun. Even Emily, who'd made it clear she didn't appreciate having an interloper like him on *her* ranch, was no longer shutting him out. In the past few days she'd turned to him more and more often, sharing her thoughts and asking his opinions.

Just the thought of Emily made his loins burn as he remembered the feel of her lips against his, her soft, supple body held so close in his arms. Each time he touched her he only wanted more. And not just physically. She had invaded his dreams and raised his hopes. When he thought of his future, he no longer saw himself as a man alone.

Could he allow himself the luxury of such dreams? Of having a home, someplace where he'd always know he was welcome, of having a wife, a woman who would love him regardless of his past or what people thought of him?

Emily was making him believe it could happen. He wasn't sure he should allow himself to even think about it, much less act on it. But what he was feeling for this stubborn, self-confident woman from back east wasn't so easily put aside. She'd crept into his thoughts. Suddenly he'd see her when his mind should have been on what he was doing, whether it was riding the boundary line or watering the ostriches. She'd be walking along the edge of the desert, and the wind would have her dress pressed tightly against the outline of her body. Her hair would be loose and blowing free, a cloud of golden red.

As he thought about her, his nostrils filled with the scent of violets and that odd mixture of womanly perfumes that clung to her very being.

He shook his head. Just thinking about her, he sometimes even forgot where he was. And that was something he couldn't afford to let happen.

There were things still left to do, men to find. He'd spent his life tracking the men he sought. He had to remember his promise and let nothing get in the way of accomplishing his goal: to punish the men who had murdered his family.

But more and more often he felt he was reciting those words as a reminder to himself. Their sense of immediacy was fading, replaced by other longings, other goals. He was changing, and he knew Emily was the cause. The question was, where did he go from here? How did he reconcile his past with this new future? Most important of all, what choice did he have?

Zach took one final look at the eggs. He had far more questions than answers, and new answers sure didn't seem to be lurking out here in the small storeroom. Or so he thought, until a dark form filled the doorway, and suddenly there stood Emily.

Zach quickly moved into the shadows in the back of the room and watched her cross toward the incubator, heading in his direction. As he watched her, a feeling of contentment and belonging rose in him, a feeling he'd never felt before. His heart picked up in excitement, and his whole body yearned for her. It was all so new, so different. He was still coming to terms with his new feelings and wasn't ready to face anyone yet, not even Emily. He needed another few minutes alone, so he stayed quietly where he was.

Emily squinted, trying to see into the darkness of the room. She'd have to remember to bring a lantern with her the next time she came. Even with the doors open, so little daylight filtered past the thick adobe walls, she could barely see where she was going.

This was the first chance she'd had to get out to the eggs since Uncle Billy arrived. It was nice to have some time away from all the others. Zach must have felt the same way, for he'd disappeared more than an hour ago. Where had he gone? Was he planning his future right this minute? Now that Billy had arrived, Zach could be on his way, released from his promise to watch the ranch. Emily didn't want to think about that, for she knew she wanted him to stay, and not just for the sake of the ranch.

Reaching the center of the room, she anxiously peered into the incubator. Three eggs, with pencil marks showing their laying dates, were nestled in one corner, leaving room for the ones she'd collected this morning. These eggs were the future of the ranch. Not to mention her own future and

Opal's. Secretly she was hoping it might be Zach's future, too.

"They'll only hatch so fast no matter how often you look at them."

Zach's voice came out of the darkness from the corner behind the incubator. She could hear its teasing tone, and her insides warmed.

"I know, but I just like to look," she said as he came to stand beside her. "Why are you out here?"

"Maybe I'm hoping they'll hatch just by watching, too," he said with a laugh. His voice was warm and inviting, but at his next words, an unexpected anger surged through her. "Think your Uncle Billy ever had this in mind when he bought the place?"

"I don't know what Uncle Billy had in mind. I'm not sure he ever gave it this much thought, if you want to know the truth. Quite frankly, I was more than a bit surprised that he showed up here at all."

"We knew he'd show up sooner or later."

"Maybe you knew that. I certainly didn't."

"Are you mad at Billy?"

"Wouldn't you be? He buys this godforsaken ranch in the middle of nowhere, uses all my money, and then leaves it for someone else to take care of. Watching Laurence waste my money on his foolish schemes was bad enough, but having it happen all over again with his crazy Uncle Billy . . ."

As her voice trailed off, she found herself pacing in the small confines of the storeroom. Uncle Billy's return had reminded her of just how difficult things were for a woman, especially since Billy wouldn't admit he'd done anything the least bit wrong or foolhardy. Just thinking about it increased her agitation and the rate of her pacing.

"Is it Billy you're mad at or the fact that your husband didn't allow you to control what was yours?" Zach asked.

Emily stopped pacing and stared at Zach.

"What are you talking about?" It frightened her that she had lost control in front of him and, even more, that he had noticed. But Billy's return had stirred up feelings she thought she'd put behind her.

"Em, maybe this is none of my business, but—" He gave her a half hopeful, half unsure look, as if he had something more to say, but wasn't sure just how she'd take it.

"Opal always says everything before the 'but' is a lie. What do you really want to say?"

It was a sign of how far her trust in him had grown that she was willing to hear him out despite the flutter of nerves in her stomach and the clamminess of her hands.

"I don't know. . . . I guess I sometimes feel like you're fighting some battle you've got to win, as if this ranch has become a field of war and every decision has to be fought over. I guess I just don't like the idea of you beating yourself against some hidden enemy.

"I've learned the hard way that you can't control everything in your life. You have to pick your battles or you'll wear yourself out. Billy really isn't your enemy, even if he does have different ideas about how to help you."

She didn't know what to say. There was a lot of truth to his perceptions, more than she would have admitted before Billy's return. But seeing Uncle Billy had brought her face to face with her hurt and anger, fanning it to full force as though she hadn't come to terms with it despite the months since Laurence's death.

"Em, I'm sorry if I've said something I shouldn't have."

Emily shook her head.

"No, you're right. I just didn't realize I was being so obvious."

"You're anything but obvious. I probably just didn't say things right. Don't forget, I'm just a simple cowboy. I don't always remember the rules around polite society. I didn't mean anything by it."

He took her hand in his and stroked his thumb back and forth over her knuckles. The warmth of his fingers against her palm was soothing, giving her a focus outside of herself and the turmoil churning inside her.

"You have nothing to apologize for. I'm the one who's sorry. I never meant for you to feel we were fighting. I simply needed to feel I could control something in my life. I guess I was angrier at Laurence than I thought, and I took it out on you and Uncle Billy. You certainly don't deserve it. But I'm not so sure about Uncle Billy. Buying an ostrich ranch wouldn't exactly be considered a wise investment by most folks."

"I agree, but then, Billy isn't most folks, is he? That's what makes him unique. Besides, you like the birds, don't you?"

Emily nodded, content to follow wherever he was heading.

"You enjoy the day-to-day work?"

Again she nodded.

"And I know you enjoy reading all those books. You certainly seem confident and in control when you correct me."

He smiled teasingly as he said the last words.

Emily had the grace to blush, for she had enjoyed correcting him when he pulled his I-know-it-all-because-I'm-the-male routine and she'd had the right answer.

"You noticed, huh?" she said with a shy smile.

"Hard to miss," he confirmed and gave her hand a squeeze. "In any case, I don't think this ranch is so bad. Billy may have done you a favor. I can see for myself you're happier now than you were when I first met you. I don't think I've ever seen you looking so pretty as you have the past few days."

Emily ducked her head at the compliment, but Zach wouldn't have it. His free hand cupped her chin and he lifted it. Their eyes met.

"You *are* beautiful, more beautiful than any woman I've ever known. You can't imagine what—"

"Zach, where are you?" Emily heard Billy call from the courtyard.

Emily bit her lip in frustration. She and Zach were really talking for the first time. She wished he'd had a chance to finish his sentence. What had he been going to say? Was he, too, wishing Billy had stayed away from the ranch a while longer so they would have more time together? Now she would have to wait to find out.

"I'll be there in a second," Zach called out to Billy. Then, in a soft voice, he whispered, "We'll finish this later. This isn't the end, Emily Crabtree, not by a long shot. I promise you that."

He quickly pressed his lips to hers, sealing the bargain.

"I'm on my way, Billy," he called again, as he turned to the door. At its threshold, he looked back at her, as if he needed some acknowledgment of what had just passed between them. He'd given her his word, and she knew he was a man of honor. She nodded her head, not totally sure what she'd agreed to, but wanting desperately to find out.

He smiled at her, his eyes glowing with promise. Then he stepped out to meet Billy.

Emily was putting the finishing touches on a letter to one of her librarian friends in Connecticut when she heard Zach yelling from the courtyard. He and Frank were supposed to be out checking the ranch for damage and clues as to who was causing all the trouble. She knew there had to be some reason for what was going on, but no one had figured out what it was yet. Zach and Frank seemed to be following some leads they hadn't told her anything about. At least she thought that was a likely possibility, since she'd seen them having very intense conversations when they thought no one else was about.

What could have brought them back to the house so soon? They weren't expected until the evening meal. She detected a note of urgency in Zach's voice when he called out again. She ran to the front door and threw it open to find Zach helping Frank up the steps.

"What happened?" Emily asked, rushing forward to support Frank's other side.

"Nothing. I'm fine. Just a small spill," Frank said, ending his sentence on a groan when he missed a step.

"He isn't fine. His horse stepped into a hole and threw him, but he should be all right in a couple of days."

Emily glanced over at Zach. His jaw was clenched tight, but when their eyes met, he merely shook his head, as if to say, "Don't worry, it was nothing." It didn't fool Emily one bit.

The door opened again just as they reached the top step, and Jewel came flying out.

"Frank honey, are you all right?" Jewel questioned, her voice thin and quavery.

"Well . . ." Frank drawled. At the sight of Jewel, he suddenly seemed to realize his injuries were not so insignificant. He groaned somewhat louder than before, and Emily caught him sneaking a peek to see what effect it was having on Jewel. She relaxed a little. If he was well enough to pull such shenanigans, he couldn't have been injured too seriously.

"Where are you hurt?" Jewel asked. Not waiting for an answer, she rattled on, "I think he should be lying down, don't you, Emily? Isn't that the best thing he could do? You never know about these things, do you? It might seem like nothing, but it could be something serious."

To calm Jewel's fear, Emily decided to follow her suggestion and get Frank to bed.

"You're quite right, Jewel. Bed would be the best place for him."

"Billy's in the spare room. Let's get Frank to mine," Zach suggested. "He'll be more comfortable there, anyway. That storeroom leaves a lot to be desired."

Zach and Emily helped Frank down the hall to Zach's room, with Jewel bringing up the rear.

After they had Frank settled in Zach's bed, Jewel suggested she get water and some ointment to soothe Frank's battered body.

"That's mighty kind of you, Jewel. I appreciate your concern," Frank said, then groaned as he shifted on the bed.

"Now, Frank honey, you just lie still, and let me take care of you."

Zach and Emily looked at each other and quietly left. They were clearly not needed.

"I'll have Eula start heating some water, and then we'll get some liniment on that shoulder. You'll be right as rain in no time," Emily heard Jewel say as she and Zach walked back to the kitchen.

"Frank doesn't strike me as the type of person to let his horse step into a hole," Emily said as she poured Zach a cup of coffee. There was more here than Zach was saying, and she wanted to know everything.

"He isn't" was Zach's terse reply.

Emily watched him as he sipped his coffee. She couldn't see his eyes, but his hand gripped his cup so tightly his knuckles looked white.

"So what happened?" she asked.

"I think someone booby-trapped that field, dammit! Hoping to cause exactly this type of incident. We're just lucky

Frank's old buckskin is so surefooted he didn't get hurt as well."

"Zach, we have to find out what these people want. Do they just want to scare us out of spite or are they after something else? Have you and Frank discovered anything you aren't telling me?"

"We don't know any more than you do. It might be a good idea if I did some investigating in town. Things are getting more serious."

"How will we manage to do that?"

"*We* won't," he said. The look on his face warned her not to argue. "*I* know a couple of people who might be willing to help—for a price. With Frank out of commission and more people to protect, we can't sit still and wait for them to act. Next time a bird might be injured—or worse, one of us. We can't take that kind of chance. Besides, I want to see if I can pick up any rumors. People'll be more likely to talk to me if I'm alone than if you're around."

Emily didn't like the idea, but she knew they had no choice. Zach was right. The kind of people with whom he would have to associate would hold their tongues if she was around. If Zach could discover who, or at least why, someone was causing trouble at the ranch, they'd know better how to defend themselves.

"What if whoever's doing this finds out you're looking for him? It could get dangerous."

"No more dangerous than sitting here like fish in a barrel, waiting for him to come after us."

Emily was forced to concede that he had a point. "You will be careful?"

"Don't worry. I can take care of myself. I've done it long enough."

"When will you start?" Emily asked, having resigned herself to the fact that he must go.

"Tomorrow's soon enough. I want to head out to the far paddock right now and see if I can find anything else. I also need to make sure the boys are on their toes tonight. Besides, you and I have unfinished business to take care of."

Her heart raced with excitement at the thought that later tonight she and Zach would spend some time together—alone. A frisson of excitement raced down her spine as she watched him walk out the door.

"Take care," she called out and wondered how she'd make it through the rest of the endless day until she and Zach could be alone together.

Emily was the first one ready for dinner. She surveyed the table and was amazed at what Eula had accomplished. Since the household numbers had grown to seven, Eula insisted they eat dinner in the formal dining room. She even wanted the hired men to dine with them, but they preferred fixing their own meals in the bunkhouse.

The Englishman had left behind his elegant china and silverware, probably because it was easier to leave than to pack. Eula had ransacked the china cabinet, bringing out the expensive linen napkins and silver napkin rings.

Emily idly straightened one of the forks, her mind straying back to her conversation with Zach. If she could just figure out why the ranch was under attack, Zach wouldn't be put in danger because of her. She didn't for one moment think a few Bible references and an excitable parson would push someone to commit such serious acts of vandalism—vandalism designed to hurt and destroy. And that was the scariest part. Someone obviously didn't care who got hurt.

"A pretty young thing like you shouldn't have such a serious look on her face," Billy said as he came in.

"I like to think, no matter what I look like, that I have the ability to think, even about important things," Emily said, facing him, "like finances."

Maybe this was as good a time as any to broach the subject of the control of her inheritance, she thought, looking at the man who had forced her to change her whole life.

"I'm sure you're a great thinker. Had to be to stay married to that nephew of mine. Laurence wasn't the most reliable person goin'." As usual, Billy managed to turn the conversation his way, but this time his comment hit close to her innermost secrets and she couldn't let it go by.

"What do you mean?" she asked nervously.

Zach paused near the doorway just outside the dining room. He could tell Billy and Emily were having a private conversation, but he couldn't make himself back off once he'd heard Laurence's name.

"It's no secret, Emmie. Laurence was a troubled boy, and he turned into an even more troubled man. I'm just sorry I couldn't do anything to help. You should never have been saddled with such a burden."

"You knew?"

Zach heard the surprise in her voice. From their conversation earlier today, he'd realized that her marriage hadn't been full of bliss. But her astonished reaction to Billy's remark indicated that things must have been worse than he'd even imagined.

"Everyone knew," Billy admitted with great sadness in his tone. "His parents thought if they ignored his problems, they'd go away. I think they hoped he'd settle down some once he was married. As for me"—he shrugged his shoulders—"maybe I was just scared. I've never been too good with woman things. And helpin' you in your marriage . . . well, I just didn't know what to do. Laurence only got worse when anyone tried to talk to him. I was hopin' by makin' you money on your inheritance, I would be makin' it up to you for not doin' somethin' when Laurence was still alive."

"You shouldn't feel bad. Nothing could help Laurence. He never wanted to help himself. I'm not even sure he could have if he'd tried."

"Even so, I am sorry, Emmie. And I didn't mean to upset you with this ranch business, neither."

"I know that," Emily said, reaching over and placing her hand on Billy's forearm. She patted him a couple of times, and then he covered her hand with his. They stood together for a few minutes before Emily drew herself up and straightened her shoulders.

"That's all in the past now," she said briskly. "The future is what's important, don't you agree? And besides," she added in a softer voice, "you want to know something? I really like these ostriches. They kind of grow on you after a time."

Billy smiled up at her as if she'd just given him the most precious gift, and Zach quietly backed away from the doorway.

CHAPTER
8

A short while after her conversation with Billy, Emily looked around the dining room table. She couldn't believe all the changes. Less than a month ago she'd been eating all by herself in the kitchen. Now she was hard-pressed to find any time alone.

"I hope Frank will be all right," Eula said as she passed the roasted potatoes around the table for the second time.

"He'll be fine now that Jewel's seeing to his injuries," Zach said with a wide grin as he spooned another helping of potatoes onto his plate.

"Frank's a mighty lucky man to have someone like Jewel taking care of him," Billy said, his eyes on Eula. "I'm sure you'd do a fine job of tending yourself, Miz Smith. Ain't nothing like a woman's comfortin' hands. Ain't that right, Zach?"

"You'd know better than me, Billy. But Frank sure does seem to be recovering nicely now."

"I suppose now that Frank's been hurt, we won't be going into town tomorrow," Opal said, making her question more of a statement as she looked over at Zach.

"It'd probably be best if I went in alone. We don't know

who's doing the damage to the ranch or what they might try. I don't think Billy and I could protect all of you if anything happened on our way into town."

Billy seemed about to protest, but after one look from Zach he shut his mouth tight. Though Zach didn't say any more, Emily knew he wanted to be free to spend his time in town trying to find out who was vandalizing the ranch.

"I understand," Opal quickly assured him. "It's just that we could ask some discreet questions around town if we did go in."

"That's mighty kind of you, Miss Opal, but I think it might be best if you let me handle this," Zach said.

"In that case," Opal advised, "you might want to check with that Dan Ebbert fellow. He seemed to know a lot about the goings-on in town. At least he sounded pretty knowledgeable last Sunday after church. Wouldn't you say so, Emily?"

"He certainly seemed friendly enough and eager to help. He even said I should feel free to call on him if any problems came up on the ranch," Emily said.

"Did he, now?" Zach drawled, looking in Emily's direction. A frown furrowed his brow.

"Surely you don't suppose that means anything, do you?" Emily asked. "I think he was just a neighbor trying to be friendly."

For a moment she thought Zach might be jealous of Dan Ebbert. Then his brow cleared and he said, "I'm sure you're right. After all, how could he resist the opportunity to come to the aid of such a lovely lady?"

Billy let out a cackle. "Why, Zach, you rascal, you sure have a way with pretty words."

Opal jabbed Billy in the ribs with her elbow. "Hush, now. Don't be embarrassing the young'uns."

"Now, Opal, I didn't mean anything by it," Billy said. "Isn't that right, Miz Smith?"

Eula looked up with a start. "I really couldn't say, Mr. Crabtree." When her eyes met his, she quickly lowered them and changed the subject. "Would anyone care for more greens?"

"Why, thank you for offering," Billy said. "I must say this is some of the best da—uh, dang cooking I've had in many a mile."

Eula blushed as she passed him the serving bowl. "I'm glad you think so, Mr. Crabtree," she said without meeting his eye.

"Just call me Billy. I always thought of Mr. Crabtree as my father and then when he was gone, my brother John." Billy stopped speaking for a moment. "Been hard since he's been gone. I'm just glad he was so happy in the time he had. He was lucky to have you, Opal."

"He was happy, wasn't he?" Opal asked. "I used to worry about that when we were first married. After all, your family never approved of John marrying an older woman. But after a time, he convinced me that we didn't need anyone's approval, and from then on, everything was wonderful." A faraway look entered her eyes. "I only wish we'd had more time together."

"I'm just sorry I never got to meet you before John died. I had great plans for visitin' when you lived in St. Joe, but I never made it. But I know you made him very happy. Yes, sir," Billy said, looking over at Eula. "'Bout as happy as you'd make some lucky man with your cookin', Miz Smith. I wouldn't mind another helpin' of your dee-licious potatoes, if'n it's all right with you."

Eula smiled shyly and got up from her place to serve him.

Billy's blue eyes glinted as she drew close. "My mama always said good food made for a good marriage."

"Did she?" Eula asked softly. She hovered over him, looking like a frightened doe, unsure whether to stay or flee.

"Yep, I reckon she did. 'Twas a mighty long time ago, but some things you never forget, not the important ones."

Eula gave him a fleeting smile, then hurried back to her seat.

"You have marriage plans, Uncle Billy?" Emily asked, surprised by his conversation, to say nothing of the way he was looking at Eula. With his roaming from one place to another, she hadn't realized he'd ever considered putting down roots.

"Every man considers marriage at some point in his life, wouldn't you say, Zach?"

"Most men, I reckon," Zach said, not quite revealing his own opinion. "If we're done here, I'd better go check on Frank," he added as he stood up.

"I've taken most of Frank's things in to him," Jewel told him as she came through the dining room carrying a tray of crockery.

"Then I guess I ought to move some of my stuff out," Zach said.

"With your shoulder, you'd best have some help," Billy put in. "If you wait a second, I'll just finish my unpacking and be right out to help you."

"There's no need," Zach countered. "I can handle it myself."

"But you shouldn't have to," said Eula. "Jewel and I can do the dishes and maybe Emily can help you."

Though she wanted nothing more than to be with Zach, Emily felt she had to protest. "But I always do the dishes, since I never cook."

"That's all right, dearie," Jewel said. "Tonight everything's turned around, anyhow. You just run along and leave the dishes to Eula and me. It'll give us a chance to talk. And besides, we wouldn't want Zach to injure himself, too, now, would we? He already has a bad shoulder, so I'm sure he could use your help." Jewel's eyes twinkled as she looked from one to the other.

Shaking her head at the obvious manipulation, Emily followed Zach to his room. She really had no other choice. For appearance' sake, he gave her a few things to carry—some shirts and his extra boots. Like all the bedrooms, his opened to an inside hall and also directly to the outside. Since Frank was asleep, they tiptoed to the outside door and out into the night.

Emily hugged Zach's clothes close. They were clean, but still smelled faintly of him. In the dark, she pressed them to her face and inhaled deeply. An ache settled low in her belly. She licked her lips and remembered Zach's taste, spicy and rich and all male.

He walked in front of her, tall and lean. She noticed that he didn't favor his right arm the way he used to. Though he was carrying the heavier things, his step was sure and purposeful. The weeks of working on the ranch had left his muscles sleek and well toned. As he passed the open windows of the dining room, Emily could see more details as the light from the lamps reached out into the darkness. She watched the muscles in his back ripple beneath his shirt with each step he took.

Her throat grew dry and she lowered her gaze. His jeans had softened with use and clung to his backside and legs, shaping his masculine form in sharp detail. She tried to swallow, but found she couldn't. It was the dry desert air, she thought, and knew she was lying to herself.

They circled the house in silence, Zach setting his pace a bit faster than Emily thought was necessary. She didn't understand his urgency until they reached the small storeroom he had converted to a bedroom so many days ago. It seemed a lifetime since she had ordered him out here and challenged his right to stay. Now she wished she could take back every negative word.

"Wait here a second," he said as he stepped inside. "Let me get the lamp so you don't trip."

She heard some rustling noises, then the sound of a match being lit. The flaring light revealed his face as he bent over the kerosene lamp. Harsh angles and shadows combined to give him a sinister look. For a moment, she felt a chill of fear. Then he looked at her, and she understood. His eyes glittered with need; his body was tense with desire. Even from this distance, she felt his heat and the power of his passion.

He set his belongings on the table and nearby chair, then came to the door and took the boots from her unresisting clasp.

"Put the shirts down anywhere," he said. His voice sounded hoarse.

She laid the shirts carefully over the back of the chair and looked around the room. It hadn't changed much. Jewel had taken the trouble to put clean linens on the bed and tidy up after Frank. Few of his possessions remained, outside of a couple of shirts on a hook near the corner and a spare pair of work gloves lying on the floor as if they'd dropped unnoticed.

Zach looked at her from across the room, his eyelids half closed, his arms at his sides.

"Do you want to go back now?" he asked, and she knew there was more to the question than the surface suggestion. She could see it in his eyes and in the way he held his body. His face was lightly flushed, and she could see the mascu-

line bulge in his pants. Still, he was leaving the decision to
her.

His question gave her a heady feeling of feminine power.
She could choose the direction the evening would take, and
he would abide by her choice. It wasn't the first time he had
yielded a decision to her, but it was by far the most important.

"I don't think the others will miss us if we stay here a
while longer," she replied. As if by magic, some of the tension dropped from him. She hadn't realized he was that unsure of her or that her decision would make such a difference
to him. She wanted to give him back something of equal
value, but she didn't know what.

"I'm sure you're right." Zach's voice sounded gravelly,
like dark velvet. As he spoke, he crossed the room and took
her hand in his.

Emily liked the feel of his hand. It was large and warm.
The calluses spoke of a life with purpose and dedication. She
felt protected with her hand in his. She'd never felt this way
before. Oh, she'd been in love with her husband when they'd
married, but she'd never felt protected. Most of the time
she'd felt that she had to protect him, and later she'd had to
protect herself. She'd enclosed herself in a hard shell, but
now she found it was only a cocoon, sheltering her until she
had changed enough that she could again emerge, not as a
shy, virginal girl, but as a strong, mature woman ready to
meet a man on equal ground.

"Where are you, Emily? You seem a million miles away."
Zach's thumb rubbed across her fingers, and a shiver went
through her.

"I'm not, really. I was just thinking about how I got here,
about the difference you've made in my life."

"Have I?" he asked with a hint of vulnerability. If her

heart hadn't already opened to let him in, that tiny insecurity would have done the trick.

"You know you have. You've helped me see what I really want in life. And that's a priceless gift."

"You've changed things for me, too," he confessed, bringing her closer. His hands moved up her arms to grasp her shoulders, and he leaned toward her. Emily closed her eyes, knowing he was going to kiss her, her insides quaking with excited anticipation. Tenderly Zach touched his lips to each of her eyelids. Then his lips trailed down to the corner of her mouth and bestowed small, soft kisses.

She felt her lips quiver. She needed more. She wanted him closer, closer than she'd ever wanted anyone before. As if he heard her wishes spoken aloud, his arms tightened around her, bringing her body into contact with his from head to toe. She opened her mouth to moisten her lips with her tongue and he swooped in.

Their mouths danced a lovers' duet, teasing and tantalizing, plundering and retreating, first one leading and then the other until they ran out of air and Emily felt she could barely stand. They stopped then and stood leaning against each other, taking deep, restoring breaths. If they didn't slow things down, they would melt from the heat they were generating. As it was, Emily could hardly support her own weight.

Zach held Emily close, so close he could feel her heart beat against his chest and smell the sweet scent of violets that clung to her skin. He couldn't believe she had agreed to stay, and yet he wanted nothing more in his life.

"You're not what I thought you were," she murmured as she snuggled against him. The way she said it, he knew it was a compliment.

"No?" He smiled into her hair. He wasn't what he'd thought he was, either. Being with Emily had made him realize how lonely his life had been. But she had changed all that, making him think of a different life, a life that looked to the future instead of only to the past.

"No. You handled that crowd today with such finesse."

"Finesse, huh?" He wasn't exactly sure what the fancy word meant, but it pleased him nonetheless, especially the way she said it. He nuzzled her hair with his cheek and ran his hand down her back, savoring the feel of her soft curves against his hardening body.

"Yes. You knew exactly what to do and when to do it. I was so scared—and so impressed, especially when you didn't draw your gun."

Her words startled him. He didn't think anyone had noticed how close he'd come to simply reacting to the taunts.

"Some people would say not drawing your gun is a sign of cowardice," he felt compelled to tell her.

She raised her head and tilted it so her dark gaze locked on his.

"They're wrong. It's far braver to take the risk and try to find a peaceful solution. When those people think about what happened here today, they're going to be ashamed. And then they're going to be thankful you saved them from doing something stupid. I was so proud of you."

Her pride shone in her eyes and melted the last of Zach's self-control. No one had ever given him such a look, full of respect and consideration and something deeper, something that matched the feelings growing in his chest, filling him so he barely had room to breathe for the joy of it. He locked his hands behind her waist and hugged her close again.

She reached up to the back of his neck and pulled him down so her lips met his. It was the first time she'd initiated a kiss, and he exulted in her action. Her mouth was primly closed as she kissed him, then parted slightly as her tongue came out to caress his lips. Her sweet taste filled him, and he opened his lips to taste her more fully. She arched against him, welcoming his tongue with her own as her hands slid from his neck into his hair. She pulled him even closer, as if she couldn't get enough of him.

He angled his head and lifted her against him, pressing his arousal into the cradle of her thighs as he showed her with his mouth what he wanted.

The kiss went on forever, growing richer with each variation as first he tempted her and then she teased him, stoking the fires of passion into a bright flame. This time there would be no slowing down, no waiting for her to be sure—she'd given him her answer a thousand times over.

The bed in the storeroom was narrow, but since they had no desire to be apart, that was no problem. Zach maneuvered them to it without breaking the kiss, then sat and pulled her down beside him. Her hands immediately went to the buttons of his shirt, opening them. He'd worn no undershirt because of the heat of the day. If she was surprised to feel his skin so quickly, she made no mention of it. He trembled as he felt her palms brush against him, skin to skin. He was burning for her. He'd thought of this, dreamed of it, so many times, yet the reality was much more potent than any fantasy.

He wanted to touch her as she was touching him, but finding his way into her clothes wasn't so easy. Though he'd thought many times of undoing the rows of tiny buttons that hugged her figure, in practice it was proving an insurmountable task.

"I can't believe this," he said with a laugh. So far, for all his efforts, only the first four buttons were undone. His entire shirt only had four buttons! "How do you get undressed at night?"

"Would you like me to show you?" she asked, her voice

low and slightly husky, her eyes black as midnight, her smile alluring and quintessentially female.

All laughter left him. "Would you?" he barely breathed.

Still smiling, she stood and slowly began undressing, one tantalizing button at a time until at last the basque top fell away. Her skirt and petticoats also fell to the floor layer by layer, as if she were peeling an exotic fruit. Unlike him, she did wear underwear, soft and frilly and edged with lace. In the flickering light of the kerosene lamp, her skin glowed a bright rosy color, and shadows beckoned his gaze to her more intimate enticements.

She stood before him then, slim and lithe, her form hidden only by a cambric chemise with delicate flowers embroidered at the neck, and drawers with matching ruffles at the knee. She bent to reach for the hem of the chemise, to draw it over her head.

"No, wait," he said, stepping to her side. "Let me."

He needed to touch her again, to know that she was real, to share every moment of this intimate ritual with her. He started with her hair, pulling out pins until it fell like a waterfall of gold, spilling over his hands in shimmering cascades of violet-scented beauty.

"How I've dreamed of you like this," he murmured.

"Have you?" she asked, looking pleased. "I've dreamed of you, too."

He couldn't believe his ears. A surge of desire raced through him, and his blood ran heavily through his veins, pooling at his very center with throbbing need.

"Oh, God," he whispered and reached for her, unable to stay even a few inches away. Her skin was soft and firm beneath his hands, warm and vibrantly alive. Her hair glimmered in the light like burnished metal and flowed over his arms like the richest silk. And everywhere he kissed her there was the scent of violets.

His lips devoured Emily, leaving little aching places all over her shoulders and neck and face as he moved from one to another, licking and nipping with open-mouthed kisses. His hands helped support her when her knees became weak, and she arched against him, desperate for the warmth of his desire. Never had she felt this burning from within, the fire stoked by the man she loved until it blazed with white-hot intensity.

She reached for the hem of his shirt and tugged it from his pants, then pushed it up his body so she could rub her cheek against his chest. The brown curls felt pleasantly rough against her face, and she couldn't resist grabbing a few hairs between her lips and tugging playfully.

"Ouch," he protested, then grinned down at her.

"Aren't you going to help me?" she asked archly.

"You seem to be doing fine on your own." He rubbed his body against her, and she wished the rest of their clothes would miraculously disappear. They didn't.

In one continuous motion he whipped off his shirt. Then, before she could catch her breath from the sight of his magnificent nakedness, he had done the same thing with her chemise.

In seconds he had shucked his pants and boots, leaving only his drawers. They were of fine wool and left little to her imagination as they clung to him like a second skin. He was a large man, though well proportioned, and fully aroused. She could see the outline of his masculinity in stark detail. A melting sensation in her abdomen sent spirals of desire spinning through her.

He knelt in front of her and tugged at the drawstring of her pantalets. She started to undo her corset, working the clasps free from the bottom. He watched, his expression rapt, as inch after inch of her torso was bared. Then he leaned forward and trailed his tongue from her navel to the shadowed valley between her breasts.

She moaned as she freed the last clasp, passion making her feel warm and liquid. His breath felt hot and cold as it fanned her skin, hot where her skin was dry and cold where he'd licked her. He turned his head and gently tongued one nipple. The liquid feeling expanded like a surging tide, washing away all thought and leaving only sensation in its wake.

His hands, large and powerful, gently stroked her back. With ever-widening circles, they slowly pushed her pantalets down past her hips until they fell of their own accord to her ankles. He raised his head, still kneeling in front of her, and their lips met for a searing kiss. She would have sunk to the floor beside him had he not chosen that moment to stand and sweep her into his arms. The sheet was cold on her back as he laid her on the bed, and she shivered, though whether from the chill or anticipation, she could not say.

"Come to me," she whispered and held out her arms.

In less than a second he was stretched out beside her, one leg draped over both of hers and his head propped up on a bent arm as he leaned over her. His other hand stroked her breast, sending ribbons of arousal to every corner of her body. He watched her, and his eyes turned a pure green, like the finest jade. A dark flush colored his cheeks, and his finely sculpted mouth looked as swollen and full as hers felt.

She raised her arms to his shoulders and pulled him more fully over her, relishing his weight and warmth. Feverishly she ran her hands over his back. Sleek muscle was overlaid by smooth skin. She couldn't get enough of him, of his strength and his gentleness, his passion and his control. His mouth dipped to her breast and she felt the heat of him envelop her. This time he suckled with urgent hunger, and she felt the impact clear down to her womb. Her legs moved apart so he could settle between them, and her hands swept down to his waist.

Smooth skin ended abruptly as she encountered his drawers. He shifted slightly as her hands pushed at him, giving her access to the last few buttons that separated them. His eager mouth moved to her other breast as he murmured encouragement to her. Her hand trembled as she brushed against his arousal. He groaned, but when she would have pulled away, he stopped her.

"Please," he murmured. "Touch me."

When she touched him again, he sighed and his whole body shook.

"This is what dreams are made of," he whispered as their lips met again.

The heat in him burned through her inhibitions, and she reached for the buttons, deftly opening them despite her shaking fingers.

"I can't wait any longer," he cried and shifted over her.

His hand found her, warm and wet, waiting for him. He stroked her, learning what she liked, making sure she was ready. Need and want consumed him. Passion fired his desire as he plunged into her and she accepted him, her fingernails digging into his back as she urged him closer. Her hips moved against his, responding to his rhythm as he slowly withdrew, then plunged even deeper, so deep he thought he felt her soul welcome his. She opened to him like a flower, giving him all she had. Never had he felt this sense of oneness, of finding himself in another, of finally being whole. He shuddered deeply at his climax, knowing she had climaxed, too, hearing her wild breathing as erratic as his own.

"Oh, God, Emily," he cried at his peak. "I never knew . . ."

He drew deep breaths as his heart raced, and slowly his body returned to itself and he became aware again of his boundaries, of where he ended and she began. His mind fought the separation, but the battle was already over. He opened his eyes and propped himself up on his elbows, afraid he would crush her with his weight.

She had made him feel as if this were his first time, and in a way, it was. This had been no quick coupling designed to assuage a masculine itch and nothing more. She had made him forget everything he thought he knew about the act of sex and replaced it with loving tenderness, with swirling feelings and strong emotions, with passion rather than lust.

Her eyes opened and she met his gaze. She smiled a smile of repletion and feminine satisfaction, a smile that acknowledged what had happened between them and invited him to share the moment.

"I've never experienced anything like that," she said in an uncanny echo of his own thoughts.

"Me, neither," he confessed.

She ran her foot along his leg. "Oh, my," she said with a laugh, "you're still tangled up in these."

He laughed with her as her foot pulled at his drawers. They'd been too eager, too involved in each other for him to completely remove them. Quickly he kicked them off.

"Better?" he asked as he settled back between her legs.

Already he wanted her again, but this time he was determined to make this experience even better than the one before—if that was possible.

When he entered her, Emily felt complete. He filled even the empty places in her soul. She had not known making love could be like this, that she could soar to such heights and know such pleasure. Always before she had thought the lack of fulfillment in her marriage was her fault. Now she knew differently.

When Zach moved, her body moved in response, perfectly attuned. He touched her, and she ached with pleasure. Simply running her fingers over his supple, muscled back was enough to start the waves shimmering inside her, and when he touched her in her most secret place, she lost all sense of herself as the waves crested and broke. But the best part of all was that he came with her, side by side, all the way there and back. And at the end he didn't turn away from her, but held her to him as if he couldn't bear to let go of what they'd found in each other's arms.

They spent the rest of the night dozing and talking until one or the other would move or stroke a hand or trail a kiss in a certain way, and passion would rise again, drawing them both into its circle of desire.

As dawn began to pinken the eastern sky, they lay together, nestled like spoons, replete but not asleep.

"Everyone will be getting up soon," Zach whispered in her ear. "I guess we better think about doing the same."

He nuzzled the tender skin at the side of her neck, and she cuddled against him.

"Seems to me you've risen already," she said in a sultry, teasing voice as she felt his arousal press against her.

"Mmmm," he murmured, sounding preoccupied as he planted a row of tiny kisses across her shoulder and down around the front of her chest, marking a path toward the tip of one breast.

In seconds they had both forgotten the encroaching day as passion claimed them again. By the time they were ready to face the morning, as well as the scrutiny of the others, the sun was high in the sky.

"I'll go check on the birds," Zach offered after they had both dressed, "if you want to go see how the others are."

She appreciated his sensitivity to what could be a delicate

issue—how much of their relationship they were ready to share with the others.

"You'll be wanting some breakfast first," she demurred, "and to check on Frank."

She felt a flush of embarrassment redden her cheeks. She hadn't given Frank and his injuries a thought all night.

"God, Frank," Zach said. "I nearly forgot about him. Not that I didn't have more important things to think about," he added with a look that had her ready to throw off her clothes again and spend the rest of the day in bed with him.

"I'm sure he's fine. Jewel would have let us know if anything was seriously wrong."

"Come on, then. We'd best get up to the kitchen. Lord knows I won't be able to control myself much longer if it's just the two of us here."

He put his arm around her waist and headed around the back of the house. When they came to the fork in the path, he led her up the rise and around its other side.

When she looked questioningly at him, he said, "I don't imagine we can hide much around here for long, but there's no point in being too obvious. I don't want anyone looking at you differently or thinking you're anything less than a lady. *My lady*," he added in a possessive tone, then stopped to kiss her in broad daylight where anyone who cared to could look up and see them.

His action reassured Emily more than any words that he cared. Though he wanted to protect her reputation, he couldn't keep away from her.

They entered the kitchen a few minutes later, side by side. Eula was already there, up to her elbows in flour as she rolled out noodle dough.

"You two were out bright and early," she said. "Everything all right out there?" She nodded her head in the direction of the low rise and the ostrich pens beyond.

"Seems to be," Zach responded, not bothering to correct her assumption that the two of them had been by the ostrich pens. Emily admired his audacity even as she felt herself blush crimson. "How's Frank doing this morning?" he added smoothly.

"Fine as can be expected," Eula replied, accepting his change of subject as though it were natural. "Jewel stayed up all night with him, and Opal and I took turns looking in on her. Hope we didn't disturb you none," she added, turning her attention to Emily.

"No, not at all," she managed to say without stumbling. How could they have disturbed her? She wasn't in her bedroom to be disturbed. She'd never been very good at deception and was thankful she was dealing with Eula rather than Opal or Jewel. The other two were much more astute and would have caught her out in an instant. "I'm glad to hear Frank's doing better. I'd better go in and say good morning."

"I'm sure Jewel'd be glad to see a new face," Eula responded. "Maybe you can persuade her to take a rest. I wouldn't want her to be getting sick or nothing."

Emily gave Zach a rather desperate glance as she made her way out of the kitchen. He turned his head so Eula couldn't see and gave her a conspiratorial wink.

"I'm sure everything will turn out just fine," he said reassuringly, though Emily wasn't quite sure whether he was reassuring her or Eula. Probably both.

To Emily's relief, the business with Frank's injury proved to be enough of a distraction that no one questioned her whereabouts, either for the night before or for the morning.

By midday Frank was feeling well enough to drag his battered body out of bed and join the others for a meal that included a big bowl of chicken soup with freshly made dumplings just for him.

"That'll fix you right up," Eula promised.

"That sure looks like wonderful soup, Miss Eula," Billy said. "Does a man have to be sick to get a taste?"

Eula looked up at him with a rather flustered expression. "No, of course not. That is . . . would you like a bowl?"

"That'd be right nice," Billy said and smiled at her.

She smiled back shyly, and Emily could hear her humming softly as she fetched a bowl and ladled out a serving for Billy.

"Maybe later you can show me around them ostriches," he said after thanking her. "Can't say I rightly know much about them birds."

Emily fully expected Eula to decline. So far she'd busied herself in the house, preferring to look after the human inhabitants of the ranch and leave the feathered flock to the others. But to Emily's surprise, Eula said, "Well, I'm afraid I don't know all that much about them myself, but I'll be glad to take you around when you have the time."

Eula blushed deeply when she saw the others all staring at her with various degrees of surprise on their faces. Emily was so dumbstruck she couldn't think of anything to say to break the sudden silence.

Frank seemed to have no such problem. "What's happening out there?" he demanded of Zach, nodding toward the window.

"Nothing new," Zach said. "I checked with the boys a while ago, and everything is quiet. There're no suspicious tracks or anything. Seems like our culprit took the night off."

"I wish I knew what he was after," Billy said. "That English lord made no mention of problems when he sold me the place. Leastways the problems he mentioned seemed more his own doing than anything from the outside."

"Did anyone else want to buy the place?" Zach asked.

"Not that I know of. The Englishman seemed pretty desperate to me."

Emily narrowed her eyes at that. What kind of investment did Billy think the ranch would be if no one else wanted it?

As if he sensed the direction her thoughts had taken, Billy turned to her and explained, "That's what made it such a good deal. I got this place for a song, and now it's going to turn into a gold mine. Why, you shoulda seen all the feathers the, uh, ladies"—Billy had the grace to turn red as he looked at Emily and conspicuously did not catch Jewel's eye— "I've, uh, met are wearin' nowadays."

"Jewel certainly enjoys wearing them. Don't ya, honey?" Frank put in helpfully, but his words only made Billy sputter and turn a deeper shade of red.

"Um, uh, yes, well . . . enough of that for now," Billy said. "When are we heading into town, Zach?"

Zach turned to look out the window. Catching sight of the angle of the sun, he said, "Not for a couple hours yet. It's too hot now, and everyone will be taking a siesta. We'll plan to get there in time for supper. Maybe we'll overhear something at Clancy's."

Clancy ran the local eating place. Emily hesitated to call it a restaurant. The food was plain and heavy, intended for a man who'd spent the day out on the range and didn't care much what he ate, as long as it was hot and filling. Guests at the boardinghouse occasionally stopped there, but more often ate in the boardinghouse dining room. Cowboys in town for the night, stage drivers, and other locals—most of them men—preferred Clancy's. It was cheaper, and no one cared if they tracked a little mud or dirt onto the floor.

"You both be careful," Emily admonished. "And don't get into any trouble. Whoever's persecuting us has a mean streak."

"She's right," Frank put in unexpectedly. "Maybe you should wait till I'm a touch better and I'll go with you."

"And who'll be here to protect the ladies?" Zach asked.

"We don't need protecting," Emily shot back. "We're not helpless, you know."

"You got a point," Frank said to Zach, ignoring Emily's outburst. She would have protested again, except that both Jewel and Eula took the opposite side, expressing their relief at having a man in charge.

As if sensing Emily's distress, Opal said soothingly, "Well, I have every faith in our ability to take care of ourselves, but it's still nice to have Frank so concerned for our welfare. If we all take care of one another, no one will be able to hurt us for long."

There was nothing Emily could say against that, so she nodded briefly.

"Good, it's settled, then," Zach said. "Billy, you and I'll meet in the barn in a couple of hours. I want to see to the birds a bit and tell the men to keep up their guard, since they'll be a little short-handed without us tonight."

They all stood and turned to their various assigned tasks. Jewel helped Frank ease his way back to his room to lie down; Eula cleared the table with Billy by her side, chattering up a storm; Opal went to the front parlor to dust, a never-ending task out here in the desert; and Emily followed Zach outside.

"We're not helpless, you know," she said as soon as they were out of sight of the main part of the house, "just because we're women."

"I know that. But Frank needed a reason he could accept to be left behind."

"That's barely a good excuse, and you know it."

He stopped in his tracks and turned to face her. She could see he was angry.

"Keeping you safe is all the excuse I need. This is no game, Emily. You may not like to face facts, but somebody could have been killed out there yesterday. Frank was lucky. He wasn't going too fast, and his horse didn't panic and tromp all over him after he fell. I hate to think what could have happened if he'd been going at a full gallop and the horse's leg had snapped."

Zach grabbed her shoulders and tried to rein in his temper. He didn't want to shout at her or scare her to death, but somehow he had to reach her—for her own safety.

"Can you even shoot a gun?" he asked in a lower voice.

She nodded, her eyes wide.

"A man's gun? To kill, if you have to?"

She paled. "It won't come to that," she said, as if wishing it were true would somehow make a difference.

He couldn't help the explosion of bitter laughter. "Let me tell you something. You can't wish trouble away. I know. I've been there. And the first time you have to shoot to kill . . . well, it takes something away from you. An innocence you don't ever get back, no matter what. I don't want that happening to you, Emily.

"You're sweet and pure. I want you to stay that way. You're a lady, and that's something special. I don't want to see the West change you the way it has so many others." He thought briefly of Lila back at the saloon, of the hardness in her eyes and the bold way she'd touched him, as if he didn't really matter except for the dollars he'd bring her. Lila hadn't started that way. Life had done that to her, and he'd do his damnedest to see that life never did that to Emily.

Emily put her hand on his cheek. Despite the work she did on the ranch, her skin was still soft, thanks to the gloves he'd given her.

"I appreciate your caring," she said. "And I hope I don't ever have to shoot at anyone. But even if I am a lady, I'm still a person—a grown-up person, not a child. You can't shield me from all life's pain. I've experienced my share, and it's made me who I am. Opal's right. We all need to take care of one another, but we can't do that if half of us don't even know what's going on."

"As soon as I know anything, I'll let you know. Is that good enough?"

She looked at him somberly, her dark eyes no longer spitting fire, and he saw the trust slowly seep in.

"That's more than good enough," she said. "And I'll tell you anything I figure out, too."

He sighed at that and rolled his eyes. "I don't seem to be able to win you over at all, do I?"

She smiled mischievously at him. "I wouldn't say that. You seem to have won me over pretty well last night."

He drew her close, and they stood in the sheltering shade of the house and kissed. She tasted sweet, and an ache filled his heart, a need to protect her and possess her, to keep her safe and hidden from life's ills, to shelter her through good times and bad. But she wouldn't let him do any of it. And maybe that was what drew him, too. She would not be like his mother, who had let his father persuade her he knew best. Emily would look out for herself, and for him, too, if need be.

As if she'd heard his thoughts, she whispered, "You take care of yourself, you hear? I don't want anything bad happening to you, either."

And then she kissed him again, and he lost all other thoughts.

The two men were greedy and unscrupulous. Ironically, that made them easier to control. He understood about greed and how to pander to it. And "unscrupulous" didn't even begin to describe him when he saw something he wanted but couldn't have—at least, not right away. In the end, everything he'd ever wanted had become his—or else he'd made sure no one else wanted it, either.

"I told you when I hired you that you'd be doing something special for me," he told them. "I'd like you to start now."

"You also mentioned extra pay," the taller one reminded him. He was the leader of the pair, short-tempered and egotistical, and thus easily manipulated.

"I did indeed. But first I need to see that you can get the job done."

"Don't worry about that none. Ray and I can handle anything that needs doing," the other one boasted, puffing out his chest.

"Good. Then let me tell you what to do." He smiled secretly. How easy they were to maneuver. "Go to Bethel Springs and make some friends. Keep reminding them of how big a threat the ostriches are. I want that Reverend Putney to feel his whole congregation is behind him. Spread whatever rumors you need to to discredit that ranch. You understand?"

Ray nodded.

"And one more thing: Don't do or say anything that jeopardizes my plan or there'll be hell to pay. Remember, I don't make idle threats."

Ray glowered at him, a spark ready to ignite, but Carl held him back.

"Don't worry none," Carl said. "We'll take care of it all. That ranch will be yours before you know it, though I don't hardly see why a body would want it."

"You just take care of things in Bethel Springs and I'll set you up so you won't have to worry again, ever."

He held out a pouch of gold coins to sweeten the deal. Ray

took it and started to count. Then he looked up. "I think we're going to enjoy doing business with you," he said, his weasel eyes bright with greed.

"I wouldn't have hired you otherwise," he told them as they headed out the door.

CHAPTER
9

The trip to Bethel Springs was disappointing. Zach was impatient. He wanted to make some progress, but the best he and Billy could do was to put out some feelers. They spent the night in town, hanging out at Clancy's for the supper hour, then staying at the saloon until the wee hours.

In the morning they decided to head back to the ranch and make sure all was well.

"Sure does beat all," Billy said as their mounts slowed to a walk up a particularly steep rise. "Everyone seems friendly enough, even that Jed fellow, but they don't know nothin' about nothin'. What d'you make of it?"

"I don't know. Someone wants something—there's no question about that—and he's taking the trouble to keep everything secret. I don't like it, not one bit."

"What about that reverend? You learn anything about him?" Billy asked, edging his horse around a large rut in the road.

"Nope. He's sure got a bee in his bonnet about the birds, but that doesn't necessarily mean anything. It's a puzzle, all right. What did you know about the ranch before you bought it?"

Billy scratched his head. "I tol' you most of it. That Englishman was pretty much a fool. Guess his family sent him here to keep him out of trouble, but some folks can't help themselves, and he was one of 'em. Sold me the place cheap. Said his father had ordered him home on the next train."

"And no one's made any offers or showed any interest in it since?"

"You'd know better'n me. You've been out here longer than I have—leastways you've been at the ranch."

Zach shook his head in frustration. Their horses picked up speed on the downhill run, effectively ending their conversation, and Zach was left to his thoughts.

By the time they reached the outskirts of the Double F, all he'd come up with was a suspicion that there was something valuable on the place—valuable enough for someone to want them off of it. That didn't leave too many options.

Zach didn't think anyone was after the ostriches. Although the market for their feathers was booming, tapping into it required hard work and time. Besides, if someone wanted to raise his own birds, it was easy enough to order some; there was no need to bother with the Double F. No, there was something on the property itself that was of value. If he could figure out what, maybe he could get a lead on who was interested in it.

"I see Hank over there by the fence," Billy called out from in front of him. "I'll ride over and see if he has anything to report. I'll meet you back at the house."

Zach nodded and kept going. If there had been any problems overnight, Hank wouldn't have been working this far out. That, at least, was reassuring.

As he got closer to the house, anticipation replaced his frustration. He could hardly wait to see Emily, to hold her in his arms again, to share the sweet intimacy they found in each other's embrace—talking, laughing, making love. In sight of the house he urged his mount into a ground-eating gallop. The animal was glad to comply, knowing his stall was close by.

As soon as he reached the courtyard, Zach pulled the roan up short. A sparkling black phaeton with blue moldings and a fine yellow stripe stenciled around the doors and body stood in front of the porch. A pair of smart bays with dark black stockings were still hitched to it and drinking from the trough, their sides heaving. Zach frowned. The animals weren't cooled down enough to be drinking like that. Flecks of foam still dotted their withers.

He clambered off his roan, which was barely spent after its short run to the house, and tugged at the bays' harness.

"Easy, now, fellas," he crooned as he pulled them back a step.

One of the horses tossed its head and whinnied in protest.

Zach stroked the animal's neck as he tightened his grip on the reins.

"I'll let you have more in a minute. You just have to catch your breath a bit first," he said in a soothing tone. Though the animal couldn't understand the words, it quickly responded to the calming cadence of Zach's voice and allowed him to maneuver both horses and the phaeton a little farther from the trough.

"What's going on here?" an imperious voice demanded from the porch.

Zach looked up to see Dan Ebbert swagger down the steps as if he owned the place. Emily quickly followed. Her face lit up when she saw Zach, but before she could speak, Dan Ebbert said, "Hey, now, what do you think you're doing to those horses?"

"I'm keeping them from killing themselves," Zach retorted, barely hanging on to his temper. It was bad enough seeing the careless way Dan Ebbert treated his animals. It was worse seeing him with Emily. "They need to be cooled down before they're allowed to drink that much water."

"Dan, this is Zach Hollis. I believe you met at church a couple of weeks ago," Emily put in as she came around to Dan's side.

"Oh, right. The foreman. In that case, carry on. You might want to unhitch the pair as well. I plan on staying awhile. Miss Emily has graciously offered to show me around the ranch."

He turned his back on Zach and held out his arm to Emily. "Come, my dear. You shouldn't be out in this heat."

Emily shot Zach a helpless look as Dan Ebbert claimed her and led her back inside.

"Come and join us when you're done," she said over her shoulder.

"I'm sure that won't be necessary," Dan countered. "Emily, you can tell me anything I care to know. Your foreman has other chores, I'm sure, and can better spend his time earning his keep."

Dan sent him a contemptuous, dismissive look the instant before he disappeared into the house with Emily.

Fury mixed with jealousy in Zach's heart as he watched them go inside together. His first inclination was to storm into the house after them and take Dan Ebbert down a peg or two. Then one of the bays tossed its head, diverting Zach's attention. He calmed the beast, and looked more closely at the entire rig.

The phaeton rolled easily. It was a carriage built for speed, lightweight and sleek, with elegant lines fit for a gentleman. This particular model even had a narrow rumble in back for a groom or servant. Everything about it, from the neatly up-holstered seats with their expensive blue cloth trimming to the shiny brass light fixture on the side, spelled quality, the kind of quality Zach could not afford, the kind of quality Emily deserved.

The horses, too, showed fine breeding. No expense had been spared in fitting them out, either. If Dan had come here to make a good impression—and Zach had no doubt that that was his intention—he'd succeeded admirably.

The first niggling doubts about him and Emily formed in his mind, and they festered as Zach unhitched the prize animals, walked them down, and put them in a stall, sheltered from the heat. He took his time unsaddling his roan, then stood at the door of the barn, unsure what to do next.

"Hey, Zach. What're you doing out here?" Billy asked as he rode up. "I expected you to be inside already."

Billy ducked his head as he rode into the barn area, then dismounted and looked around.

"What's this?" he asked, his eyes nearly popping at the color and size of the newest arrival to the barn.

"It's a carriage. Can't you tell?"

Billy whistled as he walked around, inspecting it from every angle.

"Sure is somethin', I'll say that for it. Who's it belong to?"

"Dan Ebbert."

Billy's face wrinkled into a frown. "Don't recognize the name."

"He owns a ranch a ways from here. Met him at the church a couple of weeks ago."

"What's he doing here?" Billy asked with a hint of suspicion in his voice.

"Came to see Emily, I guess."

"Might have a fancy carriage, but it's what's inside that counts, you know."

Billy gave him a pointed stare, but Zach ignored it. It was just like Billy to be loyal to someone he knew over a stran-

ger. But was Dan Ebbert a stranger? There was something
vaguely familiar about him, with his arrogant ways and pro-
prietary air. Even his disdain for others touched a distant
chord in Zach's memory.

"Maybe," he conceded. "But you have to admit he's fit
out with the best. He's got money and he's got style."

"What's that mean?" Billy asked with a touch of belliger-
ence in his tone.

"It means he's the type of man a lady deserves. He can
give her all the finer things, take her to the proper places.
Hell, he probably reads all those scholarly books, like she
does."

"Huh," Billy snorted. "Shows what you know. If you're
talking about my Emmie, she knows better. She's had all that
highfalutin folderol, and she knows it don't mean diddly."

"Has she? That's not what I heard."

Billy flushed. "All right. So maybe Laurence wasn't perfect. But you know what I mean. If Emmie wanted all that
swanky stuff she coulda stayed back east. And that's all I've
got to say on it," he said before stomping out and heading for
the back of the house.

Zach guessed he was going to the kitchen to see Eula.
With a sigh, he added a handful of oats to his roan's feed,
then brushed his hands off on the back of his jeans—just another sign of how much he differed from Dan Ebbert.

The rancher wore the latest fashion, a dark four-button
cutaway over a matching vest and finely checked trousers. A
neatly folded handkerchief protruded from the pocket high
on the left side of his chest, and the thick gold chains from
his watch were displayed at the opening of the coat by his
waist. Peeking out of the neck opening of the high-buttoned
jacket were the tight collar of his shirt and the knot of his tie.

He looked like the pictures of important men Zach had
seen in the papers. That was probably why he seemed famil-

iar. In contrast, Zach wore faded blue Levi's and a work shirt. Never mind that he had purposely dressed down to blend in with the rowdies at Clancy's and the saloon. Even at his finest, Zach didn't own a suit like Ebbert's.

But Emily owned the dresses to match. Zach knew that for a fact. He'd seen her in them: fine silks and satins, plainer seersuckers and poplins, all of them elegantly trimmed with lace or flowers or ribbons of one kind or another.

Zach closed his eyes and saw her entering the house with Dan Ebbert at her side. They looked like a real couple, both elegant and refined, dressed in the finest clothes, the kind that appeared in magazines and fancy catalogs. Right now they were probably sitting in the front parlor drinking tea from the Englishman's finest china and talking about world events. What did he know of such things?

Nothing.

He couldn't give Emily the kind of life she deserved, the kind of life Dan Ebbert could offer. It never occurred to him to question whether or not she wanted that kind of life. He simply took it for granted and set about thinking of ways he could make sure she got it. The first thing that came to his mind was to stay out of her way, to give Dan Ebbert a chance to sway her, no matter how much it hurt.

Having made his decision, Zach followed the path Billy had taken, circling around toward the back of the house rather than entering by the front parlor.

As he passed the room that had been his, Frank called out through the open window, "That you, Zach?"

Though he didn't feel like talking, he couldn't find it in him to ignore his injured friend. "Yeah, it's me. How're you doing?"

He stepped into the bedroom and leaned against the wall. Frank was ensconced on the bed like a king, with food and

drink at his fingertips and Jewel coming in and out every so
often to make sure he wanted for nothing.

"Why don't you close that door?" Frank suggested, nodding toward the interior hallway of the bedroom wing. "I
want to tell you something important."

Zach quirked an eyebrow but crossed the room and did as
instructed.

"Pull up that chair," Frank ordered and pointed to a spot
near the bed. When Zach was seated, Frank continued, his
voice low, "I'm expecting a telegram today. Phillips said
he'd send word if he managed to dig up any more information about Earl Darnell. I kinda hate to leave it hanging
around the telegraph office too long. Wouldn't want the stationmaster to start asking after us if it's not picked up. Word
could get out."

"You want me to go get it?"

"If it wouldn't be too much of an imposition. I know you
just got back, but I was too sore to remember yesterday afore
you went." Frank smiled apologetically.

"No problem. I'll leave right away." Zach stood and
started to put the chair back in its place. "Will you tell the
others where I've gone?"

"Me? Don't you think you should at least let Miss Emily
know? I know she's been waiting anxiously for you to get
back."

Zach smiled grimly. The telegram about Earl Darnell was
a vivid reminder that he had other obligations. Though
Darnell had never been far from his mind, he'd let himself
get distracted. He had to remember his first duty was to the
promise he'd made to his family. He closed his eyes and saw
his sister's face and knew he could not allow himself to be
diverted from his quest.

Besides, Emily Crabtree needed a different life from the
one he could offer. The best thing he could do for her was to

go back to his old life. Thank goodness Frank had reminded him of his duty, even if his friend wasn't aware of it himself.

"Emily has other things on her mind right now. If you'll take care of it, I'd be mighty obliged."

Without giving Frank a chance to protest, Zach headed for the door.

"When'll you be back?" Frank called out, sounding bewildered by the sudden turn of events.

Zach paused on the threshold. "Don't rightly know. Maybe tonight. More likely tomorrow or the next day, depending on what I find out. The boys can keep to the schedule we worked out for last night."

With that, he slipped his hat on and strode into the fierce noonday heat.

Emily sat in the front parlor with Dan Ebbert. She'd offered him some libations to pass the time until Zach arrived. But though she watched the door anxiously, Zach did not appear. Dan didn't seem to mind.

"I can see why you don't miss the city, Miss Emily," Dan said after taking a sip of his tea. "This is a mighty fine set of china, if I do say so. I've never seen such fine quality. I'm sure no place around, even Phoenix itself, can boast of such excellence."

His gaze quickly swept the room, lingering here and there as one object or another caught his eye. Emily couldn't help but notice he had an uncanny instinct for picking out the most valuable items.

"The former owner sold the ranch together with most of the furnishings," she explained. By now she should have been used to the directness of these westerners, but it still made her uncomfortable.

"Have you been out over the property much?" he asked.

"Not to the far corners. Mostly I stay around here. I like working with the birds."

He looked shocked. "Surely you don't venture into our hot Arizona sun, Miss Emily. I just can't imagine a fine lady like yourself laboring in the fields. Why, your foreman should be horsewhipped if he can't take proper care of this place alone."

Emily knew he was speaking with the best of intentions, but his attitude rankled, not only because he dismissed her efforts but even more so because he had maligned Zach. Not that it was solely his fault, of course. She and Zach had gone out of their way to promote the illusion that he was merely an employee. Still, even if she couldn't tell him the truth about Zach, she could make it clear that she worked on the ranch because she wanted to.

"I'm sure Zach could handle this place on his own if he had to. In fact, he probably would have preferred it that way. Like you, he seems to feel only a man can accomplish such things. But I must confess, nothing gives me greater pleasure than to see this ranch thrive and to be a part of it."

"I can appreciate that," he said, smiling jovially, though she sensed his smile was forced. "There's nothing like success to make a body proud. But you should be careful not to overextend yourself. This climate's tough on the strongest, most able-bodied men. And you're a woman. You should have someone to care for you."

"It's kind of you to be concerned," she said, knowing she would never change his opinion. Like most of the men she knew, he thought a woman's place was in the domestic sphere, while a man's domain was outside the home, in commerce and political matters. "Perhaps you'd like to see the birds for yourself before we're called to lunch. You are staying, are you not?"

"You are too kind. I should be delighted, both to see your

fine acreage and to stay for the meal, if that isn't too much of an imposition, of course."

She smiled at him. Dan Ebbert seemed eager to please, and no doubt most women would have been extremely flattered to have a man of his caliber come to call. Unfortunately Emily was not most women. She would have preferred to spend the time with Zach. She looked again at the door, but it stubbornly stayed closed.

"I'm sure it's no problem. We'd be most honored to have you stay," she said. "Let me just inform Eula we'll have an extra person, and then we can go out. You might want to look at some of the books on ostrich farming. They're over there on the bookshelf."

She rose and left the room, restraining herself to a modulated walk when she really wanted to run outside and see what had happened to Zach. She knew there was no need to tell Eula about their guest. The older woman would have already taken his presence into account. But it was just the excuse she needed.

In the kitchen she ran into Jewel.

"Have you seen Zach?" she asked.

"Not for a while. But he was talking to Frank earlier."

"They seem to talk a lot, don't they?" Emily said, shamelessly leading Jewel on so as to see what she could discover.

"Come to think of it, you're right," Jewel confirmed. "Probably one of those men's things. You know, the price of horses or cattle or some such nonsense. Men have the most peculiar interests when they're alone together."

"You think that's all it is?" Emily was surprised. She'd never thought the men's conversation would be about anything so mundane, not the way they looked as they spoke, their faces so intent, their voices secretively low.

"Well, I can't say for sure. But what else could they possibly have to talk about?" Jewel smiled, pleased with her deduction.

Emily could think of any number of things the men might have to discuss, but she didn't want to scare Jewel by divulging them.

"I'm sure you're right," she said. "I'll just check with Frank and see if Zach mentioned what he might be doing today."

She hurried down the hall to Frank's bedroom. She no longer thought of it as Zach's. Whenever her thoughts turned to Zach, she saw him in the storeroom he'd converted that first night, the storeroom where they'd made love.

Unbidden, the image of him naked and undeniably male came to her mind. She could almost imagine his taste on her lips, his scent on her skin. A frisson of longing ran down her spine, and her stomach contracted. Where was he? Why hadn't he come in?

He'd hardly been gone twenty-four hours, yet it seemed like an eternity. She'd been plotting all day how to make her escape out to his bedroom tonight once everyone else had gone to bed, how she'd find him in the dark with no one the wiser. She could hardly wait for their first kiss since his return. Her lips burned at the thought, and she stroked them with her fingertips.

Frank was alone in his bedroom when she knocked.

"Excuse me, Frank. I hope I'm not disturbing you?"

Frank looked uneasy at her approach, but smiled nonetheless. "No, no," he said gruffly. "It's always a pleasure."

"Is something the matter?" she quickly asked.

"Oh, no. Why? Do you have some problem?"

"Uh, no. That is, I was just wondering if you knew where Zach is. Jewel said he'd been by and talked to you."

He didn't meet her eyes. "Yes, he was here."

"And?"

"I beg your pardon?" he asked.

Frank appeared to be hedging, stalling for time. But to what end?

"Where is he now?"

Frank looked uncomfortable as he cleared his throat. "I guess he went back to town," he mumbled.

"Back to town? You mean Bethel Springs?"

Frank nodded, looking very unhappy.

Emily couldn't believe it. Surely Frank must be mistaken.

"But he just got here," she exclaimed. "What made him go back?"

Frank looked even more uncomfortable than before. His face turned red, and he stared at the floor. An awful thought flitted into Emily's mind. Could Dan Ebbert's visit have had something to do with Zach's precipitate departure? She remembered the look on Zach's face when Dan had taken her into the house. Dan hadn't intended to be insulting, but he wasn't in command of all the facts. He'd treated Zach like a common laborer, and she'd let him, Emily remembered. A cold chill went through her, making her feel hollow and vulnerable.

"Did he say when he'd be back?"

"Maybe tomorrow. More likely the next day."

"I see," she replied, though she really didn't. Why hadn't Zach given her a chance to explain? The ache inside her grew and threatened to overwhelm her. There was nothing she could do about it, short of riding after Zach to Bethel Springs. And what would Dan Ebbert think then? she wondered, feeling the edge of hysteria grip her.

Fortunately, Jewel entered at that moment.

"Oh, good, you're still here. Eula said to tell you that she's just about to get lunch on the table. Is that nice Mr. Ebbert staying?"

"Yes, he is," Emily said, knowing it was too late to send

the man on his way, no matter how much she might wish to. There'd be time to work things out with Zach later. Right now she had company to entertain, and good manners dictated that he not be subjected to her anxious mood.

Besides, hadn't Opal said just the other day that Dan Ebbert seemed to know a lot about what went on in Bethel Springs? Maybe the meal wouldn't be a total loss. She could use the time to question him and see if he knew anything that might be of use in tracking down the reason for the vandalism on the ranch.

Straightening her shoulders, she smiled bravely at Jewel and Frank. "I'll go help Eula with the table, Jewel. It seems we'll have one fewer than expected. Zach's gone back to Bethel Springs."

She left so she wouldn't have to see the worried looks fly between Frank and Jewel. It was bad enough having to cope with her own confusion.

The streets of Bethel Springs were virtually deserted when Zach rode in. No one else was foolish enough to be out with the sun at its highest point, baking the earth like an overheated oven. Zach dropped his roan off with Jackson at the livery and tipped the man above his usual fee to take extra care of his horse after the grueling trip. Not that it was necessary. Jackson's fondness for horses was well known; he didn't need any special incentive.

Zach decided it was guilt money, guilt for having ridden his horse back to town in this heat, guilt for having left the Double F without a word to Emily. He sighed. Paying the money did little to ease his conscience or to assuage the ache in his heart. Giving up Emily was going to be every bit as hard as losing his family. The only way he could handle it was to stay away from her. If it weren't for the troubles at the ranch, he would have left today and never returned, continuing on his own mission. With Billy back, he'd fulfilled his obligation and was free to go.

But he couldn't leave with this ominous and pervasive threat hanging over the place, so he'd do the next best thing. He'd do his damnedest to find out what was going on, and he would stay out of Emily's way to give Dan Ebbert a clear field. That decided, he headed for the stationmaster's office to get Frank's telegram.

The telegram was in a code Zach had used with Frank many times himself, so he had no trouble deciphering the message: "Trailed E.D. south to Winslow. Changed name to Edward Davies, then David Edwards. Lost trail outside Flagstaff, heading south with new, unknown alias. Will report next week. Phillips."

The message was a welcome distraction. For the first time in weeks, Zach felt the excitement of the chase come over him. It sounded as if Darnell had been heading this way. Now all Zach had to do was find out exactly where the man had settled. Frank was right: Earl had probably fixed himself a hiding place, anticipating a time when he would need to go to ground. All he had to do was find it and he'd have Darnell. There'd be no more escapes.

Zach made his way to the saloon, which was fairly empty at this time of day. The piano player was sleeping with his head cushioned on the keys, his snoring a soft rumble. The bartender was serving another customer. Lila was seated alone at the far end of the bar. She looked up as Zach walked in.

"Thirsty?" she asked in her throaty voice.

"Wouldn't mind something wet," he agreed.

She called to the bartender, who provided a bottle and a couple of glasses.

"This way," she said and led him to a table in back.

Zach followed, watching the provocative sway of her hips

and wishing he found some attraction in them. But Emily had filled his heart, and no other woman would do. Maybe Lila had been right the first time when she'd said he had a woman of his own; maybe his heart had already known what his head had refused to admit.

Lila sat and poured two drinks, a large one for him, a smaller one for herself. She set his glass down on the table in front of the chair beside her and patted its seat.

"Come and sit down, sugar," she drawled. "Tell Lila your troubles."

He sat, but leaned both elbows on the table as he took a sip from his glass. It burned rawly all the way down. He took another sip as he felt life closing in on him.

Lila put her hand on his shoulder and leaned against him. He could smell the whiskey on her breath and wondered if she, too, felt the urge to drown her sorrows.

"I'm afraid I'm no more interested than the last time," he told her in a low voice.

"Woman trouble?" she guessed.

"Maybe," he said, then changed the subject. "I'm looking for someone. Think you might have heard of him?"

And he put out another feeler, telling her enough so that she could remember if she'd ever met his quarry, but not enough to cause him problems if she talked to the wrong person.

"This is quite some place," Dan said as they walked back over the rise toward the house. "I can see you've done a lot here."

"Yes, we have," Emily responded, pleased with the signs of progress she'd been able to show him on their tour. "Zach has done wonders, hiring the help and organizing everything. We've already extended some of the irrigation canals and soon we'll start stringing more pens. The yearlings won't be ready to breed for a couple more years, but if we can pull together some extra income, we might be able to buy another pair or two."

"Buy more?" Dan frowned. "Don't you think you should wait and see how you do with these first? You don't want to get overextended."

"I agree. We're taking things one step at a time. But I'm determined we'll succeed. Just look around you," she said, pausing at the top of the rise so they could look over the ostrich pens and irrigated alfalfa fields. "All of this richness was just sitting here waiting, looking like arid land. All it took was a little water, and it's turned into a veritable Garden of Eden."

"I don't know that Reverend Putney would agree with you putting your ostriches in the Garden of Eden. Sounds like he'd think it was blasphemy."

He observed her closely, as if gauging her reaction to the mention of Reverend Putney.

"You're probably right," she conceded with a smile. "He's a hard one to win over. But I think we got through to some of the congregation when they came out here this past week."

"They came out here?"

He sounded surprised, more surprised than Emily would have thought warranted. Probably it was out of concern for her.

"Just a few of them," she quickly reassured him. "But there wasn't any trouble. We just showed them around, and by the time they left, I think they were on our side. I'm hoping it's just a matter of time before the preacher himself sees how harmless the birds really are. You seem surprised."

"Only because I hadn't heard about it. Usually I'm fairly well informed about the goings-on in Bethel Springs. You never know when it might be helpful to my business interests."

It wasn't really polite for a person, especially a woman, to question someone about his business interests, but this was the first opening she'd had to see what Dan might know about Bethel Springs, so she plunged ahead. "What sorts of business interests do you have?"

"Oh, I'm involved in a number of enterprises. I believe I told you about the ranch. I run cattle there, but I also have other holdings. There's a lot of mining hereabouts, you know."

Again she had the feeling he was watching her closely. Maybe he wasn't sure a woman would be interested in hearing the details of his businesses.

"Yes, I've heard a little about that," she said. "Why don't we go inside where it's cooler and you can tell me more?" She gave him her best hostess's smile and he grinned back, his eyes lighting up in a way that made her a little uncomfortable. But she brushed off the feeling. Dan was a gentleman. Besides, with Eula, Jewel, and Frank in the house, she felt safe from any unwanted attentions.

The adobe house was cool and welcoming after the heat and brightness outside.

"Can I offer you some fruit juice? Eula has some chilling in the cellar."

"That'd be most welcome," Dan replied.

"I'll be right back. Have a seat and make yourself comfortable."

She made her way back to the kitchen.

"Is that Ebbert fella still here?" Opal demanded, her tone none too friendly.

"Shush," Emily admonished, "he'll hear you. What have you got against him?"

"Nothing. Where's Zach?"

"He's gone back to Bethel Springs." The hurt returned in full force.

As if Opal knew what she was feeling, she said, "I'm sure he must have important business there or he wouldn't have gone off again."

"You're most likely right," Emily conceded, then changed the subject. It was just too hard to think about right now. "Where's Eula?"

She'd just now noticed that Eula wasn't in her usual place—baking or cooking something in the kitchen.

Opal's eyes turned mysterious and evasive. "I believe she's around someplace," she said without meeting Emily's eye.

"With Uncle Billy, you mean?" Emily asked with a wry smile.

"Now, Emily, idle gossip is unbecoming in a young lady. I'm sure your mother told you that when you were growing up."

Emily burst out in laughter. "So where did they go?"

Opal drew herself up to her full, if minuscule, height. "I assure you I did not ask. Nor did they volunteer to tell me."

Emily rolled her eyes. "All right. I won't say a word. Satisfied?"

"It's not a question of being satisfied; it's a matter of propriety. Now, what can I do to help you?"

Opal certainly picked her times to stand on propriety, Emily thought, recalling some of the embarrassing comments with which she'd had to cope.

"I was looking for some juice to serve Dan," Emily explained.

"Dan, is it?" Opal asked, raising her eyebrows.

"He said I should call him that, since we're practically neighbors. Besides, I thought you were the one who was so eager to have him here. Didn't you say he knew everything there was to know about Bethel Springs?"

Emily watched beneath her eyelashes as Opal considered the full implication of her words.

"Yes, I did, didn't I?" she finally said with a gleam in her eye. "Why don't you go back inside and I'll bring the juice in myself? We wouldn't want him to leave too soon or anything, would we?"

With a smug expression on her face, Emily returned to the front parlor and awaited the arrival of her ally. When Opal joined them, the two women led Dan on a merry chase, discreetly pumping him for everything he knew.

Dan turned out to be a wily prey, neatly avoiding questions he didn't want to answer, providing them with just enough information to be polite but not enough for them to figure out what was going on.

As the sun began to set, he prepared to leave. One of the hands rehitched his team to the phaeton.

"What a lovely equipage you have," Opal said. "Looks like it cost a pretty penny."

Emily's eyes nearly popped from their sockets. Hadn't Opal been lecturing her on propriety earlier today? But Dan Ebbert took the comment as a compliment.

"You're mighty perceptive, Mrs. Crabtree. I thought Miss Emily might enjoy taking a drive in it. This pair is particularly well matched, don't you think?"

"Yes, the horses are beautiful," Emily agreed honestly, even though seeing them reminded her of the scene with Zach and left an aching void in her heart.

"Your ranch must be truly successful," Opal said, a sly look in her eye. Though Emily caught that look, Dan was too busy being flattered to notice. "You must be doing extremely well. I had no idea ranching could be so profitable."

The last comment seemed to bother Dan. "Well," he

hedged, "you never know, with ranching. That's what I've been telling Miss Emily. Things can look like they're going well, and suddenly, without warning, you've got more problems than you can shake a stick at." He sent her a smile of knowing male superiority. "That's why I said I'd be glad to be of assistance, especially if you should decide this life is not for you. I could even take this place off your hands until another buyer could be found. After all, I understand the previous owner had a dickens of a time trying to sell before."

"That's most kind of you." Emily smiled, though her patience was becoming more than a little strained by his continual masculine presumption, to say nothing of his emphasis on how difficult it would be to make the ranch a success. "But at the moment we are doing very well indeed, and we have no intention of leaving. Do we, Opal?"

"That's right. After all, Mr. Ebbert, your success stands as a shining example of what can be accomplished." Opal gave him a fawning smile, guaranteed to pander to his male ego.

"I am indeed most flattered by your praise," Dan replied. "But let me assure you, my ranch is simply one of my many holdings. And I expect a windfall very shortly."

"Oh?" Opal prompted.

"Yes. Some luck has come my way. Nothing I can talk about yet, you understand. Until a deal is consummated, it is bad luck to talk of the details. But I am close to realizing my goal." He smiled, and his light eyes took on a distinctive predatory gleam. "Well, enough of that. I wouldn't want to bore you ladies, but I would be most pleased if you would visit my ranch sometime. I think you would find it most pleasant."

Though he extended the invitation to both women, Dan clearly intended it more for Emily, since he didn't take his gaze off her.

"I-I'm not sure when we could manage it," she stam-

mered, unwilling to commit herself to a particular date until
she worked things out with Zach. "Can we confirm a time
later? Things are still somewhat hectic here."

"That'd be fine. I don't want to rush you, but I hope to see
you again soon, Miss Emily."

He smiled at her, his teeth showing white in contrast to his
reddish brown beard. The hairs tickled her hand as he raised
it to his lips for a brief kiss.

"Perhaps you can tell me when would be convenient next
Sunday at church. If that would be all right?"

"Yes, I'll try," she promised. Surely she could work things
out with Zach before then. And she could honestly tell Dan
she had other commitments.

As Dan drove off, Emily looked after him, wondering if
he would run into Zach in Bethel Springs. How she wished
she were a man, free to come and go as she pleased, to ride
out at night or in the light of day without fear of the conse-
quences. But with the problems they'd been having, she
didn't dare leave the ranch on her own, not even to find
Zach—especially not to find Zach. For all she knew, he was
in the worst part of town, trying to discover who had plans to
run them off the Double F.

Zach left the saloon just after eleven at night. As far as he
could tell, no one had any more to say than on the previous
night. To tell the truth, he didn't want to be here. Though
he'd thirsted for revenge for so many years, tonight his heart
was someplace else. What was Emily doing now? he wondered. Had Dan Ebbert stayed on for the evening meal? Had
he invited her to see his place—and had she accepted?

The questions tore at his concentration and opened raw
wounds in his heart. Though he'd gotten himself a room in
the boardinghouse, he didn't feel ready to face it quite yet, so
he strolled aimlessly through the town. As he passed a dark-

ened alley, he heard low voices faintly echoing out into the street. Idly curious, he stopped for a second, just out of sight but not out of earshot.

"We just wanted you to know what a great job you've been doing," he heard a male voice say. "Everyone we've talked to thinks so."

"That's right," a second voice concurred. "We have it on the highest authority. You just look at your collection plate next Sunday, and you'll see how much you're appreciated."

The voices sounded ominously familiar, but Zach couldn't place them. He flattened his body against the wall of the nearest building and carefully edged his way around the corner into the alley. A scrubby plant grew against the same wall and shielded his body from view. The light was too dim to make out the faces of the three men who were talking less than ten feet away.

Then one of them struck a match and raised it to his face to light a cigarette. Carl Hudson. The light flared bright enough so that Zach could make out the man next to him as well—Carl's brother, Ray: the two men who had ambushed him in Colorado after killing their young confederate and leaving him to die unburied on the trail.

Red-hot fury surged in him, and it was all he could do to keep from leaving his hiding place. What were these low-lifes doing here? That they were up to no good went without saying, but their involvement with the third man, whose voice he recognized from his last visit to church, troubled him.

"I am glad to have your support," Reverend Putney was saying. "And I appreciate your bringing these other matters to my attention. Make no mistake, the Lord does not tolerate sinners of any type, rich or poor, hungry or well fed. As I've told my flock, the ways of sin are many and varied. Satan can appear in any guise, even that of a bird of the field, so we all must be on guard.

"Your support of the Lord's testament will be rewarded in heaven, as I'm sure you know. And I will continue to strike out against blasphemy, wherever it's found, most particularly out there on that ranch. My sermon will take care of it all, don't you worry," he concluded.

"We knew we picked the right person to come to," Ray Hudson said as he patted the pastor on the shoulder.

"We thought it best to confide in you and let you handle it from here," Carl concurred. "We'll be in touch if anything new comes up."

"I appreciate it. I was put on earth to do my duty for the Lord, and any additional information you provide can only help me spread the Good Word."

The Hudsons did not immediately leave the alley after the preacher left.

"So, what have you found out?" Ray asked.

"Not much," Carl answered. "But I'll tell you one thing. The boss sure has his hands in a lot of pots. And even if only half the rumors I've heard between here and Phoenix are true, there's gold and silver out here just waiting to be found."

"Gold and silver, huh?" Ray said as he lit up a cigar. In the brief seconds the flame lit his face, his beady eyes took on a greedy, calculating look. "I think I'm beginning to understand," he continued cryptically.

"What do you mean?" Carl asked.

"I'll let you know in good time, brother, all in good time."

Zach could hear the smug satisfaction in the man's tone and knew it boded ill for the town. Gold and silver brought pain and heartache in their wake. He knew that from bitter experience. And the Hudsons were the kind of scum precious metals attracted in great supply. He'd have to drop a word in the sheriff's ear.

The men walked toward Zach, heading for the main street. Zach moved back and out of their sight, but remained in hearing distance. He wanted to know everything they had to say, but he didn't want them to recognize him.

"Where to now?" Carl inquired.

"Let's drop in at Flora's for a while, and then I have plans for the rest of the night."

"Sounds good to me," Carl said, the edge of excitement in his voice warning Zach the pair was up to no good.

He hid in the shadows as they walked by, listening to their ribald comments about Flora's girls. Once they were gone, he went to the sheriff's office, but the place was empty. Unable to do anything further, he turned his steps toward the center of town.

Briefly he wondered if the Hudson brothers could have had anything to do with the problems at the ranch, then dismissed the idea. From what he'd overheard, they'd only been in town a short while, not long enough to have been involved in the early vandalism. And the recent attacks were apparently done by one person, not two, judging from the tracks. From what he could tell, the Hudsons never did anything alone. Comforted by that thought, he made for his room.

As he passed the livery stable, Jackson came out the door, cursing.

"Something wrong?" Zach asked the man. He'd never seen Jackson this lively.

Jackson paused, then spit on the ground. "Some people ain't fit to walk on this earth, let alone own a horse."

Zach smiled to himself. Jackson was known for throwing a fit whenever a horse came into his stable a bit overheated from a good run. Usually it didn't mean a thing.

"You don't believe me?" Jackson demanded, having seen Zach's disbelief. "You want to see for yourself?"

He made as if to push the barn door open again.

"I'll take your word for it, Jackson. What happened?"

"Got a pair of bays like you wouldn't believe in there," the older man said, indicating his barn with a toss of his head. "And they're as whupped as could be, marks on their backs and everything. You'd think with breeding like theirs, there'd be no need to touch 'em with a whip, or nothin'!"

The man was incensed. ——

"Bays, huh?" Zach questioned. "Hitched to a fancy carriage with blue and yellow trim?"

"Yeah? How'd you know?"

"Saw it earlier today. Quite a pair, as I recall."

"You're right about that," Jackson said emphatically and joined Zach as he walked to the boardinghouse, expounding on the finer points of the pair's breeding and conformation. Zach listened with half an ear. All he could think of was that Dan Ebbert had left the Double F, and from what Jackson had said, Emily had not come with him.

For the first time all day Zach felt a lightening in his heart. Not that it meant anything, or that his circumstances had changed, but he couldn't help but rejoice that Dan hadn't won Emily over quite so quickly. Only later would he realize he should have paid more attention to what Jackson had said.

Dawn was breaking on the horizon when Carl and Ray returned to Bethel Springs. Using the back entrance to the small second-floor office, they let themselves up the stairs.

"You here, boss?" Ray called out.

"Shut up," came the snarling reply. Impeccably dressed as always, the bearded man came out to the landing. "Someone might hear you, you fools."

Carl tugged on Ray's arm. "Sorry. Guess we just got carried away," he said apologetically.

"You have good news, then?"

"You might say that," Ray said with his customary swagger. "We destroyed most of their irrigation canals. It won't be no easy task to repair them, neither. We went after their main canal, then plugged up the leadoffs to them damn birds."

"Oh, and we talked to Putney, too. He's being most cooperative, as I'm sure you'll see for yourself next Sunday," Carl added with a grin.

"Good." The man smiled, his teeth showing white against his beard. "Very good. Things are coming together just the way I planned."

CHAPTER
10

By Sunday Emily was beginning to despair of ever getting on Zach's good side again. Since the vandals had destroyed the irrigation lines, he'd been spending more and more time trying to find out who was undermining the ranch and less and less time with her. He'd been out on the range helping the men restore the canals or back in town virtually every day, even going so far as to skip meals. With a heavy heart, she realized he was avoiding her.

"You ready to leave yet?" Opal called to her.

"Almost," she replied. Going to church was the last thing she needed today. She didn't feel up to small talk and banter when her heart felt so wounded. The only thing that kept her going was the thought that Zach would be there, too, close enough to touch. If only they could talk, she was sure she could straighten things out.

But Zach eluded her again. When the buckboard pulled up in the courtyard, Frank held the reins.

"Mornin', ladies," he said as he clambered down from the seat. "Mighty nice day out, don't you think?"

He smiled at the two of them and helped Opal into the back.

"Where'd you like to sit, Miss Emily? Up front with me or in the back with Miz Crabtree?"

Emily's heart sank. Ordinarily she would have been glad to sit up front with Zach. Now it hardly mattered.

"Whatever is more convenient for you," she said.

"Well, why don't I help you in back, then?" he said. "I think Hank will be coming along as well, and the two of us can talk up here while you keep your aunt company. How's that sound?"

"Fine," she replied with a false smile.

The trip to Bethel Springs seemed longer than ever. The dust seemed dustier, and the heat seemed hotter. Even the cactus seemed pricklier and more forbidding.

Worst of all were the covert glances she knew she was getting, not just from Opal, but also from the men in the front seat.

"We're almost there," Frank said at long last. "I'll drop you off at the church. Then Hank and I will wait outside till you're ready to leave. That all right with you?"

"That's fine. But if you'd prefer waiting somewhere else, please don't let us keep you in the sun."

"That's right kind of you, ma'am," Hank said, "but we've got our orders."

From the guilty expression on Frank's face, Emily realized who'd issued those orders. Zach.

It was small comfort to think that he cared enough for her welfare to make the men stay nearby to guard her, but not enough to come himself.

At the church they greeted Bea, who was tactful enough for once not to inquire about Zach.

The services had just begun as they entered the sanctuary, so they took seats near the rear. Several of the townsfolk who had visited the ranch looked up and nodded in greeting. A few sent friendly smiles in her direction.

By the time Reverend Putney approached the pulpit to deliver his sermon, Emily had begun putting her worries behind her.

"The Lord will not tolerate sin," he intoned. "Let the sinner beware His wrath. Though the sinner may think to fool us one and all, the Lord knows the truth. As it has been written in Amos, 'For I know how many are your transgressions and how great are your sins—you who afflict the righteous.'

"And we are afflicted here. There is sin all around. I have pointed it out, but you do not believe. You question my word, as Israel questioned the Lord. And the Lord grew angry when Israel turned from His teachings, as you have turned from mine. Woe to those who do not listen and heed.

"You have embraced the birds, those spawn of Satan, and their keepers. Have you no fear of their sin? Do you know how they live, men and women together, yet none of them wed? They have no shame, yet you do not revile them."

A murmur went through the congregation, and some of the people shifted in their seats to look surreptitiously over their shoulders at Emily and Opal.

Reverend Putney continued his impassioned speech, and Emily became more and more discomfited.

"Why is he doing this?" she whispered, mortified beyond her wildest imaginations as the pastor implied they ran a house of sin, taking in strange men and offering shelter to women of the streets.

Opal shrugged, trying to keep her poise, but Emily could see the tears collecting in her eyes. Bea appeared to be the only person present who shared their outrage over the minister's words, but before she could speak out, a man stood up near the front of the church.

"Excuse me, Reverend Putney. I mean no disrespect, but I

fear you may be mistaken, at least about the ladies present here today."

It was Dan Ebbert. He was in the pew where Emily had sat the last time, undoubtedly waiting for her arrival.

"I can't speak about the others, but I know Emily Crabtree and her aunt can be nothing but victims themselves. They've led sheltered lives and came west only recently. Surely you cannot blame them for what's happening. They've been mis-led, and I'm sure it won't take much doing to figure out by whom."

The various townspeople nodded and murmured. Words like "drifters," "gunslingers," and "soiled doves" reached her ears.

Incensed, she was about to speak out, to tell them how hard it was for a woman to survive in this harsh country, to remind them how Zach had saved the townspeople from themselves when they'd come out to the ranch to do harm, but Opal forestalled her.

"Let's just leave," she whispered, holding back her tears, "before there's serious trouble here. I don't trust that preacher. He has a fanatical look in his eye."

Emily looked again and had to agree. Dan Ebbert's words had turned aside the most personal of the man's attacks, but he'd already made his point. As she and Opal quietly left the church, no one met their eyes, and Emily could hear a susur-ration of whispers follow them out the door.

"I am truly sorry about that," Dan Ebbert said. He, too, had left the building, going out the side door to meet them in the front.

"What happened?" Frank said as he came up to them from his spot in the shade of a nearby building.

"It doesn't matter," Emily said, still too upset to discuss the attack. "Let's just go home."

Frank nodded and ran off to get the buckboard from around the other side of the building.

Dan shook his head. "This is really a shame," he said. "Just when it looked like everything was going so well for you, my dear. If there is any way I can be of help, do let me know. Would you like me to escort you back to your ranch?"

"It's kind of you to offer, but I think we'd best go alone."

"Don't worry about this overmuch. I'm sure it'll blow over in a while. After all, there is no question at all but that you're a lady. And you, too, ma'am."

The last words were for Opal. She smiled weakly in response just as Frank brought up the buckboard.

Frank helped her into the back while Hank held the horses' heads.

"Thank you for your help," Emily told Dan. "It took courage to speak out back there, and I do appreciate it. I'm just a little overwhelmed right now."

Dan took her hand in both of his, the gold ring on his left hand flashing in the early morning sunlight. "I understand. I still would like you to visit my place, but today is not the time to talk of it. I'll be in touch soon. You take care of yourself, now, you hear?"

As he had on all the other occasions when she'd seen him, Dan pressed a kiss to the back of her hand. Then he helped her into the buckboard and watched as they drove away.

"I sure wish I could like that Dan Ebbert more," Opal commented.

Emily could only nod. Dan had been more than kind, standing up for her and Opal today. Emily just wished he had defended the others, too.

Though neither Emily nor Opal spoke of the incident, word filtered back to the ranch. Within a day Zach knew the whole story, including the fact that Dan Ebbert had defended Emily's reputation, a reputation he and the others supposedly had tarnished.

Guilt rode him hard. This was what he'd feared most, and the townspeople didn't even know how right they were about him. He had taken advantage of her. The fact that Emily had been a married woman and should have known what she was about meant nothing. Zach knew her marriage had left her vulnerable. He should have been looking out for her.

Worst of all, Dan Ebbert had spoken up for her whereas Zach could not have even if he'd wanted to. He knew the town was rife with rumors about his unsavory past. The fact that he wore his gun strapped to his leg branded him a gunman, no matter the reality. That he was bringing dishonor onto Emily's head pained him more than he could bear.

His suppositions were confirmed by the sheriff when he came out to investigate the damage to the irrigation canals.

"Did you hear what happened at the church?" he asked Zach as they walked out to see the damage.

"Yes. Were you there?"

"Yup. Got kinda nasty. Made me think the ladies might want to leave. Sell the ranch, maybe. This seems like a lot of trouble, one way or the other, just to raise some damn birds."

"This is more than just raising birds for the ladies," Zach said. "This is their home."

"Maybe so," the sheriff said, "but if it wasn't for Mr. Ebbert, the ladies might not have had a home to come back to. He stood up for them, you know, and the people listened, even the reverend. Mr. Ebbert is a very important man around these parts. What he says goes."

"Then it's good he was there to speak up for them."

"I also heard rumors you were a fair hand with a gun.

Folks are afeard you're one of them gunmen. They don't like the idea of having someone like that around these parts. It's always been fairly peaceable here."

"That so?" Zach drawled. "Then how come we've had so many problems on the ranch?"

"Could be some of your own men, for all I know. They're not locals. Who knows what kind of background they have?"

Zach knew. And so did Frank, but they weren't about to tell. And because of their secrets, Emily and the others were suffering. It didn't take much imagination to realize the sheriff thought the problems at the ranch were all internal—local to the ranch because of its unsavory residents.

After surveying the damage, the sheriff scratched his head and said, "Doesn't look like there's much I can do. The only strangers hereabouts are your own men. You want me to take them in for questioning?"

"I can assure you whoever did this was not from the ranch," Zach bit out.

The sheriff merely shrugged, and Zach knew the man would be of no help.

Emily cornered Zach when he came into the house after the sheriff had left.

"What did he have to say?" she asked. In her eyes he could see the hurt and confusion his withdrawal had caused.

"Not much," he replied.

"Is he going to find who did this?"

"I doubt it. He seems to think it was done by someone here," Zach answered bluntly.

"What makes him think so?" she asked, her expression mirroring the surprise in her voice.

"He's heard all sorts of rumors."

"So? Rumors don't mean a thing, Zach. You hired these people. Surely you don't believe what's being said."

"What I believe doesn't matter, Emily. You can't just ignore what's going on in town, what they're all saying. No one else is."

She seemed about to protest, and he knew what she was going to say. She was as stubborn and loyal and headstrong as ever, his Emily, but he couldn't let her be hurt. Before she could open her mouth, he walked out, slamming the door behind him.

Having no choice, he avoided her more assiduously than before. He knew he was hurting her by his supposed indifference, but what else could he do? Dan Ebbert could offer her respectability and acceptance by the town. Zach could offer nothing to compare with that. But that didn't stop him from disliking the man more than any man he'd ever met, save one.

Over the next few days Emily longed for Zach's company, for the companionship they'd enjoyed even before they'd made love. She remembered with wistful longing their arguments and banter over everything. At least they'd been talking then, sharing their thoughts and spending time together. But lately Zach was never around. If he'd been withdrawn after Dan's visit, he seemed to have disappeared since the incident at the church, taking Frank and Billy with him.

Emily sensed they were hard at work following every lead, doing the sheriff's job as well as their own. But she suspected they were also trying to give lie to the rumors Reverend Putney had started. For herself, Emily sought solace in her work, hoping the routine that had become so central to her life would carry her through these difficult times.

"I heard there's a circus coming to town," Jewel said one morning over breakfast. "From Mexico."

"Oh?" Opal said encouragingly.

"Yes. One of the hands mentioned it, even brought a poster back from Bethel Springs. They'll be here for the day. I think we should all go see it."

"Sounds interesting," Opal put in.

"It should be grand. I saw one once when I lived in Texas. It's a sight not to be missed. What do you think, Eula?"

"I don't know. Should we go with all these problems here-abouts?"

Jewel jumped from her seat and stood with her fists on her hips. "Now is the perfect time to go," she declared. "You can't let these people, whoever they are, win the fight. Why, if we start hiding out, they'll think they're winning and so will the town."

"Jewel's right," Opal agreed. "If we stay out here all the time, the townsfolk'll think we have something to hide for sure."

"Good. Then it's settled," Jewel said. "I'll have Frank make arrangements with the men to guard this place while we're gone. Then he and Zach and Billy can take us in. You all had best get ready."

She left the room with a determined step, heading for the barn where Frank was working.

Emily suspected that Jewel and Opal had deliberately set up this outing for her sake. Although they hadn't said anything, they were well aware that she and Zach hardly exchanged two words a day. They were giving her an opportunity to spend some time with him, an opportunity of which she planned to take full advantage.

As soon as they reached Bethel Springs, Opal hurried over to Bea's, Frank and Jewel set off for the general store, and Uncle Billy convinced Eula he knew the best place from which to view the circus parade. Only she and Zach remained at the door of the livery stable once Jackson took the wagons and horses inside.

"Have you ever seen a Mexican circus before?" Emily asked, holding her bonnet in place as a gust of hot wind blew past.

Zach had been silent for almost the entire trip into town. She took hope from the fact that he hadn't refused outright to join them, but he seemed as distant now as ever.

"Can't say that I have," he finally said, but his eyes were trained on something down the street.

The only thing Emily could see was a woman dressed in bright pink standing on the plank sidewalk a block away.

"Since everyone's deserted us, what do you think we should do first?" she said, deciding that she wasn't going to let him get away with avoiding her this easily.

"Whatever you like," he said, but his attention still seemed centered on whatever was happening down the street.

She bit her lip. What they'd experienced together was too important to simply let go of. "I need to pick up a few things from the mercantile before the parade starts. Shall we start there?"

Zach nodded and took her arm, but he held her at an overly respectable distance, making sure they didn't touch except where his hand held her elbow.

When they reached the store, Zach finally spoke. "While you're inside, I have some business to take care of."

"But—" Emily started to protest but stopped short. If he didn't want to spend time with her, forcing him to do so would accomplish nothing. For all she knew, he really did have some business in town. Still she felt compelled to ask, "When do you think you'll be back?"

"I'll try to make it back before the parade starts. Frank and Jewel are still inside, so you won't be alone. I'll meet you in front of Bea's shop if I don't get back in time to escort you to the parade."

Before Emily could say another word, he was out the door. She peeked out the window and watched him walk down the sidewalk till he disappeared from sight. Her heart ached, and she felt her lip begin to tremble. Blinking quickly, she turned away from the window and pretended to examine some dry goods. It wouldn't do to let anyone see her like this. She had too much pride.

But, oh, how it hurt to have him pull away. Something had changed, at least for him. She wished she knew what it was. If she did, she could make it disappear like a puff of smoke and recapture the elusive sense of belonging that had held them in thrall. But if her experience just now was any indication, it would be no easy task to find out what was troubling him.

Zach leaned against the side of the bordello waiting for Flora. From where he stood he could see everyone who walked by, but few would notice him.

He'd talked to the madam yesterday when he was in town, and she'd promised to meet him here today. It'd been all he could do to get away from Emily in time. He was eager to hear what Flora had to say, but the hurt look in Emily's eyes had been almost more than he could bear. When he'd decided he had to back away from her, he hadn't realized how much it was going to hurt them both.

Flora was late, or maybe she'd gotten tired of waiting for him. He'd noticed her earlier, in her bright pink dress, when he and Emily had first arrived, but he couldn't have gotten away then. Maybe she was getting back at him. Flora liked her little games.

He remembered when he'd first spoken with her. It had been the morning after he'd overheard the Hudson brothers mention her place. Zach figured they were the type to boast about their conquests, whether with women or money. They'd done it back in Colorado when he'd first met them, and he had no reason to think they'd changed.

Flora had agreed, for a price, to keep an eye open for any sign of Earl Darnell or the Hudsons.

The Hudsons worried him the most right now. He didn't think they were smart enough to plan anything out on their own. That meant they were working for somebody. And until he figured out for whom and what they were up to, his best course was to sit back and watch them. He knew any confrontation would get ugly and end up reflecting badly on the Double F. After all, hadn't the sheriff already said the town considered him no more than a gunman? If any trouble arose, he'd be blamed, and by association, so would Emily, even if the Hudsons started it.

Since that first meeting, he and Flora had met again a couple of times. She'd given him some information on the Hudsons, but nothing on Earl Darnell or anyone who might resemble him. Not that Zach knew exactly how to describe him. The man changed his appearance as he moved from one place to another. Sometimes he was clean-shaven; sometimes he wore a mustache or beard. His hair had been darkened and lightened. Once he'd even shaved most of it off to make his escape.

All Zach had to go on was his reputation for beating up women and the hope that, if he really was in the area, one of these days he'd come by Flora's and she'd remember him.

Now, as he walked down the plank sidewalk, Zach kept his eyes open for a flash of pink.

Suddenly he heard the madam's voice.

"Hello, handsome. It's about time you showed up. Any chance I could change your mind about the afternoon's activities?" Flora asked suggestively. The strap of her tight-fitting pink dress slipped off her shoulder as she sidled up to him.

"Not today, I'm afraid. Anything new happen?" he asked, getting right down to business. The only woman he wanted was the one he couldn't have. The ache in his loins was the least of his worries, and that was all Flora had the cure for. The ache in his heart was a bottomless pit that sucked all the joy from his life and left him with only one goal: solving the ranch's problems and getting on with his quest for Earl Darnell.

"Walk with me," Flora instructed, and she led him down the sidewalk toward her house. She smiled and tilted her head as she talked, seeming to flirt shamelessly at least as far as any observer could tell. Only Zach knew that what she was saying had nothing to do with sex and everything to do with Carl and Ray Hudson.

"They haven't said anything outright," she told Zach, "but they've been hinting mighty strongly. Especially the older one, Ray."

"What's he have to say?"

"He's spouting off about a lot of gold and silver around these parts." Flora frowned. "I get the feeling something's going to happen soon, or maybe he's involved in something that will give him a windfall. As I said, he's not too specific."

"And the other one? Carl? He have anything to add?"

"Carl's more of a follower. My guess is Ray isn't telling him any more than he needs to know."

Zach nodded. That had been his impression as well.

"You've heard about the troubles at the ranch?" he asked as they reached Flora's house and went in the back way.

"Who hasn't? Even in my part of town, the good reverend's words get around." She gave a mocking smile as she led him into her office.

"I meant the attacks on the stock and the property."

"I've heard of those, too. I wouldn't want to drop any names, but we get a wide variety of men out our way."

"Including some of ours?"

"Could be. No one's indiscreet, if that's what you're getting at. Whatever Mr. Putney learned, he found it on his own, not from one of your men. They're pretty closemouthed about what they're doing."

"Any idea who might be behind the vandalism?"

"No, but it sure is interesting—all that talk about gold and silver cropping up just when you're having troubles. Bears looking into, I'd say."

That was what Zach thought, too. After all, he'd lived through a similar terror campaign just before his family was killed, and for nearly the same reason.

"If you get wind of who the Hudsons work for, I'll double our deal," Zach said, as he pulled out his money and laid the agreed-upon price on Flora's desk.

"I'll keep that in mind," she said with a grin. "Now, if you want something a touch more personal, I'd be glad to give it to you—on the house."

She gazed at him with an appreciative eye, making no attempt to hide her perusal of his most intimate parts.

"I appreciate the offer, but . . ."

Flora sighed. "Too bad. As always, it's been a pleasure doing business with you," she said as she scooped up the coins from her desk.

Zach looked at his pocket watch as he hurried out to meet Emily. He knew he was late; he had stayed longer with Flora than he'd expected to. Emily had been excited about seeing this circus, and as much as he knew he had to draw away from her, he couldn't disappoint her. He'd just have to keep his distance today as best he could. He walked a tightrope of pleasure and pain, knowing how much he wanted her, but knowing even more that he couldn't have her.

"I thought you might not be coming," she said when he approached her in front of the general store.

"It took me longer than I thought it would. I didn't mean to keep you waiting," he said in apology. "Where're Bea and Opal?"

"They've decided not to watch the parade. They'll just wait until later and see the performance."

"Wise thing to do, considering this heat. Maybe you should do the same."

"This may be my only chance to see a circus, and I don't want to miss a minute of it. My friends back home can't believe the things I've done since coming here."

"Probably think you've lost your senses."

"Do you think I have?"

"Doesn't matter what I think," he said, and then, not giving her a chance to object, continued on. "I think I hear the parade starting. We'd better move up by the sheriff's office if you want a good view."

Zach gestured to Emily to precede him up the sidewalk, then fell into step beside her, carefully avoiding touching her. He didn't even offer to take her packages. He didn't dare. Even from this close, the scent of violets filled his every breath, and the sight of her red-gold hair and fair skin reminded him of how silky soft she was to the touch. If he touched her once, he knew he wouldn't be able to stop.

He'd already caught a glimpse of her face. Seeing the hurt in her eyes, it was all he could do to keep himself from sweeping her up in his arms and kissing her until neither of them could remain standing. But it was better to hurt her a little now than to have her wake up some morning and realize all she'd lost by settling for him. That would be a lifetime of pain. He couldn't do that to her, and he couldn't do it to himself. It would break his heart even more than losing her now.

Billy and Eula were waiting for them, and Frank and Jewel arrived within moments. Zach was glad for the distraction. It was much easier if he had a buffer when he was with Emily.

Eula and Jewel greeted Emily and, seeing her packages, asked what she'd bought at the store. They exchanged small talk, while the men huddled together conversing on their own.

Emily kept sneaking glances in Zach's direction, but if he saw her, he kept the knowledge to himself. He continued talking with the other men and only stopped when the parade started.

For the short time that the parade passed by, Emily forgot about her problems with Zach and watched in amazement.

First came a man dressed as a clown riding a big black horse. He had a painted and powdered face and called out in Spanish that the circus was coming. He also enticed the crowd with a description of what people could see if they came to the performance down behind the livery. Billy translated his speech, since no one else in the group spoke Spanish.

Next came a large open cart. It carried four men, all wearing masks, plus an old man playing a cracked violin. He was dressed as a monkey and had a group of young boys dancing around him. The music was terrible, but no one noticed.

Following the cart came several jugglers, each tossing three or four balls in the air and never letting one hit the ground. Behind the jugglers came the acrobats. Dressed in blue tights and spangles, they rode pure white horses.

The parade ended with a man leading a long line of dogs, each one following the other and never moving out of step. When he called out a command, the dogs broke rank and lined up into three rows of three, never looking right or left. They reminded Emily of the soldiers she'd seen marching in the Decoration Day parades.

"Well, can you imagine that?" Jewel said. "I've never seen such smart dogs. Most I've ever seen them do is run in the streets or fight."

"They certainly are amazing," Emily agreed. She'd never seen dogs so well trained, but then, Jewel had been able to work wonders with Baby, too. The ostrich did whatever Jewel told it to do. Maybe it was just a matter of love and patience.

"I can't wait to see the whole performance," Eula added. "When does it start?"

"As soon as they get enough people paying admission," Billy answered. "They usually set up seating of some type, so if we want good seats, we'd best hurry."

Before long they had paid their admission and followed the crowd in. They found that Bea and Opal had saved them seats on makeshift benches placed in a semicircle around a crude circus ring. Now all they had to do was wait for the first performers to appear.

Emily noticed that Zach was sitting as far away from her as possible. He'd even made sure he hadn't walked beside her on the way down here from the parade. She made a pretense of chatting with Opal and Bea, asking about their morning and all they had done together, but her mind was elsewhere.

All she could think about was Zach. She went over all that had happened in the last few weeks. She remembered the good times they'd had just walking together in the desert, admiring the sunset behind the mountains, watching the sunrise beyond the tops of the farthest saguaros. Being together had given everything she did new meaning, from working with the ostriches to just eating a meal. And the time they'd spent in each other's arms had filled her life with wonder beyond anything she'd ever imagined. Her whole life had taken on a richness, a sense of fulfillment because of Zach.

Then suddenly everything had changed. At first she'd blamed his withdrawal on the way Dan had treated him, but she'd apologized for that day and explained what had happened, and yet he still stayed away. Something fundamental had gone wrong between them. Maybe it was something in her, she thought with a sinking feeling, for Laurence, too, had turned away from her.

She was jostled from her thoughts by an elbow nudging her side.

"Emily, how'd you enjoy the dog act?" Opal asked after getting her attention. Opal's tone told her this wasn't the first time she'd asked the question.

Emily looked around. People were already starting to leave. She'd been so caught up in her own thoughts, she'd missed the entire circus. She made a general comment, which seemed to satisfy Opal, and followed her back to Bea's, letting the conversation flow around her. Zach had already disappeared, leaving Frank and Billy with the task of getting them back home. Emily couldn't even summon the energy to be surprised. It was almost as if she had expected it deep down inside.

She was going to have to do something about herself, she realized. She couldn't spend her whole life wondering what had changed Zach and longing for his return. She had no choice but to get on with her life as she'd done before.

If nothing else, she was a survivor, but this was the most painful episode she'd yet had to survive. Seeing Zach, knowing he was near, yet not being able to touch him or reach him hurt her very soul. She felt older and sadder as she put away her dreams. Fantasies had no place in the West, she discovered. The price of loving was too high, the cost of losing immeasurable.

CHAPTER
11

"Dan wants you to visit today," Opal reminded her a few days later.

"I know," Emily responded listlessly. "You've only been telling me every day this week."

"Well, you don't seem to remember anything much from one minute to the next. I didn't want you to forget this."

"I thought you didn't like the man," Emily pointed out.

"My liking him has nothing to do with it. He seems a passable man—just to know, that is. Besides, I think you could do with a change. What do you think, Jewel?"

The other woman looked up from her sweeping. "I agree with Miss Opal. An outing would put the roses back in your cheeks. Besides, that Mr. Ebbert is a persistent fella. If you don't go there, I reckon he'll show up here before too long."

Emily considered Jewel's words. If there was one thing she didn't want, it was another confrontation between Zach and Dan Ebbert. The two men rubbed each other the wrong way.

"Maybe you're right," she conceded.

"I know I am," Opal insisted. "Besides, Billy has to go

down that way to get some new equipment, so he can take you and bring you back with no problem."

At that, Emily knew she'd run out of excuses. A day away from the Double F might be just what she needed to lift her spirits. At least she wouldn't spend half of her time waiting for a glimpse of Zach. For no matter how she tried, she could not put him out of her mind.

"All right, I'll go. Tell Uncle Billy not to leave without me."

Opal beamed at her and went off to find her brother-in-law while Emily dressed for her trip.

The Ebbert ranch rose out of the flatness of the desert and was one of the most beautiful Emily had ever seen. The Spanish hacienda style house, while built in the same manner as her own, was of far greater grandeur and size. Hers still needed a coat of whitewash and some broken roof tiles repaired, while this one was a dazzling white with a perfect red-tiled roof. Dan Ebbert certainly knew how to live in style.

"This place is beautiful, don't you think?" Emily said as Billy drove their buckboard through large iron gates and into a graveled, walled-in courtyard filled with cactus and large clay pots overflowing with flowers. Someone spent a great deal of time with a watering can in his hand, Emily thought. Flowers didn't bloom in such abundance out here without lots of care and attention.

Uncle Billy merely grunted.

"You've been grouchy all during this trip. Is something bothering you?" she asked in exasperation.

"Lots of things, if you want to know the truth."

Emily narrowed her eyes. "Are you going to tell me or just sulk out here all day?"

"Don't you get fresh with me, young lady. I'm older and wiser'n you are."

"Older, I'll grant you," Emily said loftily, knowing it would provoke him into telling her what was eating at him.

"All I can say is, be careful, Emmie. I don't rightly trust that fella," Uncle Billy said before stepping down and helping her out of the buckboard. He'd been less than enthusiastic about her visit from the beginning, but Opal and Jewel had prevailed, convincing him that the trip was a good idea.

"Why don't you like him?"

Uncle Billy looked sheepish. "I ain't got a reason. Leastways, not one I can explain. But I got a good sense about people, and my sense is telling me to watch out. Don't get in deeper than you want with Mr. Ebbert."

"I don't plan to. This is just a visit, neighbor to neighbor. Is that all right?"

Uncle Billy scrunched up his face and looked at the imposing house with its beautiful landscaping. "I guess so. Long as you know what you're doing. You want me to stay?"

She knew his offer came from the heart, but she didn't think it was necessary. From what she'd heard, Dan Ebbert had a full staff of household help, to say nothing of the fact that everyone in Bethel Springs had only the best opinion of him.

"I thought you had important business in Shiloh," she reminded him, mentioning the nearby town.

"It can wait if'n you don't want to be left alone out here."

"I should do just fine. You're worrying for nothing," she assured the older man. "Besides, you won't be gone all that long."

Billy didn't say anything to that.

"Look, there's Dan," Emily said as she noticed the man emerge from a door in one of the walls surrounding the courtyard.

"Emily," Dan called out, "I'm so glad you decided to visit." He drew close and reached for her hand, raising it to his lips. "I have waited for this a long time."

"It was kind of you to invite me," she said. As she pulled her hand from his, she noticed the ring he was wearing. "What an interesting piece of jewelry."

"You like it?" His eyes gleamed in the bright light as he brought his hand up to show off the ring. "It's been in my family for years."

"It's very impressive," Emily said as the blood-red stone glittered in the sun.

Uncle Billy didn't bother to look at the ring. He climbed back onto the buckboard and picked up the horse's reins. "I'd best be going," he said.

"Mr. Crabtree, are you sure you can't stay for some refreshment?" Dan asked, looking up at Billy.

"Got business in town. I'll pick up Emmie in two hours. Don't forget what I said," he added, looking pointedly at her. Then he slapped the reins and set off out the gates without looking back.

"It's a shame he couldn't stay. But in a way, this is better. I fear I am a selfish man when it comes to the company of a beautiful woman."

Emily blushed, embarrassed both by the flowery sentiment and by Billy's abrupt departure. At least it was reassuring to know that Dan would have welcomed her uncle if he had elected to stay.

"I'm afraid Uncle Billy was in somewhat of a hurry. He has business nearby."

"I understand. Why don't you let me show you around? Then we'll have some refreshments," Dan said. "Or would you rather have something to drink first?"

Now that she was here, she was glad she'd come. Dan

looked genuinely happy to see her, and as always, Opal was right: The change was doing her good.

"I'm fine right now. Why don't we do the tour first? I can't wait to see everything. Your place is so lovely. Have you lived here long?"

"About a year, though I only moved in permanently about four months ago."

"Where did you move from?" Emily asked, more to keep the conversation going than out of real curiosity.

"Out west," he said in a clipped tone of voice. Then, before she could continue that line of questioning, he went back to their original topic. "Where would you like to start your tour?"

Emily was a bit startled at his brusqueness. He seemed different from the last time she'd seen him. She couldn't put her finger on it, but somehow he'd changed. He was both friendlier and more impatient. She didn't understand his impatience except that maybe he was reluctant to talk about his past. She could understand that; she didn't like talking about her life back in Connecticut, either.

"Wherever you'd like to start would be fine," she answered politely.

"This way, then," he said and took her arm. In contrast to Zach, he held her close, almost too close. But he was careful. Every time she might have spoken out, he stepped back subtly, giving her the room for which she would have asked.

First he took her around the carriage courtyard and pointed out the various types of flowers and cacti he'd cultivated in his unusual garden.

"This is really beautiful," Emily commented. "It must take a great deal of work."

"That's what I hire the natives for. They don't seem to mind the heat or the work. Brought up to it, I guess. If you like this, wait until you see the patio."

"What's a patio?" She'd never heard that word back east.
"Come this way."

They entered through the door in the wall where Emily
had first seen Dan. At the time she'd been too anxious about
Billy's discouraging remarks to wonder what was behind it.
Now, as she stepped inside, she couldn't believe her eyes.
Before her stretched a beautifully mown green lawn. In the
far back corner stood a windmill, towering gracefully above
the ranch's roof.

A portico shaded the other three sides of the patio, shield-
ing the windows of the house from the intense heat of the Arizona sun. A wooden floor ran along the base of the house
under the sloping portico roof, which was covered with the
same red tiles as the house. The contrast with the green lawn
was eye-catching. Everything had a well-tended look.

"The kitchen backs onto the patio, and quite often we
have dinner served out here in the evening. Once the weather
cools, it's quite pleasant," Dan told her. "I think you would
enjoy that, no?"

He quirked a brow at her, as if he were picturing her here,
seated at a meal or sharing an evening with him and his
friends. His assessing glance was too personal.

"This is all so fascinating. I've never seen anything like
it," she chattered, wanting to end the suddenly intimate moment. "Back home we have nothing like this. It's really
lovely."

"When I first saw this house I knew I had to have it. And
I didn't let anything stop me. Fortunately the owner was
willing to sell," Dan said with a strange laugh.

Emily looked up at him quickly, but aside from a fleeting
burning look in his eye, his expression was bland, so bland
she was sure she'd imagined that spark of something dark
and forbidding.

"You were indeed fortunate. The grounds are exquisite," she said.

"No more so than you, my dear. You bring grace and beauty with you to surpass anything mere nature has to offer."

Once again, his compliment left her feeling uncomfortable.

"I can see you've done a lot of work on the outside," she said. "Is the inside as lovely?"

Fortunately he took the hint, interpreting her comment as an indication of a deeper interest in his property rather than an excuse to get out of a vexing predicament.

"Come, let me show you," he offered, "and you can judge for yourself."

After crossing the wooden floor edging the patio, they entered the house. When her eyes adjusted to the darker interior, she saw they were standing in an attractive sitting room decorated in the latest fashion. A large tiled fireplace dominated one wall, giving the room a character all its own. Above it a clock, the kind that chimed on the hour, perched on the mantelshelf, and an arrangement of dried flowers sat on the hearth.

"Shall we have our refreshments now?" Dan asked as he gestured for her to be seated.

"Thank you," Emily said, sinking down onto a tufted green velvet chair. "I'm still adjusting to the heat and seem to require more tea breaks than I did back east."

"Though I'm pleased you're here, for I like nothing better than having such delightful company, I'm surprised you've lasted as long as you have. As you said, this heat is more than you're used to."

"I'm learning to cope with it," Emily said with a laugh. "I've even gotten to the point where I no longer put cold compresses on my wrists to cool down."

"If the heat doesn't bother you, doesn't the threat of Indians have you ready to pack up and go home?"

"We haven't had any problems, and I think we're close enough to town to keep us safe. I see you have gun ports. Do you think you might be in danger?" Emily hadn't really given too much thought to an attack by Indians and was interested in what Dan Ebbert might have to say on the subject.

"I always like to be safe rather than sorry. You might give some consideration to the possibility yourself. This is wild country, even if it looks civilized."

At that moment a maid came into the room.

"You like tea served now, señor?" she asked, balancing a heavy tray.

"Put it over here, Maria, in front of Miss Emily."

His voice when he spoke to his maid had none of the gentle tones he used with her, Emily noted. As unobtrusively as possible Maria moved forward and placed the tray on the table he'd indicated. As she turned to go, Emily noticed the younger woman had a large bruise on the left side of her face. Running down the middle of the bruise was a jagged cut that was only partially healed. The injury looked fairly recent.

Emily sucked in her breath. The faint noise had the maid looking up for a second. When their eyes met, Maria lowered hers and quickly left the room.

"Is she all right?" Emily asked, concern for the young maid overcoming her training. Servants were to be ignored, she'd been taught. Their function was to serve without drawing attention to themselves. But Emily couldn't ignore what she'd seen. "She looks hurt."

"She's fine. Probably fell down some steps or walked into a door. You know how these peasants are—terribly clumsy. Lazy, too, for that matter. She'll be fine in a few days. It's nothing for you to worry about."

"Are you sure?" Emily asked hesitantly. Maria didn't look as if she'd walked into a door. She looked as if she'd been hit, and hit hard.

"I said she'll be fine in a few days," Dan repeated, his voice cold and implacable as he looked toward the door through which Maria had exited. But when he spoke again, he sounded as charming and warm as before. "Now, if you'd be so kind as to pour."

He smiled at her, and Emily had the distinct impression he wanted her to forget about the servant with the bruised face.

"I hope you enjoy this new blend of tea I just ordered in," he was saying, as if nothing untoward had occurred. "The aroma is wonderful. I'm sure you'll appreciate the bouquet and the combination of subtle flavors."

Emily poured the tea and then picked up her own cup, but as she sipped she couldn't help but wonder at Dan's total lack of concern for the well-being of one of his household. In his place she would have demanded to know what had happened, and if, as Emily suspected, she'd discovered that the woman had been beaten, she would have taken immediate steps to get rid of whoever had hurt her.

Though Dan tried to engage her in small talk, Emily found her concentration wandering. Dan seemed to have no such problem; he was more charming and witty than ever, his manner slightly flirtatious.

After they finished their tea, he showed her the rest of the house before taking her out to the barn and tack rooms. Her interest was piqued when she saw the clever use of a hole in the roof of the barn to let daylight into the otherwise dark interior. She'd have to talk to Zach about doing that at the Double F, she thought to herself, but didn't bring his name up with Dan.

When they finished their tour, a manservant came to tell Dan that Billy had arrived to pick up Emily. In a way she was relieved, for as beautiful as she'd found the ranch, the incident with Maria refused to leave her mind.

"What a shame that you have to leave already," Dan said. "Perhaps next time you can come for a longer visit."

"We'll have to see," she answered noncommittally, then thanked him for having her. "You'll have to come back to my ranch next time," she added, more out of politeness than real feeling.

"I would be most happy to see you again, whether here or at the Double F. You are always welcome to visit," he said and gallantly kissed the back of her hand. The metal from his heavy ring was cold against her palm and sent a shiver down her spine.

Billy scowled, and Emily withdrew her hand from Dan's.

"Thank you, again," she said as Dan helped her into the buckboard.

"Was your visit all right?" Billy demanded when they had driven out the gate.

"Yes, it was fine," she replied, but the memory of Maria's bruised face and Dan's indifference stayed with her all the way back to the ranch.

Maybe Billy and Zach had better instincts than she had, she thought. Neither cared for Dan Ebbert, and after today she wasn't sure about her own feelings. His charm no longer worked for her, and his strange mood swings had left her feeling uncomfortable and disturbed. She'd lived with that once and had no desire to repeat the experience, even in a casual acquaintance.

As she and Billy drove into the courtyard at the Double F, Emily decided she'd had enough of men, from Dan Ebbert to Zach Hollis. She'd had the right idea when she first came west. An independent woman fared much better than one who had to look to a man to care for her, either physically or emotionally. From now on, she would do her best to regain that sense of independence, and this time she wouldn't let anyone change her mind.

Zach knew Emily had spent the day at Dan Ebbert's ranch, and the thought had put him in a bad mood. Just how bad he'd only realized when Frank turned to him and said, "Don't you have to go to Bethel Springs for something?"

He'd said no, but when Frank had fired back, "Too bad," and then gone off in a huff, Zach decided he'd better get away from the ranch. It was bad enough being miserable himself; he didn't need to inflict misery on the others as well.

"I guess I will head into town," he said when he found Frank working around the back of the house.

"Good idea," his friend muttered under his breath, but loud enough to ensure that Zach heard him.

"I'm sorry, Frank. I guess things have been hard lately. I didn't mean to take it out on you."

"You want my opinion, just ask. Otherwise I'll keep my mouth shut."

Frank's expression dared him to ask, but Zach already knew what his friend was going to say. Frank didn't understand why Zach felt the need to give Emily her own life, a life free of Zach's burdens, a life of respectability.

"It wouldn't work," Zach told him, anticipating his words.

"You don't know that," Frank expostulated. "Listen to me, Zach. I always thought I was a wanderer, that I'd never settle down and want roots. But now that I've met Jewel, things are different."

"Maybe for you."

"How's that? You think just because Jewel's life wasn't as respectable as Emily's that she doesn't want some of the same things?"

Frank's tone had an angry tinge as he spoke in defense of his ladylove.

"That's not what I meant, and you know it. For you, trailing outlaws has always been a job—an important job, but still, just a job. If you'd wanted to, you could've switched from it to something else at any time. Hell, you can switch right now, if you want.

"But this isn't a job to me, Frank. This is my family. I didn't choose to go after the Darnells. They chose me the day they decided to burn our ranch, the day they left me alive and the rest of my family dead."

Even Frank didn't know the full details of that horrible night. No one did, except Zach and Earl Darnell. Zach had never been able to talk of it or to forget it. It had given shape and direction to his life from his youngest days. That was why losing track of Earl Darnell always caused such anguish. Until the man was punished for his sins, Zach could have no rest.

"I can't stop looking, Frank. And I can't give Emily that kind of life. I want to see him brought to justice, no matter how long it takes. Can you understand that?"

There was no need to define who the "him" was. They both knew it was Earl.

"I understand, Zach, but I can't say I agree." Frank regarded him with sad eyes. "You've given twenty years of your life to this. Do you think that's what your mama and papa would have wanted?"

"Maybe not, but they sure didn't want me to be an orphan, either. If I let Earl Darnell go, who's to say he won't do the same thing to somebody else? As it is, he's spread more than his share of suffering, and you know it. I'm not asking you to find him with me. If you want to settle down, I'll be the first to wish you well.

"But don't ask me to do what I can't. And don't tempt me

to take Emily with me. I'd rather die than do anything to harm her."

For several moments neither spoke. Then Frank said in a husky voice, "If I can help in any way, you be sure to tell me, understand?"

Zach nodded, then went to get his mount, too preoccupied to notice the expressions chasing across Frank's face— compassion, understanding, disagreement, and determination. Had he seen them, he would have realized just what a good friend he had in Frank, if he hadn't known already.

Late Sunday morning Emily sat in the front parlor with her needlework lying unnoticed by her side. She'd finished all her chores earlier, from watering the breeding pairs to checking the eggs in the incubator, and now had nothing to do but think. After the bad experience with Mr. Putney, she and Opal had decided to forgo church services for a while.

"Emily?" Eula asked as she entered the room, feather duster in hand. "Are you all right, dear?"

"I'm fine," she replied, although it was far from true, but she didn't see how anyone could help her.

"You don't seem fine to me. Is there anything I can do?"

Emily was surprised at Eula's reply. Since she and Uncle Billy had started keeping company, Eula was speaking up a lot more and taking a more active interest in other people's lives.

"Thanks for asking, but this is a problem only I can solve."

"It might help to have someone just listen—if you want to talk, that is."

Emily wavered. Would it help just to talk about what was happening? She certainly hadn't done too well on her own. Maybe it wouldn't hurt.

"Do you have all afternoon?" she asked with a smile in her voice.

"I have all the time you need," Eula replied and sat down on the settee beside Emily's forgotten needlework. She put down her feather duster, then picked up the swatch of fabric and held it out to Emily. "Did you do lots of needlework back east?"

"Some. Laurence claimed he liked watching me sew. I guess he thought it was the proper kind of work for a lady," Emily said as she took the partially completed chair cover from Eula's hand.

"Laurence was your husband?"

"Yes. He died almost two years ago, leaving my inheritance under Billy's management."

Eula must have heard the trace of resentment in her voice, for she quickly jumped to Billy's defense.

"Billy's a fine man, you know. Just too well meaning. But let me tell you, well meaning is a wonderful quality to possess. Better'n most."

"I don't know that I'd consider buying an ostrich ranch well meaning. In fact, I'd consider it foolhardy."

"Didn't you say the feather merchant you'd contacted had offered you top dollar for all the feathers you can send him?"

Emily nodded.

"Then this wasn't such a foolhardy investment, was it?"

Emily had the grace to look down. Eula was right. As far as the ostriches were concerned, things had worked out surprisingly well.

"You're right. It's just that after Laurence threw away our money on one 'well-meaning' investment after another . . ." Emily let her voice trail away.

"That wasn't well meaning. That sounds more like trying to get rich without having to work. I should know. My husband did the same thing. At least you ended up with something for Billy to manage. My Howard was a bully and a spendthrift. If it hadn't been for Jewel, I'd be out on the street."

"I didn't realize," Emily said, finally understanding some of the reasons for Eula's behavior.

"The last place we lived before Howard disappeared was next to Jewel's. When he didn't come home one day, I didn't know what to do. Jewel just sorta stepped in and has been there ever since."

"So you don't know where your husband is?"

Eula shook her head, and her eyes filled with tears. "Not that I miss him. He wasn't any good, and I'm better off without him. Jewel tells me that every time I start thinking about him." She smiled through her tears. "But it's Billy who worries me now."

"Billy is really quite taken with you, you know."

Eula sniffed and pulled a handkerchief from the sleeve of her shirtwaist to wipe her eyes.

"I know. That's what's so hard. Billy knows about my husband, but I just don't feel right even considering a life with Billy when Howard is still out there somewhere."

Emily didn't know what to say. She patted Eula's hand, and they sat together, letting the silence communicate for them.

"A bad marriage is hard to get over," Emily said after a while, her voice barely audible. "I don't always trust my judgment anymore. When things don't go the way I want them to, I always wonder . . ."

"Whether it's your fault?" Eula finished for her. "I know. Me, too. That's one of the things I admire about Jewel—her confidence in herself. She doesn't worry overmuch about what anyone thinks. She just does what she has to and expects the rest of us to fall in with her plans."

Emily smiled. She knew Jewel wasn't all that sure of herself, but she put up a good front. And sometimes that was enough. If you acted as if you believed in yourself, you could fool people into believing in you. Then, before you knew it, you'd begin to really believe in yourself, too.

Emily wished she could do that, but it just wasn't her way.

"Jewel's had a hard life, too," Eula went on. "She doesn't talk about it much. She says you have to put your past behind you and get on with the rest of your life."

"I've tried that," Emily replied. "That's one of the reasons I came out here. Besides, it isn't just my past that's causing problems. It's—" She cut herself off, biting her lip for fear she'd revealed too much.

"It's Zach," Eula said, once again finishing her thought with uncanny accuracy.

Emily got up from the settee and walked to the window, her needlework dropping from her lap, unnoticed.

"I've tried putting him behind me, too."

"He's not part of your past," Eula pointed out gently, coming up behind Emily.

"Isn't he?" Emily said, bitterness making her eyes blur as tears gathered. She blinked quickly, unwilling to waste another moment crying over what couldn't be.

Only the other day she'd overheard Frank tell one of the hands that Zach was with someone named Flora. Up till then Emily had thought she was doing well with her resolution to become independent again. But the thought of Zach with another woman had been more than she could bear. She'd spent the afternoon alone, trying desperately to gain control over her emotions, and though she'd succeeded, it was a fragile control at best.

She couldn't help but remember the woman in the pink dress the day of the circus and Zach's apparent interest in her. Had that been Flora? A shudder ripped through her.

"I know things are hard right now," Eula said, placing her

hand on Emily's shoulder. "I also know you think everything's over between you and Zach, but I've seen how that boy looks at you. There's something else going on, Emily."

"I know what it is, too," Emily said, the words bursting out of her. "Another woman."

Shocked that she'd revealed so much, Emily clamped both hands over her mouth.

"Oh, Emily, you don't really believe that, do you?" Eula asked as she pulled Emily into her embrace. The bitter tears Emily had managed to hold at bay now ran down her cheeks, and sob after wrenching sob escaped from her throat. "There, there," Eula crooned. "Get it all out and then we can talk."

Eula walked them both back to the settee and sat holding Emily, much like a mother calming her child, until she was all cried out.

"I'm sorry," Emily mumbled when she regained control over herself. She straightened and wiped her fingers over each cheek, drying away her unruly tears. She was too embarrassed to meet Eula's eyes.

"For what? I've cried my share of tears, too. What's important is what you're going to do now that you've finished crying. Don't do what I did; don't drift along hoping someone will come and save you. Decide what's important to you and do something about it."

Emily considered all Eula had told her, especially about Zach. Did she really believe he had another woman? That he no longer cared for her and could turn away from her so easily? If she did, then she would never be free of Laurence and what he'd done to her. It would mean she thought so little of herself that she couldn't imagine Zach having any lasting feelings for her.

Even worse, it meant she thought Zach a shallow, uncaring man, unable to commit himself to any ideal. But Zach wasn't shallow. She'd seen too much good in him, seen his loyalty and bravery, known his kisses and his heart.

"You're right," she said slowly. "I have to figure out what's really going on. That's the only way I can get Zach back, isn't it?"

Eula nodded. "It'd be a start, wouldn't it?"

"I wish I knew what was happening. Sometimes when I was with Zach, he'd get this sad, faraway look on his face. I always wondered what he was thinking then."

"I reckon you aren't the only one with a past," Eula said. "Zach's may have a stronger claim on him, something he can't simply put behind him. I've watched him for a long time, too, him and Frank and all their conversations. Don't you ever wonder what they're talking about?"

Emily turned to look at Eula. She'd underestimated the woman all this time, dismissing her simply because she seemed timid and scared. But there was more to Eula than met the eye.

"I've always wondered," Emily admitted, "but Jewel said they probably discussed men's things—cattle prices and such."

"Did you believe her?" Eula asked astutely.

"Well, no, not really."

"Neither do I. It's easier to think that's all they talk about. Saves a body from having to face what they might really be saying. It's a way of surviving—Jewel's way. But I don't think it's yours." Eula got up and walked back to the window. She stood there looking out. "You want to know what they're talking about, ask the source."

Emily got up and walked to her side, then followed her gaze. Outside in the courtyard she saw Frank helping Jewel with Baby.

"You think I should talk with Frank?"

"Couldn't hurt, could it? I'd say he and Zach have known

each other for a while. Longer'n they've been here, don't you think?"

Emily didn't just think it; she knew it for a fact.

"You're right," Emily decided. She couldn't just sit back and let the man she loved walk away. "I know there's something Zach hasn't told me. Maybe Frank knows what it is. The only question is, will he tell me?"

"Only one person can answer that," Eula said meaningfully before she picked up her feather duster and went back to work.

An hour later Emily saw her chance to talk with Frank. She'd seen him head out toward the paddocks and followed him.

He was checking the alfalfa growth in one of the empty pens when Emily caught up with him.

"Afternoon, Miss Emily," Frank called when he saw her walking over to the fence.

"Frank, do you have a few minutes to spare? I want to ask you something," Emily said.

She felt nervous and unsure of herself. She didn't know quite how to start this conversation and was relieved when Frank smiled and said, "Sure do. Just let me finish up in here, and I'll be right out."

Emily watched as he finished raking, then placed the rake against the outside of the fence.

"Shall we walk?" Emily suggested when he had closed the fence gate behind him. She felt it might be easier to question him if she didn't have to do it face-to-face.

They walked out into the desert while Emily tried to put her questions into words. She still hadn't decided how to ask him when he stopped by a tall saguaro cactus.

"You planning on hiking all the way to Bethel Springs?" he asked with a smile.

She looked around, a bit startled at how far they'd come.

"Oh, I'm sorry. I didn't mean to come this far."

"It's no problem. We can go back easily enough—more easily than you can start this conversation, I'd guess."

"You noticed?"

"It's a bit hard to miss," he said dryly. "Maybe I can help. Why don't you tell me what it is you want to know and I promise not to bite you or laugh at you. Does that cover all the possibilities?"

She smiled, as he'd intended her to. She'd never felt tongue-tied before in front of him, but then, she'd never had anything this important to say to him, either.

"You and Zach have been friends a long time, haven't you?" she asked.

"Yes, we have. Quite a few years, as a matter of fact, on and off like, depending on where we were and what we were doing."

She breathed a sigh of relief. Frank was trying to be helpful. She just wasn't sure how he would react to a more personal question.

As if he'd read her mind, he said, "Why don't you just ask it, Miss Emily? I don't know if I can answer or not, but I'll try. Zach's been my friend a long time. I owe him my loyalty, so if I can't answer, I'll just say so. Fair enough?"

"More than fair," she conceded. "I want to know what happened to him. What gnaws at him when he gets that faraway look in his eyes and becomes very quiet? He looks so sad and empty, as if he's lost everything he ever wanted."

"You love him, don't you?"

"More than I thought I could ever love anyone."

"I figured as much." Frank took off his hat and scratched his head, looking as if he wasn't sure he should be saying what he was about to. Emily held her breath. "Well," he said at last, "you guessed right about him. He did lose everything he ever wanted—leastways, everything he wanted before he met you." Frank squinted into the distance. "This ain't a story for a woman's ears. I don't know if I should tell you more."

"Frank, I really need to know what makes Zach the way he is. If I'm ever going to be able to make a life with him, I need to know what haunts him. Right now it's driving us apart, and if I don't understand, I can't bring us back together."

This time Frank was the one to suggest they walk, though he headed back toward the house. He kept his eyes straight ahead, not looking at her.

"Zach lost his family when he was eleven. He's been on his own since," Frank said, his voice flat, devoid of all emotion.

Emily realized this was the only way he could bring himself to tell the story and swallowed her gasp, afraid to do anything that might make him stop.

"They was all killed, except for him. He was there when it happened."

"How terrible!" Emily exclaimed, unable to keep from crying out her dismay. She felt Zach's pain as if it were her own. How horrible to be left alone at such a tender age. She could imagine how frightened he must have been, having to fend for himself. "What happened to them?"

"His family had a place in Colorado till the Darnell brothers decided they wanted it. From what I understand, they'd bought out most of the other ranchers, but Zach's father wouldn't sell. The Darnells tried using force to persuade him, but Zach's father wouldn't budge. One night the Darnells decided to burn the Hollis family out. His father, mother, and sister all died in that fire. Only Zach escaped."

"How did he manage to go on after losing so much?"

"I don't know. He's got a strong character . . . and he wanted revenge."

"You mean the Darnells weren't punished?" She couldn't believe it! All the nightmares she'd ever had about living in the lawless West were coming painfully true.

"Not right away. They owned the town by then. Who was going to stand up to them? An eleven-year-old boy?"

"No, but I bet he tried." Her heart ached for Zach. She could see him in her mind, a skinny lad, not yet grown, with his dark brown hair mussed and his hazel eyes lonely and determined.

"He did more than try. He promised his family that night that someday he'd avenge them, and then he set about acquiring the skills he thought he'd need."

"Like using a gun?" Emily asked, understanding at last the enigma of Zach's tied-down gun. No wonder he'd become a fast draw.

Frank nodded. "He also learned to track, to hide when he needed to, and to come out fighting when there was no other choice. I don't think he'll rest until everyone connected with his family's murder is dead or behind bars."

"You mean for twenty years the promise he made to his family has kept him on the trail of their killers?" Emily asked, unable to believe such sacrifice. Zach had consigned himself to living on the edges of society, driven by a seemingly elusive goal. She couldn't begin to imagine how lonely his life must have been. "Didn't anyone help him? Couldn't the government step in?"

"We tried," Frank said. "That is to say—" He caught himself up, then blushed.

"You work for the government?" Emily asked, suddenly remembering the day he'd been so uncomfortable when Jewel had mentioned the U.S. marshal.

He nodded. "I met Zach when we were both going after James Darnell. Since then we've put away some other members of the gang."

"But not all?"

"No. Not all."

Emily suddenly shivered despite the heat, knowing she wasn't going to like his next answer, but having to ask the question nonetheless. "Who's still out there?"

"Mostly just minor gang members, people who worked for the Darnells many years ago." Frank looked troubled as he kicked at a small piece of scrub by his feet. "And one more person, the one Zach's spent most every minute of the past few years trying to find. He's one of the Darnells, and Zach says he won't stop until he's found them all."

Emily had known Zach had secrets. She'd just never realized how devastating they were and how committed he was. He'd never said he'd be staying on forever, only until Billy came back to take over, but she had hoped he'd want to stay. Now she knew wanting had nothing to do with it: Zach had made a promise, and he was a man of his word. Even if he'd wanted her more than life itself, he wouldn't have been able to stay.

She had hoped that hearing Zach's story would reveal to her what to do, that it would give her the key to his heart. Now that she knew the truth, she realized Zach had thrown the key away long ago. Not that she could fault him; his reasons were painfully noble. But they wouldn't keep him warm at night.

And they wouldn't bring his family back. Twenty years was a long time to deny oneself, to put off living one's own life in order to avenge someone else's. Surely Zach had sacrificed enough. But how could she convince him of that? And was she right to even try?

"Thank you, Frank. I appreciate all you've told me," she said tightly. "And I won't tell anyone else, so you don't have to worry."

"That's not what has me worried, Miss Emily," Frank replied. "I just hope knowing what happened helps some. Zach don't mean to hurt you none."

"I know that," she said, matching his solemnity. "I don't want to hurt him, either, but it seems we're both hurting, doesn't it?"

Frank merely nodded, his face filled with sympathy and just the barest hint of hope.

CHAPTER
12

Trying to talk to someone who was avoiding you was never an easy job, Emily discovered over the next few days. Trying to talk to someone who was avoiding you for a good reason, a reason you understood and maybe even respected, was even harder. Torn between her own desires and what she knew Zach would prefer had her in a quandary.

One minute she wanted to throw herself in Zach's arms and plead with him to give up his chase, to get on with his life, and to let her get with hers, by his side. The next minute she berated herself for being selfish, for wanting Zach to turn away from a deathbed promise so she could have the life she'd always dreamed of, regardless of his needs.

She held countless mental conversations, twisting and turning his answers and hers to find an answer with which they both could live. There was none, so she put off starting a conversation she wasn't sure how to finish.

The only thing she knew for certain was that she didn't want to see Zach spend the rest of his life alone. He had so much to offer, despite his own deprived childhood. Whatever time his parents had had with him, they had used well. Though he'd been a loner for most of his life, beneath the surface layer was a depth of feeling waiting to be tapped. Emily had touched these depths when they'd made love, finding generosity and patience, passion tempered with empathy, desire fueled by deeper feelings. He'd never given a name to those feelings, but then, neither had she until she'd talked to Frank.

How could she have spoken of her love to his best friend but never to Zach himself? Surely if he'd known, it would have made a difference. He wouldn't have been able to put her out of his life so easily.

But as she waited to talk to him, she realized that turning away from her hadn't been easy for Zach. If it had, he wouldn't be so hard to find. He would have been there for every meal, able to ignore her presence, oblivious to her pain. New memories assailed her, memories of things she'd barely been aware of at the time they'd happened. The way Zach had watched her during the circus parade; she'd felt his eyes on her every moment, as if he couldn't get enough of the sight of her. The way he'd sat so far from her, yet still sent tiny glances at her whenever he thought she wasn't looking. The way he'd disappeared so quickly right after the show. She'd been half aware of the longing in his gaze, the tight self-control in his every move, the lines in his face that seemed deeper and more filled with sorrow.

Suddenly she didn't care that she couldn't figure out every last detail by herself. She wanted to talk to Zach immediately, to express her feelings and her fears, her doubts and her longings. She wanted to see his face when she told him she loved him, to know in her heart how he felt about her. She was ready to risk everything, to take a chance on happiness, and to persuade him to risk love, too. So it was that she was standing at a window overlooking the courtyard when Dan Ebbert came to call.

She was out on the porch by the time he'd climbed down

from his phaeton. As before, his horses were winded, foam dropping from their mouths and dotting their backs.

"Hello, Dan. This is a surprise. What brings you out our way?" she asked, not at all sure she was pleased to see him.

He gave her his most charming smile. "I just felt I had to see you again. Is there ever any better reason to come visit a beautiful woman?"

Behind him his horses strained toward the watering trough. Remembering his last visit, Emily asked, "Should your horses be drinking yet?"

Dan turned around and pushed the horses back, threatening the more persistent one with the whip when it didn't move fast enough. The horse jerked its head high and a quantity of foam broke free from its mouth.

"Damn foolish beasts," Dan said angrily as the foam fell onto his jacket. He shook it off viciously and then brought the whip down across the animal's face.

Emily stepped forward instinctively, wanting to intervene, though she wasn't really all that experienced yet in handling horses. Just then, drawn by the commotion, Hank appeared.

"Need some help?" the hand asked Emily.

Gratefully she turned to him. "Yes, if you wouldn't mind. Perhaps you could take care of Mr. Ebbert's team? They need cooling down and then some water."

"Sure thing, Miss Emily," Hank assured her. She didn't miss the disdain in his expression as he eyed the whip in Dan's hand. Crooning to the animals in much the same way as Zach had the previous time, Hank coaxed them back, then led them around toward the barn.

"Wait! You forgot this," Dan called, holding out the whip.

"I won't be needing it," Hank said and kept walking.

Dan muttered something under his breath, then tossed the whip into the phaeton when it became clear Hank wasn't coming back for it.

"Your employees leave something to be desired," he declared when he came up the porch steps. "They're surly and too independent. I've been giving your problems a lot of thought lately, and I think I've come up with a solution that should please us both."

Thoroughly bewildered, Emily could think of nothing to say. Whatever problems she had were nothing Dan Ebbert could help out with. And after this last exhibition of temper, she didn't feel kindly disposed to him in the least.

At a loss for words, she simply said, "Oh?"

"Yes, my dear. Why don't we go inside out of this heat, and we can talk more comfortably?"

Emily didn't really want him inside. The other women were out in a far storeroom they'd set up for quilting and other domestic work. They'd invited Emily to join them, but she hadn't been in the mood. All she'd wanted to do was wait for Zach. Frank had mentioned he was expected back this afternoon. Now she half dreaded his return, not wanting him to find her with Dan, especially alone.

But Dan didn't wait for her agreement. He opened the door to the house and ushered her in, heading for the parlor where they'd talked the last time.

Once inside, he reached for his pocket handkerchief and wiped away the last traces of horse spittle from his coat.

"Would you like some water to wash up?" Emily offered.

"Perhaps that would be a good idea," Dan agreed, looking down at his hands with distaste.

She led him out to the kitchen and got him a basin and pitcher. When he finished washing up, she offered him a drink.

"And where is your charming aunt?" he asked, having noticed the house was empty.

"She's with Jewel and Eula, sewing in one of the storerooms."

"Good, then we're alone. All the better. What I have to say to you is personal and best discussed without an audience."

Emily felt a sinking sensation in her stomach. "That would hardly be proper," she said in an attempt to divert him.

But Dan was not to be swayed. "Don't look so worried. What I have to say is extremely proper. However, I think the setting could be improved. Why don't we go back to the parlor?"

Emily nodded and headed for the front of the house, racking her brain for a way to keep Dan from taking the conversation in a more intimate direction, as he seemed inclined to do.

"Here, sit beside me," he ordered and stopped by the settee.

Emily would have preferred the chair on the other side of the low table, but not wanting to be obviously rude, she sat on the settee, as far from him as she could get.

Dan gave her one of his practiced smiles. "I am sure that by now you have guessed what I have to say." He took her hand into his. "Nevertheless, let me say it so we have no misunderstanding."

He raised her hand to his lips for a quick kiss. She resisted the urge to yank it out of his grasp, but when she tugged gently, he would not let go.

"Please, Dan. I think we are at cross-purposes," she said with a growing sense of desperation.

"Not for long, I'm sure," he countered. "I intend to bring our purposes into alignment as soon as possible." His light eyes took on a bright gleam. "I want you to marry me, Emily," he said boldly, then continued, ignoring her gasp, "I know this is sudden, but after I saw you at my house I couldn't wait any longer. You fit perfectly, like a jewel in its proper setting."

"But—" she started to protest, but he put a finger against her lips.

"Listen to me," he commanded. "This place is too much for you to run. And why should you have to? I can take care of all this for you. I'll make you richer than you've ever dreamed of being. And all you have to do is become my wife. We can be married by the end of this week. I'll even let you bring your aunt to live with us, if you want."

Standing abruptly, she pulled free of his hold. Her breath was coming fast, and her heart pounded in her chest. The gleam in his eye was no benign light. He was determined and, for some reason, had elected her as the focus of his interest.

"I couldn't possibly marry you," she said. "Why, we hardly know each other. We've only met on one or two occasions. And as to this ranch, I must differ with you. I don't need to be cared for. I'm doing quite well on my own."

"You can't possibly mean that," he countered, rising from his seat. "I've heard of your problems. This place is too much for a woman to deal with. I'm offering you everything. And in exchange I'll take care of your ranch as well as my own."

"I'm sorry, Dan, but there seems to have been a misunderstanding between us."

"There's been no misunderstanding. I know all about you." His voice turned cold and harsh, as it had when he'd spoken about his servant, Maria. "Who doesn't? It's all over town. Do you think you can turn me down, a woman of your morals?"

His eyes looked feral, reminding her of a wild beast, as if he'd lost some inner control. He grabbed her roughly by the shoulders, then clamped his arms around her when she tried to pull away.

"Why should you waste your favors on others?" he demanded. "I'm willing to make an honest woman of you. What more can you want?"

With those words he lowered his mouth to hers. She tried frantically to turn her head away, but he wouldn't allow it, grabbing her face with one hand, his fingers and thumb digging into her cheeks as he held her in place.

His lips were unpleasantly moist, and his breath was hot and fetid. She pressed her lips tightly together, refusing him, but he bit her lower lip, gaining entrance to her mouth when she gasped in pain.

His taste overwhelmed her, making her gag. She groaned and tried to kick him, but his high boots protected his shins from her attack. His only reaction was to tighten his grip on her face. The more she struggled, the stronger he seemed to get, as if he were feeding on her desperation. Finally she went limp in his arms, hoping to fool him into thinking she had stopped struggling. When she felt his grip loosen, she gathered her strength and gave one last, frantic push.

She caught him by surprise and backed away when he let her go, her hand over her mouth. She felt her stomach turn and fought being sick.

"Get away from me," she said in a hoarse voice. "Get away and don't come back. If you ever so much as touch me again, I'll call the sheriff. Is that clear?"

He looked at her with contempt. "What makes you think he'll believe you?"

"If he can't handle the problem, I'll find somebody who can. Now leave."

"You're making a mistake, Emily," he said threateningly, and took a step closer to her. She stepped back. "I mean it. If you think you've had problems so far, you haven't seen anything. The West is no place for a woman on her own. My offer won't last long, so you'd better make up your mind quickly."

"I've made up my mind. I wouldn't marry you under any circumstances. Don't bother coming back."

He raised his left hand and she shrank back from it. His blood-red ring caught the light and glittered evilly. For a panicked second she wondered if that was what had left the mark on Maria's face. But Dan didn't strike her. He simply cursed fluently, using the most pungent language she'd ever heard.

The front door opened with its distinctive squeak. Billy stepped in, then glanced into the front parlor.

"What's going on here?" he demanded, his voice none too polite.

"Nothing," Emily managed. "Mr. Ebbert was just leaving."

"Fine. I'll be glad to see him out, then," Billy said, eyeing the man assessingly.

Dan grabbed for his hat, which he'd placed on a marble-topped table by the entrance.

"No need," he said. His face was flushed with the heat of his anger, and his shoulders were stiff as he headed out the door.

"It'd be my pleasure," Billy said back, his voice equally unfriendly, and followed him out.

Emily lingered behind for a couple of minutes, trying to still the trembling in her limbs, then followed just to the door. She saw Hank at some distance heading for the barn, no doubt to retrieve Dan Ebbert's bays and phaeton. Billy and Dan seemed to be having a heated conversation. The wind eddied and changed direction, carrying only Dan's words to her.

"I'm a powerful man in town, Mr. Crabtree, powerful

enough to make things mighty uncomfortable for you and your friends if you won't see things my way."

Then Billy said something back to him.

"You're a foolish old man," Ebbert replied. "You won't get a better deal from anyone."

Whatever Billy said in response made Dan's face close up tight, and Emily could see his anger building.

"What I want it for is my business. My money speaks for itself. Take it or leave it."

As Hank brought the phaeton out, Emily saw Uncle Billy shake his head. Dan climbed onto the driver's seat and reached for the whip still lying where he'd thrown it on his arrival. She wanted to call out to Billy to beware. Dan had an evil temper, as she'd discovered to her dismay, and it flared wildly out of control when he was crossed.

But Billy didn't need her help. He simply whacked the nearest animal hard on the rump and sent the phaeton flying forward. Dan was barely able to keep his seat as the vehicle took off out the gates.

Billy turned to look at her. "You all right?" he asked.

She nodded.

"You don't look it from here. What'd he do? Did he lay a hand on you?" His voice sounded angrier than before. "It's not too late to go after him and horsewhip him good."

Emily shook her head. "He tried," she admitted, knowing how bad she must look. "But I managed to throw him off."

"I warned you the man was no good," Billy said in a gentler tone. He came up the porch steps and looked at her more closely.

"I know, and I believed you. I just didn't know what to do when he came visiting."

"Well, I'll tell you what to do. Next time he shows up, you take a gun to him. I don't want him anywhere near this property or you. What'd he want, anyway?"

"I don't know. He asked to marry me, but I don't think he really wanted me at all. Isn't that strange?"

Billy frowned as he thought things through. "Let me know the second Zach gets here. I don't like the sound of things. Where're Eula and the others?"

"Out in the sewing room, next door to the incubator."

"I'll go check on them," he said. "Will you be all right alone? You want me to send one of them back?"

"No, don't send them in yet," she answered hurriedly. "I'd rather have a few minutes to myself."

Billy gave her another piercing look, as if deciding for himself whether she was really all right. "I feel real bad about this. I should have been here when he arrived. Zach told me to look after you, and I let you both down."

"He didn't really hurt me, Uncle Billy," Emily said, reaching out to touch his shoulder. "It wasn't your fault."

He merely shook his head, still frowning, and said, "I'd best go and give you some time alone. Everybody'll be showing up for supper before you know it. You need anything, just give a holler. I'll have Hank stay out here in the courtyard."

"Thanks, Uncle Billy," she said in a small voice, grateful for his thoughtfulness. To tell the truth, she didn't want to be utterly alone if there was even the slightest possibility that Dan Ebbert might return.

In her room she sank down onto the bed, trembling and shivery now that she could loosen her control a little. How had she ever thought Dan Ebbert charming? How could she have missed the man's barely controlled violent streak? She shuddered and felt suddenly unclean. Getting unsteadily to her feet, she stripped off her dress and started to wash.

She dressed in clean clothes, then went to the kitchen and made herself a snack, which she carried back to her room. She wasn't really hungry, but she didn't want to face the others over the evening meal. This way she had an excuse. After placing the untouched tray on the Eastlake side table by her bed, she went to the rocking chair in the corner and sat. Wrapping her arms around herself, she started to rock, losing herself in the rhythm of the motion, closing her mind to the thoughts and memories of her upsetting afternoon.

"Where's your brother?" the bearded man snarled as Carl came up the stairs.

"He'll be here in a minute. What's the problem?"

"No problem. I just got something that needs doing."

"Another special project?"

"I'll tell you when he gets here. There's no point in going over everything twice."

Carl noticed the tension that came from the man. He'd never seen him like this, with his eyes glittering angrily and the muscle in his cheek twitching wildly.

Ray came up a few minutes later—none too soon, in Carl's opinion. He didn't relish hanging out with the boss when he was in this mood. It made chills run down his spine.

"Time you got here," the boss growled at Ray.

Ray sent his brother a questioning look, and Carl just shrugged.

"I didn't think we were meeting again so soon," Ray explained. "I only got word a few minutes ago and came as fast as I could. Usually we don't meet in the middle of the day like this."

"Something's come up that can't wait. We've got to move and move fast. Here's what I want you to do. Hire some men and attack that ranch. Make it look like it was Indians or outlaws. Anything you want. Just make sure no one's left when you're done. I want that place now, one way or another."

Ray's eyes lit up the way they always did at the prospect of taking action.

"How soon you want this done?" he asked.

"Tonight, if possible. The sooner, the better."

"Tonight it'll be," Ray promised. "Come on, brother, we've got work to do."

Zach opened the bedroom door without even knocking. The room was dark, but not silent. He heard a rhythmic creaking sound coming from the corner. He stepped inside, his eyes slowly adjusting to the darkness. No lamp had been lit, not even a candle.

"Emily," he whispered when he saw her huddled figure in the rocking chair, "can I come in?"

She didn't answer, nor did she look at him. She just kept rocking, back and forth, back and forth.

A chill ran down his spine, and fury bubbled inside him at the man who'd done this to her. He tamped it down. The last thing she needed was to witness more anger.

"Billy told me Dan Ebbert dropped by," he said, keeping his voice soft as he knelt on the floor in front of her. "Said the man spent some time with you today."

She stopped rocking and looked around her as if she felt confused. "It's dark already," she murmured.

Zach followed her gaze to the gauze-covered window. The drapes were pulled back, leaving only the filmy curtains to let in the light during the day while screening out the direct sunlight. Now the window showed only the black of night.

"It's after nine. You've been here a long time. Everyone's finished supper already. They were worried about you."

She still didn't look at him. "I'm fine," she said, but her voice sounded thin, and he wasn't convinced.

Maybe he should have let one of the women come in to her. Her aunt or even Eula might know better how to offer comfort. That was something he'd never learned, or if he had, he'd long since forgotten. Besides, he wasn't sure she would even accept comfort from him after the way he'd treated her, pulling away without explanation, purposely keeping to himself despite the pain he'd seen in her eyes.

He had thought it would get easier over time. He'd been wrong. Every morning he woke up longing for her; every night he went to bed aching for her touch, the sound of her voice, the whisper of her breath. The scent of violets lingered in his mind, and sometimes he'd whip around in a circle, certain he'd caught a whiff of her elusive scent on the desert air. But she was never there.

He'd worked himself to exhaustion day after day, to no avail. This was a battle he could not win, a battle he was no longer sure he wanted to win. Frank's words haunted him as much as his memories. How much of his life did he owe to others? What was the price of justice? Had he paid enough? What if he never found Earl Darnell? Would he have lost him and Emily, too? His thoughts had been too painful to bear, but he'd resisted yielding to his needs. He'd thought he was doing the best for Emily; that was the only thing keeping him from her side, until Billy told him what had happened today.

He'd rushed straight to her room, not stopping to eat or say hello to the others, wanting to take her into his arms, to make everything right for her. Now, kneeling by her side, he was unsure what to do. He lit the candle on the table behind her, then reached out tentatively and gently stroked her hand. She felt small and fragile, her fingers delicate and fine-boned compared to his. He knew it was an illusion. She was strong and determined despite her smaller form, willing to pull her weight and then some, on the ranch and in life.

He'd made a mistake in not telling her about his past. He'd thought he was sparing her greater pain by withdrawing, but he'd been wrong. Instead of protecting her, he'd brought her this.

"Can you tell me what happened today?" he asked.

"I was waiting for you," she said, still not looking at him. "There was so much I wanted to tell you, so much I wanted to say. . . ."

His grasp tightened around her hand. "I'm sorry I wasn't here, Emily. I should have been."

She looked at him then, and he saw in her eyes a depth of sorrow that he'd never seen before, even when she'd spoken of her marriage. She sighed and laid her free hand over both of his.

"You know, it's almost laughable. I came west vowing never to have to deal with another man. Not after Laurence. And now look at me. Wanted by a man I can't stand, and not—"

Her voice broke, and she turned her face away from him.

"And not what?" he pressed her.

"And not by the man I . . . want."

He heard the brief hesitation as she spoke and knew she'd been thinking of another word. Was it the same word that lived in his heart, longing to burst free?

"Do you want me, Emmie?" he asked tenderly.

The look in her eyes answered his question as no mere words could.

"Oh, Emily," he said on a groan. In one quick movement, he pulled her out of the chair and into his arms. "I never thought I'd hold you like this again."

His lips touched hers, and she melted against him; the scent of violets filled his lungs as he breathed deeply. And then all was sensation, her hands tangling in his hair, her mouth clinging to his, her skin gliding beneath his fingertips as they both frantically tore away at their clothes. Somehow they made their way to the bed, their muscles turning languid and weak as they caressed and kissed each other. She touched him and he thought he would explode. He felt propelled by an urgency he couldn't explain to claim her, to make her so irrevocably his that she could never deny it— and neither could he.

Her skin felt smoother than the richest silk as his hands skimmed past her waist and over her belly until they reached the tops of her thighs. Her legs parted for him, revealing her most intimate, secret places to his touch. The tiny sounds of pleasure coming from her throat egged him on. He needed to know her as he'd known no other woman.

"Oh, God, Zach," she moaned as once again she threaded her fingers through his hair. She'd never felt like this in her life. Waves of pleasure crested inside her, and still she wanted more, needing with every fiber of her being to have him closer. "Come to me," she pleaded, even as the waves began to break.

He rose above her, and in seconds they were one. She felt completed and replete. When his mouth covered hers, she lost all sense of herself, caught up in the oneness of the moment, the fleeting instant when she had no separate existence, when all was Zach and Zach was all.

They lay together, side by side, as they slowly caught their breath, reveling in the aftermath of a pleasure so intense they did not know how they'd survived it.

The interlude healed her soul, and as her body regained its breath, she scattered tiny kisses on every part of him she could reach. Zach was kissing her back when the first shout came.

She felt him tense and listened more closely. The shout came again, closer this time.

"What is it?" she asked, sitting up.

"I don't know," Zach replied and threw off the covers.

Emily could hear him feeling around the floor for his clothes.

"I'll light the lamp," she offered. The candle had long since sputtered out.

"Wait. I don't want anyone to be able to see in here."

She saw his dark shape move to the window, then stand to one side as he carefully pulled back the lacy curtain and peered out.

"Can you see anything?" she whispered, holding the sheet to her chest, suddenly aware of how vulnerable she was, sitting naked on the bed.

"No," he whispered back. "I think the sound came from the other side of the house. I'll go check. You stay here until we know what's going on."

She said nothing, understanding his need to protect her, even if it was misplaced. He pulled the heavy drapery over the window, then lit the small candle she kept by her bedside.

"I'll let you know what's going on as soon as I find out," he told her, then quickly brushed his lips over hers and left the room.

Emily scrambled off the bed and dressed as fast as she could. Heavy footsteps passed by her room, and she knew that Frank was joining Zach at the front of the house.

"Emily, come quickly," Opal's panicked voice suddenly sounded, and Emily raced from her room, heedless of the fact that her top buttons were still open.

In the front foyer, one of the men Zach had hired lay in a puddle of his own blood.

"Help me," Opal said, her eyes desperate as she pressed a white cloth to the man's chest. Emily recognized it as the damask tablecloth they used for Sunday dinners, though now it had a bright scarlet hue instead of its usual snowy white.

"Indians," the ranch hand mumbled frantically. "They're attacking. We have to save ourselves."

"Hush, now," Opal crooned as Emily took over the task of trying to stop the bleeding, leaning hard against the make-shift bandage to apply more pressure. A part of her knew she was working in vain, but another part wouldn't let her stop while the man was still breathing. "You're doing just fine. Zach and Frank will take care of everything. Don't you worry none."

"What happened?" Emily asked.

"Ned here just rode in from out on the range, just beyond the ostrich pens. Said the lot of them were attacked by Indi-ans. Zach and Frank just took off with Billy to see if they could help."

"Where are Eula and Jewel?"

"They're getting all the guns and ammunition ready, in case the attack comes closer to the house."

Opal looked as pale and scared as Emily felt.

"Will they be all right?" Emily asked.

"The men, you mean?" Opal asked.

Emily nodded.

"I hope so," Opal said, but the look she gave Emily re-vealed just how unsure she was. "Why don't you go help Eula and Jewel? I'll stay here with Ned."

"Are you sure you'll be all right?" Emily whispered. The man was fading fast. It was just a question of time before he would be gone.

Opal nodded her head, then turned her attention back to the dying man, making soothing noises as she stroked his hand. Emily watched for a while, wishing she could do something more but she couldn't. At least, not for Ned.

Leaving Opal to her sad task, she ran to the kitchen. Jewel was stacking ammunition on the table.

"Eula's getting the sheets in case we need bandages. You want to make sure we have enough hot water?" Jewel said.

Emily nodded and went to work. From this part of the house, they could hear gunfire in the distance. After a particularly long volley, both Emily and Jewel stopped working and looked at each other, their fear echoing back and forth.

Emily's hands trembled. All she could think of was Zach, how warm and alive he'd felt in her arms, how vital. How could it be that just moments ago they'd held the world in their arms and now it was being ripped from their hands with no mercy?

"What if they need more ammunition out there?" Emily asked frantically. "Maybe one of us should take a couple of rifles to them. I can sneak out the back and work my way past the ostriches if I dress all in black."

She took a step toward the bedrooms.

"Are you crazy?" Jewel shouted, grabbing hold of her arm. "You'll just get yourself killed, and maybe them as well. You think Zach will be able to concentrate if he's worried every second about you?"

Emily knew Jewel was right, but it was simply too hard to wait and hope for the best. She wished she could at least see the battle rather than just hear the shots. How many Indians were out there? she wondered. How badly were their men outnumbered?

She'd heard the stories of Indian massacres, knew the tribes felt this was their land and resented the encroaching white man. The Apache had been particularly warlike and had terrorized the area for many years, escaping time and again from their reservations to reclaim the lands that had traditionally been theirs. But there had been no attacks recently, not since Cochise had surrendered to the army. Was this an escaped renegade band?

Her fear for Zach overwhelmed any concerns she might

have had about her personal safety. When she heard a horse whinny in the courtyard, she ran to the front door and flung it open.

Zach and Frank were out there supporting two injured ranch hands. Hank stood slightly behind them, holding a gun on two other men—men Emily had never seen before.

"Who are they?" she asked, bewildered.

"Our 'Indians,' " Zach said contemptuously. "They attacked with about a dozen other white men, all dressed in buckskins and war paint like these two. Fortunately Ned and Hank saw them before they could attack the house. How's Ned?"

He looked up from helping the injured man off his horse. Emily shook her head to indicate that Ned hadn't made it.

"Damn," Zach said and looked away, his jaw clenched.

"Here, let me help with Jake," Emily said, coming forward. She touched Zach on the arm, and he looked down at her.

"This was my fault," he said, his voice raw. "I brought Ned out here."

"You couldn't have anticipated this attack," she pointed out. "And who knows? If it hadn't been for the hired men, even more of us could have been killed."

"It wasn't your fault, boss," Jake confirmed. " 'Tweren't nobody's fault but the men who attacked us. And we got rid of them, thanks to your quick thinkin'."

Emily was relieved to see some of the tension leave Zach's face. He didn't need the burden of yet more deaths on his conscience.

Eula came out of the house then. "Where's Billy?" she called out anxiously.

"He's still at the paddock with Tex, checking out the birds," Frank told her. "He's fine. I'm not too sure about some of the birds, though."

Jewel followed Eula. "Thank God, you're all right," she said when she reached Frank and grabbed on to him, not letting go even when he turned to help the remaining hand off his horse. Blood dripped from the man's arm, and he wobbled when he tried to stand on his own.

"Easy, there," Frank said and started walking him up to the house, one arm around the wounded man, the other around Jewel.

Opal directed them to bring the injured men into the bedrooms, where she and Eula could clean and bandage their wounds.

"What about those two men outside?" Emily asked. "Who are they? Did they say why they attacked?"

"Not yet. I wanted to make sure everyone here was taken care of first. You stay inside, Emily. I don't want anything to happen to you."

The look of vulnerability in his eyes made her realize how afraid he'd been for her.

"I'm fine, Zach." She reached up to the errant lock of hair that fell over his forehead and brushed it back. Then her hand caressed his cheek and slipped down past his jaw to the heat of his throat. She reveled in the feel of his warm flesh and drew comfort from the strength of his pulse, beating so regularly, the symbol of life. "I was so afraid for you," she confessed. "I couldn't even worry about myself or the others here at the house. I wanted to rush out there to be by your side."

He reached for her shoulders and looked into her eyes. "Thank goodness you didn't. For a while there we were caught in a cross fire. You could have been killed."

He pulled her close and wrapped his arms around her. She nestled her head in the hollow of his shoulder, content just to hold him for a couple of minutes, knowing that much still had to be done before this night was over. His scent surrounded her, masculine and unique, making her feel safe and cared for.

"Zach, you coming?" Frank called from the courtyard. "We still have to take care of these two outlaws."

"I'll be right there," Zach called out.

Emily tightened her arms around his waist, wanting to have him to herself for just another minute. As if he understood her need, he lowered his mouth to hers in a kiss of comfort and affirmation, a remembrance of wonders past and a promise of better things yet to come. Slowly he released her and stepped away.

"Take care, now," he murmured. "I'll be back as soon as I can."

She nodded and stood by the open door, watching him until he disappeared around the corner of the house.

So much had been left unsaid, and so much still needed to be determined, but one thing she knew in her heart: She would never love another the way she loved Zach Hollis. And in the morning she would tell him so.

CHAPTER
13

Emily awoke to find that Zach and Frank still hadn't returned from Bethel Springs after taking the prisoners in. It seemed fate was conspiring against her. On top of that, Billy had come in late last night with the report that three birds had been killed, a male from one of the breeding pairs and a couple of the yearlings. The only good news was that one of the eggs in the incubator showed signs of being on the verge of hatching, the chick inside making tiny peeping noises in response to Emily's voice.

When Zach and Frank didn't show up by the time breakfast was over, Billy grew too impatient to wait for their return.

"I'm goin' into town," he declared. "I want to see what's goin' on."

"We'll come, too," Jewel said, looking at the other women at the table. "It'll do us all good to get away from here for a spell. Don't you think so, Eula?"

"Oh, yes. I agree, Billy, providing you don't mind," Eula chimed in.

Billy's eyes lit up as he looked at her. "I don't ever mind

spending time with you," he said. "Just hurry and get ready, now. I don't want to miss the others."

Opal decided she'd go along as well. She could visit with Bea and tell her about the happenings at the ranch. Emily was the only one who was reluctant to leave. She felt the loss of the ostriches keenly and wanted to be around in case one of the eggs actually hatched.

"I'd rather stay here, if it's all the same to you," she said.

More than just the ostriches kept her home, however; she wanted time with Zach alone. That was something she wouldn't get in town or on the way home, where she'd have to share him with everyone else. Better to wait for him here, knowing that as soon as he arrived, they could slip away together and make a start on their new life.

Although the others were disinclined to leave her, eventually they agreed.

"You take care, now," Billy ordered before climbing up into the buckboard. "Don't leave the house or go out and about on your own. Hank and Jess will be nearby, keeping an eye on the place. I don't think anyone'll be back. We showed them rascals a thing or two last night, and they won't forget that in a hurry."

Once they were gone, Emily made her way to the middle storeroom and checked on the eggs. So much had happened in the last twenty-four hours, she needed some time to take it all in, to try to make sense of the fierce range of emotions she'd experienced in such a short time.

All of her thoughts centered on Zach and on the changes he'd made in her life and her outlook. She'd come out west vowing that she'd never again give her soul to a man, and then Zach Hollis had appeared. She couldn't imagine a life without him, and after what they'd shared last night, she felt for the first time that her dreams might just be coming true.

Holding the lantern above the incubator, she looked down

at the eggs. Every egg was as smooth as it had been when she'd first put it in, so many weeks ago. She chirped at the eggs, and one chick chirped back, making her smile. They would hatch soon now, she was convinced.

She gazed at the eggs for a few more minutes, then remembered Zach telling her that watching didn't make them hatch any faster. She smiled as the memories tumbled through her mind, making her lips tingle and her heart ache. She missed him already, though he'd been gone only a few hours. Deciding that the eggs could take care of themselves for a while, she headed back to the main house.

She was in the kitchen having a cup of tea when she heard the front door crash against the wall behind it, as if someone had flung it forcefully open. Running to the front of the house, she was stopped in her tracks by the sight of Dan Ebbert in the front hall.

"What are you doing here?" she asked, feigning a calmness she did not feel.

Beyond him, through the open door, she could see a large closed carriage, not his usual phaeton. Stranger still, she saw that he had a driver with him.

"Why, I've come to see *you*, of course," he replied.

Something in his voice sent shivers down her spine.

"This isn't a good time," she said and edged her way back toward the kitchen. She didn't like being alone with him, especially in the house where no one could see them.

"I think it's the perfect time. Everyone else has gone to town, so there's just the two of us. Most convenient." He took a step in her direction, keeping the distance between them too small for her to make good an escape.

The look in his eyes scared her. They had that strange glitter she'd noticed other times, always before he said or did something violent or cruel. She backed up another step and was poised to turn and run when he made a grab for her.

Emily tried to dodge him, but he was too fast. Within seconds he had her arms immobilized and was dragging her out the front door.

Seeing his driver, she opened her mouth and screamed, hoping for some aid from that quarter. She knew Hank and Jess were out mending the fencing that had been torn down last night, close enough to hear the alarm bell, but not the human voice.

Dan clamped his arm roughly around her neck, briefly cutting off her air supply. The scream died in her throat as black spots danced before her eyes.

"Do that again and I won't be responsible for what happens," he growled in her ear. "You understand?"

She nodded her head, and he loosened his grip just enough to let her catch her breath. He began tugging her across the porch. She tried planting her heels on the wooden planks, but could find no traction. She'd never thought of him as particularly muscular, but he was much stronger than he looked. His hands were the size of hams, and one of them easily captured the two of hers, holding them together in front of her as he pushed her toward the steps.

Just when she thought she'd lost all chance of escape, she heard him cry out and loosen his grip slightly. But before she could pull away, he again tightened his hold, quickly recovering from whatever had distracted him.

To her surprise, Emily saw Baby's head bobbing back and forth and looking at her from between the rungs of the porch railing.

"Get the hell out of here, you damned bird," Dan spat out, taking a swing at the ostrich's head with his foot, but missing when Baby backed up. "Putney was right. These damn birds are from hell."

Emily started to protest Dan's attempts to hit Baby, but he clamped his hand over her mouth, his fingers biting into her cheeks, muffling her words. Fed up with her resistance, he jerked her off her feet and half carried, half dragged her down the steps to his new carriage.

Her heart stopped beating as she realized he was planning to take her away from the ranch. How would Zach be able to find her if he succeeded? She twisted her head and tried to scream through his hand, frantic now that she understood what he had in mind. She attempted to bite him, but he held her jaw too tightly.

Baby must have heard her muffled screams because out of the corner of her eye, Emily saw the bird come rushing in her direction. But the young ostrich was no match for the determined man. With one well-aimed kick, Dan sent the bird flying, and it landed in a heap by the front steps just as Dan maneuvered them to the carriage. Emily tried to catch just one glimpse of movement from her beloved pet, but Baby lay still.

Made reckless by her rage and anger, Emily kicked out at Dan's legs, trying to hurt him the same way he'd hurt Baby, but her soft slippers did little damage. She continued to lash out at him, not caring that her feet were getting the worst of the bargain. All she wanted was revenge on the man who had killed her ostrich.

He didn't like her little attempt at retribution, and he tightened his grip on her wrists. With just the least bit more pressure, her bones would snap. Then, before she knew what he was about, his other hand came out and hit her across her cheekbone. She felt as if the world had exploded in front of her eyes, but the pain radiating through her didn't blot out his voice.

"Kick me again, bitch, and I'll give you something else to remember," he said as he tightened his grip just the smallest bit more.

Emily went limp from the pain and the realization that she

couldn't win this battle. She had to save her strength and bide her time until the opportunity to escape presented itself.

"Carl, where the hell are you?" she heard Dan call out.

"Here, boss," a voice replied from the far side of the carriage.

"I brought you along to help, not to sit in the shade and sleep," Ebbert snapped, still holding her as tightly as before. "Now get around here, so we can head out to San Miguel."

The sound of lazy footsteps reached Emily's ears. Whatever hope she'd entertained of getting help from Ebbert's driver died as the tall, blond man walked around the front of the carriage and looked expectantly at Dan.

"Hurry up and open the damn door," Dan ordered him.

The man did as he was told. In one swift movement Ebbert lifted Emily off her feet and threw her onto the carriage floor. She tried to work herself into a sitting position, but Dan grabbed both her hands and tied them behind her. Then he fastened her shackled hands to a ring located under the maroon leather seat.

Her cheek was beginning to throb with every beat of her heart. She felt a warm trickle run down the side of her face where his ring had struck her. A vivid image of Maria's cheek came to mind. No wonder he'd been indifferent to the servant's injuries. He'd inflicted them. A sick feeling gripped her stomach.

From a distance she could hear him and his driver talking.

"What are you planning to do with her, boss?"

"She's the reason we're going to San Miguel. Now get up there and drive, Carl."

"Are you sure you want to do this? I mean that's an awful long distance from here."

"Just do what I say, dammit."

"We can get the gold without her, you know," Carl said in

a coaxing tone. "Ray and I had them on the run, especially after that Apache attack we put on."

"Don't be stupid," Ebbert said with disgust in his voice. "She and that old man will never leave. Didn't matter what I offered, he wouldn't sell. Then he had the gall to threaten me! Well, I'll show him. With her, it'll *all* be mine."

"Ray said he thought we would split it with you."

"He did, did he?" Ebbert said, his voice steely, without a trace of emotion. Just the sound of those four words sent shivers through Emily. "Seems to me your brother thought a little too much."

"What are you doin'?" Carl asked, his nervous surprise evident to Emily even through her haze of pain.

"Too bad your brother Ray was so smart," Ebbert said, then added with a laugh, "Too bad for you, that is."

Emily flinched at the sound of the shot. Something hit the ground with a dull thud, and she could only assume it was Carl's body. Unbridled fear curled in her stomach. Dan Ebbert was a very dangerous man, much more dangerous than she'd ever imagined.

Rolling to one side, she tried to loosen the rope tied around her hands; her one thought was to get away. But the rope was too tight. She heard the sound of the body being dragged away from the carriage and shuddered to think what Dan must be up to.

She pushed herself as far away as possible from the open door. No sooner had she moved than Ebbert was at the opening looking in on her.

"Did you kill him?" Emily whispered, afraid to ask, but unable to stop.

"He doesn't matter. He's lost his value. You, on the other hand," Ebbert said, his eyes glowing the way they had in the parlor the day before, his excitement evident in the way he moved and in his tone of voice, "there's a lot I can do with you."

She could sense the thrill of violence running through his veins even as she was unable to believe he'd shot a man in cold blood.

"You can't think you'll get away with this!" she cried out. "When Zach finds out, he'll—"

Emily swallowed the rest of her words as he raised his arm again, poised to strike her a second time.

"Ah, I see you learn quickly, my dear," he crooned. "Too bad. I could enjoy teaching you how to behave. Most women do once they find out a man won't take any lip. You will be quiet now, won't you?"

Emily was able to nod her head, but the pain was still intense enough to keep her from moving it too quickly.

"I thought so." He smiled at her as if they were having tea together in the front parlor of the ranch. "Too bad you weren't as cooperative about the ranch," he said with a sigh of regret. "You just wouldn't go along with me, would you?"

Emily watched him through eyes filled with terror. She didn't know what he had in mind or to what lengths he might go. His utter calmness was more frightening than any ranting he could have done. Her heart was beating so hard she could barely make sense of what he was saying. His words floated in and out of her consciousness.

"That crazy old uncle . . . wouldn't sell, no . . . what I offered. If you'd sold it . . . none of this . . . happened, you know. You forced me . . . They all did."

He shoved her feet around so that she was propped up against the opposite door, then he sat down on the seat beside her. He sat quietly for a moment and Emily could only imagine what horrors he was considering. She was afraid to look at him, afraid to draw any more attention to herself. She trained her gaze on the maroon leather on the seat across from her and forced herself to breathe.

Then she felt his hand on her hair.

She tried to move her head away from him, but the way he'd tied her prevented her from moving more than a few inches in any direction. Her breath caught when he spoke, his voice low and confiding.

"The first time I saw you at church, I thought how sweet you'd be. You can't imagine the thoughts I was having there in Pastor Putney's front yard. What would he have said if he'd known? I really didn't want to upset him, though; he was such a help to me in gettin' the whole congregation riled up against you. And everything was goin' along fine until your foreman stepped in. Knew he was trouble from the first. Something about him . . . Well, he won't be able to stop me now."

She felt his hand move away from her hair, but before she could breathe a sigh of relief, he'd grabbed her chin and tilted her face toward him. "So sweet," he said musingly. He just stared at her for a moment, then asked, "Do you understand what I mean by sweet?"

Fearful anticipation coursed through her, weakening her limbs. She stayed silent, afraid of inciting him to further violence if she said the wrong thing.

Dan raised his other hand and traced her mouth with his fingers. Then, forcing her lips apart, he ran his finger against her tongue.

"See, I told you. Sweet," he reiterated as he touched his finger to his own lips.

Silence surrounded them, and Emily had to fight to remain calm. She wouldn't let herself think about what could happen next . . . she wouldn't. When she thought she might faint from the tension filling her, Ebbert's fingers left his mouth only to move to the back of her neck. The feel of his hand on her skin sent shivers of revulsion through her entire body. She wanted to shake him off, but she was too afraid. He'd just shot a man—a friend of his, by all accounts. What would he do to her if she resisted?

His fingers trailed down to her shoulder, then around to the front of her dress. One of the buttons had been ripped off in their struggle, and the bodice gaped open just above her breasts. He reached for that opening and laid his fingers on her bare skin, and for a moment she thought she would be sick.

At that instant the carriage lurched. His hand stopped its movement, resting on the upper slope of her breast. Slowly he pressed his fingers into her soft flesh, then slid his hand back out of her dress.

"Maybe this isn't the best time." He paused, then added, "We'll have all night, after all."

He leered at her, enjoying his superiority, then shoved a dirty piece of material into her mouth and jumped down to the ground. With careful attention, he closed and locked the door of the carriage behind him.

Zach was hungry for the sight of Emily. He'd left her only a short time ago, but already he missed her and wanted her with him. Frank had been right. When you found something as special as what he had with Emily, you didn't just throw it away.

He'd already met with the circuit judge and given him all the information he needed for the time being. The judge promised to have the sheriff investigate what had happened so there could be a speedy trial.

"Now what?" Frank asked.

"I don't know," Zach said. "The men claim the Hudson brothers hired them, but I can't believe they're behind all this. Neither Ray nor Carl is smart enough to pull off the things that have been going on at the ranch and not get caught. They'd be boasting all over town, and we'd have heard something about it."

"What should we do? We can't force them to tell what they don't know."

Though Zach wanted nothing more than to go back to the ranch and be with Emily, he forced himself to think about this latest problem. "My guess is that sooner or later whoever is behind everything will show his face. Someone that careful is sure to try to contact the two prisoners to make sure they don't talk. And when that time comes, we'll be there to see who it is."

"You want to take turns?" Frank asked. "That way one of us can get some rest while the other watches."

"Good idea. I'll take the first shift. You go get some sleep. You look even more tired than I feel. Besides, I sleep better when it's dark. You take the daylight."

"Thanks," Frank said with suitable sarcasm, but Zach noticed that the older man didn't fight him.

They left the jail, and Frank headed for the boardinghouse to get a room while Zach crossed the street to keep his vigil from a less conspicuous place. As he walked toward the mercantile, he saw Jewel and Eula heading in his direction. Why were they in town? Had something else happened on the ranch? He hurried to meet them.

"Ladies," Zach said, tipping his hat. "What brings you to town? Where's everyone else?"

"We know what he means by 'everyone else,' don't we, Eula?" Jewel looked coyly at him.

"Do we?" Eula replied in a teasing tone. "I just can't imagine who."

"Who what?" Billy asked, coming up beside Eula and putting his arm around her waist.

"Nothing," Zach said. He could feel himself beginning to

turn red. Obviously nothing was wrong or they wouldn't be carrying on like this. "Now, if one of you would tell me what store Emily's in, I'll go find her and we can see about getting some lunch."

The thought of seeing Emily sooner than he'd expected brought a rush of excitement to him. They had so much to say to each other, so much to work out; he couldn't wait to begin. He wanted to savor the comfort of her touch, to see the look of longing in her eyes—to know that she wanted to be with him the way he wanted to be with her.

"Emily's not in town," Eula told him. "She said she wanted to keep an eye on the eggs that were about to hatch, so she stayed at the ranch."

Zach turned to Billy and sent him a quelling look.

"She's not out there by herself," Billy said, defending himself. "Hank and Jess are with her, and Hank said he'd stay within hearing distance of the house while we were gone. I told her if there was any trouble to ring the bell, and Hank would come in."

"If you say so," Zach replied, but he was uneasy. Maybe it was just the disappointment of having to wait to see Emily. Billy was probably right; he was just being overly anxious. Still, the sooner he was back at the ranch the better. "I think maybe I'll head on out to the ranch right away."

"We're headin' back ourselves," Billy said. "We stopped off at the judge's to find you. He had some questions for us. Told 'im everything we know. Now we're plannin' on pickin' up Opal over at Bea's and then headin' back."

"I'll ride with you," Zach replied. "I just want to go to the boardinghouse and let Frank know. I'll meet you at the livery."

But before they could go their separate ways, Flora came running up to them. She looked at the others for just a minute as she caught her breath, then turned to Zach.

"I need to talk to you. Something's come up," she said haltingly.

Zach's pulse sped up. Whatever Flora had to say, Zach knew it had to be terribly urgent. They'd decided their arrangement would be kept in the utmost confidence, and only a major emergency would have her accosting him like this.

"What is it?" he asked.

"It's Lila. She's been beat up real bad. You said you wanted to know. I came as fast as I could."

Zach heard Jewel and Eula gasp, but his main concern now was to find out all Flora knew.

"When?"

"Early this morning."

"Did you talk with her?"

Flora nodded, then said, "She's in a lot of pain. Looks like whoever beat on her busted her nose and maybe her arm. There's also this real deep, ragged tear across her left cheek. Doc's havin' a devil of a time stitching it up."

A cold wave of certainty ran through Zach. This was what he'd been waiting for all these weeks, the break he'd longed for with desperate intensity. The jagged tear on Lila's left cheek was the sign. Only one man left that as his trademark, along with all the other hurts and bruises. Something clenched in the pit of Zach's stomach. He knew in his soul the identity of the man who had inflicted those wounds on Lila: Earl Darnell.

"Who did it?" Zach asked, though he already knew the answer.

"Lila says it was Dan Ebbert."

"Dan Ebbert? That can't be right." When Zach got this feeling, he was never wrong or at least he'd never . . . And then it hit him.

Now he knew why Dan Ebbert had seemed so familiar all along, why he'd had this strange, hostile feeling every time

he'd been around him. Dan Ebbert and Earl Darnell were
one and the same. If you lightened Ebbert's hair and shaved
off his beard, took away a few wrinkles and several pounds,
you had the one Darnell with whom he'd been obsessed
since the night of the fire, the one who had stood foremost in
Zach's mind. At last his enemy was within his reach.

All this time that bastard was right under his nose, living
almost next door and courting Emily.

Courting Emily.

The horror of it washed over Zach. That son of a bitch had
had his hands on Emily! That day in front of the church
passed in front of his eyes. He could still see Ebbert hovering over her, his lips pressed to the back of her hand. And
more recently he'd come to the ranch and scared her so.
Now Zach had yet another reason—if he needed any more
reasons—to see that Earl Darnell never took another breath.

Emily twisted, trying to loosen the ropes around her
wrists. She hadn't been able to free herself, though she'd
been trying for quite some time. Her wrists ached; the skin
around them was abraded so badly she could feel blood
seeping, but she didn't dare stop trying. She eased herself
back against the seat of the carriage to rest for a few minutes
before resuming her attempt.

She gagged again in reaction to the wad of material
stuffed in her mouth, then talked herself into regaining her
calm. She couldn't help herself if she let panic take over. She
had to think and plan, and somehow she would survive this.
The words became a litany every time the horror of her situation threatened to overwhelm her.

She'd been in the carriage for about three hours on roads
that had gotten steadily worse. She'd been thrown between
the seat and the door for most of the trip, and her arms felt as
if they had been pulled out of their sockets. When she could,

she focused on the watch pinned to the bodice of her dress, concentrating on the movement of the second hand.

As each minute ticked by, she'd count it off, trying to take her mind off the heat that was building up inside the small closed compartment. She wished now that she'd told Zach how much she loved him when she'd had the chance, that she wanted to spend the rest of her life with him. Now she wasn't sure she'd ever get to.

Perspiration covered her body, and her clothes were plastered against her. She had no doubt the temperature was well over one hundred degrees inside the shut compartment. She craved something cool to drink. She could see the juice Eula had sitting on the table in the kitchen. The condensation was slowly rolling down the sides of the glass. She could almost taste the tartness of the fruit on the tip of her tongue.

At that moment the carriage hit a rut in the road.

Why was she thinking about such things? She'd be better off thinking about what would happen at the end of this trip. She wasn't naive enough to believe Dan didn't have plans for her. The most obvious one made her skin crawl. Just thinking about him touching her made her stomach heave.

What had he mumbled when he'd first gotten into the carriage? She searched her mind. At the time, she'd been in too much pain to pay close attention. Now she used her pain to make her mind function, to piece together her fragmented memories and try to make sense of what was going on.

Dan had said he'd wanted to buy the ranch from Uncle Billy, but Billy had refused to sell. And gold had been mentioned. Dan had been very upset about not getting the ranch. Somehow he must have found gold on the property and decided he wanted to have it all to himself.

That made more and more sense to Emily as she remembered how often Dan had spoken discouragingly about her chances of success, how he'd offered to take the ranch off her hands until another buyer could be found. Now she suspected that he had no interest in another buyer; he simply wanted to be sure she never guessed why he wanted the ranch.

All she'd accomplished by taking him on a tour of the Double F and showing him her success was to make him more desperate. She recalled how often he'd hinted at unexpected problems that plagued ranchers, and she wondered if that was when he'd thought of his plans for scaring them off. When that didn't work, he'd tried courting her, again without success.

So what was he up to now? She made herself go over every word that had been said since he'd shown up at the ranch. And then she remembered Carl had said they were going to a place called San Miguel.

Emily had heard the town mentioned before. It was a small village inhabited mainly by Mexican peasants. They did a little farming and some prospecting—nothing that could help her in her quest to understand Ebbert's plans.

Just then the coach stopped and the door to the carriage flew open. She no longer had to speculate on Dan's plans. She was about to find out exactly what they were.

Zach knew the minute he got to the ranch that something was wrong. There was a strange feel to the place. When he saw the body lying by the porch, the coldness he'd felt before increased tenfold.

It was the body of a good-sized man, but that didn't relieve any of Zach's uneasiness.

"You ladies stay in the wagon," Zach commanded as he quickly dismounted. He pulled his gun from its holster and walked over to the body. With the tip of his boot, he pushed the body over onto its back. Then he heard a low moan.

"Billy, see if Emily's inside. Be sure to check the barn and storerooms, too," Zach yelled, sliding his gun back into its holster when he knew it was safe to do so.

"Recognize him?" Frank said as he came up alongside Zach.

"It's Carl Hudson, the one I told you I'd seen in town. He's still alive, but he doesn't look like he'll last too long."

He'd been shot in the back, Zach noticed, and knelt beside the body. There was a certain irony to coming upon one of the Hudsons shot in the back and left to die. It was what they'd done to him so many weeks ago, but Zach had no interest in irony. All he wanted was to find Emily. He leaned over the man. "Carl, can you hear me?"

"Ray, is that you?" Carl replied, his voice weak from the loss of blood. He didn't open his eyes.

Zach looked over at Frank who simply nodded.

"Yeah, it's me, Carl," Zach answered. "Who did this to you?"

"Shouldn't have trusted . . . didn't like . . . but you . . . said."

"Who, Carl? Who didn't you trust?"

"Didn't like . . . but you wanted . . . Ebbert's secret . . ."

Ebbert. The fear that had hovered in the back of Zach's mind since he'd entered the courtyard surged back through him.

"Emily's not inside," Billy said, running out onto the porch.

"I was afraid of that."

Visions sprang before Zach's eyes. Visions that now contained Emily instead of his sister. Zach closed his eyes and shook his head, trying to clear away the images. Then he turned back to Carl.

"Where'd Ebbert go, Carl? Where did he go?" The urgency in Zach's voice increased; he wanted to shake the man to make him talk, but realized that that would be of no use.

"San . . ." Carl began to say and then started to cough.

Zach lifted him up a little higher, and the coughing stopped.

"San what?" Zach prompted, desperate for his answer. He had to find Emily. He couldn't go through this again.

"Miguel," he whispered. "He shot me. . . . Ray . . . don't leave. . . . I'm . . ."

Carl's head rolled to one side, and blood ran out of the side of his mouth.

Zach lowered the body back to the ground and stood up. He looked over at Frank.

"San Miguel is about three hours away," Frank told him. "To the south."

"He's been lying here about an hour, I'd say, by the looks of the blood on the ground."

Frank nodded his agreement, just as Hank and Jess rode up.

"What happened?" Hank called out. "More trouble?"

"I thought we caught all them bastards or scared them away," Jess put in as they jumped off their mounts and ran up.

"We didn't catch the right one. Yet," Zach said. There was no point in getting mad at them. Like the others, they had assumed the ranch was safe now that most of the attackers had been rounded up or chased off. The important thing was to find Emily. He quickly explained the situation to the two men, then added, "Hank, I want you to head into town and find out what's happening there. See if you can find out anything about Ray Hudson."

Hank nodded, and Zach turned to Jess. "You stay here and look after the ladies. And bury him," Zach finished, nodding toward the body. "It's more than he did for his own."

Within minutes Zach, Frank, and Billy had everything they needed for the ride to San Miguel.

* * *

For the past half hour Emily had sat on a low wooden stool in the back room of a small adobe building. Her wrists were raw and aching from trying to loosen the heavy hemp rope Ebbert had used to tie her up, and her cheek burned where he'd struck her. At least he'd removed the gag from her mouth.

Ebbert had said nothing to her when he left her at the house. He knew no matter how much she talked or yelled, no one would help her. This was obviously his town. The locals had bowed and scraped when he arrived, not a one questioning him about the woman tied up with rope.

She'd heard him talking to several other men right after he left her in the room. They were speaking in English, but their voices were muffled so she couldn't understand what they were saying. From the sounds that reached her, though, she could tell they were joking and laughing, so she realized he hadn't been lying to Carl when he'd said he had friends in the small town.

Since then she'd been left alone with only her terrifying thoughts. The longer she waited in the small airless room, the more terrifying her thoughts became.

The door opened and Emily looked up with a start. A small, stooped Mexican woman came in carrying an earthen jug. She brought it to Emily without a word and held it up to her mouth. Water. Emily was so thirsty she didn't even mind its bitter flavor. All she wanted was something to wash away the taste of the gag.

After gulping down every last drop, she tried to ask the woman some questions, but the old lady rattled off something in Spanish and hurriedly left the room. It was apparent she'd been warned against talking to the gringa and feared the punishment for disobeying.

If only she could get her hands untied, Emily thought,

she'd have a better chance of getting away. Where she would go, she hadn't the slightest idea. She just wanted to get out of there.

The room seemed to float around her, closing in. She took a deep breath, and it settled down enough so that she could look around for something, anything, to aid her escape. She noticed a clay pot sitting in the corner. If she broke it and used the jagged edge, she might be able to cut the rope and free her hands.

Eagerly she stood up, but she felt herself sway and sat back down. The room was floating again, worse than before, and she was floating with it. How strange, she thought with a distant part of her mind. Everything was getting a little hazy. Then the room started getting darker and darker.

When she opened her eyes again, Dan Ebbert stood in front of her.

"Time to wake up, my sweet. The wedding is about to begin."

Emily tried to remember where she was. Groggily, she looked around the room. It was unfamiliar. And then it came back to her in a rush, but the room was no longer empty; Dan Ebbert and three other men stood before her.

How long had she been asleep? She couldn't remember anything past seeing the clay jug. She looked down and saw that her hands had been untied and the sleeves of her dress pulled down to cover her reddened wrists.

"Come, come. We don't want to keep the padre waiting after he's been kind enough to fit us into his schedule," he said, taking her by the arm and slipping his other arm around her waist.

The men standing behind him parted, and he steadied her as she walked out onto the dusty street.

Now that she was outside in the air, her mind was beginning to clear. She looked down the street and saw the church.

It came to her then what he intended. He planned to get control of the ranch by marrying her.

"No," she tried to yell, but her voice came out as a whisper.

She stopped walking, but Ebbert pulled her forward, allowing his hand to move up higher and brush the bottom of her breast. She slumped away from him, allowing him to think she was still under the influence of whatever drug he had given her. He shifted his hand lower to help support her, and she continued walking as slowly as she could.

She might have been moving slowly, but her mind was racing. What could she do? The three men accompanying them were obviously Dan Ebbert's hired hands. Not only would they be of no help, they'd make sure she did whatever Ebbert said.

She looked up and down the street, but there was no one else in sight. All the residents of the small town had apparently decided to stay out of Ebbert's way. But surely no minister would marry them, even under the kind of pressure Dan Ebbert exerted.

"See the church there at the end? That's where we'll take our wedding vows. I can hardly wait—especially for the favors that will come afterward," he said and then leaned down and pressed his lips to her cold ones.

She shook her head and wiped her mouth with the back of her hand, but he paid her little attention. He threw back his head and gave a demonic laugh. With a motion of his hand, the men moved off ahead of them and entered the church.

Minutes later they were back outside with a man dressed in a hand-woven brown cassock, his head covered by a hood. He wore a cross on a long leather thong hanging around his neck.

One of Ebbert's men had a gun pressed to his head.

"This is the man who'll soon marry us," Dan said, his eyes sparkling with good cheer.

The priest looked as terrified as she felt, and she knew in that instant that no one could save her—not she herself, not Zach, not anyone.

CHAPTER
14

Zach watched as they brought out the priest. His jaw clenched, and every muscle in his body pulled tight. From the shelter of a small hut next to the church, he'd seen Darnell bring Emily out of the house on the corner and parade her up the street to the steps of the tiny church. Frank had had to hold him back when Darnell leaned down and kissed her.

Never had he felt such hate. During the ride from the Double F, his only thoughts had been about Emily. He'd been so afraid for her. Not since the day his family was murdered had he suffered the churning emotions that raged through him right now—the helplessness and fear, the anguish and determination. And under it all lay a fury so overwhelming he could hardly think. But think he must.

"Any ideas, Frank? Billy?" Zach asked over his shoulder.

"We might have a better chance after they go inside the church," Frank said in a hushed voice. Billy nodded behind him.

"I think you're right," Zach answered in a whisper and motioned him and Billy out the back door. "And I know just the way to do it."

* * *

Emily glanced around the church, hardly daring to believe the immorality of the men who had kidnapped her. They knew no honor, for they were even willing to desecrate the sanctity of a church. Her hands were clammy and her heart was beating frantically. They'd been in the church about ten minutes, and she'd spent the entire time searching for a way to escape.

A part of her felt this couldn't be happening, that it was all some horrible nightmare from which she would wake, sweaty and out of breath, but safe. Another part of her realized this was all too real. Her legs had turned rubbery long ago, and her head throbbed from the aftereffects of the sleeping drug and the blow from Dan Ebbert. Even if she managed to find a hiding place, she wasn't sure she was steady enough on her feet to make a run for it.

Worst of all was having to handle the volatile man beside her. Ebbert bore no resemblance to the man she'd met in the churchyard in what now seemed like another lifetime ago. His eyes glittered like those of a madman, and he alternated between impatiently yelling at his friends and looking at her as if she were a luscious dessert and he a starving man. The thought of him touching her intimately and trying to take his pleasure nearly robbed her of all breath, making her light-headed.

She swayed, and Dan pushed her into the front pew.

"Sit here before you faint on me. I've had it with things going wrong," he snarled. "Now I'm going to do things my way."

He looked toward the door near the altar. "Isn't that priest ready yet?" he shouted.

"He said he had to change into his wedding clothes," the man named Slim called out from near the sacristy.

"Well, how long does that take?"

Slim just shrugged his shoulders.

"Bang on that door and tell him to hurry. I can't wait much longer. I'm getting impatient to sample the wedding night delights." He sent Slim a man-to-man grin filled with lustful meaning.

Slim gave Emily an assessing look, as if he were trying to guess what she looked like without any clothes on. She looked back at him haughtily, refusing to let him see how intimidated she felt. A shiver ran through her, and she had to bite her lips to keep her teeth from chattering.

There had to be something she could do, but what? If Dan thought she would willingly go with him to the marriage bed, he'd better think again. She promised herself that, one way or another, she would find a way to evade him before that moment came. Once again she thought of Zach, of how she had to survive so she could get back to him. The thought calmed her and gave her strength; it was almost as though he were by her side.

Then she looked up and saw the priest walking out of the sacristy followed by two other celebrants carrying a chalice and a censer. All three wore hooded white cassocks, over which were surplices embroidered with intricate Spanish designs. Their faces were entirely hidden within the folds of their hoods.

Desperately Emily looked around the empty sanctuary, but there was no source of help, no way out. She wanted the life back she'd had last night, lying in Zach's arms. She wanted him to feel her love and to know that love was returned. What was happening now couldn't be true. It couldn't.

But it was. At that moment Ebbert grabbed her arm and pulled her toward the altar where the three clergy were praying, apparently saying the blessings in preparation for the ceremony.

"Smile, my sweet," Ebbert said. "This is supposed to be your happiest day."

She pulled away from him and stumbled on the three steps leading to the altar. Tripping over her blue gabardine skirt, she fell at the feet of the head priest.

First she saw his robes and then his hand as he offered to help her up from her sprawled position on the floor. And finally she saw his boots. Something was wrong, she realized. She looked more closely as her heart raced.

She raised her head and nearly fell again. For in place of the priest she'd seen out in the street, she was looking into the blue eyes of her own uncle Billy. He winked and then stepped back to his original position. She wanted to cry out with joy, but she knew she still wasn't out of danger. There were four burly men against her and Uncle Billy—not exactly even odds. But the sense of relief was paramount.

She took a deep breath and slowly climbed to her feet. Pulling her dirty navy blue shirtwaist down into place, she walked up the final steps and stood in front of the altar beside Dan Ebbert. At least now she had a chance, a real chance.

When Uncle Billy started speaking in Spanish, Emily heard Ebbert mumble something to one of his men. Interrupting the service, the man spoke to Uncle Billy in Spanish, and Billy replied, shaking his head.

"He says he doesn't speak English," the man told Ebbert.

"Damned foreigners. They should learn to speak like the rest of us," Dan said in a disgruntled tone. "Tell him to go ahead."

Just when Uncle Billy started speaking again, there was a commotion in the back of the church. Suddenly a goat was running up the center aisle.

When Ebbert's men turned to catch the animal, Emily heard one of the celebrants shout out, "Now," in a familiar voice, and then she was grabbed by the shoulders and pulled away from Dan Ebbert and the altar.

This time her heart actually stopped beating for an instant. She knew that touch, would have known it in the darkest night, in the blackest cave. Zach!

With his free hand Zach pushed back the hood of his cassock. He looked down at Emily and gave a brief prayer of thanks before pulling her into his embrace.

"Are you all right?" he asked. She nodded and relief flowed through him. He reached out to touch the bruise on her face, then stopped, knowing how painful it must be. A dark and terrible rage filled him at the thought of Earl Darnell daring to touch her, let alone inflict this kind of injury. "Are you sure you weren't hurt?" he asked again, his voice hoarse.

"He didn't hurt me that way," she answered, understanding the unspoken question. "I was lucky. He didn't want to waste any time marrying me; otherwise . . ." He could feel the tremors that shook her as they both contemplated what might have happened if he hadn't caught up with Earl so quickly.

Around them the fight raged, and Zach knew they hadn't won yet. "Stay here out of harm's way, and . . ." He hesitated, too filled with emotion to continue for a second. Finally he said, "And next time *please* come to town with everyone else."

She gave him a tremulous smile, and he knew in that instant that she really was all right, not just putting on a show for him. He gave her a quick kiss, then raced down the steps and leaped onto the back of a man who was about to hit Billy with the censer. He knocked the man to the floor and then hit him a second time, making sure he wouldn't get up again.

Zach double-checked to make sure the man was truly out, and then looked around the sanctuary. Frank was tying up

the hands of one of Darnell's men, while Billy was strad-
dling the third one and waiting for Frank to bring over the
rope.

Zach looked under the pews and elsewhere but found no
trace of Darnell, only the goat, which had found a new home
in a saint's alcove.

"Where'd he go?" Zach called out when he couldn't find
Earl anywhere.

Both Frank and Billy looked around, but the man passing
himself off as Dan Ebbert was nowhere in sight.

"He went out that door and headed up the street," Emily
told him and pointed to the side door, which was now standing wide open.

Without a backward glance, Zach ran for the door. He
couldn't let Earl escape after getting this close, after seeing
him face to face and knowing he was as evil as ever. Although Emily had said she was all right, he knew what
Darnell could be like and knew that Emily must have been
scared out of her wits.

As Zach ran, all he could see was Darnell as he used to
be—younger, slimmer, his hair fuller and lighter. In those
days he'd had no beard, probably hadn't needed to shave
more than a couple times a week. No wonder Zach hadn't
recognized him. With the changes time and artifice had
wrought, his identity as Earl Darnell had been almost completely obliterated unless you knew what to look for.

And now Zach did, not that it mattered. He wasn't going
to let the man escape this town. One way or the other, Earl
Darnell had reached the end of the line. Zach headed for the
stable where he, Frank, and Billy had discovered Darnell's
carriage. If Darnell wanted to get out of town, he'd need a
horse, and where better to find one?

Zach drew his gun, then quietly opened the side door and
slid inside, allowing the door to close noiselessly behind

him. The interior was dim, but Zach managed to find his way over to a stall. He searched the immediate area, but Darnell was nowhere in sight.

Zach set his back against the wall and waited for the other man to make his move. Everything in him demanded he get Earl Darnell. It was what he had worked for his entire life, and now it was only minutes away. The others he'd wanted, but not like Earl. Earl had been the one. The one who . . .

He heard a faint noise, the barest whisper of a sound. He stood away from the wall, gun in hand, alert and ready. He heard the sound again, closer this time. And then Earl Darnell dropped on him from above, where he'd been hiding in the loft. He clipped Zach on the side of the head, then scrambled for Zach's gun. Zach resisted and they exchanged blows, each fighting for supremacy. Though Zach had the advantage in height and reach, Darnell had surprise and greater bulk on his side. On top of that, Zach felt dizzy from the blow to his head. After a few moments of struggling, Earl managed to pin Zach against the stall, his gun arm stretched out, the gun pointing uselessly toward the far wall.

"Couldn't just leave, could you?" Darnell huffed between deep, gasping breaths. "You're not stupid. You knew someone wanted that ranch, but you just wouldn't leave."

"Where'd you want me to go, Darnell?"

Darnell nodded his head at the use of his real name. "So you know me, do you?"

"Like my father, I don't like to be run off what's mine."

"This ranch wasn't yours, so why'd you care?"

"I just don't like to see people getting pushed around."

Zach made use of the conversation to get his breath back and to get over that dizzy feeling. But if he waited too long, the older man would also catch his breath. Choosing his moment, he gave a shove and caught Darnell unprepared.

Earl stumbled back a step, but before Zach could coordinate his movements, Earl grabbed a pitchfork and managed to knock the gun out of his hand with a sharp blow to the wrist. He quickly turned the pitchfork so its tines pointed at Zach.

"So we've met before, have we? I always knew there was someone after me," Darnell said, keeping the pitchfork out of Zach's reach, feinting a couple of times in an attempt to catch him off guard. Zach kept his eyes on Earl, watching his every move. His life depended on it. His gun lay on the floor, buried in hay, too far away to be of any use. "Too bad I didn't take care of things better the last time. I won't make that mistake again."

Earl's eyes glittered with fiendish intensity as he feinted with the pitchfork, moving to the left, then reversing to strike with all his strength on the right. But Zach anticipated him and jumped out of the way, then grabbed the handle of the pitchfork and jerked quickly, wrenching it out of Darnell's grasp.

Darnell surged forward, and Zach dropped the pitchfork to grab him around the waist and wrestle him to the floor. Earl fought dirty, going so far as to grab a handful of dirt and hay and throw it at Zach's face. Zach ducked and avoided the worst of it, but enough grit got into his eyes to be painful. Earl used that moment to pull free. Zach lunged after him, grabbed his ankle, and yanked him back. Darnell kicked out viciously with his other foot, aiming for Zach's face but hitting only his upraised arm. Then Zach launched himself head first into Earl's belly, knocking him down.

They rolled over and over across the hay-scattered floor until Zach gained the advantage, ending up on top with his hands around Darnell's neck. He did not squeeze hard enough to kill him, but he came close. Just the slightest bit tighter and . . .

"You lousy son of a bitch," Zach ground out, his jaw

clenched as he looked down into the eyes of the man who'd helped kill his family. "Day and night for twenty years I've dreamed of this. I hunted you in six states, but you always managed to slip away."

Darnell didn't say a word. He spent his energy trying to gulp as much air as he could while he clawed at Zach's hands, desperate to dislodge him. But Zach was past feeling pain, he was lost in a netherworld between memory and reality.

He looked at Dan Ebbert but saw Earl Darnell's face as it had been long ago. The smoke was all around him, and every breath he took was an agony. The back of the house was burning now, and so was the side. His mother came running out of the rear room, blinded by smoke and headed for the front door. As she pulled the door open to get a breath of fresh air, a single shot rang out. The impact threw her back into the room where she lay sprawled on the floor, a red stain growing on her chest.

Zach ran to her, but it was too late. When his father tried to pull him away, a volley of shots came through the doorway, killing him, too. Zach grabbed a handful of bullets and his own pistol and fired back, uncaring of his own safety. All he wanted was to take as many of the attackers with him as he could.

It was a futile wish. Within seconds the burning building groaned and a roof beam crashed to the floor, bringing the red hot fire with it.

"Papa, Mama, help!" his sister Becky screamed as she ran into the front room, the back of her dress in flames. Zach tackled her, knocked her to the floor, and tried to smother the fire. He managed to beat out the flames, impervious to the burns on his hands, but the house groaned again, and before he could react, another timber fell to the floor, giving him a glancing blow to the head. Everything turned black.

The next thing he remembered was James Darnell's voice cutting across his consciousness.

"Get a move on, Earl. We don't have time for this," he'd said.

Zach had no idea who Earl was. He moved his head slightly, ignoring the pain, fighting the dizziness, desperate to find Becky. But all he saw through the open door was Earl Darnell's face, the same face that now lay before him.

"I'm near done here," Earl had said before he shimmied up his pants. "You want a turn?"

"Nah. I want to get out of here before anyone gets too curious. I can have my fun in town. Now get moving."

Earl got to his feet and adjusted his pants, then kicked aside something on the porch floor and walked down the steps into the yard.

When Zach turned his head a little farther to see what Earl had kicked aside, all he saw was a fragment of Becky's skirt blowing in the evening breeze. . . .

"Why?" he asked now, with the same desperation he'd felt that night. "For the land?"

The man beneath him had no breath to answer as Zach's hands tightened on his neck. But deep inside, Zach knew the truth.

"You're not happy unless you're killing, are you? Well, now there'll be a killing, all right, but you won't be doing it. You're finally going to pay for everything you've done and everything you've even thought of doing. There won't be any more ranches to take over, any more people to kill or burn out. And you'll never rape another woman like you raped my sister, you bastard. You'll never be able to touch Emily," Zach cried, tears flowing down his face. "Never. *Never!*"

A rattling sound started in Darnell's throat, but Zach didn't hear it, nor would he have cared if he had. He was too caught up in the agonies of the past, in the desperate longing for revenge that had directed his life for nearly twenty years. Earl was everything that was evil, and he hadn't changed one bit. He didn't deserve to live, to be able to spread his poison and ruin more and more lives.

But Zach was not so intent on his goal that he didn't hear a familiar voice.

"Zach!" Emily begged. "Zach, you mustn't. You have to stop. Please."

"She's right, my friend," Frank said in a calm voice and laid his hand on Zach's shoulder. "He's not worth it."

Zach wanted to ignore them, to squeeze just that little bit tighter and crush the man's windpipe, to know that the world was rid of Earl Darnell once and for all. But something stopped him, something inside that made him listen, that let Emily's voice penetrate the images in his head and reach the very core of him.

"Zach, please, your parents wouldn't want you to do this," she was saying between sobs. "Neither would your sister. Let him up and allow Frank to take care of him. Please, for me."

He wanted to explain it to her, to make her understand that he couldn't stop now. He'd waited too long for this moment, much too long. It was all he'd ever wanted . . . wasn't it? He shook his head to clear his thoughts. He needed . . . What did he need?

Emily. He needed Emily, not Darnell or anything else. Only Emily. Slowly he released his grip on Darnell's neck.

They made a pair, the two of them both bruised and filthy, their clothes torn and ragged. Yet she'd never seen a more welcome sight in her life than his bruised and battered face, Emily thought as they walked arm and arm into the board-inghouse. This was all she'd ever wanted, to have the man she loved by her side, to know in her deepest being that there was a future for them. All she had to do was convince Zach. But this wasn't the right moment.

First he had to heal, to put the past behind him, to know that Earl Darnell was getting the punishment he deserved. Then Zach would be able to look forward, and for the first time in his life he would have choices. She could only pray that he would choose her.

They had tied Dan Ebbert and his cohorts to their horses and led them back to Bethel Springs. By the time they arrived, it was late at night. The only person at the jail was the deputy. They woke the circuit judge, who was still in town, and he ordered the prisoners held in jail until the next day.

Zach had been unusually silent, letting Frank do the talking. Then they'd been too exhausted to return to the ranch house.

"Stay in town tonight," Frank had said. "I'll head back to the Double F and check on the others. In the morning, I'll bring in your clothes and things. Jewel and Eula will pack some things for you, Miss Emily," he added with a slight reddening of his face.

Back east, Emily would have been appalled at the thought of staying at a hotel without any luggage, and she would never have considered going in with a single man. It was a sign of how well she'd adjusted to the freer spirit of her new home that she merely nodded and thanked Frank for his thoughtfulness.

"I got two rooms on the top floor, if that's all right," said Mrs. Stratton, the boardinghouse owner, with a huge yawn. She didn't seem at all surprised at being wakened in the middle of the night to check in new boarders, even scruffy boarders.

Zach nodded, and she pushed the keys across the table toward him.

"Breakfast's included," she told them. "Table's set at seven." Then she turned around on another sleepy yawn and went through the door leading to her private quarters. "Everything you need is in the rooms—sheets, towels and such," she said before the door shut behind her.

Emily looked up at Zach, intending to give him a quick smile. The smile died when she saw the deep grooves etched by fatigue on either side of his mouth. His eyes also looked weary and a little vulnerable, as if he'd lost his bearings for a while and didn't know quite what to do next. And in a way, he had, Emily realized. His whole life had been directed at one goal: finding Earl Darnell and making sure he was punished for his sins. Now Zach had all but accomplished that goal.

Had he ever given thought to what lay beyond? Had he ever had the dreams most people had or allowed himself the luxury of needs and desires? Emily thought not, or if he had, he had hidden those wishes deep inside, seeing them as a betrayal of his promise to his family.

"Come on," she said softly. "Let's go upstairs. I've got the keys."

She put her arm around his waist, and like a sleepwalker, he let her lead him to the staircase. As they climbed, she felt his arm creep around her and she couldn't resist snuggling against him.

They reached the first room, and Emily unlocked the door. The small chamber was tucked under the eaves and looked warm and welcoming despite its size. In the center was a comfortable-looking four-poster bed. Emily didn't even bother checking the second room. She knew where they were going to spend the night.

"Sit here and take off your boots," she ordered Zach, then bent to light the fire. As soon as she was satisfied that the fire would catch, she turned back to the room. Zach was just sitting there in the half-light, unmoving.

"Do you want a drink?" she asked.

He looked at her with a kind of open vulnerability she'd never seen in him before. She came to his side and sat down with him on the bed, then reached for his hand. But he pulled it out of her grasp.

"You shouldn't be touching me," he said in a voice that seemed to come from his very soul.

She looked up into his eyes. "Why not?" she asked, worried about the strain on his face. Why was he so upset now? The worst was behind him.

"I nearly killed a man today," he replied, his tone raw as he looked down at his hands, turning them over and back so he could inspect both their tops and palms, as if he couldn't believe what he'd nearly done.

She grabbed his hands, then held on tight when he would have withdrawn. "But you didn't," she reminded him fiercely. "Do you think he would have done the same for you if he'd had the chance?"

"No," Zach admitted, "but—"

"There is no 'but.' You're a good man, Zach Hollis, the best I've ever known and we've both had a terrible day. Don't think of it another minute. Tomorrow morning, when it's daylight, you'll look back and see that you did the right thing. Right now you're torturing yourself for no reason. Dan Ebbert or Earl Darnell, or whatever he chooses to call himself, should be feeling like this. Not you."

He looked at her and she could see the aching longing. He wanted to believe her with everything inside him.

"Come on," she said firmly. "Let's go to bed."

Without waiting for permission, she began undressing him, helping him ease off his boots, then unbuttoning his shirt. He let her care for him, much like a sleepy child with a parent. As soon as he was in his undershirt and long johns, she stripped off her own clothes. She knew she would never wear them again, even if Eula washed them clean and pressed out every wrinkle. She let them drop to the floor and crawled into the bed next to Zach, clad only in her chemise.

"You shouldn't be here, Emily," he said wearily. "You don't know what you're doing."

"Now, Zach, you've said that to me from the day we met, and you haven't been right yet," she answered, keeping her voice light.

In the light from the fireplace, half his face was illuminated, the other half dark. He reminded her of the Roman god Janus, one face looking forward, one face looking back; one face in the dark of the past, the other in the light of the future. She remembered then that Janus was the god of new beginnings, of *good* beginnings. That thought gave her the courage to reach out with one hand and cup his chin, to turn his face in her direction, fully into the light, fully into the future.

"I'm almost exactly where I want to be," she murmured. She saw the look of hope kindle in his eyes.

"Are you?" he whispered.

She nodded, and as he raised his hand to stroke her hair, she leaned forward and touched her lips to his. She held her breath as her mouth gently worked over his, waiting for his response, aching for it. She didn't have to wait long. As her lips stroked his, his mouth opened to receive her and his hand threaded through her hair, holding her tightly against him as he ravished her, leaving no corner of her mouth unexplored.

He maneuvered his free arm beneath her, then brought her to lie on top of him, her length along his own. She could feel his every breath, his heart beating beneath hers, his body warmer than the fire, heating her from the inside out. She moaned her pleasure as the kiss deepened and his hands stroked her body, lifting her chemise higher with each pass. And then his fingers were against her skin, tracing the valley of her spine, smoothing over her shoulders and down past her ribs to her bottom and back again, hypnotizing her as her bones turned to liquid and her insides melted.

Feverishly she began unbuttoning his undershirt. At last she could touch him, but it still wasn't what she wanted. She struggled with his shirt until he broke their kiss and quickly pulled the shirt off. Without waiting for her, he undid the buttons on his long johns and slid them off as well. Then, after turning to her, he removed her chemise.

Then his lips were on hers again, and she felt the smoothness of his skin against her body. He rolled her onto her back and came down on top of her, one leg between hers. She felt the different textures of him, the roughness of the hair on his legs, the warmth and dark maleness of his mouth, the strength in his arms as they took the brunt of his weight.

"Now I'm *exactly* where I want to be," she said, her voice husky with desire.

He raised his head and looked into her eyes, smoothing her hair back from her face with his hands.

"Are you sure?" he asked her, his expression as serious as she'd ever seen it. "There's no going back from this, Emily, not anymore. I won't be able to let you go if we make love. I tried before, and it didn't work. I know I don't deserve you, but I can't seem to help myself. If you have any doubts, any at all, now's the time—"

"I love you, Zach," she said, interrupting him. She cradled his face in her hands. "I've been wanting to tell you for the longest time. I promised myself, when Earl Darnell had me, that if I got away, I'd tell you first thing. That was what scared me the most—thinking that if something happened to me, you'd never know, that I'd have missed the chance to tell you."

"But that was before—"

"Hush." She put one hand over his mouth. "There is no before. I love you, Zach Hollis, just the way you are, knowing everything I know about you. Walking away from Earl Darnell was probably the hardest thing you've ever had to do, but you did it, Zach. I've never known a stronger man. That's part of what I love about you. Don't you see, Zach? I can trust you and know you'll always do the best you can. Not many men are like that. I know. I was married to a weak man."

"Can you tell me about it?" he asked. "I want to know everything about you, Emily Crabtree. Everything."

"I'll tell you everything tomorrow. Right now let's put the past away and take this moment for ourselves."

Zach understood her need and nodded his head. Tomorrow would be soon enough.

He lowered his mouth to hers, and she wrapped her arms around his shoulders. She tasted of life, of promise, of everything he'd ever dreamed of. Her skin was softer than satin beneath his fingertips, and with every kiss, every touch, every sweet caress, she let him know how much she wanted him. Him! He couldn't believe it, and he couldn't resist her siren song. Desire burned in him like a wildfire raging out of control. He'd almost lost her, and to his worst enemy. Somehow, though, he hadn't. The miracle had occurred, and here she was, in his arms, in his life, loving him as he loved her.

The words tumbled out of him. "Oh, God, how I love you, Emily."

He didn't wait to hear her response. He needed to taste her again, to feel her beneath him, to reaffirm life and love and everything good. For the first time in his life, his mind's eye saw more than revenge; it saw possibilities unbounded.

Anything he wanted could now be his; he could go anywhere, live where he pleased, wander or settle down. The
choices were his to make. But there was only one place he
wanted to be, one choice he wanted to make, and with a single thrust, he went home, sinking into Emily as far as he
could, sharing his very essence with her, knowing she was
his future, his life.

He felt her tighten beneath him, sensed the waves of pleasure that made her muscles tighten rhythmically, and felt his
own climax match hers. And still it didn't end, the feeling
that this was where he belonged, that this was the home that
would welcome him no matter what. This was the place
where he belonged forever—by Emily's side.

CHAPTER
15

Emily and Zach left the sheriff's office, followed by Billy and Eula. Emily watched Zach shake his head, as if it would somehow put the world back to rights. He'd been doing that since the judge had made his decision.

"What are you going to do?" Emily asked him.

The decision he had to make wouldn't be an easy one, she knew, after all that lay between him and Earl Darnell.

"I still can't believe it," Zach said, looking around at the others.

"Dammit, boy, you deserve it and more," Billy put in. "That judge knew what he was doing when he gave you Ebbert's—uh, Darnell's spread. What'd he call it? Restitution. That means getting what you deserve as payment for what happened to you and your family. Take it and don't look back," Billy advised as they stood in front of the sheriff's office.

"The judge knew it couldn't make up for everything you've been through, but he figured it would be a start to a new life," Emily said quietly. "That is, if you think you can handle living there. Do you want to?"

For a moment Zach didn't speak; he only looked deep into

her eyes. "As long as we'll be making a new life together, that's all that matters."

Leaning over, he kissed Emily on the lips, sealing his words with a promise of love. Her heart filled, and she knew she'd never been as happy as she was this very minute.

"Guess that leaves you and me, Eula. Think you could settle here with someone like me?" Billy asked, a gleam in his eye.

"Oh, Billy, how could you even ask a silly question like that? You know how I feel about you, but you also know I'm not free," Eula said, looking uncomfortable about alluding to her husband with others around.

"Eula, I should have told you this before, but"—Billy stopped speaking and cleared his throat—"for the last two months I've been tracking your husband. Had a friend of mine doing most of the hunting. Got a telegram last week, but just didn't know how to tell you."

"The best way is straight out, Billy," Eula said, straightening her shoulders as if ready to take on a heavy burden.

Billy looked over at Emily, and she nodded. Billy had told her only this morning what he'd learned about Eula's husband, and she had urged him to tell Eula as quickly as possible.

"He met with an accident in Kansas City, a fatal one," Billy told her and then waited.

"How'd it happen?"

"Seems he tried to pull a deal with the wrong man and got a bullet for his efforts." As Billy finished speaking, he put his arm around Eula's shoulders, offering her any support she might need.

"I'm all right," she said, patting his hand. "I lost whatever feeling I had for Howard a long time ago. It's just sad, you know. He didn't have to go that way."

"Maybe I should wait a decent amount of time before I

say this, but I'm asking you right here and now. Eula Smith, will you be my wife?"

Eula's face flooded with color, but she nodded in the affirmative.

Billy grinned and kissed her on the cheek. "We'd better tell the judge we'll be needing his services."

"The judge said he'd be glad to marry anyone who asked," Emily said, smiling up at Zach.

Zach had asked the judge to marry them this afternoon, promising Emily a church wedding when they found a minister to their liking. After all that had happened, Emily felt Reverend Putney wasn't the right choice.

Just as they were heading up to Bea's to tell Opal, Jewel, and Frank the good news, they were confronted by a large group of people.

"Mr. Hollis?" one of the men called out. Emily remembered him as the man who'd done the talking out at the ranch once before. "Maybe you remember me. I'm Sam Dawson. We'd like a word with you, if you can spare the time."

Zach nodded, tensing. They didn't look angry, but who could tell? Best to hear them out and then decide what to do.

"As you know, the sheriff ran off after we found out he'd been in cahoots with Dan Ebbert. Also looks like the sheriff was the one who killed that Ray Hudson. Someone heard them having an argument about who was in charge. Anyway, now that we're without a sheriff, folks hereabouts were thinkin' you might be interested in the job."

A few people in the crowd called out their approval, one voice in particular louder than the others.

"Sure would like to see someone like yourself in that position, Mr. Hollis," Jed Danner called out. "We need someone respectable in that job."

"That's right," another man called out. "Someone we all look up to."

Zach felt his heart fill to bursting. He'd thought earlier
that he would never be happier than he was with Emily by
his side, but now he knew there was one more thing he
needed. His whole life he'd been looking for something,
never sure what it was, but always knowing he hadn't found
it. For most of his life he'd thought it was Earl Darnell. Now
he knew differently.

What he'd been searching for was what his father had had:
a loving family and the respect of his neighbors and friends,
the knowledge that he belonged. That was what it had been
all along, something that most men took for granted, something Zach had never had.

"This is quite an honor. I can't tell you what it means to
me that you've asked, but I'm afraid I have to decline."

The crowd grew silent. Then murmurs of disappointment
began rippling through the group.

"You see, Emily and I will be married this afternoon, and
our lives will be going in another direction."

In the crowd there were murmurs of approval, but some
were still disappointed.

Then Zach thought of something. "If you'll take my recommendation, I think I know someone who would be perfect
for the job."

The crowd stood silent waiting for his suggestion.

"Most of you know my friend, Frank Ross, and the way
he's worked on getting Earl Darnell to the proper authorities.
Well, you see, he did all that because he's a U.S. marshal.
And I know for a fact that he's thinking about retiring. An
offer of the sheriff's job might be all the persuasion he needs
to settle down right here."

A murmur rose from the crowd as they argued over what
to do next, some still hoping to convince Zach, others resigned to the fact that he had other, more important plans.
Zach wasn't sure what they would decide, though he was

flattered that so many of them persisted in thinking he was the best man for the job.

Then a new voice broke in, hushing the crowd.

"I wholeheartedly support Mr. Hollis's recommendation."

Zach turned and saw Mr. Putney pushing his way forward from the back of the crowd.

What was he doing here? Zach didn't like it one bit. He wasn't going to tolerate a single negative word said against Emily. He stepped forward protectively, ready to do battle if need be.

As if sensing Zach's hostility, Putney held up one hand, palm out, and said, "First, let me apologize, to you and to the members of my congregation. I want you all to know how wrong I was when I spoke out against the folks at the Double F."

Putney moved farther to the front and climbed up on the seat of a nearby wagon. He held his hands up for silence as the people began to talk among themselves.

"I truly believe that I was led astray by Satan in the earthly form of Dan Ebbert. I know I've done wrong, not only against you and Miz Crabtree," he said, looking over his shoulder at Zach and Emily, "but also to the members of my flock. I haven't been a good shepherd, and for that I'll be eternally sorry. I've asked the forgiveness of my Lord, and I'm hoping that you'll forgive me, too."

Zach knew he wasn't the one who'd borne the brunt of the reverend's tongue. Emily would have to answer his plea. If he knew Emily, she'd forgive him and probably make him take an ostrich chick himself to see how harmless they were.

"As you said, Mr. Putney, it's the Lord who forgives and hears our prayers. I'm lucky enough to have had mine answered just today," Emily said, sending Zach a warm, loving look. "We'd be pleased if you'd do us the honor of helping the judge officiate at our wedding this afternoon."

"Ladies, I think we have our work cut out for us," Putney declared. "We have a wedding to plan, and our church is the only place for it."

Emily looked out over the paddock to the mountains in the west. She had slipped out of the house for a few minutes of quiet. After the wedding everyone had come to the Double F, bringing all they needed for a festive wedding supper. She'd loved every minute of it, but now she wanted a few minutes on her own. She'd never expected to be this happy in her life. Zach was loving and caring, and more wonderful than she'd ever hoped for.

The wedding had been beautiful. Bea had provided her with the perfect dress, Billy had walked her down the aisle, and Opal, Jewel, and Eula had stood beside her as she and Zach exchanged their vows. Frank had even been persuaded to put on a suit and serve as best man. Nothing could have made her happier.

"Could you use some company, Mrs. Hollis?" Zach whispered from behind her.

"From you, always," Emily replied as he put his arms around her and pulled her close. How she liked the sound of her new name, Emily Hollis.

"I brought more than just me," he said and nodded for her to look behind him.

Emily laughed as she saw who'd followed him.

"Baby looks none the worse for wear," Zach commented, nestling his chin in her hair.

Emily nodded. "I thought for sure Dan Ebbert had killed her. She sort of crumpled, and then when she didn't move. . . ."

Emily could feel tears start to well up in her eyes. The memories of that day still had the power to overwhelm her. To think she'd come so close to losing all this.

Zach squeezed her and, reading her mind, said, "It all worked out, Em. Even Baby's fine, and not only that, she has a new little friend."

Emily looked down at the tiny ostrich that followed right behind Baby, imitating her every move.

"Isn't he sweet?" she crooned. "Jewel's already named him Shadow, since he's always following someone around."

Emily knelt beside the infant bird, then pulled Zach down beside her.

"Feel that," she said as she ran her hand over the back of the baby bird. "He feels more like a little pin cushion than a bird, with these spiky little feathers."

The brownish yellow bird looked like a medium-sized chicken except for its funny feet with their two toes, one so much larger than the other.

"How do you know it's a he?" Zach asked, looking skeptically at the bird.

Emily laughed. "I don't, really. I just get this feeling . . ."

Her voice trailed off at the look in his eyes. "I get this feeling, too," he said and leaned over to kiss her.

She forgot all about Baby and Shadow as she let herself go in the pleasure of his kiss, the feel of his lips against hers, the touch of his hands on her shoulders, the tug of his fingers in her hair.

With a start, she realized Zach didn't have that many hands.

"What?" she sputtered. "Baby!"

But it was too late. Baby had snatched her new silver comb right out of her hair and taken off.

"Do you want me to go after her?" Zach asked with a grin as he helped her back onto her feet.

Emily watched the bird run out into the desert, the way it had the very first time she'd met Zach. She smiled at the memory. Catching Zach's eye, she knew he was remembering the very same thing.

"No, I guess if she really wants it, she can have it. After all, I've got an even better treasure right here."

She raised her face for a kiss, and Zach complied, his arms closing around her as he brought her firmly into his embrace. After a while Shadow peeped and began pecking at her shoe. Emily leaned down and picked up the bird.

"Will you be able to leave all this behind?" Zach asked, looking over her shoulder at the ostrich.

Emily nodded, but she wasn't as sure as she pretended to be. When the chick had first peeped at her and then hatched, she had felt something she'd never felt before.

"I've been giving it all some thought, and I have an idea," Zach said as he brushed his hand over the baby ostrich's back.

"You're full of ideas today—from our wedding to the new house to getting Frank the job of sheriff, which he's very happy about, by the way, as is Jewel. I think the two of them are ready to settle down, too. So what's your newest idea?"

"I've been thinking there's no reason why we can't hatch the eggs at our new place. There's plenty of room. All we need is the incubator. If you want to, we can handle that end of the operation, then bring the chicks back here when they're a little older, for Eula and Billy to raise. How's that sound?"

Emily smiled at him. Zach knew her so well. The eggs and chicks had been her fondest interest, and now he was making sure she'd still have them when they started their own home.

She had come out west to salvage what she could of her inheritance and had found so much more than she'd bargained for. She'd thought every spark of love inside her had died, that happiness was out of her reach. She had been ready to settle for a life on her own, for contentedness rather than passion, for independence rather than love. But she hadn't counted on Zach.

He'd found the tiniest ember buried in her heart and fanned it into a burning flame of love, a flame that burned in them both, hotter than the desert sun, longer-lasting than the rugged desert mountains. They'd been tested by the worst this land had to offer, and they had come out stronger than before. With Zach by her side, she knew she could face every challenge. With his love melding with hers, she would satisfy his every dream.

"I think that would be perfect," she said, and turned into his embrace. He was waiting for her, his eyes finally showing his peace, the haunting shadows now gone.

The past was, at last, truly buried. The future was finally theirs.

ROMANCE FROM THE HEART OF AMERICA

Diamond *Homespun* Romance

Homespun novels are touching, captivating romances from the heartland of America that combine the laughter and tears of family life with the tender warmth of true love.

__GOLDEN CHANCES 1-55773-750-9/$4.99
  by Rebecca Lee Hagan
__SPRING BLOSSOM 1-55773-751-7/$4.99
  by Jill Metcalf
__MOUNTAIN DAWN 1-55773-765-7/$4.99
  by Kathleen Kane
__PRAIRIE DREAMS 1-55773-798-3/$4.99
  by Teresa Warfield
__SWEET JASMINE 1-55773-810-6/$4.99
  by Alyssa Lee
__HOME FIRES 1-55773-823-8/$4.99
  by Linda Shertzer
__HARVEST SONG 1-55773-841-6/$4.99
  by Karen Lockwood (January 1993)